Praise for *The Stone M...*
(FIRST BOOK OF TH...)

"... a powerful tone of mystery ..."
Tim Lloyd, *Adelaide Advertiser*

"Sean Williams' *The Stone Mage & the Sea* is an
alchemical blend of elemental magic, tragic romance and
the coming of age of a young boy. Poised between
Earthsea and Mad Max, the magic of fantasy meets the
wonder of science fiction in one of the most rewarding
genre novels to come out of Australia this year."
Jonathan Strahan, *Locus* Reviews Editor

"A wonderful, magical fantasy set in a landscape that
is both eerily familiar and strangely alien, and peopled
with mages and villains and heroes that keep the
story pounding along."
Simon Brown, author of *Inheritance* and *Fire & Sword*
(Books 1 & 2 of THE KEYS OF POWER TRILOGY)

"Magical and mesmerising, *The Stone Mage & the Sea* is
a story to disappear into, whether you're 15 or 50."
Kim Wilkins, author of *Angel of Ruin*

"A stunning new fantasy set in a world where the
raw talent for magic of a young fugitive is the greatest
risk of all. Williams has a sure touch: he invents a time
that feels as real as today."
Janeen Webb, author of *The Sinbad Chronicles*

Sean Williams lives in the centre of Adelaide, South Australia — a city Salman Rushdie once described as the ideal setting for a horror story — with his partner, Kirsty Brooks, writer and director of Driftwood Manuscripts. A multiple Ditmar and Aurealis Award-winner, he is the author of over fifty published short stories and an increasing number of novels, among them the award-winning *Metal Fatigue* and *The Resurrected Man*. He is co-author, with Shane Dix, of the best-selling Evergence Trilogy. As well as their latest novel, *Echoes of Earth*, the first book in the Orphans Trilogy, they have been commissioned to write three novels in the Star Wars: New Jedi Order series.

Sean is the Chair of the SA Writers' Centre and a recipient of the SA Great Award for Literature. When not writing, he enjoys DJing and cooking curries.

THE
SKY WARDEN
& THE SUN

SEAN WILLIAMS

Second Book of The Change

Voyager
An imprint of HarperCollins*Publishers*

The lines quoted in Chapter 8 are taken from the short story
"William Wilson" by Edgar Allen Poe.

Australia Council
for the Arts

This project has been assisted by the Commonwealth Government
through the Australia Council, its arts funding and advisory body.

Voyager
An imprint of HarperCollins*Publishers,* Australia

First published in Australia in 2002
by HarperCollins*Publishers* Pty Limited
ABN 36 009 913 517
A member of the HarperCollins*Publishers* (Australia) Pty Limited Group
www.harpercollins.com.au

HarperCollins*Publishers*
25 Ryde Road, Pymble, Sydney, NSW 2073, Australia
31 View Road, Glenfield, Auckland 10, New Zealand
77–85 Fulham Palace Road, London W6 8JB, United Kingdom
Hazelton Lanes, 55 Avenue Road, Suite 2900, Toronto, Ontario M5R 3L2
and 1995 Markham Road, Scarborough, Ontario M1B 5M8, Canada
10 East 53rd Street, New York NY 10022, USA

National Library of Australia Cataloguing-in-Publication data:

Williams, Sean, 1967– .
The sky warden and the sun.
ISBN 0 7322 6996 2.
I. Title. (Series: Williams, Sean,
1967– Change; bk. 2).
A823.3

Cover illustration: Shaun Tan
Designed by Darian Causby, HarperCollins Design Studio
Typeset in 11.5/17 Sabon by HarperCollins Design Studio
Printed and bound in Australia by Griffin Press on 80gsm Bulky Book Ivory

7 6 5 4 3 2 1   02 03 04 05

For Jessica

ACKNOWLEDGMENTS:

Thanks to: Jo McNamara & Ben Mountford for Spider Lake; Ryan Meyer for writing down names on the way back from Cowell; the staff at the Prairie Hotel, Parachilna, for local knowledge and great food; Rob & Claire Brooks for the loan of their car (and their lovely daughter); Nick Linke and Simon Brown for providing valuable feedback on an early draft; Ian Hall for tech support; Shaun Tan for another wonderful cover; Rodney Stuard for excellence in nitpicking; Stephanie Smith for editorial sainthood; Richard Curtis for patience and good humour; and Jonathan Strahan, Heather Williams, Shane Dix, and Bill Gee for varying but all very deserving reasons.

The "strandbeasts" referred to in Chapter Fifteen are very real. These amazing creations are the work of Dutch artist Theo Jansen. Images of them (under their real name: "strandbeests") can be found at various locations on the World Wide Web.

The support of the Australia Council, HarperCollins Australia, the SA Writer's Centre and the Mount Lawley Mafia was essential during the writing of this book. Inspiration came courtesy of South Australia's superb Flinders Ranges and Yorke Peninsula, plus a number of the City of Adelaide's fine statues.

But once again it is a certainty that without the many sacrifices made by Kirsty Brooks this book (and its author) would have been a much shabbier beast. For all those tyres we blew, for hiking in the rain, and for very much more, I will always be in her debt.

CONTENTS

PART ONE

RUNNING

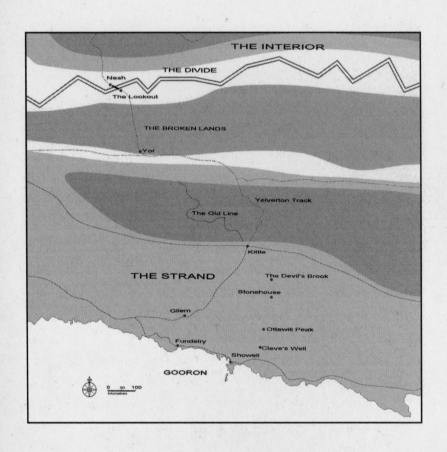

CHAPTER 1

BETWEEN SKY
AND STONE

They were being hunted.

At first, Sal wasn't certain of it. When he and Shilly fled Fundelry ahead of the storm Lodo had summoned, he thought they might outrun pursuit. They drove furiously, pushing the buggy and themselves as hard as they could in the least obvious direction, heading east across the rolling, water-logged dunes, avoiding roads and all signs of life until dawn lightened the sky ahead of them.

Crudely covered by a waterproofed tarpaulin, nestled between the banks of a narrow, stony-bedded creek, Sal and Shilly, with the machine that was their greatest hope of obtaining freedom, waited out the day in a state of feverish dread. Half-expecting capture at any moment, they slept fitfully. Silent under the shade, exhausted and grieving, neither dared voice the fears that urged them to keep running.

And as the sun rode higher in the sky, burning the storm away, Sal found reason to be afraid.

Bridging all the distance they had covered in an instant, the Syndic's mental eye swept over them. Sal closed his mind tightly and concentrated on the exercises Lodo had given him, picturing himself as a slippery ball bearing that the Syndic's fingers could not grasp. Once he had thought the owner of that far-seeing, unearthly gaze to be almost god-like, but he knew better now: she was just a woman, a person with limitations like anyone else.

The last time Sal had seen her, his paternal great-aunt, she had been sprawled at the base of a dune, knocked flat by a raw outpouring of the Change that had come from somewhere within him when she tried to take him captive. The memory of that outpouring left him cold; he never dreamed he had anything like that at his beck and call.

He had wondered then if she was dead, if he had killed her, but Nu Zanshin of Farrow clearly didn't give up easily, or quickly.

Her fingers did slip. Clumsy in their eagerness, they went reaching away past the two fugitives, heading northeast. He didn't allow himself to relax. They might have evaded her this time, but he would have to be careful in future or their freedom would be short-lived.

When night fell, they followed the creek inland as far as they could go. The buggy was no stranger to rugged terrain, but Sal was unused to driving and didn't want to risk a broken axle on the jagged rocks and crumbling banks. He figured that slow progress was better than none at all. Taking that into account, and the need to avoid human contact wherever possible, he didn't let himself hope to travel more than a hundred kilometres that second night. The buggy had fuel to last almost a week at that rate of travel, and the more ground he could put between them and Fundelry, the better.

They hit relatively open country shortly after midnight, under cold skies with stars glinting like hail waiting to fall. Sal focused his attention on the buggy and the controls he had watched his father use so many times before. He tried not to think about his father's death or the revelation that had preceded it: that the man he thought of as his father might not have been his father at all. Instead, he concentrated on the roughness of the ground ahead, glowing faintly in the light from the shuttered headlamps, on the gears and on the whine of the motor. He felt the mental wheels of the exercise Lodo called the Cellaton Mandala turning behind the effort of driving, and had faith that it would deflect any further attempts to find him by the Syndic. He ignored the rumble in his stomach telling him that they hadn't eaten the previous day; not since the Alders' Feast in Fundelry, the night before last, when his father had still been alive and it had seemed there was still a chance that Lodo could save them from the Sky Wardens.

Driving gave him an excuse for not talking, although the truth was that he couldn't find the words to express what he wanted to say. He wanted to tell Shilly that he was sorry. He wanted to say, *You don't have to come with me; this isn't your problem; you can leave whenever you want*, but he was afraid. What would he do if she *did* leave? He didn't want to be alone. And he didn't know how to say that, either. So he said nothing.

They drove straight through the second day and slept that night in a Ruin he knew of near an abandoned town called Cleve's Well. There they were safe from the Syndic, since the signature of his mind would disappear in the ancient place's unique aura. The ambient levels of the Change were strong there, not rooted so much in living things or particular rock formations, but in events that had taken place long ago and left their mark forever. The high level of background potential had an additional effect on them beyond providing security. He dreamed that night that he was being followed, among other things, and woke to find Shilly crying silently in her sleep.

The next morning, after a breakfast consisting solely of the fruit and bark from a desert pear bush, he tried to talk to her.

He told her the story of his parents: how his mother, Seirian Mierlo, had married an ambitious older man named Highson Sparre in order to increase the prestige of her family. Lodo, who had explained this to Sal, had known little more about the history of Seirian's family beyond the fact that they had emigrated from the Interior to the Strand in order to escape a scandal. That was enough, however, to place the rest in context. Sal's mother had fallen in love with Dafis Hrvati, a journeyman bound in service to an acquaintance of her husband, and neither her divorce nor their union had been condoned by any of the families involved.

So the lovers had run away together, into the borderlands. They had remained fugitives for a year, until the Sky Wardens, led by Highson and his aunt, Nu Zanshin — who was not yet Syndic, but would be before long — located Seirian by virtue of her use of the Change. They spirited her back to the Haunted City, whereupon they had learnt of Sayed, her son, who had been given the use-name of Sal. Why his existence made so much difference, Sal didn't know, but it seemed to. For some reason the Sky Wardens were more interested in him than either of his parents.

Although the Sky Wardens recommenced their search immediately, Sal had disappeared along with his father. The two of them had remained hidden ever since, protected by the father's denial of everything he had ever known in the past:

music, the Change, and his lover. His priority was to protect Sal, as his mother would surely have wanted. In the end, only Sal's growing potential at the Change — and his father's attempt to hide it by seeking help from Lodo, a renegade Stone Mage — had given them away. It was then that they had learned, from the Alcaide himself, of Sal's mother's death: she had wasted away when attempts to find Sal and his father had failed. Despairing of ever seeing them again, she had died of a broken heart.

Shilly listened patiently — or seemed to, at least — as he spoke. Everything after his arrival in Fundelry she knew about, since she had been involved in it. Although she, like Sal's father, had no natural talent, Lodo had been her teacher too, and his instruction had enabled her to bend another's talent to her own will. In many respects, her understanding of the Change was much deeper than Sal's, who had, until two weeks earlier, never suspected what potential he had. When the Sky Wardens had come to take him so they could train him in their way, he had decided to keep running, and Shilly had been swept up in the storm.

He didn't need to tell her about that, just as he didn't want to tell her how to think or to feel about it, since he himself was still trying to work that out. He just wanted her to know the full story.

If she understood it, or him, any better when he had finished, she gave no sign. She sat silently beside him in the buggy, as dark-skinned as he was fair, skinny under the simple cotton dress she wore everywhere. Her sun-bleached hair strayed across her face and her green eyes revealed nothing, betraying not the slightest hint of what she was feeling behind the mask. One finger doodled patterns in the dust that caked the side of the buggy.

Eventually she said, "Your mother had family in the Interior, right?"

"Yes." He knew very little about them except that they had come from somewhere called Mount Birrinah and been expelled from the Strand following his parents' elopement. "The Mierlos."

"You'll be looking for them, I suppose."

Sal opened his mouth to tell her that he hadn't decided where he wanted to go. But he didn't say it. After a lifetime of following his father around, he wasn't used to making decisions.

"I was thinking about Skender Van Haasteren," she said.

"Lodo's teacher? What about him?"

"He'd help us, I'm sure." She turned to look at him. Her face was expressionless, but her eyes were brimming over with tears. "That's where *I* want to go. You can drop me off on the way to visit your family. You don't have to come with me all the way."

Sal nodded. Lodo's teacher was from the Desert Port region; the old man had told him that much. Sal didn't know exactly where that was, but he knew one thing: both Mount Birrinah and Skender Van Haasteren were in the Interior. Maybe, he thought, the details weren't important. For the moment, his destination and Shilly's could lie in the same direction, if he so chose. Away from Fundelry. Away from the Syndic and her Sky Warden bloodhounds.

"Do you think Lodo is dead?" he asked her.

Her eyes were red. "They killed your father, didn't they?"

He nodded. It seemed too much to hope that Lodo had somehow beaten the Sky Wardens and escaped. They had heard nothing from him since they had fled the tremor that had saved them. The obvious assumption was that Lodo had been overwhelmed by the Alcaide in the same way that his father had been.

"It'll be tough," he said. "It's a long way."

"But we can make it, can't we?"

He shrugged. "We might just get there in the end, if we work together."

Only then did he remember that she had never been more than a few hundred metres away from the sea, not once in her entire life. Confronted by the distance they had to travel, *he* quailed inside. He had been to the Divide several times, but never beyond it, and that had been with his father, whose absence ached inside his chest as if a hole had been opened there. If he was uncertain, he thought, then she must be terrified.

But if she could do it, so could he.

"North it is," she said, her gaze returning to the horizon ahead. "Together."

And that was that. He turned the steering wheel to point the buggy inland, and he drove.

And they drove: out of the sand dunes and into firmer country, with round, weathered hills the colour of brown, lifeless dirt. They stuck to dry riverbeds and isolated road fragments as often as they could. Maps in the buggy's tool box gave them a rough idea of where to head, although many of the landmarks had changed over the years and they were passing through places Sal had not visited before. They travelled under the cover of night when there were signs of habitation, but the daylight was better for navigation. With the sun burning down on them out of a sky now utterly free of clouds, they took great care to maintain a shade, unfurling the buggy's tarpaulin to act as a roof which flapped noisily as they drove. But still they burned. Even Shilly's dark skin was tender for the first few days, and peeled after a week.

They passed ancient and recent life, among them spindly metal towers, many metres high, that had rusted and then slumped when their bases could no longer support their weight. A craterous mine ate into a hillside like a terrible, wasting disease, grey around the edges and half-filled with black water. By its edge rested an enormous crane, gutted for its parts but still glittering with the Change. Crumbling cemeteries made poignant companions to equally derelict buildings, some little more than chimneys and hearths standing alone in fields untended for decades. Some structures were welcome shelter from the heat, the best of them hollow, gap-toothed silos that reverberated with the buggy's engine when the two runaways arrived, and hummed with the wind when all was still again.

Shilly lay awake in the silos, listening to the hum and feeling as though she was privy to one side of a conversation between gods, so slow and ponderous that she couldn't decipher individual words.

But it was the landscape that threw her off-balance the most. It smelled different, and it looked different. She was used to gently rolling sand dunes and the occasional cliff face, a world defined by its relationship with the sea.

Here, the world extended in all directions the same, and it was alien in ways that weren't immediately obvious. The ground, for a start, grew redder the further north they travelled. The trees were taller and less bushy than the ones she was used to. Once they came across a forest of slender trees that had been burned in a recent bushfire; their hearts still lived, and new leaves grew green in vivid contrast to the blackened bark. As with the trees, the distant hills were larger, but had fewer angles than those closer to the coast; they were like the rolling shoulders and hips of reclining giants, their eyes closed just over the horizon. Everything around her was worn and dusty and hot — and seemed utterly empty.

Up close there was detail aplenty. Three-cornered jacks waited for her if she was careless enough to wander off in bare feet. Insects jumped around them in great hordes — tiny flying ones that stung, and heavy hoppers that could hurt from momentum alone. Fat, black flies dangled in the air as though on the end of invisible strings, and many-legged creatures left furrowed tracks in the dirt. Birds with wings like outstretched hands drifted in updrafts, sharp eyes seeking insects and small animals below. Shilly hadn't seen any of the latter yet, although she heard them rustling at night.

The bugs and sun didn't seem to bother Sal as much as they did her, thanks to the protective earring he wore through a hole in his ear. There was no point to wishing she had a ward like that. She gathered that they were very rare; it was one of the things that had tipped Lodo to Sal's importance when he had arrived in Fundelry. His mother had given it to him when he had been born to protect him from minor injuries.

But they weren't so minor, she thought, when there were lots of them at once. All she could was grit her teeth and endure.

By Ottewill Peak, Stonehouse and the Devil's Brook they went, across fields once sown but now fallow and stony. Some were infested with purple-flowering weeds that Sal called "the curse" but which Shilly found startlingly beautiful. Sal let her handle the navigation, while he drove. The maps didn't tell her anything about where she was going: they didn't describe how the air smelt, or if there would be people nearby, or what there might be to eat. It was simply her job to read the names and watch the places go by, having learned little more about them in the process. They didn't stop anywhere interesting — if there *was* anything of interest in this arid, stony land. All they did was travel and sleep. She forced herself not to fight the buggy as it bounced across the hard, new world she had been propelled into, even when it felt like her muscles had been pounded to jelly and her bones were on the verge of shattering.

On the fifth day, with the sun high in the sky, she begged for a rest stop. A headache painted bright, flashing dots behind her eyelids and she was afraid she might scream the next time she had to get out and push the buggy from a sandy patch. While she leaned back into the seat with her hat over her eyes, trying to remember why she was putting herself through this, Sal ducked away to investigate a nearby patch of vegetation.

"This is from the yukuri vine," he said when he returned, holding up a number of small, greenish fruit. He opened one and removed some of the pulp within. "I chose this spot because I recognised its leaves. Close your eyes."

She did so warily, lifting her hat when he asked, and letting him rub the moist flesh across her eyelids and forehead. It felt cool against her skin, although it had a bitter smell. His touch was soft.

"This'll make you feel better."

It did. Within a few minutes, her headache had ebbed to the point where it only nagged rather than dominated. She didn't move, letting the seat take her weight while Sal clattered about with their stuff, unfurling the sleeping bag they shared if it was cold at night and preparing the tarp to cover the buggy. He had decided to make the rest stop more permanent without consulting her, and she was more grateful than she could say for that. She knew she should be helping him, but she had no energy; she seemed to weigh as much as one of the giants whose backs they traversed every day. Tears pricked at her closed eyes: she was a dead weight, but he never complained.

She said nothing, either. Every time she opened her mouth, she was afraid of what might come out. She didn't want to blame him for the mess they were in for he had as little control over it as she did. If she was caught up with him, that was just bad luck; it could have happened to anyone. And wishing that she had never met him was like wishing the sun wouldn't rise in the east. She couldn't change anything about it now, unable as she was to drive, and having nowhere near enough money to pay someone else for passage to the Interior. She could only float with the current and see where it took her.

Floating: that was what she was doing. For the first time in her life, control of her immediate fate had been turned over to someone else, and it didn't sit well with her. She knew Sal would rather she talked to him about it, but she wasn't ready for that and didn't know when she would be. When Sal stopped running, perhaps then she would talk. Running was, she knew, his preferred means of avoiding anything too difficult to deal with, the same in principle to her silence. If they could meet halfway, perhaps then they would make the distance together.

The next day, they dared human contact to buy fuel for the buggy, and food, using the small amount of change they had between them. She went through the motions while Sal stayed out of sight in the buggy. If the landowners had been told to keep an eye out for anyone on the run from the Sky Wardens, they showed no sign of it. They accepted the fake name she offered, took her money, filled the buggy's tanks with alcohol, and let them go.

"We can't afford to relax yet," Sal said that night, as they took shelter in yet another dry creek bed. Being close to a major town, they didn't draw attention to themselves by travelling with lights on during the darkness. "I can still feel her looking."

Shilly nodded, having nothing to add. He was right: they couldn't relax yet. According to her map, they weren't even a quarter of the way to where she wanted to be. The only way she could think of possibly surviving the journey was to forget about the past — and even the present. Their destination was all that mattered, no matter how far away it seemed or what she had to put up with on the way. It would be worth it, she told herself. It had to be.

Northwest of Kittle they found one end of an old railway line that wound up through the hills. The terrain ahead was rugged. Long since stripped of its valuable metals, Sal hoped that the Old Line, as the ancient railway was called, would be a passable track. His father had never travelled that route, but had talked of it once, when they wound their way along the usual road between the Broken Lands and the more gentle plains of the Strand. That route, the Yelverton Track, was relatively wide and safe, but well used because of it and an obvious place for the Sky Wardens to lie in wait for them.

"We have two choices," he told Shilly at the base of the Old Line. "We take the buggy and hope for the best, or we leave the buggy behind and make our way on foot. What do you think?"

She seemed to consider the options, but didn't offer an opinion beyond shrugging.

"If we walk," he went on, "obviously it'll take longer, but it will be safer. That's assuming we can find a path if the Old Line peters out, or can make our own. It's tough in there and I can't guarantee anything."

He didn't bother to explain why they needed to head in that direction in the first place. There were only two safe places to cross the Divide; that was clear from the map before him. The pass they were heading for, to the west, was the least travelled.

"I think we should take the buggy," he concluded. "There'll be a long way to go when we reach the far side. The Divide is still 600 kilometres away. Without the buggy it'll take months to reach the Interior. It's worth the risk now to save time later. Do you agree?"

She frowned, her expression saying more clearly than words: *Why are you asking me this? It's clear you've already made up your mind.*

"We can talk about it, if you want," he said. "Maybe I've missed something."

She shook her head and adjusted her hat so the shadow covered her eyes. With one hand she pointed irritably forward, to the Old Line.

He waited a moment to give her a chance to speak, but that was clearly all he was going to get. It was the closest he had come all day to provoking a genuine reaction out of her, so he didn't mind so much. And he had her tacit approval to proceed. It would have to be enough.

They discovered that the Old Line consisted of a rutted, gravely surface. Erosion by rain and wind made it uneven and treacherous. He proceeded slowly and carefully, even along straight sections. Sometimes the missing railway sloped upward into the hills, or it snaked around slabs of rock larger than houses and through earth that had been laid down millions of years before. The scenery, when he had time to look at it, was magnificent in a bleak, time worn way.

Nightfall — their seventh since leaving Fundelry — brought an end to the day's sightseeing and to the first leg of their journey on the Old Line. The way was dangerous enough by daylight, when the frequent cracks and rockfalls could be clearly seen and negotiated. During the dark it would be suicidal to continue on. They camped in the lee of an overhanging cliff, the same red-brown colour as dried blood, under which the Old Line passed. In its shadows Sal noted an effect his father had once spoken of, but which he had never before felt: under the cliff face the background potential faded to zero, and he lost all sense of the world around him. It was as though the Change had been sucked out of him and drawn into the ground, where it dissipated and vanished. The feeling was unnerving, but not one that threatened any harm.

Figuring that he would be as safe here as he was in a Ruin, he didn't mind camping for the night. They even risked a fire and boiled a measure of their precious water for their first cooked meal in a week. Sal had been collecting fruit and edible leaves everywhere they stopped. He added these to a number of small grubs he had dug out from under a tree that morning and created what his father had named a 'desert stew'. Shilly's skin went a shade lighter when she saw him put in the grubs, but she ate her half without complaint. She couldn't complain, he supposed, if she wouldn't talk.

The night was cold. Shilly slept under the tarp while he sat up to watch the stars. Humming an old tune to himself, enjoying this time of relative privacy, he went through the contents of his pack by feel until he found his way to the clasp wrapped in soft leather near the bottom; it had belonged to his mother and, Lodo said, symbolised the Earth. But that wasn't what he was looking for. Deeper still lay the heavy, grey globe that the old man had given him on his last night in Fundelry. It was like one of the powerful globes Lodo had used to store light during the day and then illuminate Fundelry at night, but this one was smaller and denser, more mysterious still. Lodo had said on giving it to him, *I think you will need a little light in the future, wherever you go*, and had bade him to keep it secret from Shilly. Sal had done so, although his conscience nagged at him.

He drew it out into the starlight and cradled it in his lap. It was as heavy as he remembered and cool to the touch. No light reflected off it. He pressed his palms against its smooth surface and enclosed it in his fingers. Shutting his eyes, he sought any sign of recognition within it, the slightest hint that it knew what it was for and could tell him how to use it. But there was nothing. His thoughts vanished into the globe like rain down a well. Part of him thought that that might be a result of the Change-deadening place they occupied, but a greater part suspected otherwise. He would have to learn how to reveal the globe's secrets, just as he had had to learn to use other Change-endowed artefacts. The Change wasn't something he could use intuitively, no matter how much innate talent he had. It was a skill acquired through hours of practice. And it was a responsibility, Shilly had said.

With that thought in his head, he put the globe back into his pack, rested his back against the wheel of the buggy and slept.

He dreamed that the globe was burning brightly, just as it had in his dream shortly after leaving Fundelry. Again he saw the bully, Kemp, in the golden tower, the ghostly city buried in sand, a tunnel mouth guarded by two swinging corpses, an old woman who looked something like himself, and a talking statue. Lodo was in the dream, and so was Tait, a journeyman like Sal's father had once been.

Tait, whose brother Tom had befriended Sal in Fundelry, was leading a Sky Warden in blue robes across a desert. The first time he had had the dream, the identity of this man eluded him. Now it came to him: it was Shom Behenna, the new Selector of the Fundelry region. More powerful than his predecessor, Amele Centofanti, he had taken over her position when she had failed to detect Sal.

It wasn't until after they woke the next morning and inched their way from beneath the shadow of the rock that Sal guessed what the man was doing in his dreams.

As soon as they left the Change-numbing bubble of safety and entered the background potential, Sal felt the Syndic's eye abroad — again scouring the Strand for any sign of him.

He evaded her with greater ease than before. Her mind was distant, diffused across the very large space she had to search. But beneath her grasping lay that of another mind, one subtler than hers, and nearer. He felt it as a gentle *tap-tap* against his defences rather than a full-scale assault. Just as an ant might find access where a human hand might not, this mind sought to insinuate itself without him noticing. It prodded at him for a while, and then went away. It returned later on, as though to check that he was still there. He knew it was Shom Behenna as surely as he knew that one misstep would send him tumbling off the Old Line to his death in the valley below.

Tap-tap.

Sal went cold at the feel of this new, more sophisticated pursuer. Had Behenna found him? Did he know where Sal and Shilly were, and where they were headed? Sal fervently hoped not. He was uncertain just how much information could be conveyed by that gentle *tap-tap*. Perhaps Behenna could tell nothing more than that Sal was still alive, and maybe roughly where he was. The latter didn't please him; he had, after all, hoped to slip out of the Strand completely unnoticed. But if Behenna *did* know, where were the gulls, descending out of the sky to confirm the location? Where were the Sky Wardens to drag them back to the Haunted City?

He didn't tell Shilly. They had enough to worry about, with the Old Line to negotiate and the Broken Lands ahead. And it didn't change anything. They were still running. They simply had a better idea, now, of who they were running from.

The last stage of the Old Line was the worst. The northern face of the range was almost sheer, as though someone had torn the range in two and they were descending the walls into the rift valley. The missing middle was nowhere to be seen, however. Shilly imagined it being thrown into the Interior, on the other side of the Divide. Or maybe it had been swallowed up by the plain like an ocean might swallow a leaky boat.

Whenever the buggy's wheels slipped beneath them, all such speculation was instantly forgotten. Sal inched the buggy forward through such areas while she walked behind, carrying their packs. That way, if the buggy did fall, they might not lose everything. Sal was ever ready to jump free; they could walk the rest of the way if necessary.

So she thought, anyway, until they came to the bridge.

The great cataclysm that had torn the mighty range in two had sent fingers of destruction into the midst of the hills. The ravine below them was one such example. Its walls were sheer and angular; the creek far below, even when full, could not have carved it. To their left and right it stretched out for kilometres. The side they occupied offered no route down to the bottom; only on the far side had the ancient builders of the line found a way to descend to the plains. There would have been no benefit in building the bridge, otherwise.

When built, she supposed, it had been a piece of engineering to be proud of: it spanned the gap in a smooth arch of around one hundred metres, with no supports, which had held up a perfectly flat length of track. Where the tracks had been were lengths of decaying concrete and rusted metal grates, forming a road of sorts wider than the buggy was long. Staring across the gap-toothed mesh the buggy would have to traverse, with the depths of the ravine below, Shilly had a sudden premonition that something was going to go wrong.

Sal threw a rock out onto the bridge. It clattered noisily. The bridge didn't suddenly crumble into dust, which was only a slight relief. They still didn't know whether to turn around and go back.

"There's a safety rail," he said, indicating the waist-high barrier on either side of the span. "That makes it stronger."

He walked twenty paces out onto the bridge and looked around. Shading his eyes, he looked along the ravine. Then he pointed into the far distance to Shilly's right.

"Yor!" he shouted to her. "That's where we're headed."

She couldn't see it from where she was standing on the last metre of road and she didn't really care at that moment. The bridge was just one more hurdle to get over on the way to Skender Van Haasteren. Sal lowered his hand and gingerly picked his way back to her.

Where the rails had been were two strips of long, plank-like beams just wide enough for the buggy's tyres. It was a close fit; the slightest deviation would threaten to slide the buggy onto the rusty grille. The grille was supported by metal bars every metre or so. If all four wheels slipped off the planks, she didn't see how they could possibly get them back up. That was, of course, assuming that the planks would take the weight of the buggy in the first place . . .

Sal sat in the driver's seat. He didn't say anything for a moment, and Shilly waited, watching him. She thought he looked older than he had before, in Fundelry, although that could just have been the effect of the freckles spreading over his pale skin, and the dirt. If he didn't look older, he definitely looked more serious.

"You go first," he said. "Take the packs. Go all the way across and wait for me there."

"Don't be stupid," she said, the first real sentence she had uttered for days.

"It's not stupid. There's no need to risk both of us. If I fall, you can keep on going."

"If you fall, I'm as good as dead. I don't know anything about this place. I'll starve, or be bitten by something, or fall foul of the locals." She felt a heavy resentment of her situation rising up inside her, but she fought through it to what really bothered her. "If you fall, I don't want to stand over there and watch you die."

"I'm not going to fall —" Sal began.

"So I won't either. To make sure, I'll walk ahead of you. If the bridge won't take *my* weight, you'll know to turn back."

For a moment he seemed about to argue. Then something like relief spread across his face, and he nodded. She turned away to get out of the buggy and put on her pack, hoping the fear she was feeling wasn't so obvious.

Sal started the buggy's engine and inched it forward until its front wheels were a metre back from the beginning of the bridge. Shilly took a deep breath and stepped onto the plank opposite the one Sal had walked along before, since she already knew the first one was safe. Even without looking around, she sensed the emptiness of the ravine enclose her as she put one step in front of the other, then another, then another. She tried not to look too far down, even though she had to make judgements about the integrity of the bridge. She just walked carefully, as she might across the beams of a rundown jetty. *I will not fall*, she told herself. *It's only a hundred paces across.*

The bridge creaked as the buggy moved slowly onto it. She felt the planks flex beneath her and refused to breathe any faster. She looked over her shoulder and saw Sal, white-faced, inching the buggy along. Its weight made rusty rivets pop and ancient metal groan; every metre or so it jerked slightly as if something small had given way beneath it.

Perhaps, she thought, they should have taken some of their supplies over first. Without the extra fuel and water tanks, it would have been lighter, less of a strain; and they could have inspected the way properly first, too. But she hadn't thought to suggest that, and it was too late now.

Looking ahead was her job. Sal gave her a quick thumbs-up, and she turned her attention forward again, watching where she placed her feet and looking for any sign of weakness. The ancient builders had done their job well. She never felt desperately unsafe, even at the halfway point, when the wind sang past the soles of her feet and the sense of space around her was at its peak.

She glanced in the direction Sal had indicated before and saw on the horizon a smudge that could have been a town. Yor, she presumed, whatever that was.

The rest of the way was in shadow, but she had the measure of it now: walk forward ten paces and wait for Sal to catch up; think of how good it would be to feel solid earth underfoot; don't look down to where that same earth waited, far, far below; savour the moment of stillness as long as it lasted, and be glad that she wasn't in the buggy with Sal, who wouldn't get to rest at all until he joined her on the far side. He could afford neither to stop nor to go too quickly. The buggy crawled along in slow motion, as if in a dream that would never end.

Yet the edge of the ravine grew clearer with every press forward. The bridge terminated in a road no different to the one they had left. Dusty, unsafe, abandoned — it looked like paradise the more she thought about it. Once there, the hurdle would be crossed, they could keep moving on.

Forty metres to go. Thirty. Twenty.

It happened just before the last rest stop, with only eleven metres left. She had barely taken her ninth step when she heard a new noise from behind her over the burbling of the buggy's engine: a groan, or a creak. It was not as dramatic as a crack, but still of concern. She turned immediately and opened her mouth to shout a question at Sal, to ask if he had heard it too, when it came again, louder, and the plank beneath her *twanged* like a plucked string.

Sal clearly felt or heard *that*. His eyes grew wide and the buggy jerked forward with a snarl as instinctive panic drove the accelerator downward. It stopped after a metre or two, and for a split second Shilly thought that that was it, that the crisis was over and their slow progress would continue. But then she realised that the engine was still snarling, and its front wheels were slipping.

Something clattered far below. She didn't look down; she didn't need to. If part of the bridge had fallen away and the buggy was teetering on the lip of a precipice, it would look exactly like this.

The buggy tipped backward slightly. Sal glanced behind him, then looked firmly forward again and put his foot down. The engine roared to no avail.

Shilly ran forward, toward him, reaching. "Give me your hand!"

"No! I can do it!"

You can't! she wanted to scream. He couldn't see what she could. Behind the front mudguards, the wheels had already lifted off the surface of the planks. He would have no traction, front or back, no matter how hard he accelerated. There was nothing he could do to arrest the buggy's slide backward. And down.

Except ... If he wouldn't jump and there wasn't time to explain, there was only one thing she could do. She leapt into the air and brought both feet down hard on its front bumper bar. Her extra weight brought the spinning wheels into contact with the planks and the buggy lurched forward. Taken by surprise, Sal struggled with the steering wheel and Shilly sprawled helplessly across the bonnet. The rear wheels screeched and the buggy slewed wildly across the bridge, crossing the remaining distance in a little more than a second — but not in a straight line. First it jumped off the planks and scraped against the left safety rail with a shower of sparks. Then it fishtailed to the right side. One metre from the edge the buggy impacted with the right rail hard enough to pivot it entirely around, so that when it finally came to rest, on the solid, red earth, it was facing the way it had come, toward the bridge that had so narrowly let them pass.

The engine died and everything was silent. But ringing in Shilly's ears was the crack she had heard when the buggy struck the right-side rail with her strewn across its bonnet. For a second, she entertained the hope that it was the buggy that was broken, not her — but then the pain hit, and she screamed.

CHAPTER 2

THE BROKEN

Sal saw stars when the buggy juddered to a halt on the road. His mind was a mess of impressions: the terrible sensation of sliding backward into the hole in the bridge, followed by the wild rush forward, out of control, when Shilly tipped the buggy so its front wheels could get a grip. He had bruised his chest on the steering wheel when they had struck one of the guard rails, and he dreaded to think how much damage had been done in the impact. If they had cracked the radiator, or the sump ...

Shilly's cry instantly cleared his head. She was hunched over on the hot bonnet of the buggy, trying to sit up. He got out to help, but she slipped off and fell onto the ground before he could reach her, and she screamed again.

When he saw the blood, his stomach seemed to plummet to the bottom of the ravine.

"Shilly!" He instantly went to her, not needing to ask where she was hurt. Her right leg lay folded beneath her in an impossible way, broken in many places when crushed between the buggy and the guardrail. Her face was a sickly yellow, and getting paler by the second. She clutched at him and pulled him closer.

"No blame," she hissed through clenched teeth, her eyes not really seeing him. "No —"

Then she was unconscious and limp in his arms, arterial blood splashing thickly over his knees and onto the road. The stink of it nearly made him gag, but he suppressed it along with the panic boiling upward in his chest. He had to think clearly. People died from injuries like this.

The most immediate problems were the bleeding and the major break in her thigh. What little herbal lore he knew would be of no use to him. There were few plants around, for a start, and none of the right type to promote clotting. Instead, he tried to wipe away the blood as best he could, but it kept flowing from the wound. He put his fingers around the tear in her thigh, holding the skin tight against the thick splinter of bone sticking out of her. That lessened the steady pulsing, giving him time to think.

His first thought was to make a splint out of the wreckage of the bridge and tie it on with strips torn from the tarpaulin. Her unconsciousness was a blessing because it would be easier for him to straighten the leg, provided she didn't remain unconscious for too long. The longer she bled the deeper into shock she would go, so the sooner he got started the better.

The moment he released his grip on the wound to go and get the things he needed, the pulsing started again. The puddle of blood had already spread all around them; he was drenched from the waist down and up to his elbows. If she had any blood left in her, which seemed incredible, he knew she couldn't afford to lose much more.

The situation couldn't possibly have been worse. He couldn't move for fear of killing her, but he couldn't save her *unless* he moved. Meanwhile, the sense of *her* that nagged at him when they were close was ebbing. All he could do was crouch by her as she slowly faded away.

Anger and frustration welled in his chest. Shilly had saved his life. He *refused* to watch her die.

His one remaining hope lay within. Reaching deep inside himself, he sought the source of the Change. There had to be something it could do to help her. If he couldn't use it to save a life, what was it good for?

He imagined a hole inside him, a tunnel leading not down or left or backward, but in an entirely new direction, one he coundn't describe. He stretched his mind along it, probing. Deeper. Something stirred, but it was formless, useless. He tried harder, reached deeper, but still nothing happened.

"Help me!" he screamed. Only echoes answered his call. The Change eluded him. "Help me save her!"

Think, he told himself. *There has to be a way*!

The answer came to him from an unexpected quarter: not from the Change, but from a voice that spoke through the Change, directly into his mind.

"*Shape*," it said.

Sal stiffened. Lodo had spoken to him this way once, during his brief training. He had the feeling of grey clouds parting — the same grey as the terrible Void Beneath — just long enough for a word to sneak through, a single word from another mind a great distance away. Then the grey crashed back in to seal the breach. He didn't recognise the mental voice.

Another word came: "*Will.*"

Understanding was like a firework going off. The Change wasn't a servant; it had no intelligence of its own. Shouting at it wasn't going to tell it what to do, no matter how much he wanted it to. He had to *explain*.

The words came again from the distant mind — "*Shape will*" — but he had the concept, now. Shilly had explained it to him in the Ruin near Fundelry, when he had tried to make light blossom from a stone. He had to picture in his mind what he wanted done before it would happen in reality.

What needed to be done most of all? The arteries had to be sealed, and that meant first moving the bone. He closed his eyes and used the information coming from his fingertips to imagine the inside of Shilly's shattered thigh. The femur had cracked *there*; one splinter went up, another down; the end poking through the wound led to her hip and would have to be retracted before the others could join it. The big veins, surging feebly now against his grip, could reconnect if he pushed them *this* way . . .

At the first movement of bone and tissue beneath his fingers, he almost let go in fright. Opening his eyes, he caught a faint orange aura dancing across Shilly's flesh — but it was gone as soon as he saw it. The bone stopped moving at the same time, and he closed his eyes to regain his concentration.

Once he had it, the bone retracted smoothly into the wound. Shilly stirred as her leg straightened of its own accord. The jagged splinters lined up and the severed ends of the arteries met.

Sal had the wound completely closed beneath his hands by then, despite the slipperiness of her skin and the strength draining from his fingers, but the blood was still flowing freely. Putting the ends of the arteries together wasn't enough. He would have to fuse them.

He was seeing stars again by this point. He dug deeper and *willed* the ends shut. A brief flower of energy blossomed beneath his palms, inside Shilly's leg, then he was drained, empty. Dizziness rushed through him, and he couldn't stop himself falling down into the grey void that had waited for him all his life.

(And all he heard for an endless instant was the hum that lay behind everything: every thought, every word, every meaning, and every *life*. It was deep and resonant, and drew him into it like the water had drawn him down into the ocean in Fundelry when he had fallen off the jetty — but this time there was no one there to call him back.)

Tap-tap.

Sal stirred. "Huh?"

Tap-tap.

Cold air and a feeling of space rushed over him, as though he was lying near a great emptiness that threatened to engulf him. He sat upright with a jerk. Everything was black, or seemed so at first. What had happened and where he was came to him in fragments: the Old Line, the ravine, the buggy, the bridge. Night had fallen and, apart from a band of stars far above him, the world was utterly dark. There was no moon. He had been unconscious for hours.

"Shilly?" He reached out for her and found her arm beside him. It was warm and she had a pulse. Her breath came evenly out of the darkness. Reaching lower he found the wound on her thigh. Blood still trickled from it, and it would need to be sewn shut with the needle and thread in the buggy's tool kit, but the bleeding was nothing like the mortal torrent that had poured out of it before. It hadn't killed her. The Change had saved her. *He* had saved her. They had saved each other.

He rose to his hands and knees and felt through the darkness for the buggy, wary of losing it and accidentally crawling over the edge of the ravine. When he found it, he collapsed into the driver's seat and reached under it for the torch in its recharge clip. Yellow light spilled out of the end of it when he flicked the switch, illuminating the scene around him.

Shilly lay on her back where she had fallen in a wash of dried blood. Her right leg needed splinting immediately. He didn't have the strength to seal the breaks; the artery alone had drained him nearly dry.

Out of the darkness, he seemed to hear Lodo's voice, cautioning him: "*Having the Change won't give you access to boundless reserves of energy. All you have is as much as you are, and no more. Take too much, and you risk losing yourself. You'd become like a ghost, or the opposite of a ghost: a body without true life, a shell of yourself, a golem, as some call them. Many wardens and mages have fallen into this trap over the centuries and some still exist. They can be dangerous, for empty vessels may be filled with other things.*"

Sal wondered, as he prepared the material necessary for a splint, how close he had come to dipping too deeply — and he contemplated how much harder it was to heal than to harm. The destructive burst he had sent against the Alcaide and the Syndic in Fundelry hadn't drained him anywhere near as much as shifting bone and fusing two ends of a severed artery.

Tap-tap.

He froze, realising only then what had woken him. The words that had come in response to his desperate plea for help came vividly to his mind. Now he knew from whom they had come, too. His urgency, his desperation when Shilly had been dying in front of him, must have been as obvious as a volcano to anyone looking. And there *had* been someone looking: Shom Behenna. Sal had exposed himself by using the Change out in the open. This, he knew, was how his parents had given themselves away when on the run from Highson Sparre. The Change stood out more clearly than a fire at night for those who could see, his father had said. He would have to be more careful in future, if it wasn't already far too late.

But he put it out of his mind for the moment. There were no words any more from the distant Sky Warden, and Shilly needed him to concentrate on her, not Behenna. Her battered leg was purple and swollen, and at risk of infection. If he could splint it and get her in the buggy, they could move on. Out of the hills there would be more ground cover, more medicinal plants. Even if he couldn't find the right ones, there was always Yor, the next town on their journey. If he moved quickly enough, they might yet stay ahead of pursuit. The fact that he couldn't feel the eye of the Syndic pressing down upon him gave him some small hope.

When Shilly's leg was bound, he carried her as gently as he could to the buggy and put her on the tray. The sweet, cinnamon smell which was usually part of her was completely buried under the stench of blood. He rearranged their supplies to give her room and laid out the tarp to act as a makeshift cushion around her. The less he jarred her leg, the better.

Only then did he get into the driver's seat and try the ignition. The engine caught immediately. Letting go of the breath he had been holding he performed a careful three-point turn, then headed off down the Old Line and left the ravine far behind him.

Bright light burned through Shilly's eyelids.

It can't be, she thought. The last thing she remembered was the shadow of the ravine. *I'm dreaming.*

She tried opening her eyes and was assaulted by sensations: light, stronger than before; the sound of the buggy rattling and roaring along a road of some kind; the taste of dust and blood in her mouth, and —

She shouldn't have tried to move. She remembered that much the next time she awoke. The pain in her leg was too big to contain. It overwhelmed her, thrust her back into the darkness. But the darkness held despair and nightmares of failure. *We didn't make it, did we?*

There was no answer. She couldn't tell if she was speaking or not, but she reached outward anyway.

Sal?

Instantly, the buggy braked and pulled over. She heard the sound of scrabbling. A shadow fell across her face. Her eyelids were stuck together, and she forced them open with an effort.

"Are you awake?" Sal asked. He was a blur looming over her, silhouetted against the bright, blue sky. She felt his hand on her forehead. "Can you hear me?"

She nodded, although the effort made her fragile grip on consciousness waver. Her stomach churned as though she was about to be sick.

He removed his hand. "I thought you were going to die." His face conveyed an almost comical mix of hope and dismay. "Your leg — can you feel it?"

She nodded again, and *was* sick, then. The nausea and the pain fought for control of her world until the darkness stepped in once more and claimed her for its own.

The next time she awoke, everything was dark and cool behind her closed eyelids. The smell of the road was gone, replaced by a pungent odour of herbs and ointments. She was lying on a bed, covered with a soft sheet. Her clothes were gone, and any embarrassment she might have felt was quashed by the sensation of being clean for the first time in days. Her hair was wet and cool against her scalp.

Her thoughts were clear enough to deduce that she had been stripped and bathed while she was unconscious. By Sal? He couldn't move her on his own, not with her leg . . .

Her leg! She tried to feel it, but could not. It was numb. *Gone?* Panic subsided when her fingertips found her thigh and followed it as far as she could. There was bandage, a splint. *They wouldn't splint a stump, would they?*

She collapsed back onto the bed, groggy and exhausted, and full of smaller aches. Cool air wafted over her in gentle waves. Wherever she was, she was glad to be off the road. If only, she thought, she could stay there forever . . .

After a while, she became aware of voices talking softly in a room nearby.

". . . good food, painkillers, antibiotics, fresh bandages. Most of all she needs time: time to rest, to heal, to get better."

The man's speech was accented in a way she had heard sometimes in market traders, as though they were speaking a slightly different language. Then someone else spoke and, although she couldn't make out the words, she recognised Sal's voice. A trickle of relief ran through her.

"That much is obvious," said the accented voice in response to what Sal had said, "but even the strongest won't recover overnight."

"We don't have time," Sal said, more loudly. "We have to get moving again, and soon."

"Well, I could supply you with what you will need, I suppose. It will be expensive."

"I don't have any money left. You know that."

"I do know that, Tom, and I have already given you more than you could afford. I am a reasonable man. I will let you stay here longer in order to help Elina. But I am not a saint. If you leave, I will not be able to help you."

Shilly was momentarily confused over the names. The reason for them came back to her only slowly through the fog in her head. In order to preserve their anonymity, she and Sal were travelling under assumed identities. The real Elina was a young girl in Fundelry with a sputtering of talent that would burn itself out before she turned five, just as Shilly's had. The real Tom had applied for Selection in order to follow his brother, but had helped her and Sal escape when his devotion had been betrayed. Shilly had no idea what had happened to them in the wake of the visit of the Alcaide and Syndic to their tiny village. Their names felt odd through her disorientation, and the memories came with a deep sense of sadness and loss.

Again Sal said something she couldn't hear properly. When the man spoke next his voice was gentler.

"I don't know, Tom. We've done everything we can. With proper care, the bones should knit well. Her thigh's as straight as anyone could make it, I guarantee you that. Given time and rest, I think she will walk again in three months."

"If not?"

The older voice hesitated. "You must understand that when I say that she will only walk given time and rest, I do not mean that she will be the same as she was. She has been seriously injured. There will be consequences. She will have a limp for the rest of her life, for starters. The risk of another break will be high. Walking might be the most she will ever do. If she *doesn't* get the time and rest, well..." Shilly heard a silence that might have been filled with a shrug. "It's a hard road to the Lookout. If you don't undo all the work I have done and she doesn't lose the leg entirely, my guess is that she will be lamed. Crippled. Do you want to risk that?"

"No." There was a slight edge of desperation to Sal's voice that sent more of a chill through her than even the word *crippled* had. "And that's what I thought you were going to say."

The older man sighed heavily. "It's not that I don't sympathise, Tom —"

"No, Engenius, I know you do. But there's nothing else you can do. I'm more grateful for what you have done than I can say. It's not your fault I don't like where that leaves me."

There was silence for a moment, then the rattling of beads in a doorway. Shilly sensed someone in the room with her, and she opened her eyes.

The first thing she saw was a fan circling overhead, stirring the air in the shadowed room. The walls were wood-panelled and carved in the likeness of animals she had never seen before. There were birds, beasts, reptiles, insects — a dizzying panorama that distracted her from the room's contents. Perhaps that was the idea. When she did notice, she saw gleaming knives, extra-long tweezers, silver pans and clamps next to a black leather bag that was old, but had been lovingly cared for. She was in some sort of surgery.

Sal stepped slowly into view, bending at the waist to look at her face. For all the attention she had received, he hadn't wasted any on himself. He was filthy, covered in red dust across every visible inch of skin. His clothes were torn and stained brown with dried blood. He looked like he hadn't slept for days.

"You're awake," he said, and she couldn't tell if he was relieved or annoyed.

The best she could manage in reply was a croak. Her mouth was parched. Sal put a tube into her mouth. The other end dipped into a glass of water and she sipped eagerly.

He looked worried. "How much did you hear?"

"You . . ." She stopped, then tried again. "You were going to leave me here, weren't you?"

His exhaustion didn't cover the surprise on his face. "What? No, Shilly, of course not."

But he was lying. She could tell that. He had come into the room to say goodbye while she slept.

"Would you have come back?"

He warred silently with himself for a moment, then said: "Yes."

Even though she had guessed, the sense of betrayal surprised her. What had happened to *together*?

"Don't go without me," she said. "Don't leave me here alone."

"I don't want to, but —"

"Just don't. We had a deal, didn't we?"

"Your leg —"

"I'm going to have a limp even if I stay here. Isn't that what he said? The chances are I won't be any worse off in the buggy. We can use the Ch—"

He put a hand across her mouth before she could finish the word and looked, alarmed, back through the beaded doorway. "Not here," he hissed. "I haven't told anyone about that."

She nodded, flushing at her lack of thought, and he took his hand away.

"Yes," he said. "I've thought of that, but I didn't want to leave you with no other option."

"What's the difference between that and abandoning me here?"

"I would have come back, really."

"If they didn't catch you first. Or me. What if you walked back into a trap? Did you think of that?"

He shook his head. If she had thought he looked older during the crossing of the ravine, he looked young and vulnerable again now.

"I don't think I can stay awake much longer," she said. And it was the truth. Whatever was keeping her leg numb was also having an effect on her mind. Her vision kept blurring no matter how hard she tried to keep it clear.

"Engenius?" Sal called. The beads rattled again, and a large, white-skinned man walked into the room. His hair and beard were grey and close-cropped. His eyes were concerned.

"You're sleepy?" he said. "Don't fight it, princess. It will make you strong."

Princess? No one had ever called her anything like that before. She wanted to ask him who he was, but the words wouldn't come.

Sal leaned close. "I won't go," he said. "I'll be here when you wake up. I promise."

She couldn't tell if he was lying or not this time, but had no choice but to let him go. His face receded to the end of a long, dark tunnel, then he vanished from sight.

Engenius Lutz was the only surgeon in Yor, and therefore the only surgeon for many hundreds of kilometres. He dressed in grey smocks that hung to his knees, regardless of the temperature, and his breath smelled of the yukuri fruit Sal had used to soothe her headache. So she learned the next day, when she woke to see her leg unbound for the first time. The sight of it appalled her — a mass of bruised flesh, all yellow and purple, looking less like a part of her than a side of meat left out in the sun too long. To take her mind off the pain, Lutz told her about how she had come to him. She had assumed that Sal knew of the surgeon from his previous travels, but Lutz explained how

Sal had roared into town during the town's afternoon siesta the previous day, honking his horn and bellowing for a doctor at the top of his lungs.

"He shook things up, let me tell you. Wouldn't take no for an answer. People will talk about it for years."

Which was exactly what Sal was afraid of, she knew. The fewer people who knew about them, the better. At least the buggy wasn't as much of an oddity as it had been in Fundelry. She heard the burbling of several similar vehicles in the street outside.

"He told me what you did on the bridge," the surgeon said, looking down at her from a great height. His face was broad and well rounded, as though moulded out of clay. "That was quick thinking, princess. You were very brave."

Was I? she thought. She'd never considered herself brave before. She'd just done what she had to do. If that was all it took, then it was easier than she'd thought.

She blacked out again when he rebound her leg, but woke feeling better some hours later. There was a grey-haired old woman in the room, cleaning. She paid no attention to Shilly at all as she dusted in the corners and took away the old bandages. The tune she hummed was soothing and lulled Shilly back to sleep, even though she fought it. She was spending too much time asleep. They were losing ground.

The next time she woke, it was night, and Sal explained that the old woman was Lutz's mother. His clothes had been washed since Shilly had last seen him. He was almost looking clean, if a little rough around the edges.

"We need to leave here," she said.

"I know. Lutz won't let us go until tomorrow, and even then he's reluctant. I don't want to push him. He knows more about this than I do, after all."

"It's *my* leg," she said, "and I decide what to do with it."

"Yes," he agreed, "but you're not really in a fit state to make decisions, are you? Look at you. You can hardly keep your eyes open."

She was about to argue, but she truly didn't have the energy. He was right: the last thing she wanted to do was go anywhere.

"Tomorrow, then. You promise?"

"I promise. We'll have you out of here before you can say 'apothecary'."

"Say what?"

He smiled and answered her, but she only saw his lips move. Sense by sense, the world drifted away, and she slept deeply, dreaming of great purple clouds that hung swollen and heavy above a land already drenched with pain.

Lutz helped Sal prepare a seat for Shilly in the back of the buggy, his features painted pink by the dawn sunlight. The big man folded the sleeping bag so it would support her back. There wasn't enough room to lie full-length comfortably, so she would have to sit partially upright all the time, no matter how ill she felt. Her leg would be supported on water and fuel containers, suspended in front of her like a jetty jutting out from shore.

"I strongly advise against this," said Engenius Lutz for the fifth time that morning, his wide face set in a lumpy frown.

"I know." Sal lashed down the tarpaulin. He had washed again while she slept, and looked rested. "But we have no choice."

"Perhaps if I came with you —"

"I'm sorry, Engenius. We've got to make it on our own. We have a long way left to go."

This was Shilly's first proper glimpse of Yor. The town consisted of a collection of sun-bleached houses on either side of a gravel road leading straight as an arrow into the town and beyond it. It was much smaller than she had imagined, little more than a place to water camels or refuel after a long journey. What exactly the countryside around it consisted of, she couldn't see, but she could smell it. The air was rich with an odour she associated with some of Lodo's more arcane experiments: harsh and tangy, vaguely distasteful. A constant haze of dust, kicked up by wheels and hoofs, hung thick in the lazy air, making her eyes water.

The thought of Lodo made her sad again, but she put aside the emotion. There were more immediate things to worry about.

The surgeon shook his head heavily. "I am a simple man, Tom. I have no concern for anything but the wellbeing of my patients. That leg, in this instance. I don't care who you're running from or what you might have done to deserve it, but I will say this: in order to make your journey easier, I'll do my best to ensure that you aren't followed."

Sal glanced up from his knots. "Thank you," he said. "You don't have to do that."

"I do. Gentle travel may make all the difference." He looked up the road at a surly cluster of people watching from the shade of the general store's verandah. "I can't say, though, that everyone will share my opinion."

Sal nodded soberly, and together they helped Shilly into her improvised seat. She bit her lip as her leg was moved. They tried to be gentle but the pain was sudden and sharp, like red-hot knives twisting in her bones.

When she was settled, Lutz pressed a small jar of tablets into her hand. "For the pain, princess."

"I'll be fine," she snapped in reply. Hurt throbbed through her, making everything difficult.

Lutz backed away and watched from the shade as Sal started the buggy's engine.

"Drive well!" the surgeon called over the sound of the engine. His expression was concerned — and something else too. Jealous, perhaps. Shilly couldn't define it.

"I will." Sal raised a hand in farewell. Dented and dirty, the battered vehicle drove off in a cloud of white dust.

Shilly waved at the doctor and his grey-haired, hunched mother. She was glad they were on their way again, but she was sad to be leaving. Lutz had been kind and persistent in his treatment; she would miss that security on the road ahead. There was a certain amount of confusion about it, too. She had missed a lot of the previous day and two nights, including the mad dash from the ravine down to Yor, and the resetting of her leg. It seemed strange to her that they were going already, when from her point of view they had only just arrived. That was just an illusion, she knew, and staying longer simply wasn't an option. The town itself would have to be a missing piece of their journey for her.

Not a large piece, she gathered. From her vantage point, she could see that the town was being slowly eaten away by the elements. There was no grass, no trees, no green at all. Everything was dead. How, she wondered, could people live there?

"We're in the Broken Lands now," Sal said as he drove up the main road. "Yor is the gateway. Do you remember my dad saying that he'd buried my body here, when the Alcaide questioned him in Fundelry?"

"Yes." She thought she did, although she was still trying not to think about the past.

"We always had to come here, to refuel and pick up water, but I wasn't intending to make such a dramatic entrance."

They passed a dozen houses, a camel pen containing six of the tall, curious beasts, and went through a rusty gate. *Not much of a gateway*, she thought. Beyond that was only road — if it could be called that. The level, white surface that had led through the small town soon became a heavily rutted track winding through deep red soil. It led perfectly north as far as she could see over a landscape as flat as anything she had ever experienced. On the horizon ahead she could see what looked like hills, but the shimmer in the air made them hard to discern. They could have been anything: buildings, trees, mirages. On her right, a ghostly willy-willy whirled the red dust into the sky like a snake.

Sal had the map unfolded next to him, in the passenger seat. Shilly couldn't quite see it.

"Do you know where we're going?"

"We're heading for a place called the Lookout," he explained. "It's on the far side of the Broken Lands but on this side of the Divide. That's where we cross — to Nesh on the other side. From that point on, we'll be in the Interior. Where exactly we'll go then, I'm not sure. We'll have fewer options than we do in the Strand. The Stone Mages prefer cities to villages, so there will be fewer places to look. That could make it easier or harder."

She couldn't imagine what it would be like, so she tried to concentrate on the immediate future. "What are the Broken Lands?"

"I don't know, exactly," Sal replied without turning his head. His attention was on the road, avoiding sudden dips or bumps. Even so, the buggy lurched all too frequently, jolting her leg. "I always thought of it as something like a Ruin, but I'm not picking up any background potential. It's just — there."

"What is?"

"You'll see. It's not all like this."

"I hope not." Yor lay behind them, swallowed by the cloud of dust they left in their wake. Her eyes could discern no detail on the terrible, flat plain — except for the enigmatic shapes far ahead. Above the horizon the sun was already burning fiercely, blinding her and boiling her at the same time. "Do we have to go through them?"

He nodded. "This is the safest and most direct route to the Lookout. The Broken Lands stretch almost two thousand kilometres from side to side, so to go around would take forever. Luckily they're narrower across than they are wide. At this point, they're only two hundred kilometres across."

She was relieved to hear that. "It shouldn't take us long, then."

"It's not all as easy as this."

"You call this easy?"

"Compared to what's ahead, yes. I've never driven it myself. I only watched while Dad did it." Sal was silent for a moment, then said: "I'm thinking at least two days."

She winced as the buggy tipped suddenly to one side then righted itself. The track's narrowness and roughness implied that it wasn't designed for motorised traffic. She saw occasional black patches on the ground as they passed by, where caravans had camped on the outskirts of Yor. But for her leg, a camel would have been much more comfortable, she thought.

The buggy lurched again and, despite her determination not to, she reached for the vial of pills Engenius Lutz had given her. Taking one of the rough, white tablets, she washed it down with a swig of water.

"It's weird," Sal said, "coming back here without my father."

Shilly couldn't tell if Sal was addressing her or just himself, but she was happy to let him talk.

"The last time we came this way, we were caught in a storm. It was amazing. The sky was black with clouds and the rain was hot and thick, like taking a shower. We couldn't drive in it; had to stop and wait it out and move on when it was over. But that wasn't the worst of it. The ground isn't good at holding water here, so the road was swept away in places, and then we came across a caravan that had been caught in a flash flood. They lost five people and two camels. We carried some of their goods in exchange for a room at Yor. Later, we heard that another caravan had been struck by lightning. The leader, a woman named Diamond Fargher, was someone we knew from the borderlands. She was hit when she was in the open and it instantly stopped her heart. Her team carried her body until the water subsided and buried her out here, somewhere. It'd be a lonely place to rest, that's for sure ..."

Shilly's eyes drifted upward, to the sky. It was blue and flawless, apart from the sun. She couldn't imagine it as Sal had described it: cloudy from horizon to horizon, teeming with rain. But she didn't disbelieve him. He wasn't the sort to exaggerate simply to impress her.

She wanted to ask him about the Divide and the Lookout, but her thoughts were clouded and her mouth wouldn't move properly. The pain had receded into the distance and she was grateful for that, but the brief memory of Yor was fading with it and she wanted to scream that it wasn't fair; couldn't she keep her mind without the pain? Why did it have to be one or the other?

The buggy moved in slow motion, rocking her gently as though floating on the sea. Sal was talking again. The words meant nothing. She couldn't sleep, but she dreamed that they had been travelling forever on a giant, bone-white ship across a desert sea. The water ran out before they got where they were going, though, and they were marooned in the middle of nowhere. The sun baked the soil rock hard, locking the ship tight in the ground. They couldn't move. She jumped out of the boat and tried to dig it free, cursing all the while, determined not to be held up a moment longer. She was late, and getting later with every minute.

The fat, blistering sun turned ponderously across the sky and descended to the opposite horizon, which for some reason was as irregular as the teeth in an ancient skull. In the darkness she could hear the wind whistling through the ravine, and felt again the awful moment of panic as the buggy had leapt forward with her sprawled across it. The crack of bone between metal and concrete snapped her back to full consciousness with a start.

"Are you all right?"

Shilly looked around, confused. It was night, and they had stopped. The buggy was off the track, sheltered behind a ruined masonry wall. The horizon on the other side matched the one in her dream perfectly.

When had the world gone from being flat to rugged again? She couldn't remember. But she wasn't still dreaming; she was sure of it. Although her head was fuzzy, her thoughts were clear.

"Just a nightmare," the voice decided. She looked up at its source. Sal was leaning over her, a half-smile making light of his concern. She nodded, knowing that the memories of the ravine would be with her forever, along with the scars. No matter what else she forgot in the long, arduous journey, that would never fade.

"Don't let me take any more of those tablets," she said. "I feel terrible."

"How's your leg?"

"Don't ask. Do I have to stay up here?" She was still slumped in the makeshift bed on the back of the buggy. Her back was aching.

"I'll get you down later. First I want to make a fire and put some food on. You need to eat to get better."

"Is that why we stopped?"

"No. The road is too bad to drive on at night. We got bogged once already."

She frowned, a vague memory of him cursing the spinning wheels drifting out of the vagueness then sinking back down again. With the memory came more images that clashed with the desert surrounding Yor. Images of crumbling riverbanks, flat boulders and shattered rock, through and over which the track wound like a snake.

"Where are we?"

"About fifty kilometres into the Broken Lands. We made good time until the last stretch. It's even rougher than I remember." He clambered down off the tray and began to unpack supplies. "If you want to do something, you can peel these."

He handed her a knife and some wizened, yellow, root vegetables. She took them, relieved that she wouldn't have to sit and watch him do everything. They were supposed to be working as a team; at some point she would have to start fulfilling her end of the deal.

When a simple stew was boiling in the pot, he helped her hop awkwardly off the tray and onto the ground. The shock of landing reverberated through her broken leg and she bit her lip to avoid crying out. He talked with unnatural animation about the wildlife he'd seen on the road while she relieved herself, leaning on him for support and not hearing a word he was saying until she was relatively comfortable by the fire. The smell of cooking was a great improvement on the pungent odour of the countryside; whatever it was, the odour was stronger than it had been at Yor and nagged at her like an itch.

They were silent as they ate their meal. She could feel the reticence of the early stages of their journey creeping back over her again, but this time she fought it. They needed to talk to each other if they were going to keep travelling together, and most of what she *needed* to say boiled down to one phrase, one she had always found difficult to say.

It finally came out when dinner was over and the fire was winding down. They were sitting opposite each other. His eyes reflected the orange light back at her.

"I want to say thank you, Sal," she said.

He looked startled. "What for?"

"You know." The words came only awkwardly. "For saving my life."

"You saved mine too."

"That was just a reflex. I didn't think about it. You went to a lot of trouble and took a great deal of risk to —"

"You don't have to thank me, Shilly. You shouldn't. I don't deserve it." He looked distinctly uncomfortable.

"Why not?"

"It's just ..."

"It's what, Sal?"

"Let's just say we're even. We saved each other. That's enough, isn't it?" He shifted restlessly. "I mean, I crashed the buggy, I dragged you away from Fundelry, I got you into trouble with the Sky Wardens —"

"And we're trying to fix all that, together. You didn't have to take me with you. Thanks for giving me a chance."

"Neither of us really has a choice," he said. "We're sort of stuck with each other."

"True. So it would be stupid to fight about who owes whom for what. We should just be grateful in general."

"I agree," he said. "Maybe this is what Lodo meant when he said we were 'destined.' Destined to help each other through this, as much as we can."

She thought about that, as she'd thought about it many times during the previous weeks. "I don't know," she eventually said. "It could be."

He nodded. "I can't see how he could know about anything else. We're just kids, really. The future could hold anything."

Shilly studied him in the fading firelight and wondered who he was trying to reassure the most: himself, or her. They were both still young, it was true, but they were on their own and were being forced to grow up fast. She could see it in him, at times, and on his face: the man he would one day become. She didn't know if he could see similar changes in her: she was older, so the difference wouldn't be so obvious. His voice hadn't broken yet. He had further to catch up.

He was right, though. Anything *could* happen. But that wasn't what she'd wanted to talk about. Far from it. She could feel herself flushing with embarrassment in the darkness and clutched at anything to change the subject.

"How long until we reach the Desert Ports?"

"A week, maybe two." He sounded relieved at the shift too. "It depends on how we get on at the Lookout and Nesh. Even if there's no one waiting for us there, we'll still have to talk our way through."

"Do you know how we're going to do that?"

"Not yet." He surprised them both with a sudden yawn. "Sorry," he said, stretching out and lying back on the sleeping bag with his hands beneath his head. "Don't worry, Shilly. I'm sure we'll think of something."

She nodded because she had to believe him. This was his territory, not hers. What little she knew about the borderlands came from Mrs Milka, Fundelry's only Schoolteacher, and she didn't trust a lot of that. The official line was that the Stone Mages of the Interior and the Sky Wardens of the Strand co-existed in harmony, having very little in common except a small amount of trade. Shilly was sure it wasn't so simple, or innocent. Sal himself was proof of that, if she needed any: a child born out of a mixed, political union who had spent most of his life between both countries, in neither one nor the other. He couldn't be the only one.

Maybe that was where the inhabitants of Yor fitted in. If someone didn't belong in either the Strand or the Interior, but didn't want to travel, there might be few places left to live. Even an isolated, derelict town would be better than nothing — and might even give someone a sense of purpose. Someone like Engenius Lutz could be important where medical help was hard to find.

She felt vaguely sorry, then, for the man who had healed her. He had saved her leg at least, if not her life. It didn't seem fair to her that *anyone* should be forced out into the fringes: Lutz, Sal, or her. But perhaps there was a reason she knew nothing about.

She lay back to watch the stars. They were brilliantly depthless, perfect for taking her mind off her worries and the pain in her leg, and her uncertain memories of all the things waiting for her in the Interior: the Advisory Synod, the Judges, the Nine Stars. At least one thing was behind her, even if her memories of that were even more uncertain and hazy. She wouldn't be unhappy if she never saw Yor again.

"Have you ever —?" she started to say, but stopped upon seeing that Sal was asleep. She went back to looking at the stars and wondering at the strange, angular nature of the northern horizon, determined to keep watch while he rested. Without taking one of Lutz's potent little pills, she doubted she would sleep anyway. She had had far too much of it lately, enough for a lifetime.

So it came as a surprise, deep in the night, to be startled awake by the sound of another vehicle chugging toward them along the track, glimmers of light from its headlamps shining around the masonry they were sheltering behind. It was even more of a shock to hear it slow as it grew near. Shilly automatically tried to sit up, but every nerve in her leg cried out in protest.

The last vestiges of sleep vanished when she heard the vehicle rattle to a halt and two men speak softly over the chugging of the motor.

She remembered in a flash Lutz's promise to deflect any pursuit if he could, and his glance at the cheerless group of villagers further along Yor's only road. There was only one conclusion she could come to.

"Sal!" she hissed. "Sal, wake up! Someone's here! They've found us!"

CHAPTER 3

WHERE CITIES DIE

Sal was on his feet without thinking. The urgency in Shilly's voice bypassed his brain and spoke directly to his limbs. He remembered to skirt the remains of the fire and was careful of her leg when he reached her, but it was a moment or two before he actually understood what was going on.

An alcohol engine chugged nearby. Light splashed around the wall hiding the buggy from view of the road. Another car! But no one travelled the Broken Lands at night, not unless it was an emergency — and if this *was* an emergency, *why* had they stopped?

"What do we do now?" Shilly whispered to him. Her eyes were wide and white — the only details in her dark face he could make out.

He was spared a vague answer by the grumble of the engine climbing up a notch in pitch, then a crunch of gears engaging. With a growl, the car began to move away from them, bouncing over the uneven surface of the track leading away from Yor, the glow of its headlights gradually fading away.

He had barely begun to relax when he heard footsteps approaching them. Shilly's hand clutched his arm and every muscle in his body unconsciously tensed to spring.

"Sal?" called a voice. "Shilly? Are you there?"

Sal froze at the sound of their real names, thinking that there was only one person who knew them who could have caught up in the night. A patch of black stepped around the deeper blackness of the wall and a torch snapped on, blinding him.

"I thought so," said the voice behind the light, and this time Sal recognised it. "It may be dark, but a blind dingo couldn't miss your tracks."

It was Engenius Lutz, a big, shadowy figure behind the glare of his torch — the most unlikely person Sal could have thought of to turn up just then. It seemed only an hour or two ago that they had left him behind in Yor.

"Where did you learn our names?" Sal asked, standing up.

"What are you *doing* here?" Shilly put in.

The surgeon came closer to the remains of the fire and averted the light. In his other hand he clutched his black leather bag and a small khaki rucksack. He looked crumpled and weary. The shadows pooled in the recesses of his earthen face.

"Just before sunset," he said, "two people came to town: a boy slightly older than you two, and a man. The man was as dark as a snake's shadow and had the look of someone getting close to something — something he wanted very badly. He sent the boy to find them a room for the night. Then he started asking questions."

Sal knew what was coming. "Did he give a name?"

"Shom Behenna."

"He's a Sky Warden. Did he tell you that?"

"Eventually, yes — and if you thought *you* made a stir, that was nothing compared to him. I don't think we've seen a Warden in Yor for twenty-five years."

Sal's head felt light. "I knew it. They've been following us. I dreamed about them. Behenna —" He was about to say that the Sky Warden had helped him save Shilly's life, but that would have revealed too much about them. The less Lutz knew about Sal's relationship with the Change, the better. He would have to explain his reticence to Shilly later.

"His young companion's name is Tait," Lutz went on. "He says he knows you, princess. He described you perfectly."

Shilly's eyes widened further in the reflected light of the torch. "Tait? But —"

"What did Behenna say, exactly?" Sal asked the surgeon.

"He wanted to know if anyone had seen you. The names he used were different to the ones you had given me, and he didn't say why he wanted to know where you were, but the descriptions matched. I knew immediately he was the one you were running from. I can see why, too, Sky Warden or not. He was eager when he heard how close he was, and he became angry when told no one would take him anywhere at night. He could practically smell you, and his hunger was terrible to see." Lutz shook his head. "I said nothing, of course. I excused myself and pretended to be out when he came knocking on my door. As soon as the sun was fully set, I arranged for a lift. There *are* some who will drive this road at night, but you have to have a good reason. Or apply sufficient leverage."

A town's only doctor would know enough to get anything he wanted, Sal guessed. A Sky Warden could apply pressure too. Behenna would be on the road first thing the next morning.

"How were they travelling?" he asked.

"On horseback. It's rare we see such beasts up here, and these had been run into the ground. They had money for stables and new mounts, but they won't find anything of that quality in Yor. When they travel again, it will be by camel or motor vehicle, or on foot."

Sal thought furiously. That meant Behenna and Tait must have ridden all the way from Fundelry, buying fresh horses every chance they could. Not limited to tracks and rough fields, they would have been able to travel on good roads and enjoy the finest hostels. That explained how they had caught up so quickly.

How they had worked out which way to go was a different question. Maybe it was simply an educated guess that had paid off. Behenna had known Sal's history and had assumed that he would head north. While the tiny *tap-taps* might not pin Sal down with any precision, the one instance of genuine contact by the ravine must have done so. Once Behenna had known exactly where Sal was, he would have known that Sal's next stop was most likely to be Yor. From then on, it had just been a matter of speed. If they had stayed one more night in Yor, as Lutz had wanted, that would have been the end of their freedom.

It made sense. The trouble was, Sal didn't know what he could do about it.

Shilly was the one who broke the silence.

"So why are *you* here?" she asked Lutz.

The big man put down his khaki rucksack and sat on it. "I came to warn you. You'll have only a night's head start, and the Sky Warden will be guided by people who know the road well. You won't be able to outrun them, not with this leg to care for, and I could not allow you to risk a patient's health by trying."

"You couldn't *allow* it?"

"Don't misunderstand me, princess. I am not here to tell you what to do! I only want to help you."

"Your lift should have stayed, then," said Sal. "That way, Shilly could have gone back with you while I went ahead. She could have waited in Yor like I originally planned."

Shilly was shaking her head before he finished the sentence, but it was Lutz who killed that argument.

"It wouldn't work. Your pursuer was asking about both of you, remember. Not just you, Sal. She wouldn't be safe if you left her behind."

So it was official, Sal thought. Shilly was a fugitive, too. They really were stuck in it together, whether they liked it or not.

In the reflected light of the torch, her expression was hard to read.

"What do you suggest we do, then?" she said. "You wouldn't have come all the way out here only to be caught with us."

"Indeed." The surgeon's smile lit up his bulbous, bearded face with a mixture of relief and something oddly like triumph. "If you take the road, you will be too easy to find. I'm proof of that: there is so little wheeled traffic through here that your tracks stood out clearly, even at night. The friend who drove me here will obscure your passage somewhat, but an experienced tracker will still find you easily. I can help you in that respect, and show you another way across the Broken Lands into the bargain. It is definitely not safe to travel at night, but I can direct you to the junction now and we can continue at dawn."

For a brief moment, Sal felt doubt. The surgeon had healed Shilly willingly enough, and for little money. He professed to be concerned only about Shilly's injury. But if his concern for the broken leg was greater than his desire to help Sal escape, and if the Sky Warden had convinced him that Shilly would receive better care away from Sal, Lutz might willingly betray them. They didn't know how far he would go to save a patient from herself.

Sal's instinct told him that they could trust the surgeon, but it didn't entirely reassure him, either. There was something behind Lutz's words that didn't entirely ring true. Had they had any other options, he might have reconsidered the decision he had to make, but as it was he had little choice.

"All right. We'll do what you say, if Shilly agrees."

Shilly nodded.

"Good. Then let's break camp." Lutz stood. "The junction is a couple of kilometres further on. I'll take you there, then find us somewhere safe to sleep. We need to get as much rest as possible. We'll be on our way again at dawn, and it's not an easy road."

Thus warned, Sal helped the surgeon place Shilly back onto the tray of the buggy, then rearranged the supplies so there would be room for their extra passenger. Lutz was happy to let Sal drive, only speaking when he knew of a hazard ahead. They bounced along the dirt track for a good thirty minutes, past strange rock formations that loomed out of the darkness on either side then fell back into shadow behind. The red desert surrounding Yor was barely an hour's drive across, and the tangled landscape now around them was closer to the true nature of the Broken Lands: uneven ground filled with the remains of ancient habitation, such as the wall they had sheltered behind, where Lutz had found them. Who had once lived there and what had happened to them, Sal didn't know. He suspected no one did.

"There." Lutz pointed at the turn-off with one long finger. Had he not done so, Sal would have driven right past it. It was little more than a gap in the landscape, a slight lightening of shadow between the remains of a low stone fence and the embankment of a dry creek bed. Even during the day it wouldn't stand out among the other odd breaks in the path.

Lutz led them a hundred metres along the new track, then had Sal bring the buggy to a halt. He disappeared for a moment to erase the marks where they had left the main road. When he returned, he unfurled a thin rug from his rucksack, lay down on the sandy ground with his head resting on his battered, black bag, and went almost instantly to sleep. They didn't light a fire.

Shilly wasn't far behind the surgeon, falling into a deep, but occasionally disturbed, slumber. Sal lay awake listening to the sounds of the Broken Lands. It was busy, filled with insects and other small creatures scurrying about in the cool night air. As always, Sal was surprised by how much the temperature dropped at night in the desert and before long he was forced to go to the back of the buggy for the sleeping bag.

Shilly stirred, moaning in her sleep. Her hands fluttered, reaching for her leg. Sal wondered if he should use the Change to help her, either to ease the pain or assist the bones as they knit. But he couldn't take the chance. Behenna was too close. It would be like sending up a flare.

So he forced himself to ignore her and curled up on the ground by the buggy, willing himself to sleep. *No blame*, she had said, but he still felt responsible. She had saved his life and was now paying the price for it. If she was lame for the rest of her life, would she really forgive him so easily?

At some point, as a quarter moon the colour of sand rose over the jagged horizon, he closed his eyes for the last time that day, and slept.

The next thing he knew, Lutz was shaking him awake.

"Come on," the surgeon said, nudging him again. "We have to get moving."

Sal struggled upright, rubbing his eyes. A dull half-light painted their impromptu campsite in pale browns and greys, barely enough to see by. The eastern sky was turning yellow. Shilly was glaring at him from her position on the buggy's tray, lines of pain around her eyes. Did they really have to move so early?

Tap-tap.

He didn't feel like sleeping after that. If Behenna was awake, too, the chase was already on. Their only hope was to beat him to the Lookout and cross into the Interior, where they would finally be safe.

They packed up their small amount of gear and had a cursory breakfast. Lutz hadn't brought any food with him, but they made do. Having Lutz along made caring for Shilly easier; Sal still felt embarrassed by some of it, but he told himself that this was what working together was all about and that he'd just have to get used to it until she was better. Regardless, he was still glad when it was over and they could set out.

Lutz guided Sal unhesitatingly forward, deeper into the Broken Lands, away from the road they had intended to travel at first, then parallel to it.

The way was indeed hard, the shattered landscape worse than he had imagined from the relative safety of the road. It seemed to consist of a vast number of fragments flung together from very different parts of the world. At times they skated across a field of loose, grey stones, polished as though by water; then they would be back on desert sand, only yellow rather than the red he was used to. Then, without transition, the earth would buckle beneath them and they would be traversing the lip of a tumbledown cliff, or negotiating what might have once been a gentle hillside but was now tipped onto its side, presenting a rugged slope. All these sorts of terrain, and more, coexisted uneasily, some of them only metres across, making travel difficult.

Sal soon learned, though, that the boundaries between the patchwork landscapes were the most treacherous places. Lutz was guiding him along the largest and most easily traversed sections, following a very faint track that frequently hairpinned to avoid obstacles. Sal's arms became tired from turning the steering wheel, and his legs ached from frequent accelerations and braking — but his discomfort was nothing compared to Shilly's. She quickly succumbed to the pain and took another of the surgeon's tablets.

That left Sal with only Lutz and Behenna's *tap-tapping* for company. The surgeon was unforthcoming on anything other than the route, wrapped deep in private thoughts. In between directions, Sal tried to draw him out.

"Turn left up here, past that rock face. The grey one."

"You know your way pretty well, Engenius. I don't know how you do it."

"A friend walked me through here once, a long time ago. If you've been once, you never forget."

His grey eyes, almost the same colour as his beard, stared patiently ahead — *through* the landscape, Sal thought.

"Have you always lived in the Broken Lands?"

"Not always. Take us through that gap by the tree, there."

"Where did you study medicine?"

"In Samimi. Be careful. It's steep."

Sal steadied the buggy as it tipped down a rough incline. "Why —? Uh." They hit bottom with a jolt, and he took a second to look behind him to make sure that Shilly was okay. She didn't stir. "The Samimi near Yunda, west of the Haunted City?"

"*In* Yunda. Have you been there?"

"No." Samimi was a large coastal town, far too deep into the Strand for his father to have felt safe. Only once had they ventured anywhere near the sea, and that had been at Fundelry. "I've only heard of it."

"You haven't missed anything." Lutz's eyes drifted off the road for a moment, then came back. Sal wondered if bitter memories clouded the man's feelings for the town, since it had a good reputation. Maybe he had lost a patient under dubious circumstances and been forced to leave. That would certainly explain why the man chose to live somewhere so isolated and with no great future.

"I'm sorry if we've put you out too much," Sal said, not wanting the conversation to stop so soon.

"Not at all. I like a change of scenery every now and again, and there's always work for me to do at the Lookout."

"How will you get back to Yor?"

"I'll get a lift with someone." Lutz's eyes drifted forward again, and his expression clouded. He started to say something, but it was mumbled so half-heartedly that Sal missed the beginning.

"What was that?" Sal prompted. Something about Lutz's father?

"I'm sorry. Nothing you need worry about, Tom — I mean, Sal." The surgeon slumped into himself. "Over that gravel, now, nice and quickly or you'll slide. When you get to the top, though, go slowly. There's another drop ahead."

That was the end of the conversation. The noise of the gravel under the wheels was too loud to talk over, and the next few kilometres were a maze of switchbacks and landfalls. It took all of Sal's skill to negotiate it; not once did Lutz offer to take a turn at the wheel.

And still, as constant as his heartbeat, came the faint *tap-tap* from Behenna. By the afternoon, Tait and the Sky Warden would most likely have reached the place where Sal and Shilly had left the main road. Only time would tell if that confused Behenna. The best Sal could hope for was that they might regain *some* of their lead on the way to the Lookout. Behenna was unlikely to be deflected forever. There was only one way to cross into the Interior for a thousand kilometres in either direction, and they were both heading there.

They stopped for lunch under the shade of a eucalyptus grove. A spring — the only flowing water Sal had ever seen in the Broken Lands — trickled from under a cluster of rocks and vanished into a crack not far away. When Sal took the opportunity to replenish their emergency tanks, he was startled by the distinct buzz of the Change in the water. Somewhere near them, or near the spring's source, was a Ruin.

He stood up and looked around. If it was in their path and they found it by nightfall, it would serve as a good hiding place from Behenna. All they had to do was convince Lutz to stop there without alerting him to the fact that Sal was sensitive to the Change.

The only things that stood out in the confused landscape ahead of them were the towering, angular shapes on the horizon. He had seen them before, from the main road, but never from this close. They were growing nearer as the day wore on, yet even from this new perspective they were still mysterious: too tall and thin to be mountains; too big to be buildings of any sort he'd seen before. Something about them made him think of the story of Polain the Butterfly Merchant and its city of metal and glass, but it couldn't possibly be the same thing, not in the middle of such a wilderness.

"Is that where we're going?" he asked Lutz, raising his voice to catch the surgeon's attention and pointing at the shapes ahead.

Lutz looked up, frowned and nodded. "We're going through there, yes."

"What is it?"

"You'll see all too soon."

"*How* soon?"

"Today."

Sal knew that had to be wrong. At the rate they were travelling, they wouldn't reach the strange silhouettes that day, maybe not even the next. But he didn't argue; there was clearly no point trying to talk to the surgeon until his mood passed. Instead, he did as he had originally intended: he filled the water bottles, and made sure afterward that Shilly drank from the Change-rich water.

Shilly awoke from her drug-induced daze to the sound of arguing.

"We have to."

"I'm telling you, it's not safe!"

"Why not?"

"It's too complicated to explain right now."

"But we *need* to go there."

"Why?"

"We just do!"

"That's not good enough, Sal. There must be a reason."

"Why should I tell you, when *you* won't tell *me* why it's unsafe in there?"

"Hey!" Shilly levered herself into an upright position, startled by the annoyed tone in Sal's voice. "*Where* do we have to go? Why isn't it safe? What's going on?"

He and Lutz were standing on the top of a slight rise, facing each other. At the sound of her voice, Sal turned and came down the hill.

"I'm sorry," he said. "I didn't mean to wake you."

But she was no longer paying attention to him. Her eyes had been caught by what lay beyond him — and what was, obviously, the cause of their argument.

She saw towers, hundreds of them facing her in a wall more than a kilometre wide. They were like nothing she had ever seen before, of varying heights and shapes, in different colours and styles. She couldn't tell how tall they were: higher than she dared imagine, if the haze between her and them was an accurate judge of their distance.

And they were old. Even from so far away she could see holes where walls had fallen away, gaping mouths where cornices had collapsed, and empty sockets where mighty sheets of glass had once hung. With the sun dipping low over the horizon behind her, its golden light catching the buildings perfectly, she was struck by their tragic, terrible beauty.

"Can you feel it?" Sal whispered.

She wrenched her eyes off the view, back to him, and was confused for a good while as to what he had meant. Then it hit her. She looked back at the towers. They were golden from more than the sun. Below the optical effect was something more unique still: the twinkling of the Change. To be visible across such a distance, she knew, it must be very strong indeed.

No wonder Sal wanted to go in. If the towers were a massive Ruin, there was no way Behenna could find them there.

Sal turned back to Lutz, making a visible effort not to let frustration get the better of him. "I want to go there and you said earlier that we were going to. What's the problem?"

"That was when I thought we'd make it before nightfall. If we pitch camp now, we can go in the morning and everything will be fine."

"I don't understand what difference it makes being at night."

"It makes all the difference. Trust me."

"But if we stop now, we'll lose the rest of the day."

"It's only an hour or so, Sal."

"It's only a *Ruin*, Engenius!"

Lutz held up a hand. "Okay, okay! We're not getting anywhere, shouting at each other. How about we let Shilly decide?"

She looked between them, reluctant to distrust their guide, but unwilling to trust him completely, either, if he wouldn't give them a reason for his opinion. Obviously Sal had tried to get him to, and just as obviously Sal didn't want to tell Lutz why *he* wanted to so badly.

"I pick the city," she said, adding, since she couldn't use the Change as a reason either: "We'll be able to light a fire in there, hidden from view. That'd make a nice change."

Lutz looked disappointed, as though he'd thought she might choose otherwise. His mood had changed dramatically since the morning, from eagerness to be on their way to something bordering on fear, and she thought he might continue to argue the point. She almost hoped he would; maybe then they would find out why he didn't want to proceed any further that night. But he gave in with a shrug.

"All right," he said, "the city it is. A fire is a good idea, but we'd better grab wood now. There'll be none from here on."

What he meant by that only became clear when the buggy was loaded up and carried them over the hill. Instead of more of the twisted landscape she had half-noticed on the journey thus far, all she saw between her and the towers was a completely flat, white plain.

"Salt lake," said Sal when she asked. "This is how we're going to make the towers by nightfall." He put his foot down on the accelerator, urging the buggy onward. Although built for reliability rather than acceleration, over an uninterrupted stretch it was capable of a surprising turn of speed.

The air — with its strange, chemical stench — whipped through Shilly's hair and stung her eyes. The surface of the salt lake was different to anything she had ever seen before; it made the desert seem normal. A dried-up sea, out in the middle of nowhere. The sparkling surface crunched under the wheels, not everywhere pure white; patches of colour rolled by like flattened reflections of a non-existent cloudy sky. Occasional rocky "islands" stood out from the perfect smoothness of the lake. From one they startled a large emu; the long-legged, awkward-looking bird stared at them and then ran for the horizon.

Even across such an expanse, it took some time to reach the base of the towers. The setting sun had painted the salt lake in pinks and reds by the time they were there. And then Shilly saw the weirdest thing of all.

The base of the towers lay beneath the dry bed of the salt lake, as though the city had been flooded before the lake dried up. She couldn't tell how deep they went. They stuck out of the ground like the pylons of a pier at low tide. There were no doors, although in numerous places broken windows were within reach or were half-buried so that a simple crawl would give access to the inside. She was curious to find out what they might contain and wondered if she could convince Sal to crawl inside for a look.

The towers loomed over her, imposing and ominous at close quarters, even with the colours of sunset across them. There were so many of them huddling so close together she couldn't see the sky between them. Peering through gaps, she saw others behind the front ones, and others behind *them* — all different, all decaying. She had no way of telling how many there might be: hundreds, maybe. It couldn't possibly be thousands, she told herself. Her mind baulked at the thought.

Sal skirted the edge of the towers, looking for a way in. There was little room between them, at times barely enough for the buggy to squeeze through, and the white ground was littered with rubble. Sometimes the sound of the buggy's engine triggered decay high up in a tower, and a rattle of falling masonry or glass greeted them, making Shilly jump. It sounded like evidence of life, but it could not be. The place was dead; she could feel it in her bones.

Yet it was vibrant with the Change. The twinkling in the air wasn't like light; she wouldn't be able to see anything by it. It was there all the same, making her nerve endings tingle.

Lutz half stood in his seat, worrying at his lip. Shilly thought he looked torn between nervousness and eagerness. "There," he said, pointing ahead at a relatively wide avenue between two particularly large, pointed towers. "If you must."

They drove through the gap as the shadow of the horizon reached for the base of the towers. The air grew instantly cooler and darker, as though a veil had been drawn. Shilly looked up in awe. The towers loomed over her, reducing the sky to a faint patch far, far above. She felt giddy looking up so high, and couldn't imagine what it would be like to scale such edifices.

Sal turned left, then right, then stopped in a clear patch where no masonry had fallen.

"A compromise," he said to Lutz. "We'll stay near the edge, but not so close that a fire could be seen from outside."

"You really think this Behenna would follow you here?" The surgeon's eyes didn't look at Sal. They roamed the growing shadows instead, nervously. "This is a cursed place."

The buggy's engine stopped under Sal's touch and the echoes took a disturbingly long time to fade. More bricks tumbled in the distance, making Shilly jump. All the windows — and there were so many of them — were empty and black. They seemed watchful, wary. She felt as though she was drowning in their age and dereliction.

Shilly wondered if they'd made the right decision, coming to this city. The small of her back itched. The air tasted of despair as much as it did of salt. She was no longer interested in knowing what the towers contained.

"The fire," Sal said, shivering. "It'll be dark soon."

Lutz helped unload the wood they had gathered with more enthusiasm than he had shown all day. Shilly could do little but watch them as they worked, cursing yet again the inconvenience of her leg, the throb in her bone that warned against even attempting to move on her own. If anything happened, she would be helpless.

When the fire was lit, they brought her down and made her comfortable on the ground. The feel of salt and sand under her buttocks was a welcome change from the tray of the buggy, despite the worsening smell.

"I'll make us something to eat," said Sal, unloading more supplies.

Lutz looked around and up. What little light remained of the sunset was dispelled by the warm crackle of the fire. The pool of yellow light surrounding it seemed very small, the darkness beyond impossibly deep. The only break in it came from shards of glass reflecting the firelight back at them, like eyes blinking.

She tugged the sleeping bag over her shoulders, chilled despite the flames.

"While you're cooking," the surgeon said, "I'll scout the area. Make sure we're safe."

"From what?"

Lutz didn't answer, just eased himself away from the fire and into the shadows. The last thing Shilly saw of him was his expression: frightened, but determined all the same. Whatever was out there, Lutz wasn't going to let himself be deterred by his fears.

Shilly helped Sal prepare vegetables, as she had done the previous night. When the stew was simmering in the pot, he came to sit by her. A wind had sprung up between the towers, carrying with it a biting chill as though somewhere deep inside the city lay a giant block of ice, untouched by the sun.

"What's got into *him?*" she asked, meaning Lutz.

Sal shrugged. "I think he's terrified. This place has him spooked."

"Understandable. But he wanted to come here."

"Not at night, remember? We blew a tyre after lunch and it took us a couple of hours to fix it. But for that, we would have made it during daylight. Maybe he would have been okay then."

"He could be afraid of the dark."

"If so, he's braver than I am, going off on his own." Sal peered out into the impenetrable darkness.

"I think he's looking for something," said Shilly, voicing a gut feeling. She remembered Lutz's envious look when they had headed off into the Broken Lands, the keenness with which he had led them off the usual road.

"Any idea what?"

"No. We'll have to ask him when he comes back."

Neither stated the obvious: *if* he came back.

"Something might well find *him*," Sal said. "This is the most amazing Ruin I've ever heard of. I dreamed about it, once. It means something, I'm sure."

Shilly gently shifted her leg. Her toes were tingling and there was an itch out of reach below her knee.

"Do you want me to — you know?" Sal asked, indicating the leg.

"Do you think it's safe?"

"Here, I'm sure it is. I can't feel Behenna at all. We're completely swamped by the background potential."

"Okay, then. Before Engenius comes back . . ."

Sal put his hands on the splint and bandages enclosing her leg and shut his eyes. Shilly did the same. The shimmer of the Change surrounding her didn't go away; if anything, it became clearer, as though normal sight was usually in the way. For a brief instant, with the potential so strong and so close all around her, she thought that she might be able to access it herself, without help — but she could not. Even here the Change was completely out of her reach. She could only see it, and use it second-hand — sensitive, but passive.

Sal's touch sent a shiver up her spine. She could feel him visualising the breaks and damaged tissues as best he could. The Change gathered under his touch. It was as if a million tiny, glowing spiders were laying webs through her flesh, tying everything together. He was clumsy, though, missing some tender spots entirely and devoting too much attention to others. She bent her own will to the effort, using his gift via the physical connection between them.

She lost track of time. The bubbling of the stew faded into the background. It could have been hours or minutes that they worked on her leg, feeling their way by instinct through the damage and doing what they could to repair it. Although she couldn't tell how much good they were doing, the injury was so severe that any improvement would be better than none. As long as they weren't doing harm — and it didn't feel like they were. It felt right. Gradually, the tingling in her toes retreated, and the ache began to ease.

That small progress encouraged speculation. How far could they go? Would it be possible for the two of them, in such a place, to heal her leg entirely? She doubted it; they didn't know exactly what to do, for a start, and it was very close work, requiring the utmost concentration. Maybe a small wound could be healed, but not something so large, affecting so great a proportion of her body. If they stayed there a week or more ... But she knew they couldn't. There was no food, for a start, and it was getting so *cold* ...

A faint noise — a footstep — distracted her, and her eyes snapped open, expecting to see that Lutz had returned and discovered their secret.

She gasped. There *was* someone standing on the other side of the fire, watching them closely, but it wasn't Lutz. Where the surgeon was tall and grey-haired across his scalp and face, this man was shorter, stockier and bald, dressed in a worn cotton top and ragged pants. His eyes and mouth were mere shadows in a heavily lined face.

Sal jumped to his feet the moment he saw the man. "Who are you? Where did you come from?"

The man smiled broadly. Even then, Shilly couldn't see his teeth. "I live here," he said. His voice was clear but seemed to come from a long way off. "I know someone you know."

"Engenius? Have you seen him?" Sal stepped forward to put himself between the man and Shilly. "If you've done anything to him —"

"Not him. He means nothing to me."

By then, all the hairs were standing up on the back of Shilly's neck. Something was terribly wrong with the man before them. It took her a long time to notice it, because it could not be true: he wasn't breathing.

A palpable chill emanated from him; the flames between them fluttered as though fanned by an icy breeze.

"*What* are you?" she asked.

Deep in the shadowy eye sockets, two invisible eyes turned on her. "Can you guess, Shilly?"

She faltered under that terrible regard. "How did you know my name?"

"I told you," said the cold voice. "I know someone you know."

"*Who?*"

"You're a golem," broke in Sal. "That's what you are."

The smile disappeared as the eyes went back to Sal. "No. The body is the golem. *I* am its resident. The distinction is important."

"What should we call you, then?" Sal's voice was firm, but there was fear behind it.

"I have been called by many names. The part of me that you see before you, through this body, is but a small part of the whole. I am in many bodies at once, many golems. I see many things through them. Not all are worth seeing. Here..." The empty gaze of the golem looked dismissively around at the towers in shadow, at the black windows, and then returned to Sal and Shilly. "*You* are worth seeing."

Shilly shifted herself closer to Sal, wishing she could stand beside him to face the creature. "I don't understand," she said. "What do you want from us?"

"Nothing," the creature said with another smile, "but to be close to you."

"Are you cold? Is that it?"

"Yes and no. It's not heat I lack, but life, *physicality*. That is what I seek, and what you have. I cannot take it from you, but I can stay near in case it is offered to me."

"Suppose we don't want you to stay."

"Well, Shilly, then you must make me go. I encourage you to try. It won't be easy, even here. How strong is your friend, do you think? Will his gift suffice?"

Sal shook his head, and squatted next to her. "Don't listen to it. It wants us to try to use the Change to get rid of it, to burn me out so it can come inside."

"Inside you? Take you over?"

"Yes," said the golem, "that's the way it works."

"How?" She looked in alarm from the creature to Sal. "What would happen to Sal if you did that?"

"Horrible things." The golem seemed to enjoy her discomfort. "He wouldn't be dead, but he wouldn't be alive either. He would be in the Void Beneath — ah ... you know the place."

Shilly felt Sal stiffen beside her, and she remembered that he had glimpsed the Void in Fundelry, while they had been spying on the Alcaide and the Syndic. He had never described what he'd seen, and that was enough to make her fear it.

"I think you're trying to frighten us," she said. "I don't think you're telling the truth."

"Oh, I am," it said. "I cannot lie. The only way I can avoid telling the truth is by saying nothing at all, so if I speak to you, you know that what I say is, well, *true*."

"But you *are* trying to frighten us."

"Yes," it admitted, "that is so."

"Why?"

"Why not?" Its smile became more natural then, which only made the face of its empty host look more unnerving. "It's boring here. There is little to do. Nothing ever changes."

"Travellers like us are your entertainment?"

"There are few enough of those, and even fewer like you. This golem I inhabit —" limp hands rose to pat the torso before them "— he was the last of any talent to come here, some years ago. He wanted to find the secret of the towers, and I wouldn't let him. He tried too hard to dispel me, so here I am. He fits well, don't you think?"

Shilly forced herself to ignore the relish with which the creature flaunted the body it inhabited. "What *is* the secret of the towers?"

The gleeful expression faded. "There is none, but that doesn't stop people like Lutz looking." Its mouth curled into a moue of distaste. "There's nothing here but death."

"Why don't you leave, then?"

The golem's empty eyes swung to Sal, who had spoken. "Because I can't," the voice spat. "Know this, Sayed Hrvati: there are three places to which creatures such as I are drawn. This one is in decay; the second is north of here, beyond my influence; the third lies far to the south. You know of the last, I suspect."

Sal frowned. "To the south ... You don't mean the Haunted City, do you?"

"Do I? We shall see. Perhaps we shall renew our acquaintance there, one day."

"How do you know that?"

"Perhaps I don't."

Sal shook his head in irritation, and Shilly sympathised. She was beginning to wonder if the creature was just playing games with them.

"Look," she said, "are you here for a reason?"

"That depends." It neither looked at her nor answered her question directly. Instead it began to walk slowly around the fire, one step at a time.

"Are you going to try healing your friend again?" it asked Sal.

"Not with you sniffing around," he replied. "You'd like that, wouldn't you?"

"Very much. It is to me as that fire is to you." For the first time a real emotion appeared on the golem's face: one of wistful desire, of longing. Of *hunger*, Shilly thought. Hunger for the Change.

"You can't have it," said Sal.

The golem kept coming around the fire. Sal edged closer to where Shilly sat.

"Stay away," he said. The flames cast the golem's face in half-shadow, making its ghastly expression stand out even more. With each step the cold became more piercing until Shilly noticed that her breath was fogging.

When it was within arm's reach, it raised a hand as though to touch them. Sal instantly knocked it aside.

"Good," it whispered, raising the hand again. "Good boy —"

A cry sounded from outside the clearing — a man's shout of fear, distant but clear. The golem, distracted, turned to look into the shadows. The cry was repeated, nearer, this time. When the golem's empty eyes fell on them again, its amused smile had returned.

"Saved by the fool," it said, backing away. "Until next time, children."

Mingled relief and dread swept through Shilly as it walked toward the edge of the firelight. The heat of the fire returned in a rush and she put a hand on Sal's leg for support. He knelt down beside her, also watching the golem's retreating back.

"It's okay," he said. "It couldn't have hurt us unless I used the Change."

She wasn't so sure. And that didn't mean it wouldn't try to hurt them in other ways.

As though it had heard her thoughts, the golem turned on the verge of the shadows. With a quick motion, it flicked an object toward them, glinting gold in the flames. She automatically flinched. Whatever it was, it fell far short, landing with a shower of sparks in the fire.

The golem smirked at their startled expressions. "I'll send Lodo your regards."

It was gone before either of them could respond.

CHAPTER 4

DIVISION

Sal jumped when the golem threw the object into the fire and vanished into the shadows of the ruined towers. Feeling foolish, he turned that motion into a step toward the woodpile. There he found a long stick with which he reached into the fire and attempted to retrieve the object. His hands were shaking, which didn't help matters.

It called me Sayed Hrvati. My heart-name; my father's surname ...

"What did it mean?" asked Shilly from behind him, her voice strained. "What does it know about Lodo?"

"I don't know," he said, forcing himself to concentrate on the matter at hand, moving around the fire to get a better angle of approach. Whatever the golem had thrown, it had fallen heavily and sunk deep into the glowing coals. "It said it knew someone we both knew. Maybe it knows him."

"But how? He can't still be alive. Can he?"

Sal paused in his task. The last evidence they had of Lodo being alive was during the earthquake the old man had summoned to help them escape. Beyond that, there had been no sign. But if he *had* survived, and if the summoning had taken too great a toll on the old man's strength . . .

They had left him to a fate worse than death — assuming, of course, that what the golem had told them really was the truth.

Shilly was obviously thinking along the same lines. Her face was etched with horror. "No. He *can't* be. I won't believe it. That *thing* — it just wants to hurt us! It's messing with our heads. It can't *actually* harm us, so —"

She stopped as someone stumbled into the clearing. Sal rounded on the figure with the smouldering branch upraised.

"Hey!" It was Lutz, white-faced. He backed away in alarm. "What's wrong?"

"Where have you been?" Sal asked.

"I was looking," he said, around heavy breaths. "There was something out there. An animal, I think." He hesitated and Shilly realised that it must have been Lutz who had distracted the golem with his cries. He hadn't been attacked, but he had been frightened. Like them.

"What were you looking for?" asked Sal.

Lutz didn't answer. He was staring at them as though seeing them for the first time. "What happened here? You two look like you've seen a ghost."

"Something like that —" Sal started to say, but Lutz broke in over him.

"No! Where is he? Where did he go?" Suddenly animated, he ran around the clearing, looking out into the shadows. "Father!" he called. "Father, come back!"

Sal watched him warily. "Was your father a Change-user?"

Lutz's eyes were wide. "No — no, he wasn't. Why?"

"This wasn't him, then. It was someone — some*thing* — else." Sal returned his attention to the object in the fire, losing patience and scattering the burning logs in order to gain access to it. It slipped under the pot of stew, which he lifted out and put carefully to one side.

"I'm sorry," said Lutz, collapsing onto his knees at a point opposite both of them. "I shouldn't have mixed you up in all this." The fire reflecting in his eyes had all the vividness of tears.

"In all what?" asked Shilly, her voice cold. "Where did you go?"

Lutz didn't look at her. "The last time someone tried to survey this place was fifty years ago," he said. "My father was part of the expedition, and he never came back. None of them came back. But I know he's still in here, somewhere. This place doesn't let go easily."

"You've tried to find him before?"

"Yes, but I don't have a vehicle and few people will come here. Those who know of it are afraid. Those who don't —"

"Like us?" she broke in, angrily. "I suppose we have to be tricked."

"No, no." He opened his hands, pleading with her to understand. "It's not like that. I swear it isn't. I lied about nothing. This really is the only way I know to get across the Broken Lands without Behenna following you. The road skirts the salt lake, so you would have passed by the city anyway. You wanted to come here as soon as you saw it. I would have been happy to wait until dawn, to look then, but it was *you* who insisted on coming here at night, when the *things* walk ..."

He faltered. Sal had managed to hook one end of the stick under the object in the fire and drew it slowly into the light. It was brass, not gold, and it had been blackened by the fire. But it still had its shape, that of a squat X with a hole through its centre, attached to a long, heavy-linked chain. The loops of the chain were tied around the cross in numerous thick knots; one broken end hung free.

"Oh, father," said Lutz, weeping openly at the sight of it. "This belonged to him. I haven't seen it for fifty years. Father!" Then he was on his feet again, railing against the figures he imagined lurking in the shadows, but never straying too far from the light. "Why did you come to *them*? Why didn't you give it to me? *Why*?"

Sal shook his head, irritated, as once again the surgeon's energy was quickly spent, leaving him hunched and deflated with self-pity. The golem hadn't been Lutz's father. Only someone with the Change would be at risk from something like that.

"What is it?" asked Shilly, nodding at where the object lay cooling on the white ground.

"It's nothing," said Lutz. "A trinket. But it was his. It's obviously a sign." His eyes stared into the fire as Sal put the logs back together. "We waited at Yor for the expedition to return, and it never did. They thought I was mad for looking for him here. My mother ... even she gave up hope. But that didn't mean there wasn't a chance he could still be here. It's a terrible place, but it has power, too. The Wardens on the expedition knew of it. They were excited to be going along, nervous. They didn't know what they might find, and we never found out. I've seen nothing here because I don't have the talent, but I've never stopped hoping. All my life I've been waiting for a sign — and now I have it."

He reached forward, heedless of the heat, grabbed the blackened cross and held it triumphantly before him. "He *was* here, and he might still be here, in one form or another. Even if it's just his body, that would be some reward. I can come back. If I look hard enough, long enough, I know I'll find something ..."

Sal nodded, understanding now why the surgeon lived so far from civilisation, but finding it difficult to believe that he would ever locate his father after so long a time. The creatures that inhabited the ruins might keep trinkets for amusement, but bodies that couldn't be inhabited would be useless. Lutz's father would have rotted away long ago.

He wondered if Lutz had become hypnotised by the place itself — by the history, the mystery.

"What difference would it make if you did find anything?" Shilly asked bluntly. "He'd still be dead."

Lutz winced, as though confronting that painful truth for the first time. He didn't answer her question. "Fifty years it took me to find this much," he said, his gaze slowly shifting to meet Sal's, "and it was *you* they gave it to."

"We didn't ask for it," Shilly snapped. "Someone's playing with us. If we hadn't come here, you'd still have nothing."

Lutz didn't say anything. Eventually he grunted, as though reluctantly taking the point. Sal was unnerved by the look in his eyes. Why he would resent them for leading him to the first positive sign in his long quest, Sal didn't know, but it was enough to make him cautious.

"You said you saw an animal out there," he prompted, hoping to change the subject. "What sort of animal?"

"It doesn't matter." The big man stretched out on his side with his back facing the flame, effectively shutting them out. "They talked to *you*, remember."

Shilly shot Sal an annoyed look that said as clearly as if she had spoken: *And* we're *supposed to be the kids.*

Sal couldn't dismiss him so easily.

"I've made stew, if you want it," he said, reaching for the plates he and his father had once shared. The metal serving spoon had seen better days, but still performed its job. Shilly accepted a bowl, even though she didn't look hungry. They ate in silence, and Lutz didn't move.

Sal slept poorly among the towers, in the midst of so much tragedy, real or imagined. He and Shilly took turns keeping watch and stoking the fire, but the golem didn't return, and there were no more disturbances. Lutz did eventually stir from his inward-gazing repose and helped himself to some food, but he slept soundly afterward, stretched out as he had been the previous night under his thin rug with his head resting on the battered black bag and both hands clutching the trinket that had once belonged to his father. If he woke, he made no sound.

There were no *tap-taps* from Behenna that night. The darkness seemed to soak up any attempts at conversation. The more it intensified, the more silent it became, until Sal began to wonder if he had become deaf. Only the soft crackling of the fire reassured him that he hadn't. He huddled in the small bubble of light it cast and waited for the sun — and sound — to return.

Dawn came gradually among the giant buildings. The light dispelled some of the anxiety he had felt during the night, but there was no birdsong to greet the sun, only a cold wind sweeping between the towers. The city's ghosts were rushing to their beds, he thought, shivering, and the shadows retreated with them.

The ruined surroundings returned in cold, pale colours. Sal stood to stretch his legs. Although he felt confident that it would be safer to explore during the day, he didn't walk far. Empty-framed windows didn't tempt him: what lay beyond them was universally dark and spooky, like the eye-sockets of the golem. He wasn't going to push fate. From those dark spaces he sensed invisible intelligences watching him, waiting for him to come closer, out of the sunlight.

The sky far above brightened quickly. By the time he returned, Shilly was up, brushing the creases out of her clothes with one hand, frown lines deep in her forehead.

"I wondered where you'd got to," she said, sounding more irritated than relieved. "I thought our friend had come back and dragged you off."

"No, but I found its tracks." He indicated the direction the golem had gone the night before. "They lead that way."

"Where did he go? Into one of the towers?"

"No. They just stop in the middle of nowhere, as though he jumped up in the air and never came down."

Shilly's look of annoyance increased.

"I'm going to wet myself if you're not quick," she said, shifting awkwardly on the spot. "Could you . . .?"

He hesitated, hoping Lutz might stir and offer his assistance, but the surgeon did not. "Of course." He helped her upright, then took her weight as she hopped along the way he had gone, to the nearest corner. She balanced herself against the building while he waited out of sight.

"How's your leg?" he asked, whispering in case Lutz was only pretending to be asleep. "Did we do any good last night?"

"It's a bit better," she said. "I can't bend it, but the pain is easing. I can think about other things, now."

He basked only briefly in the warmth of her gratitude. "That's good," he said, "because we have a long way to go yet."

"To find Skender Van Haasteren?"

And to get away from Behenna, he added to himself. "If that's still what you want to do."

"Finished," she said, hopping awkwardly back into sight. Her expression was cautious, as though she was afraid he might try to talk her out of her destination. "It's not much to go on, I know," she conceded as he helped her back to the campsite. "But it's better than nothing at all. He was a teacher of the Change, so he must've been someone important — a Stone Mage, at least. He gave Lodo the scourge because he had high hopes for him."

The Scourge of Aneshti was a whip-like charm used to test which particular skill a student possessed; Sal had experienced it once, and it hadn't been pleasant. *Every great teacher of the Change has had one or something very much like it*, Lodo had said. The same man had given Lodo *yadeh-tash*, the amulet he had worn around his neck and used to predict the weather.

"It's not as if we have any choice, now," said Sal. "We can't go back."

"I know. But it'll be okay. We'll find him. Someone will know who and where he is."

"And what then?"

"We talk to him. We tell him Lodo started our training and failed to finish it. That we came to him because we had no one else to turn to. He doesn't have to train us himself. He must be a very old man now, not taking students. But he'll know someone. He must be able to help."

"We'll be lucky if he even talks to us."

"Do you think so?" Her expression was uncertain for a fleeting instant.

"I don't really know what to think. All I know is that Lodo ran out on him. He might not want anything to do with us, all these years later."

"I'm sure he will," she said, "when he meets us."

"Right." He smiled. "How could he possibly resist?"

But she wasn't joking. "He'll want you just as much as everyone else does: the Alcaide, the Syndic, Shom Behenna . . ."

The conversation ended on that unsettling note. They had reached the campsite and, although Lutz was still asleep, Sal wasn't prepared to risk the surgeon overhearing anything to do with their past. The less he knew, the better.

As it turned out, Lutz only woke when everything was stowed back into the buggy and Sal had finished burying the embers.

"What, no breakfast?" the surgeon asked, sitting up and rubbing his eyes.

"I want to get moving," Sal replied. "If we push hard, we might make the Lookout today."

"We should be there this afternoon." Lutz's joints cracked as he got up and began rolling up his rug. "The ground eases once we're out of the Broken Lands. We'll make good time, the last hundred kilometres or so."

"Can we avoid the main road?"

"I suggest coming in from the east. That means going out of our way for a stretch, but it'll be safer. There's a chance your Sky Warden friend might get there before us, and I'd hate to lead you straight into a trap."

Sal was all too aware of that possibility. He had been to the Lookout before, and remembered it as a large tower overlooking the bridge across the Divide. It had once been just a guard post with room enough for a garrison inside, but a fluctuating community had grown around it like coral, living off the proceeds of trade between the Interior and the Strand. It wasn't a proper town, lacking permanent buildings and all but the meanest of streets, but it would give them numbers to hide among. He didn't know exactly how many people passed through there, but it had seemed like a lot when he was younger. More than Yor, easily.

He accepted the surgeon's plan with a nod, knowing too little about the surrounding terrain to propose another one.

The morning passed much as it had the previous day. The Change-rich ambience of the city was soon behind them. Once they crossed the northernmost banks of the blissfully flat surface of the lake and re-entered the Broken Lands proper, heading north, it was back to numerous terrain changes and constant vigilance. Lutz was incommunicative, except to give directions; he was obviously troubled by their encounter with the golem and refused to talk about it, but his resentment seemed to have turned into determination during the night. He urged them on with eyes firmly forward and white-knuckled hands gripping his father's blackened cross.

Shilly forewent her daily painkiller and remarked on how unusual the jumbled terrain looked to her. Sal wished only that it would end. He felt as though he had been driving forever. A poor night's sleep didn't help his mood.

And as soon as they left the salt lake Behenna's faint *tap-tap* returned, an endless reminder of why they were running.

By mid-afternoon they had reached a stretch of red sand not dissimilar to that surrounding Yor. Sal's hopes rose as the patches of jarringly out of place terrain thinned out, then fell behind them entirely. The way became easier, less circuitous.

Navigating by the sun, they headed north-northeast in a straight line. Although glad of the speed, Sal was acutely aware of the cloud of dust they were throwing up behind them. It would be visible for kilometres.

"How far to the main road?" he asked Lutz.

"Forty to fifty kilometres that way," the surgeon said, pointing west. "Have you thought about how you're going to cross the Divide?"

Sal hesitated for a second, then said: "Not really." He'd been concentrating more on driving, not what he would do when they got there. "There are caravans crossing all the time. I thought I'd pay my way across." Where he would get the money, though, was a problem he preferred not to examine until he had to.

"I can help you with that, too, if you wish," Lutz said. "There is a trader whose child I saved. He owes me a favour. If he is there, he will smuggle you across the Divide, I'm sure."

Sal took his eyes off the road to study the surgeon. "You'd do that for us?"

Lutz patted him reassuringly on the shoulder. "For the leg, Sal. For the leg."

His answer only made Sal suspicious; Lutz had made no effort in that regard since the previous day. He hadn't helped Sal tend to Shilly at all. Only with great reluctance had he bothered to help put her back in her place on the buggy.

But Sal nodded as though he thought the idea a good one. They said no more of it until a muddy haze appeared on the forward horizon, indicating that they were nearing the Lookout. Sal knew he should be relieved to be so close, yet he felt nothing but a rising tension. If Behenna had overtaken them, he would be waiting for them at the Lookout. And even if he *hadn't* overtaken them, he wouldn't be far behind. He wished he had a glamour like the one Lodo had used in Fundelry, to hide himself from prying eyes.

"What's that?" asked Shilly, pointing northward, to their right.

Sal looked. They were within sight of the Divide. Not much could be seen through the heat-hazed air, but it was apparent that a vast chasm lay to the north. The southernmost edge gave the horizon a foreshortened appearance. The northern side was too distant to be seen at all. Mrs Milka had apparently neglected to describe the Divide, for Shilly plainly had no idea what she was looking at.

"Wait and see for yourself," Sal said. "We're not far away now."

"Is it the Interior?"

"Not quite." The Divide remained a steady distance away as they drove to the Lookout. He hoped that Lutz wouldn't give anything away.

Lutz didn't. Now that the job of getting them to the Lookout was almost done, the surgeon said nothing for the rest of the drive. He stared ahead with a fierce concentration as the sun sank slowly toward the horizon. Only as the brown haze resolved into the dust thrown up by a small town did he speak.

"Join that track, over there. It's not often used. People here go either north or south, rarely anywhere else."

"Won't we stand out?" Sal asked.

"No one will notice. Trust me."

Sal's fingers tightened around the steering wheel as he did as he was told. Before long, he could see that Lutz was right.

There was no clear-cut edge to the town, consisting as it did of white and brown cloth tents spreading in vaguely ordered rows across a slight rise in the surroundings. The air was full of strange smells and noises, and the buggy blended in perfectly with other vehicles weaving through it all. Scores of camels strode regally about in enclosures set well back from the main encampments, and it was between two such enclosures that Sal guided the buggy. Most of the tents opened inward, away from them, facing into the centre of the makeshift town. There, shorter than he remembered, stood the white tower of the Lookout, visible over the tops of tents.

"It's a lighthouse," said Shilly, "without an ocean."

"Function dictates form," said Lutz, directing Sal down another side street. Surrounded by tents, Sal felt less exposed. There were other buggies and people everywhere: dark-skinned and fair, dusty from travel, and none wearing the blue of the Sky Wardens. The air was full of shouts, engines chugging, clanging metal, and even music.

"Let's find somewhere to put the buggy," the surgeon said, looking through every gap they passed. "That's our greatest risk at the moment. Kids your age are common enough, but few of them drive." He half-stood in the passenger seat. "Over there."

There was an unattended space between three tents just wide enough for the buggy and deep enough so people walking by wouldn't notice them. Sal slowed and backed in. The engine rattled to a halt as though pleased to be resting.

Lutz got out.

"Where are you going?" Sal asked.

"To find Favi Kalish. He's the leader of the caravan I told you about. If he's here, your troubles will be over."

Sal settled back into his seat as Lutz slipped out of their hiding space. Looking up at Shilly, he saw her face was drawn with pain and concern. She was watching him right back.

"I have a bad feeling about this," he said.

"Me too."

"I should follow him."

"Go, then. We need to be sure."

"But you —"

"I'll be okay," she said. "Don't let me hold you back. I'm just annoyed I can't do anything to help."

"Shilly —"

She shook her head and made a shooing gesture. He slipped off after the surgeon.

At first he thought he had left it too late. Many men around the Lookout shared Lutz's desert dress sense, and Sal couldn't find him straightaway. Then he caught a glimpse of the surgeon's grey-stubbled scalp a little further along the street, and he immediately set out in pursuit, ensuring there were people between them at all times.

The crowd grew denser as they neared the Lookout, giving Sal more opportunities to hide but making it harder to keep up. There was an open-air market taking place on the northern slopes of the Lookout, between the tower and the way to the Interior. A large number of wagons and merchants had gathered there to trade stock and negotiate haulage. Some were clearly from the Interior, as pale as the robes they wore, while others were dark, hailing from deep in the Strand. Most lay between those two extremes, the inevitable result of mixing populations.

Sal saw several black-clad Syndic representatives, checking to make sure that the laws of the Strand were being observed, but nowhere did he see any sign of the Sky Wardens. Lutz walked unhesitatingly into the market and looked around as though searching, then headed off to his left. He walked up to a tight knot of wagons and asked one of the men attending it a question. The trader nodded, listened some more, then nodded again. Lutz slipped him something that looked like a coin, and the man walked off.

He returned a moment later with a tall, white-haired man wearing a long, black shift patterned with red flowers. They embraced and walked out of sight behind one of the wagons, talking intently, frowning.

Sal couldn't get any closer without drawing attention to himself, and he doubted the wisdom of trying. So far everything Lutz had said was true: the surgeon had gone to look for a caravan, the leader of which, if that was who the man in the black shift was, he knew well. But still the doubt nagged. There was too much riding on the surgeon's honesty. Sal didn't know him well enough to place their fate in his hands so absolutely, and he had been in an odd mood ever since the ruined towers. They had glimpsed a dark current running through the surgeon the night before, after the golem had come. Who knew how deep it ran, or where it might lead?

He waited a minute longer to see if the two men emerged. As he watched, a lanky, pale-skinned woman in dirty grey riding clothes approached the first man Lutz had spoken to and initiated an angry exchange Sal could half-hear from the other side of the market. Something about a quota infringement. It was clear the woman held the entire caravan in poor regard. When the object of her anger shook his head and laughed, she spat onto the ground by his feet and stalked away.

Sal watched her return to her own caravan, a larger affair than the other with solid, wide-wheelbase carriages designed to carry machine parts or other heavy goods as well as fabric and spices. The people working there deferred to her, and shook their heads when she explained what had happened.

Sal would have watched longer but for a flash of blue nearby. A Sky Warden. He shrank back into the shadow of a nearby tent, his pulse pounding in his throat. Not Behenna. This was a woman with brown curly hair. But the robes were the same, and there was no mistaking the crystal torc at her throat.

Sal retreated through the crowd, newly mindful of everyone around him. He didn't know how many Sky Wardens maintained the Lookout, but there were bound to be more than one. Even if Behenna hadn't arrived, they could communicate through the Void Beneath using thought — the same way Behenna had talked to Sal by the ravine. He didn't doubt that they knew about him and Shilly, and would be keeping an eye out for them. Behenna was still *tap-tapping* for him. Half afraid that Shilly had already been discovered, he hurried back through the narrow alleys between tents and wagons to where the buggy was hidden.

She was still there. He almost collapsed with relief. The sweat was dripping off him by the time he sat down under the shade and took a long drink of water.

"What did you see?" Shilly asked.

"Nothing suspicious," he admitted, outlining Lutz's actions in as much detail as he could remember.

"That's good, isn't it?" she said when he had finished. "There was no one here waiting for us, no one's seen us since we arrived, and Lutz is doing everything he can to get us out of here. Why would he betray us now, after all he's done?"

"I don't know." Sal had pondered this all the way back to the buggy. It was clear that Lutz was determined to strike a deal with Favi Kalish, just as he had been determined to help Sal and Shilly reach the Lookout safely. It was also clear, however, that Lutz had used them to conduct another, brief search for his father's remains, and he had clearly resented them for being the ones the golem had spoken to. That resentment seemed to be gone — but was it really?

Suddenly Lutz was there, flushed, out of breath, and alone.

"It's all arranged," he said. "We'll wait until it's fully dark, then move."

Sal looked at the sky. An hour at most. "What do we do?"

"Drive to the crossing point. It's always chaotic there, no one will notice an extra buggy among the rest. The caravan you want has a red flower painted on each cart. The leader, Kalish, will be expecting you. He knows what you look like and will delay customs until you arrive. Once you are there, he'll move out, taking you across with the rest of the caravan. You'll be safe on the other side."

"And you?" Shilly asked. "What happens to you after we're gone?"

The surgeon shrugged bonily. "Don't worry about me, princess. Just you concentrate on getting away and looking after that leg."

He smiled up at her and patted her hand. Sal could tell that she was ready to believe Lutz, and he was tempted to. Perhaps the weird behaviour in and since the Broken Lands had been nothing more than an aberration, the product of a bad mood brought on by difficult memories. Sal could understand that, he supposed.

He just couldn't believe that their escape would go so easily. The Sky Wardens would be watching every caravan closely as it went over to the Interior. Without some form of distraction, they would never slip by.

Lutz resumed his seat as the day faded around them, but he soon became restless and fidgeted. Sal tried to distract himself by thinking about the Interior, thinking ahead rather than looking behind him, at what was chasing them. They would be there very soon, if everything went well, yet he had only a vague idea what to expect. For all that he had spent a lot of his life in the borderlands, he had never before made the leap across. The distance was relatively small, but crucial.

And how much stranger it must be, he thought, for Shilly, who would soon be not only out of her depth but also completely out of her home country as well. At least there would be no Sky Wardens looking for her over there. The rest of their journey, he hoped, would continue uneventfully.

The first stars were beginning to appear when Lutz's barely-contained energy overflowed.

"I'm going to make sure everything's ready," he said. "I'll come back if it isn't — so if I don't come back, you'll know that it is."

Or that something has gone badly wrong, Sal thought to himself, unable to sit passively by while a trap might be springing shut around them.

"Be careful," said Shilly.

"I will, princess. I will." He slipped out of their hiding place and disappeared up the street.

Sal waited thirty seconds, then started the engine.

"What are you doing?" Shilly leaned forward to grip his shoulder. "You can't go early. They won't be ready."

"I'm not going early. I just want to get closer." He turned to look at her. "Also, Behenna *must* be here by now. If Engenius is caught and they make him talk, they'll know exactly where to look."

She nodded. The nervousness in her eyes perfectly matched the way he felt. They were coming to the crunch. After the accident in the ravine, the golem, all the hundreds of kilometres they had put behind them, this was it.

He kept the headlights off as he inched the car out of the niche and onto the narrow roadway. It was cooler at night, and busier. People were everywhere, and none of them gave the buggy any special notice. Sal kept to the side ways, approaching the heart of the tent town by the most circuitous route, ever watchful for blue of any kind. When someone so much as glanced at him, he looked away then back again a moment later, to make sure no scrutiny lingered too long.

His route was either well chosen or lucky, for they reached the edge of the market without incident. There the ring of wagons and caravans gave way to the customs staging area. Sal parked the buggy behind a large, empty wagon. They were within sight of the staging area but not likely to be seen. From their position they could watch what was going on, and finally Shilly could see what awaited them.

Even by night the Divide was impressive. The Lookout was situated on the inner lip of a chunk taken out of the side of a massive canyon which was kilometres across and seemingly bottomless in the dark. A wide, iron bridge, lit by lanterns all along its length, crossed the gap from the Strand to the Interior, but not in one single span. Instead the bridge comprised several stages. The first led from the Lookout to the top of a conical "island" standing upright in the canyon, where time had eroded the soft rock around a hardier central core. There were several such islands in a rough line, and the bridge leapt from one to the other, zigzagging across the gap until the two sides were joined. The bridge was a glowing thread hanging in darkness, a frozen lightning bolt arcing through space.

Activity on the bridge provided the only true sense of scale. A single cart, dwarfed by the gulf around it, was travelling from where the much larger settlement of Nesh shone brightly on the Interior side of the Divide to the Strand side. A medium-sized caravan crawled to meet it, strung out in a line even though there was enough room for four wagons to proceed side-by-side. At the Lookout end, three other caravans queued at the staging area, their leaders completing declaration forms and waiting their turn to proceed out over the abyss.

Shilly's hand had stayed on Sal's shoulder through their short journey, and it gripped him tightly now. "It's beautiful."

He could appreciate what she meant. As on the other occasions he had seen the Divide, Sal couldn't help the feeling of awe that overtook him. It was too big to truly comprehend, wider across than the city in the Broken Lands was long. Sal knew that in its length, the chasm divided Strand and Interior across the entirety of the two lands, as though the continent had been rent in two by some unimaginable force.

Its nature was as mysterious as its size was awe-inspiring. The Divide wasn't a canyon for there was no river at its heart; it wasn't a rift valley, either, for its sides were almost vertical. The air at the base of the winding cliff faces seemed to boil during the day, strange sandstorms swirling and dancing even though no air stirred on the top. It was, Sal thought, a crack in the landscape, a break in reality that might let something strange and unknowable in.

But there were more important things than sightseeing on his mind. Two caravans were vying for seniority at the Lookout checkpoint. One belonged to Favi Kalish and was the one they were supposed to join. The tall woman who had argued earlier with one of Kalish's riders led the other. The two of them and a Syndic representative were arguing heatedly, although Sal couldn't make out their words over the clatter of axles, the snorting and stamping of camels and the sound of orders being shouted. The geniality of the market was gone, replaced by the pressing need to move on, either home or to another marketplace.

As Sal watched, a Sky Warden stepped out of a guardhouse and approached the arguing trio. He spoke a few words, rebuffed another angry outburst from the female caravan leader, and then gestured for them to disperse. Sal watched with interest as the tall woman strode back to where her wagons were assembled, waiting to move out. But they didn't move. They just sat there, waiting. Meanwhile Favi Kalish walked back to his own caravan to talk to none other than Engenius Lutz. Kalish looked pleased, while the surgeon was the picture of nervousness.

Tap-tap.

Sal felt like Lutz looked. One thing bothered him: if the surgeon *had* sold Sal and Shilly out, why hadn't the Sky

Wardens just taken them there and then? It would have been easier than mounting such an elaborate deception and risking a double-cross. They had no reason not to trust Lutz, who had actively helped the pair escape from Yor and knew exactly where they were. How could the Wardens possibly hope to benefit from delaying?

Sal couldn't answer that question, but it wasn't going away. And the more it nagged, the more important it became. The next question was: what to do about it? If he tried to explain it to Shilly, he was afraid he'd make himself look stupid, but he couldn't just sit there, either, waiting for the axe to fall.

Finally, he could take it no more. He slid out of the driver's seat. "I won't be long," he said, ignoring Shilly's startled query.

He ducked and wove through the chaos to where the lanky woman stood fuming, watching Favi Kalish and his caravan on the other side of the staging area.

"Excuse me." Sal didn't want to come too close for fear of exposing himself. The woman turned at the sound of the voice, and saw him in the shadows.

"What do you want?" she snapped.

"My father is in the caravan behind yours and he sent me to find out what the hold-up is."

The woman looked past him as though trying to find evidence to disprove his story. "The problem isn't mine," she said. "The Wardens have given Kalish preference but he won't go through. There's a problem with one of his axles, apparently. A replacement is coming, he says; it won't take a moment. But he is just stalling. I can tell. He is enjoying making me wait."

That accorded with Lutz's plan perfectly. Kalish was waiting for Sal and Shilly to appear before making his move across the bridge. Lutz looked nervous because defying the Sky Wardens was dangerous even on the northern edge of their territory. Sal had no reason to be suspicious ...

Except he still was.

"So you *are* going across," he said. "After Kalish?"

"That's right. We're headed for Ulum." The woman's lips and cheeks were tattooed with fine, grey lines as though she was wearing a mask. Numerous black rings hung in her ears. She was studying Sal just as closely as he was studying her. "Why do you ask?"

He warred with himself for a split second, then opted to follow his instinct.

"I'm not really with another caravan," he said. "I want to get across the bridge, and quickly. Is there any way to get Kalish moving?"

"None. He's as stubborn as a camel. The harder I push, the deeper he digs his heels in."

"Couldn't you jump the queue?"

"Sure, and I've done it before, but tonight the Syndics are on edge. They're jumpy, and I don't want to..." She stopped. "Wait. I know who you are. You're one of those kids the Wardens are looking for."

His blood congealed in his stomach. "Which kids?"

"Don't play dumb. I hear things. No wonder you want to get across so quickly. I should turn you in before I get myself into trouble."

Her voice was disapproving, but she stayed exactly where she was.

"Or you could help us," he said.

"Tell me how I might."

"Let us mix with your caravan while you jump the queue."

"In return for what?"

This was the weakest point of his argument, such as it was. "For the look on Favi Kalish's face."

"That's a small price for pissing off the Wardens."

"You said you've done it before."

"I have, yes, but not when things were like this." She nodded slowly. "Yes, I see it now. Kalish is waiting for *you*, isn't he? Not for some busted axle to be fixed. And you're selling him over."

"He might be selling us over first." That was true enough: even if Lutz was innocent, there was always the possibility that the caravan leader had other ideas. "If he is, the Wardens will catch us when he goes to cross. That's what they're waiting for. They're distracted from everything else. They won't, therefore, be ready for you when you break the queue. We'll take them by surprise and get past easily."

"And it'd be in character for me to do something like that, so they won't be suspicious." She nodded as though the plan met her approval. "Fine. But it's still a risk. Why shouldn't I just hand you over and see if there's a reward? That way, I ingratiate myself with the Wardens for a change, maybe make some easy money, *and* still get to put one past Kalish. What do you say to that?"

He thought desperately. "That it's not your style?"

"No, but I'm no fool, either."

"I haven't got any money —"

"That's a shame."

"I can offer you . . ." He stopped, knowing that the moment he had dreaded had come. For all his hoping that another idea would occur to him at the last moment, it hadn't. "I can offer you our buggy. It's in perfect working order. Get us across, and it's yours."

She raised her eyebrows. "Working vehicles are rare. People don't just give them away on a whim."

"I'm not."

"You must really need to get across."

"I do."

She regarded him a moment longer, then said: "Okay, I'm interested, despite myself. Reward or no reward, I don't like anyone screwing over a customer. It's bad for our reputation. And Kalish is far from a friend. I'll have a look at your buggy and see what we can do. If it's in good condition, you have a deal."

Sal kept any relief he felt off his face. "Thank you."

"Don't thank me," she said. "Thank your own resourcefulness. I think you're more right than you realise about Favi Kalish and his intentions. The last I heard, he was heading south, not north."

The woman's words echoed in his mind as she whistled and two burly men appeared by her side. She spoke to them in a trader's language and then waved them away. "Okay," she said, turning back to Sal. "Show me."

He retraced his steps to where the buggy nestled in the shadows. He didn't know what he would have done had it not been there, but it was, with Shilly, looking puzzled and concerned, still in her spot.

"Sal, what's going on? Who is she?"

"I don't have time to explain." He could do little to ease her mind while the woman looked over the vehicle. "We're moving out."

"Where's Engenius?"

"He's with Kalish, waiting for us." That wasn't a lie, but he still felt bad about it. He just didn't have time to explain.

The woman straightened from an inspection of the exhaust. "It's been a long way."

"It has, but it has been cared for."

"I can see that." She came around the buggy to where he stood. He waited anxiously for a second, then took her hand when it was offered to him. "We have a deal," she said. "My name is Belilanca Brokate. Call me Beli, never Bel or Bela. I'll make arrangements in the caravan for somewhere for you to ride. Do you object to one of my men driving during the crossing?"

Sal hesitated, but could see the sense in it. "No."

"Good. That increases our chances of success."

She whistled softly and the two men appeared again. They had obviously followed her and awaited her signal. Once again she spoke to them in a tongue Sal couldn't follow. The two men nodded and disappeared. Moment later, the snorting of two camels announced their return with a light wagon.

"Your friend is injured, yes?" Brokate indicated Shilly, who was watching with a stunned expression on her face.

"Her leg is broken."

"It would be better to have names, if we are to do business together."

"Of course." Sal kicked himself for not thinking of it earlier; traders set great store in knowing who they were talking to. Unhesitatingly, he gave their real names, since Brokate had already guessed who they were. "I'm Sal, and this is Shilly."

"A pleasure." The woman nodded once, then waved the two men forward.

"Hey — careful." Shilly resisted their touch at first, but had no choice other than to let herself be lifted off the buggy and placed gently into the wagon. Sal grabbed their packs from among their supplies and followed her. Brokate unloaded some of the boxes from the wagon and put them on the back of the buggy to change its profile, then lashed the tarpaulin back into place. One of the men produced a small bottle of paint and daubed a black circle on the bonnet.

And it was done. Sal hoisted himself into the wagon and let it be drawn away. Behind them, in full view, he watched the men climb into the buggy, start it, and follow. There was a hollow ache in his chest as he watched. What if he was wrong about Lutz and Kalish and had given away the buggy for nothing?

"I hope you know what you're doing, Sal." Shilly sat stiff and silent by his side. He couldn't tell if she was in pain or annoyed. Probably both, he assumed, and there was nothing to be done about either. All he could do was sit and hope that he did know what he was doing, and that Behenna's ceaseless *tap-tapping* wouldn't discover them.

"We're almost there, Shilly," he whispered. "Almost there."

When they reached the rest of Brokate's caravan, the wagon shuddered to a halt. Its leader appeared once more, to tie a flap over where they sat, leaving a gap for air and so they could peer out. She pressed battered binoculars into each of their hands. "For the view. It'll be good from where you're sitting. But I want them back, mind." Then she was gone.

The rocking motion of the wagon started up again as the rest of her people stirred, responding to her whispered orders to get ready. Then they began to move out. The roaring of engines, the braying of camels and the shouting of humans was deafening. Sal peered anxiously out at chaos behind them as the caravan rolled slowly forward. It was dusty and hot, and he was terrified, but it was good to be moving. They were committed. There was nothing more he could do. Brokate would either get them to the other side or not — and he would worry then, either way, about what would happen next.

At first he saw little but the wagons around them. The buggy had nipped ahead, presumably to take a position at the heart of the caravan. The men and women leading the camels were too busy to notice the two pairs of eyes peering out from one particular wagon, and Sal felt easier for that. The fewer who actually knew about them, the better.

Then the shouting reached a new height, and the wagon slowed. He presumed they had reached the final checkpoint and were braving the resistance of the people who manned it. Sky Wardens were sticklers for organisation and efficiency at the best of times. When they were trying to trap two fugitives, they would only be more so.

Of course, though, that was also the exact moment when it would be best for Brokate to turn them in. He had no more reason to trust her than he did Favi Kalish. What if he had foolishly led them into the worst possible situation?

The *tap-tapping* grew more urgent as the caravan lurched forward through the checkpoint. Sal concentrated on making his mind smooth and impenetrable, but the Sky Warden's touch was too strong, too insistent, too urgent. He knew something was up. Sal had to bite his lip to quell the panic rising in him. At any moment, he expected to be discovered.

Then Shilly's hand was gripping his upper arm. They were passing the checkpoint. Through the flap they could see Kalish, red-faced and shouting at the Warden in charge of the crossing. Engenius Lutz was standing beside him, looking around anxiously. Behind him, dressed in the dirty brown robes of a traveller, standing behind a sheet of cloth so he would be hidden from the staging area but not from the road, was —

Tait. The young journeyman looked annoyed, as though at a sudden change of plans. Sal sat upright and put his nose as close to the slit as he dared. If Tait was there, Behenna wouldn't be far away. He crouched down in the back of the wagon as Tait looked over his left shoulder at someone who had spoken, then stepped to one side.

And there he was: their pursuer, Shom Behenna, of moderate height yet solidly built, skin deep black and hair to match. His powerful gaze cast about the dusty air, as though he could see through wood, through canvas, to what lay hidden in the caravan passing them. He saw nothing, but clearly he suspected.

Lutz said something Sal couldn't make out. The Sky Warden reached out to take a handful of Lutz's smock and pulled the surgeon closer. Even though the surgeon was taller than the Sky Warden, Lutz shrank at the touch. Behenna said something through tight lips. His words weren't clear, but their relationship was.

"You *knew*," whispered Shilly. "Lutz betrayed us!"

"Or Kalish did." A feeling that wasn't quite relief flooded through him: he *was* profoundly relieved to have evaded the trap but dismayed at the same time that his suspicious instinct had proven right. "I didn't know for sure."

"Do you think he was hoping for a reward? Enough to mount an expedition back to the city, perhaps?"

Sal shook his head. He hadn't thought of that. If finding his father meant more to Lutz than Sal and Shilly's freedom, then it was certainly possible that that was why he had tried to turn them in — especially when he could justify it to himself as trying to save Shilly's leg.

Sal was more concerned for the moment about getting away. Just because they had slipped past Behenna didn't mean that they were going to make it to the other side unchallenged.

The sound from hoofs and wheels and feet had changed; their wagon had made it past the crossing and onto the bridge itself. With every extra metre between him and the Lookout, the tension coursing through him rose slightly. By the time they reached the first "island" and turned to enter the new section of bridge, he was trembling. It couldn't happen so easily.

Through the binoculars, Sal watched furious activity unfolding through the customs and market areas. It was being searched, he guessed, along with the rest of the town, and when it came up empty, Behenna finally knew for certain that he had been tricked. Abandoning all attempts to hide himself from general view, the Sky Warden strode out onto the road and stared at the retreating caravan, a hundred metres away and barely onto the second stretch of bridge. Brokate must have seen him too, for shrill whistles urged the caravan faster.

The Sky Warden rolled up the sleeves of his dusty blue robes and raised his hands. He closed his eyes for a moment. A glint of light reflected from the glass torc he wore around his neck. Sal held his breath, wondering what would come next and what he could possibly do to counter a direct attack from someone like Behenna. What if the caravan was destroyed simply in order to recapture him? How far would the Sky Warden go to get what he wanted?

The expression on Behenna's face was taut with strain and Sal suddenly realised why he had gone to such lengths to trap them unawares. Behenna was *afraid* of him! After the outburst that had almost killed the Alcaide and the Syndic, Behenna was doing everything he could to avoid a direct confrontation.

It was too late for subtlety now, though. Behenna shouted in a loud voice, and the cry vanished into the air of the Divide. Seconds later, a reply came from the walls of the canyon — an echo of the shout magnified into a twisting gale that tore at the canvas and sent the wagons skidding across the bridge into the stone guard rails protecting them from a fall to the bottom of the canyon far below. Shilly grabbed Sal to stop herself from falling as their wagon bounced sideways, such was the strength of the wind. Sal's ears popped, and he couldn't even hear himself shouting in alarm.

The wagons were jammed against the guardrail by the wind. They couldn't move forward, no matter how their drivers cursed. The Sky Warden had effectively pinned them in place. All he had to do was keep them there until a delegation arrived from the Lookout, and Sal would be theirs.

Sal reached deep into himself for a way to counteract the Sky Warden's summoning of the wind. What he lacked in skill, he might be able to make up for in brute strength. He'd give Behenna a *reason* to be afraid.

Before he could try, fire sprang into life along both sides of their section of the bridge — towering sheets of yellow flame that burned so hotly they produced a wind of their own, buffeting the caravan from all sides, but not burning a single hair. The elements clashed around them. The Sky Warden's unnatural gale fought the updraught from the fire, but without success. Strength was gradually leached out of the hurricane until nothing remained but a loud moan.

Sal's hearing returned. The force building up in his chest drained away as he looked around in amazement. This hadn't come from him, but from somewhere else. He heard more whistles and shouts as, slowly and carefully, the wagons began to move. He also heard enough voices asking where the flames had come from to realise that they weren't from Brokate, either. This was something beyond her control. It was as though the bridge itself had risen up to defend them, to protect them from the Sky Warden, although he couldn't imagine how or why. He could only watch breathlessly as they inched their way forward.

The Lookout was no longer visible, let alone Behenna's small figure. Sal's world had narrowed to a wide thoroughfare between two walls of fire. Time slowed as they wound their way along, following the turns of each junction with even more care than usual. Brokate's voice rang out clearly from the front, urging her team on and berating anyone whose courage flagged.

After what felt like an eternity, the flames fell behind them, and they were on the last section of bridge. The air felt instantly cooler and a natural breeze swept away the stench of fear and fire. Cooking smells, and incense, gradually took its place. The lights of Nesh weren't visible from Sal and Shilly's backward-facing vantage point, but every metal surface glimmered. Every trader's eye gleamed.

Then the hoofs, feet and wheels were rattling on solid ground. The flames burning along the greater length of the bridge died away entirely, and the Divide was again dark.

Sal raised the binoculars to see what was happening at the Lookout, and saw that things had finally calmed down. Kalish had gone, and so had Lutz. No one waited to travel across the bridge; the conflagration had made them nervous. Only Behenna remained, watching Brokate's caravan limp onto the far side of the canyon, slightly battered and shocked, but intact.

Across the gulf, Sal felt the mind of the Sky Warden grope for him, parting the suffocating fog of the Void Beneath to send him one brief message: "*Clever boy.*"

Then Shom Behenna turned and walked away.

Brokate appeared before them, untying and pulling back the canvas that had hidden them from view. Her face was flushed and very much alive.

"We made it!" she said, looking as though she didn't quite believe it herself. "*You* made it, Sal and Shilly. You're safe now. You're on the other side. How does it feel to be here?"

As much to his surprise as Shilly and Brokate's, Sal burst helplessly into tears.

PART TWO

LEARNING

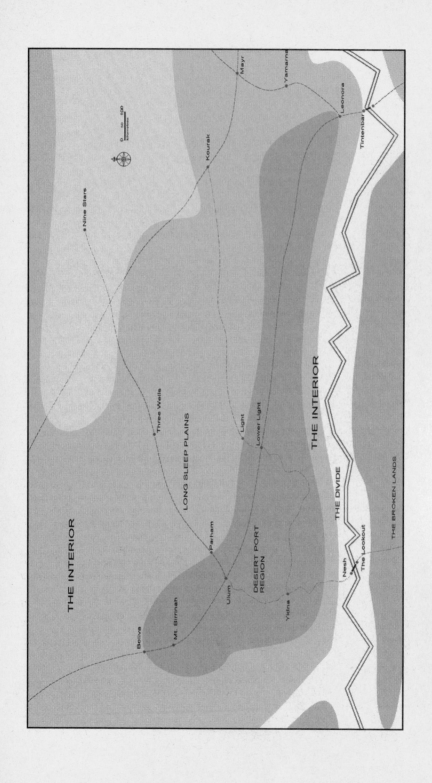

CHAPTER 5

DEATH, THE GREAT CHANGE-MAKER

Belilanca Brokate's caravan plodded slowly but steadily along the winding road from Nesh to Ulum, trailing a cloud of dust behind it. Shilly was in a bad mood — and knowing it didn't help. They had been travelling for seven days, stopping every night by the side of the road.

Judging by the smell of the dust during the day, she decided it must have risen from dried-up animal droppings disturbed by the wheels of wagons, carts and the occasional motorised truck. The path was obviously well used and the road camels, especially bred to haul wagons across long Interior highways, were not the sweetest-smelling creatures she had encountered. Their fresh deposits, baked by the relentless sun, soon crumbled to powder, ready for the next set of wheels to run over them.

Brokate had made her a bed in one of the leading wagons from which she could comfortably watch the land approaching and falling by. The view had soon worn as thin as the cushions beneath her. The landscape of the Interior so far was little different to that which she and Sal had crossed on the Old Line: hilly and uninteresting. She had heard, as a child, stories set in landscapes of towering peaks tipped with ice, of sheer walls of rock so high and steep that they could topple at any moment, and she had assumed that the Interior would be like that, immediately and obviously different. But these hills were little more than bumps in the landscape they had to either get over or go around — which they did with relaxed ease. Brokate and her team had clearly travelled this way many times before. They knew the road better than they knew each other. Shilly didn't know how they endured it, or the flies.

As anticlimactic as the view was, though, it was nowhere near as bad as the heat. If she had thought it hot in the northern fringes of the Strand, she now knew better. By day the air boiled. The sun pounded down like a hammer on molten iron. The wind only brought more heat from the north and burnt as easily as the sun. She consumed litres of water and sweated most of it out. She felt as though she was drying up like the camel turds, and suspected she smelt as bad. The only thing that made it bearable was the thought that she had to go this way to get where she wanted to be. It would be cool where Skender Van Haasteren lived, she hoped; maybe there would be mountains and snow. Until then, she just had to endure.

The fact that Sal hadn't complained even once only made it harder for her to say anything. Quite apart from the ward easing some of life's little annoyances for him, he got to sit at the front of the wagon with Brokate, trading stories and songs to while the time away. Shilly could see the back of their heads from where she lay and heard their voices clearly. It was all right for him, she thought: he'd achieved what he wanted. Brokate had confirmed that the Sky Wardens never came into the Interior if they could help it. They were a long, long way from the sea, the source of the Wardens' power, and getting further away every day. He was safe from Behenna, from his great-aunt the Syndic, and from the Alcaide. Sal had put it all behind him, and could afford to relax.

Shilly wished she had it so easy.

"Between the old times and these," Brokate said, her accented voice as rolling and dusty as the road they travelled, "the face of the world changed many times. Not in the way a person's face changes when they look happy or sad, for the bones below a face don't move: it remains, always, the same face. The Earth's bones *themselves* moved. When this happened, many things came into being that had not existed before, and others that had once been familiar were gone forever, sometimes overnight.

"In those in-between times, there lived a baker. He wasn't a famous baker, a maker of delicate pastries or towering cakes or anything like that. He lived in a small village on the slopes of a tall mountain. This village was no different to any other. Its name was La Menz and, as well as the baker, it had a blacksmith, a mayor, a butcher, tailor, and so on. The only thing that makes it memorable is that, on one of those nights when the bones of the world moved, everyone who lived there died."

She paused.

"Go on," said Sal. "I think I know it, but in the version I've heard the baker was a carpenter. There might be other differences. And Shilly will want to hear it. Won't you, Shilly?"

"I don't mind." She looked up from a pattern she was sketching with charcoal on the wagon's canvas sides. In truth, she didn't care either way. The stories provided only a distraction from the monotony of the scenery.

"The baker never learned why everyone died," Brokate continued. "He didn't even notice it at first, for he had had reason to be out of the village's bounds for most of the night. He came home before dawn and napped on a couch so as not to disturb his wife or children. When the sun rose in the morning so did he, sleepily, not noting the silence in the house as he went about his work."

Brokate's voice took on the rhythms of the wagon's wheels and the camels' hoof steps. "The village bread was late that morning, but no one complained. The baker presumed that his wife had given the villagers warning the night before, telling them that he had been called away and would be too tired to keep his usual schedule. But as time rolled on and the steaming loaves cooled, and still no one came to collect them, he began to wonder. Had his bread been spurned by even those who had once been his most loyal customers? Would people go to work hungry just to make a point?

"He called out to his wife and received silence in reply; this was not unexpected. But his children hadn't bidden him good morning, as he demanded that they, at the least, should do. Neither could he hear them squabbling in the kitchen while they ate breakfast.

"He wasn't an imaginative man, but by then even he felt something like sand slipping under his feet. It was the bones of his world moving — shifting, sliding, falling away ..."

I know how he feels, Shilly thought, her mind wandering. Everything about the traders unsettled her: the tattoos and piercings, the strange incense they burned, the metal coins they traded with, the strange, rhythmic songs they sang, their accents.

Nesh had been a bewildering kaleidoscope of colours and sounds that had quickly undermined any gladness she had felt about achieving their goal of crossing to the Interior. The people there dressed in robes and kept rat-like creatures called quolls as pets. They shouted in strange languages and stared openly at her dark skin. The caravan had only stayed a night, but that had been more than enough for her. She could understand now why Sal had preferred a life on the road to the towns he and his father had occasionally visited. She had never before felt so isolated, even after years of being Fundelry's odd girl out.

Caught up in her thoughts, she missed a sentence or two, and she surprised herself by being annoyed when she realised it.

"His wife lay on the family bed," Brokate was saying, "cold and still. His son, barely old enough to grow a beard, huddled in a ball in one corner of the room, while his sister, older but smaller, lay spreadeagled on her stomach as though dropped from a great height. They were stiff but not yet beginning to smell. A red dust like fine sand or pollen lay across their skin.

"The baker ran from the room in horror. It was too terrible: it couldn't be true. But it was the same in every home he visited: families lay dead in their beds or nearby, coated in the crimson ash. Some had died sleeping, others looked as though they had woken long enough to cry out in pain, then expired. And it wasn't just the people: the blacksmith, the mayor, the butcher, the tailor and the others. The livestock had succumbed too. All through the village nothing moved. No birds sang. No insects crawled or flew to inspect the dead. Nothing but himself, the baker, had survived.

"He spent all day trying to work out what had happened. Had the red dust killed them, or was it just a residue left behind by some terrible poison? Whatever was behind the mysterious deaths, it must have struck everywhere at once, for nowhere was there a sign of disturbance; no one had alerted family members or neighbours. They seemed to have died in their sleep or shortly after waking. The red ash remained a mystery no matter how hard he searched. All he could tell for certain — the unimaginative, unremarkable baker — was that he was alone. He had been spared purely because he hadn't been there.

"Crying silently he walked the empty streets where he had once strolled with his family, feeling the hands of children in his, the warmth of his wife's love buoying him upward. He lost track of time. He sat, stunned, in the town's only bar, drinking on his own. The fact that everyone was dead only sank in at the thought that he could leap the counter and take anything he wanted. He didn't have to pay because there was no one left to care. They were all gone.

"Night fell. The sun set over the deserted town and no lights came on to greet the stars. The rows of windows were cold and empty. Doors no longer offered protection from the night; instead they locked in a darkness that the baker was reluctant to see or even think of. The baker was alone in a town of the dead. How long, the baker wondered, until the stench drove him away? Or the killer, the source of the red ash, returned? Perhaps, he thought, if the killer *did* return to correct its mistake, to collect the one who had slipped through its net, that would solve his problems.

"And at that precise moment," Brokate said, her voice deepening, "the baker heard footsteps coming up the street into the heart of town. Hard shoes clunked on the cobbles: heavy shoes and a heavy walker, slow and measured. Whoever was out that night had no fear of the fate that had befallen the village.

"Terrified, the baker ducked behind the counter of the bar and hid. The footsteps grew nearer, as clear as ice in the empty night, along the road, across the pavement, and into the bar.

"'Come out,' said a voice which he felt in his heart and gut, rather than heard with his ears. 'Come out of hiding and see my face.'

"Quivering, the baker rose to his feet and faced the visitor. He had expected a man; the owner of such hard shoes and heavy stride simply *had* to be male. But what he saw was no person at all.

"'I am Death,' said the figure before him. The baker received a confused impression of many things at once: leathery bat wings; a bright red insect carapace; wide-spaced spider eyes; long, black limbs with joints higher than his head. The creature's appearance was constantly shifting, accompanied by the sound of moth's wings rustling, dead leaves falling, ghosts whispering.

"'H-have you come to take me?' the baker asked it.

"'You called me,' it said. 'Is that what you want me to do?'

"The baker didn't realise that Death could be summoned simply by thinking about it, and he was far from certain that Death was what he actually wanted. By way of answering the question, he stammered out as good an explanation of what had happened as he could manage under the circumstances: he had been called away the previous night and when he returned everyone had been dead. He was the only one left alive. Perhaps there had been a mistake, and Death could correct it.

"The apparition watched him closely through its many eyes. 'Do you think you should have died with your family?' it asked.

"The baker didn't honestly know. 'Can you tell me what happened to them?' he asked.

"'They stopped living,' Death said.

"'But why?'

"'I don't know. All I can do is show them to you.'

"The baker thought of the bodies decomposing in the rooms behind the bakery. 'I don't want to see them as they are.'

"'As they have always been, then,' said Death, and with that, what little light there remained in the world drained away around them, and darkness closed in."

Brokate paused to take a sip of water, and Sal took the opportunity to compare versions again.

"The red dust is different. I heard that they died in their sleep, with their eyes shut and mouths open. The only odd thing was a black smudge on their foreheads, as though someone had marked them with charcoal."

"It doesn't surprise me," Brokate said. "These stories are told and retold many times, and every teller adds something of his or her own culture in the process. As long as the essential details remain the same, it doesn't matter. The charcoal marking is an interesting one, though. Where I come from, in Kourak, there was a religious sect near our village. If you were favoured by them, they would mark you like that at certain times of the year."

"Why?"

"Your guess is as good as mine." She twitched the reins leading to the camels, and settled more comfortably in her seat. "Where were we? Oh, yes. Death took the baker to the other side of life, where there exists a realm living humans can only rarely visit. It is a shadow world, but not in the sense of darkness and absence of light. Death is a shadow cast by life, not the absence of life. When you take away all that a person is, all that remains is what they have become.

"The simple baker found much to puzzle him there. The first thing he saw was a replica of the village and its inhabitants, all seeming as solid as ever. The blacksmith stood by his bellows, staring at the baker as he walked past. The mayor scowled at him. The butcher's silver blade flashed onto an empty chopping block while the tailor's needle swooped and dove into black, leathery fabric. None of them said a word.

"Death walked beside him, its heavy steps the only sound in the dull world. No one acknowledged it, the baker noticed; maybe, he thought, they couldn't see it. Death led the baker along the street to his house and up the short flight of steps. On the threshold, he heard the sounds of an argument. His wife and children were bickering, as usual.

"They fell silent when he walked into the kitchen, the feathery whisper of Death at his heels. His wife, son and daughter stared at him for a timeless moment.

"'Franic,' he began, but his son spun angrily on his heel and walked out.

"He tried again. 'Tulpil —' but his daughter crossed the room in two strides and slapped him across the face, then also left the room.

"That left only: 'Elsa?'

"'You weren't with us when we needed you,' his wife said, glaring.

"He couldn't meet her stare. 'Elsa, what happened to you? Do you know?'

"'We died, of course!'

"'Do you know what did it?'

"For a moment, her anger faded. Her eyes took on a faraway look. 'I dreamed of a cloud. A red cloud. It rolled down the hill and engulfed the town. It buried us. Everything went dark. I woke up here.' She came back to herself. 'And you weren't here, damn you. You weren't here.'

"'I came back and found you'... he began.

"'I don't care what you did, you fool,' she broke in. 'You've never been any good when it counted. You're weak-willed, useless. It should be you that died, not us.' She turned her back on him and walked out, spurning him as his children had.

"When she was gone, the baker turned to Death and said that he had seen enough. He was crying. He hadn't expected tears in the realm of Death. He had thought that they would be left behind, along with cruelty, disdain and scorn.

"Death raised an arm and the grey of the shadow-world faded. 'Is it true?' Death asked him, before taking him back to the real world.

"'Which part?'

"'That you should have died instead of them,' Death said, 'not with them.'

"'I don't know. What difference does it make now?'

"'I have the power to change some things,' said the apparition. 'If you would die to return them to life, I can make it so.'

"The baker looked at Death in surprise. It didn't seem possible that he would be able to change places with his family — but, then, none of what had happened to him seemed possible. Why not this, too?

"But the baker remembered the shadow-realm version of his family's kitchen. It was empty. The hearth was grey and cold; there was no food in the larder and no water in the sink. It was a dead place.

"'Take me home,' the baker said, and Death did just that."

Brokate paused again, but this time Sal didn't interrupt. Shilly was glad for that. A nagging uncertainty had crept into the tale; there was more underlying it than she had at first suspected. In simpler tales, the baker would gladly have given his life to bring back his loved ones.

"The apparition didn't leave the baker after that as he had thought it might," Brokate went on. "It hovered in a corner while he tried to get things in order. He had to eat, or he might as well let Death take him. He had to sleep. Deep down he knew that, even when bones shift or break, the flesh persists. It may be lame or scarred, but it heals. And sometimes it heals stronger than before.

"Besides, he had graves to dig. Had there been insects left in the wake of the red dust, the bodies of his fellow villagers would have made meals for numerous tiny mouths; instead they just sagged, wilted, putrefied. The dust didn't hurt him when he moved them. On the beds, on the floors and in the hallways, red outlines revealed where they had fallen and died. From a population of over one hundred, that would soon be all that remained of them.

"On the third morning after the village had died, when his job was only half-done, a pale, thin hand on his shoulder shook him awake from a deep sleep.

"'Bern,' a voice said into his ear, for that was his name. 'Bern, wake up. Wake up!'

"He jerked upright with such force that he startled the person who had been shaking him. She was a young woman dressed in a farmworker's shift. Her hair was blonde and long, and her eyes were grey-blue, like old ice. She was looking at him with concern, and he didn't know how to reassure her.

"'Oh, Bern,' she said, 'you had me worried. I thought you were dead, too.'

"'You've seen them?' he asked her.

"She screwed up her nose. 'I can smell them. What happened?'

"'I don't know.' His eyes wandered to the stairwell and found the shifting, eerie form of Death watching closely from under the stairs. 'Monca, you shouldn't be here.'

"'Da asked me to come,' she said. 'He's heard nothing from Dedrick since Wednesday, and they were supposed to meet. He sent me to see what was wrong.' Her words faltered.

"'Did you kill them?' she asked.

"'No,' he said. 'Do you really think I'd do that?'

"She flushed. 'The last time I saw you, you said they were angry with you.'

"'Deservedly so, Monca. I didn't hate them for it.'

"'People have killed for lesser things than hate, Bern.'

"'Not me,' he said, suddenly hearing exactly what people would say when word spread of the catastrophe. Everyone in La Menz had died except Bern the Baker, the one sowing his oats with the pretty farm girl from the neighbouring village. The one who would abandon his wife and children, given half a chance. The one who deserved it most. That it was partly true didn't make it any easier to bear.

"'I didn't do it,' he reiterated with as much force as he could muster, hearing only hollowness in his voice. He was empty, unable to raise enough passion even to defend his innocence.

"'I believe you, Bern, my love.' She leant closer and tried to embrace him, but he pushed her away and stood up.

"'I'm sorry,' he said. 'Everything is wrong. I should have been here, with them, when it happened.'

"'With that bitch and those two brats?' Her temper flared as it only did when he talked about his family. 'You didn't leave them: they all but cast you out. You were lucky you *weren't* here when it happened. Now you're free. You can do whatever you want. We can be together.'

"'It's not that simple, Monca,' he said. 'There are things I have to do. I have responsibilities —'

"'To the dead?' she interrupted.

"'To myself,' he said. His heart ached to see her looking so upset. Before, when his family had been alive, he had blamed them for her pain. Now he wasn't so sure. Perhaps he would never be able to give her what she needed.

"'I love you, Bern,' she said.

He couldn't answer. Tears filled his eyes, the memories of walking together as a family through the streets of his village coming to him again. The children's hands had been much smaller than his, then, and his wife's love had faded since. 'All things change,' he said. 'All things die. We can't fight that.'

"He headed for the stairs.

"'Do *you* love *me*, Bern?' Monca wanted to know. He didn't have an answer for her. His simple heart ached from the confusion of his life. Once, he had loved his wife as much as he had thought, just days ago, that he loved Monca. He had loved his children, too. Somewhere along the way it had all gone wrong and he didn't know how to make it right. He didn't know who he loved. All he knew was how to make bread, and that was worthless in an empty village.

"He walked up the stairs without looking back. Monca must have noted the smell issuing from the bedroom before she had woken him, for only Death followed him now.

"'Why are you still here?' he asked the apparition.

"'I still await your decision,' it said. 'I note that you haven't buried your family yet. Until that is done, nothing is binding.'

"He nodded. The bodies of his wife and two children lay where they had fallen. He had resolved to deal with them last of all, even if they came apart in his hands. Not until his mind and heart were certain that he was making the right decision would he condemn them to the grave.

"'I feel guilty,' he said. 'I wanted to leave them, and I did, that night, to see Monca. They died while I was gone. But they hadn't really wanted me there; they just wanted security. I gave them that, at least, and took my own needs elsewhere. I came back to them to ease my conscience, not my heart.'

"Death said nothing.

"'They died,' he went on, 'and at first I was glad I wasn't with them.' It felt good to confess the dark secret that lurked in his heart, where Monca had been unable to free it. 'I was glad to be alive. But can I really live like this, feeling guilty for my good fortune? Monca doesn't know what it is like to have had a family and lost them, to death or to anything else. Monca is young. She doesn't deserve this — complication.' He felt terribly sad, thinking of the woman waiting for him below, wondering what he was doing.

"Death watched him from a point near the doorway, whispering to itself. The baker saw his own face staring back at him, momentarily, from the chaos of body parts and textures. It frightened him to see it, but it excited him, too. A vacancy opened in his chest, as though, just for a moment, he was falling. There was one simple answer to his confusion, and he was, after all, a simple man.

"It was time to act.

"'You'll take me, and bring them back?'

"'If you have decided,' said Death, 'it will be so.'

"'And I'll be able to watch them?'

"'If you want to badly enough.'

"'I think I will,' he said.

"Death moved closer, until it was looming over him. The smell of old bird wings and sun bleached rabbit bones buried him in musty darkness.

"And it was done."

The baker's decision took Shilly completely by surprise — although it was the one she had thought he should make, originally. This wasn't the way such tales normally worked. Simple men didn't have affairs — and if they did, if they loved another more than someone else, surely they would stay with their lover, not sacrifice themselves and lose their chance to find happiness. Why would he give up everything for a family who had died through no fault of his own? A living love had to be better than dead grief.

It didn't make sense to her. What was the baker seeing that she wasn't?

Brokate continued:

"The baker found his afterlife mercifully uncomplicated. He moved into the pale echo of his old home, where the cupboards were bare and the air was dry, and learned how to live in the land of the dead. With no need to eat or drink, he found himself, for the first time in his life, with plenty of time to think.

"His family, meanwhile, rejoined the living. What they did, at first, he didn't know. It took him some weeks to get the knack of seeing through the death-realm to the land of light and life. Even then, it was ghostly and faint, like pictures on gauze held up to the sun. But it was clear enough — *too* clear, at times.

"In the time since the red cloud, families and friends of the dead had repopulated the village. The grave the baker had half-filled was now smoothed over and marked with a statue honouring those who had died that night. The village had a new blacksmith, mayor, butcher and tailor, and when they spoke of what had happened it was with awe and reverence, not fear. The village became a symbol of the new, changeable world, not of an uncaring destiny that might strike at any moment.

"But there was still sadness, and he wasn't the only one who felt it. He had opened a window onto the square, and invited the villagers to see what he saw. They were wary at first. Many avoided him, not understanding how the exchange between him and his family had taken place, and perhaps fearing the touch of Death even in this lifeless place. But one by one they came to witness what had happened since their departure. Curiosity overpowered disapproval, as it so often does.

"The spirits of the dead, watching the world the baker had chosen to leave, watched as the words of Death — that the baker's family would appear to him as they had always been — came vividly true.

"His wife didn't even pretend to mourn. She sold the bakery to a man from another village — a gambling drunk with a temper to match her own — and he soon moved into her bed. His son took to roaming the streets of the village and nearby towns, stealing what he could and vandalising what he couldn't. He was arrested many times, but that only encouraged his wilfulness. His daughter took work with the village tailor, but skimped on her chores and made mistakes. When caught out, she lied about her fellow workers to cover herself.

"And yet somehow they thought themselves happy. On the first anniversary of the death of the village, the baker's family, the sole survivors of the red dust, gathered to toast their good luck, and to mock the fool who had chosen death over life in the real world. They raised their glasses to the dry, empty realm they had visited briefly and to the ghosts who were still trapped there. The ringing of their laughter echoed through the afterlife, hurting the baker's ears and heart, and all those who heard it.

"There was a silence afterward, when he closed the peephole between life and death forever. One by one, the dead villagers gathered around him to offer their silent sympathy. Once, they had spurned him; now their touches were like snow falling — cold and almost weightless — but he felt each keenly. He was embraced by their sorrow and made one of them again. Although the bones of his world had shattered into unrecognisable fragments, his spirit soared. He was forgiven at last. He was free."

Ah, Shilly thought, beginning to understand. That was it. The baker wanted understanding: he wanted the villagers to know what his family had been like, so they would accept why he had left them. They might have been his family, but even the love of a family member must be earned, and they no longer deserved his. Yet he had stuck by them, supported them, even maintained the fiction that they were still a family when everyone knew that his heart had fallen elsewhere. Instead of blaming him, the villagers should have celebrated him for his perseverance and set him free to do what he wanted, whether that was to be with Monca or not. Even with his family dead, he couldn't be with her in good conscience. He couldn't live until he had proven his accusers wrong, and he couldn't love under a cloud of death.

But where *was* the love? Was death his only reward? That seemed a harsh lesson to her.

"Does it end there?" asked Sal.

"Doesn't yours?" challenged Brokate.

"It changed halfway through. It didn't go where I thought it would." Shilly was gratified to hear that it wasn't just her who was surprised.

Brokate's voice took on a provocative edge: "How would *you* end it, then, if you had the choice?"

"Me?" The question took Sal off guard. "I don't know."

"Make something up," she said. "Tell me what you want to happen."

Sal thought for a long time — so long that Shilly began to wonder if he was going to say anything at all. When he did finally speak, he had adopted a softer, singing tone, one she recognised from his father's storytelling.

"I would end the story like this," he said. "The baker hadn't been able to watch Monca through the peephole because she lived in another village. Since he could only see La Menz, he had no idea what had happened to her after he died.

"On the night he was forgiven by his villagers, she was brought to him in the shadow world. She had called Death and asked for him, and the apparition had come to take her with its heavy footsteps and strange whispering.

"The baker couldn't have been more surprised. 'You don't belong here,' he told her.

"'I do now,' she said in reply, stepping away from Death to stand before him.

"'You died for me?' he asked, as dumbfounded by her as he was by any of the turns his life had taken.

"'I loved you, Bern. Life without you had little appeal.'

"'But I'm just a baker,' he said. 'No one needs bread here.'

"'You *were* a baker,' she corrected him. 'And *I* need you for more than your bread.'

"'How do you know that I love you in return?'

"'I don't,' she smiled. 'But we have the chance to find out, now.'"

Brokate interrupted with a brisk laugh. "Very romantic," she said. "And let me guess: the two of them are still there now, watching over the village as time passes. Is that right?"

"That's right. The baker's family all met bitter ends, one by one, and found no kind welcome in the afterlife."

"And the red dust never returned, for the bones of the Earth had settled finally into their new positions." She laughed again. "That's some ending."

Shilly agreed, although it didn't solve everything.

"Do you think any of it's true?" asked Sal, after a short pause. "Do you think there might once have been a village like that, in which everyone died?"

"Undoubtedly. Lots of things have happened in the past that we can barely imagine. But as for the rest ... Well, only Death, the great change maker itself, knows for sure."

She clicked her reins and for a minute or two they rode in silence, bumping along the winding path between and over the barren hills.

Shilly tried to relax in the heat and the smell of camel. Every shuddering metre she travelled was one less between her and Skender Van Haasteren.

"Your turn, Sal," said Brokate.

"But I gave you an ending," he protested.

"Only an ending. That doesn't count."

"The only story I can think of at the moment is about a butterfly merchant named Polain." Shilly heard a note of reluctance in his voice, and she knew he didn't really want to tell the story. Or maybe he did; he had brought it up, after all. Maybe he wanted to get it out of his system — the last story his father had ever told.

"Butterflies," repeated Brokate. "Not moths?"

"Not moths. In a city of metal and glass larger than any built before or since." Shilly thought of the city in the Broken Lands, its bleak testimony to the ways that had been lost and the sheer weight of time that was gradually tearing the towers down. The empty windows of the towers reminded her of the village in the land of the dead, where people saw things as they really were.

"And every one of the butterflies was different? Is that right, Sal?"

"Yes. You've heard it." Shilly couldn't tell if he was relieved or disappointed.

"Not your version. Tell it to me, and we can compare. In some ways, that's more interesting than the tale itself — the tales *between* tales, if you like."

So Sal began the story and Shilly turned her attention inward. She had heard this one before, and it reminded her too much of places and people she had lost: Fundelry, Lodo, Von, Aunty Merinda, Mrs Milka, Derksen ... She wondered if Thess had had her baby, and if shy, vulnerable Tom been forced to go to the Haunted City against his will. Had Kemp been punished for faking the thefts that had got Sal in trouble, then letting them take the buggy as the Sky Wardens had closed in? There were too many things to think about, and she was afraid to start.

Outside held nothing but the baked earth of the Interior and the blast-furnace sun. She hadn't heard Sal ask for details about their destination, not even once. Wouldn't he *ever* get tired of stories and talk about something real?

She couldn't have sweated out all the water she'd drunk that day, for by the time they stopped for the night her bladder was bursting. At the heart of a round depression, surrounded by low hills, Brokate and Sal lifted her off the wagon and helped her to a relatively private patch of ground near the campsite. As she crouched, Sal helped her maintain her balance with his usual red-faced silence, as though determined, too late, not to say or do anything that might betray his embarrassment. When she pulled aside her dress this time, she felt warmth trickle down her thigh, and thought in horror: *Bloody hell, I've pissed myself! That's all I need.*

Then suddenly, Brokate elbowed Sal aside and was simultaneously trying to hold Shilly up and gesturing that he should leave. He started to protest, then glanced down, and his face turned an even darker crimson. He instantly turned and hurried away.

Only then did Shilly herself realise what had happened.

Brokate was soothing, reassuring her that nothing was wrong while Shilly relieved herself — there was no way she could hold on any longer — then fetching rags to soak up the flow of blood. It was perfectly natural, and it happened to every girl as she grew up. Shilly knew all that; Aunty Merinda had taught her about menses years ago. The surprise was simply that it had happened to *her*. Part of her had dreaded it; another part had looked forward to it, especially as she had lagged increasingly behind the other girls in Fundelry. Now that it was here, she didn't know how to react.

She did feel awkward for Sal, though, and was glad for Brokate's help — especially on overhearing part of the caravan leader's conversation with him when they returned to the camp.

"It's nothing to worry about," Brokate said, softly but firmly. "Don't go treating her any different because it's happened. There's no reason why you should. And I'll hear none of this *now she's a woman* crap, thank you. She's the same Shilly you ever knew. She's just had her period, that's all."

What Sal said in reply Shilly couldn't hear, but Brokate laughed heartily.

"You won't need to worry about that. I'll show her anything she needs to do and she can look after herself. It's different for every girl. Let her find her own rhythm, and she can tell you about it if she wants to. I know it's awkward, but in a way this is a blessing. It would be more awkward if it had happened and you didn't know anything."

To which Sal uncertainly agreed, and the conversation ended there. Shilly lay in the close comfort of the wagon, wondering what she'd say if Sal came to her to stammer some awkward apology or offer his support or whatever came into his head. But luckily he left her alone, and so did Brokate. The caravan leader had more important work to do, making sure that the wagons, trucks and buggies were secured for the night, the camels fed, tents erected, toilets dug, fires lit and meals prepared. Voices rang out in the deepening twilight as members of the caravan caught up on the day's events. There was laughter, song, playful ribbing and, occasionally, grumbling from the normally reticent camels. Just another night on the road to Ulum.

She wondered if she should feel more. The blood on her thighs meant that having children would be an option, one day, and that thought made her stomach roll. The Sky Wardens taught through their system of Schools that people should wait until they were secure in their lives before contemplating bringing another into the world. Most people, according to Aunty Merinda, took precautions against unwanted childbirth until they were absolutely certain of their decision. The village seer had left no doubts as to the causal connection between pregnancy and sex. But just because she could, technically, grow a child inside her didn't mean that she was about to rush out and get herself knocked up. There had to be a father in the equation. That was the thought she found most frightening to contemplate.

When dinner was cooked, Sal brought her a bowl of stew made from a dark brown meat and lots of vegetables. The gravy was pungent with unfamiliar spices and hot on the tongue. She wasn't sure she liked it, and watched enviously as Sal ate his with relish.

He didn't say anything about what had happened, but she could sense his nervousness. She wondered if Brokate had forced him to bring her the meal, as he normally would, or if he had made the gesture of his own accord.

"How long until we get there?" she asked, desperate to break the silence.

"Two days," he said around a mouthful. "Beli says we're right on schedule."

Beli says ... Shilly couldn't help the stab of resentment at the familiar way Sal talked about the caravan leader. "What happens then?"

He didn't say anything for several mouthfuls. "I don't know. Ulum is a big place, from what I hear. Bigger than anywhere I've been before. Bigger than Yidna, that's for sure." They had passed through the town called Yidna on the fifth day and dropped off some of the caravan's other passengers. It had been the size of two Fundelry's, a small community by Interior standards, eking out a living from travellers in the shade of a narrow ravine, hardly the sort of city she had been expecting. "Beli might be able to ask around for us. I don't want to push my luck with her, though. She likes us, but she has a business to run. I don't want to get her into trouble, if anyone follows us."

"Who would follow us?"

"I don't know." He looked uncomfortable, as though she had touched a nerve. Maybe, she thought, he was so used to running that he didn't know how to think otherwise.

"So we're just going to walk through the city gates and start asking around?" she asked.

"If you can think of a better plan, I'd be glad to hear it."

They ate the rest of their meal in silence, deep in thought. They were getting closer to the end of their journey, to Skender Van Haasteren. The more she thought about it, the more the name carried with it an air of mystery as well as promise: What was the man who had taught the young Lodo like? Would he still be alive? Would he help the friends of a man who had abandoned his vocation for a life of poverty in another land?

When the meal was over, preparation for the night began in earnest. The stars were out in the cloudless sky, and a half moon rode over the eastern horizon. Shilly watched it as the caravan riders cleaned up after the meal, banked up the fires and slowly put themselves to bed. One by one exhausted team members retired to their tents until only a handful were left by the fires, Sal and Brokate among them. Shilly dozed fitfully throughout the evening, then woke up with a start at midnight to find the camp silent and the fires reduced to embers. A chill wind swept through the tent ropes, making them hum. Sal lay curled around himself behind her, deeper in the shadow of the wagon, his breathing regular and deep.

Nothing has changed, she told herself. Yet everything had. Lodo was gone; they were in the Interior; she was having her first period. She didn't know what else the future held for her.

With a snort, she told herself to stop being melodramatic and go back to sleep. *I will not think*, she told herself. *My body can look after itself, and there's nothing I can do, for the moment, about the rest.*

But it wasn't any of those concerns that kept her awake. It was the story Brokate had told that day, about the baker who had given his family a second chance to live at the expense of his own life, simply in order to prove himself blameless. And Monca, who had loved him and ultimately summoned death to prove it. That Shilly couldn't understand at all, and she feared she never would.

CHAPTER 6

THE CROSSROADS

On the day they were due to reach Ulum, Sal crawled out of his sleeping bag before dawn. He was turning into an early riser, much to Shilly's dismay. Nervous and excited at the same time, he slipped off the wagon and went for a walk.

The camp was quiet apart from the occasional snore from human and camel. By night the landscape lacked the brown, baked aspect it showed during the day; it was inviting, almost gentle. The air was still and frigid, biting with the deep, desert chill he remembered from his days travelling the borderlands with his father — only here, further north, it was even more pronounced.

In the days since they had joined the caravan, they had travelled five hundred kilometres into the Interior, and since leaving Fundelry, he and Shilly had put more than one and a half thousand kilometres behind them. That thought, instead of making him proud, made him feel very small, and more than a little humble.

He was in his mother's country. This was the land in which she had been raised: as defined by the sun as the sea defined the Strand. Before coming to the Haunted City to marry Highson Sparre, nephew of the woman who would one day become the Syndic of the Strand, Seirian Mierlo had spent her life in landscape much like this and perhaps even seen the very things he was seeing now. The Interior was as much a part of his heritage as her family name and the Change. It was finally time to become acquainted with it.

He climbed a short distance up the side of a hill and sat on a protruding lip of rock to wait for the sunrise. Molash, the cook, was always up at dawn, and would soon have the fires stoked for a breakfast of fried eggs and onion with herbs and plants scavenged from the area around the campsite, only some of which Sal recognised. The camels would wake then, too; their noise, along with the smell of food, would rouse the rest of the camp. Then it would be all noise and fuss until everyone had dressed and eaten, and everything was stowed for the day's journey. Then they would be off.

Had they been closer to Ulum, Sal would have seriously considered leaving — before anyone woke, to save awkward questions. But Shilly couldn't get very far, even on the crutches one of the caravan workers had made for her, carved with the repeated circular motif of Belilanca Brokate. The dry hills were unkind to travellers on foot.

In the buggy, it would have been a simple journey, but that wasn't an option any more. Brokate had sold it to a vehicle trader in Nesh, the night they had crossed the Divide. He had only learned of its loss when he had offered to show the caravan mechanic how to service it.

"It's too incriminating," she had said when confronted. "Too hard to hide. If someone follows you, we'll stand out because of it. And besides —" she had displayed an awkward smile, teeth flashing in the yellow sunlight "— it was too good a deal. Passage to Ulum isn't worth what I got for your buggy, even taking into account the crossing we went through, so you get to keep the difference. Here..." She had reached under the seat at the front of the caravan's leading wagon, and held out a purse full of metal and ceramic coins. "This is yours. I was going to give it to you when we reached Yidna, but you might as well have it now. I don't think I need to tell you to spend it wisely."

Through a strong sense of betrayal and hurt, he had known that what she had done not only made sense, but was needlessly honourable. Their deal had not required her to give him anything. He was quite happy to let her take the lot in the knowledge that, without her help, they would never have made it to the Interior in the first place.

But she wouldn't let him say no. As a result, he and Shilly now had money for when they arrived in Ulum. Enough to cover accommodation and food for a couple of weeks if they were careful. Enough, maybe, to bribe an official or two. Enough, he hoped, to get them where Shilly wanted to go.

Exactly where *he* was going, he hadn't worked out yet.

The thought of being unable to travel gnawed at him. All his life had been spent on the road; that was what he considered normal. Losing the buggy was like losing a home as well as a way of life.

A faint smudge of light crept into the eastern sky as he remembered the rest of that conversation with Brokate.

"Have I earned your story now, Sal?" she had asked, glancing cannily at him from her position at the reins.

"What story?"

"Why you're here. Who you were running from."

Squirming, he had replied: "It's not that interesting, really."

"I'll bet it is. I've barely known you a day, and you've already given me the most exciting Divide crossing I'm ever likely to have." Again, her smile had flashed at him from her tattooed, pale-skinned face. "Give me something to tell my nephews and nieces when I get home, Sal. Don't leave me wondering who you were for the rest of my life. I've no doubt you and Shilly are *someone*."

"Well," he had begun, hesitating over almost every word. "My father, he stole something from the Sky Wardens, and they wanted it so badly they chased him all over the Strand to get it."

"And I presume they didn't get it, in the end, otherwise they wouldn't be after you now."

"They did get it, sort of. But it wasn't a thing so much."

"Then what?"

"It was my mother."

"Ah." She had leaned back slightly and nodded. "I think I see now. They got her, and now they want you."

"Yes."

"But you didn't want to go with them, so you ran. Why here?"

"Shilly thinks — that is, *we* think — there's someone in the Desert Ports who might be able to help us."

"The biggest and best Desert Port is Ulum, so you're heading in the right direction. Who is it you're looking for?"

He had stalled at saying the name. It was all very well revealing their history to someone who was, basically, a complete stranger, but their future was another thing entirely. "A Stone Mage," had been all that he would admit, in the end.

That had surprised her. "Really? You could be heading off the griddle and on to the grate, my friend."

"Why?"

"Who's to say that he or she will be any different from those you're running from? Whether they throw rocks around or whistle at the wind, they're all after the same thing. If you have a knack with the Change, if you have their way in your blood, they'll want you, no matter where you came from and no matter what *you* want. It's as simple as that."

"Really?" On one level, hearing her say that had comforted him. It reinforced something Shilly had said earlier, about everyone wanting him. If it *was* as simple as that, then all their problems were solved. Skender Van Haasteren would be only too pleased to teach someone with Sal's innate talent, and Shilly with him. They would receive all the welcome they hoped for when they found him.

Brokate had chuckled throatily. "We have a saying where I come from: if the Stone Mages don't get you, the Weavers will. We're a backward bunch, you see. Although the talent is prized we don't like being told what to do, and we don't like those who'll tell us, either. I'm sure half my bias is a result of that attitude, drummed into me as a child."

"Who are the Weavers?" Sal had asked, remembering when Lodo had mentioned them once without explanation.

"You don't know? I don't either, to tell you the truth. Not really. They come at night, it's said, and they take anyone with the talent who uses it for evil, or out of selfishness, or tries to bottle it up inside so no one will know it's there. They take children away and never bring them back. Sometimes they take women of childbearing age and force them to have children, or take men and force them to sire more — which wouldn't be hard, some men I know."

"They really do that?"

A quick shrug had demonstrated that she didn't take the stories especially seriously. "We also have *erges* and *djinns* back home, if that's any consolation."

He had taken her point: it could have been nothing more than a story to frighten kids with at night. But her words about jumping from the griddle to the grate stuck with him. He didn't want to be with the Alcaide or the Syndic because they had kidnapped his mother and killed his father. What if the Stone Mages were just as bad? What would happen if he changed his mind and decided to leave — perhaps to join his mother's family in Mount Birrinah? Would they let him go? What would he do if they didn't?

There was no point worrying about that until he met them, he knew, but the thought was in his head, and there it stayed, nagging at him.

The sky was changing colour by the minute as the sun began to rise. Molash the cook was up and relieving himself. Sal averted his eyes and wondered how he and Shilly were ever going to sort things out on their own. Even with the occasional Change-assisted massage, her leg was slow to heal. She was far from able to rest her weight on it. If their search for Van Haasteren failed in Ulum and they ran out of money, they would be stuck in an unfamiliar city, alone. His only hope then would be to find his mother's estranged family and hope that they would help him despite everything; it was his mother's fault, after all, that her family had been expelled from the Haunted City and sent back to the Interior.

Maybe, he thought, if all else failed he could work for Brokate. She might need a weather-worker on her journeys across the Interior. With Shilly's help, he could light fires and provide illumination; they could learn to do other things, like mend axles or pottery, heal minor injuries, tell fortunes. Their life wouldn't be glamorous, but it was better than having no other options at all. His parents had lived and worked just like that: his mother with the Change, his father knowing how to use it.

But there was no point in worrying about it until they found Skender Van Haasteren, and they wouldn't find him until they reached Ulum. He told himself to let it go and enjoy the journey while it lasted. He was seeing things he'd never seen before. He was going places his father had never travelled. He was looking after himself and Shilly as best as he was able, and he had kept both the Syndic and Behenna off his back. That was something to be proud of, no matter where he ended up. Although the thought of getting to know an entire country was daunting, taking it one piece at a time was the best way, he decided. He would have the rest of his life to put those pieces together.

A sharp whistle brought him back to the present. It was Shilly, leaning awkwardly out of the wagon and waving at him. He scrambled to his feet and hurried down the slope. Brokate had insisted that he continue assisting Shilly with her toilet, since the caravan leader wouldn't be with them forever. He didn't know what to say or where to look, and he felt like his face was flaming red every time, but he knew it would be wrong to avoid it. It was perfectly natural and nothing to be ashamed of. He might as well wish that his voice wouldn't break, as he knew it inevitably would.

Perhaps, he thought, Lodo had meant that the two of them were destined to embarrass each other.

"Today's the day," she said, when he came to a halt at the back of the wagon. Her hair was painted gold by the dawn, sun-bleached tips reflecting the clarity of the new morning. She seemed excited by the thought.

He nodded, glad that at least one of them was absolutely certain they were doing the right thing.

The hills, no longer mere bumps on the landscape, grew angular and steeper as the day wore on. Brokate sensed his mood and let him ride with her in silence, but the rest of the caravan became increasingly boisterous as their destination approached. They joked, sang bawdy songs, and argued about who owed who how many drinks at which establishment. Only the bean counters, as Brokate called them, wondered aloud what sort of price they would get for the goods they carried for themselves, or worried about whether the cargo they carried for others would be collected and paid for in good order. Everyone was concerned with making money, since that was the nature of their business, but at the end of their week long trip, conversation concentrated mainly on the pleasures of being home.

When Ulum finally came into sight, a cheer went up. The road ahead zigzagged along the lip of a steep incline, then dipped out of sight behind a sloping wall easily ten metres high, topped with outward-leaning battlements. Beyond the wall, Sal could see numerous painted spires and domes glinting in the sunlight.

Shilly whistled from the back of the wagon. "That's some town."

"Home to fifty thousand people according to the last census," said Brokate, "each and every one of them needing to eat, drink and amuse themselves. A lot of trade comes through here because it sits on a crossroads. Most of the human traffic comes southeast along the hills, from Mount Birrinah, heading through Lower Light and Carslake and ultimately back to the Strand the longer but safer way. Grain and stock come from the Long Sleep Plains to the northeast. Traders like us bring more exotic goods from the southwest, through the hills. There are things you can only get from the south, even though the road's harder that way."

Sal was only half-listening to Brokate's words. As he squinted to get a better look at the city, wishing he had the binoculars he had studied the Divide through, he realised that something wasn't quite right.

"Is this the biggest town in the Interior?" Shilly asked.

"Not at all, but it's definitely one of the top ten or so. Boliva and Parham are twice as large. I've been to them and can attest to that. They're not as well managed as Ulum, though. Mount Birrinah is about the same in size, and one of the nicest to look at, but that's because it's much richer."

"What about the Nine Stars?"

"That's different again. No city is the same as any other; that's the most important thing to remember. The Interior is a very big place, and there's a lot of variety."

Just like the Strand, Sal thought. There was, perhaps, as much difference between the far east and west of both lands as there was between deep north and south. Only someone who hadn't travelled would expect it to be otherwise.

Perhaps the oddest thing about *this* city was the lack of flags, banners, lines of washing, signs flapping in the wind . . .

Something in his head clicked. He knew what was bothering him about Ulum, now. He could see everything with unnatural clarity. The air was smoke-free, except for two dense columns on the far side, rising thickly into the sky where fierce winds high up tore them to ribbons. There was no dust, no haze, no blurring of the details at all. He would have thought fifty thousand people would leave more evidence of their presence in the air.

"Where are they all?" he asked.

Brokate turned to look at him with a slight smile on her lips. "Underground, of course. It's the only civilised place to live around here. You'll see."

She snapped her reins and the camels lumbered forward. Sal glanced at Shilly, whose expression didn't change from one of puzzlement.

The sound of the caravan riders ebbed as they concentrated on the many sharp turns in the road, followed by a steep descent to the city gates themselves. The shadow of the hills enveloped them, and the air became uneasy, as though many winds tried to cram into one narrow space at once. The wall of the city stood at the higher end of a shallow valley, and the gates were set into the base of the wall — a stone archway eight metres high, and the same in width, that could be sealed by solid doors of wood and steel. The doors were open, and the caravan slid unchallenged between them.

"This is the workers' entrance," said Brokate. "As I said, not many people come from the southwest, compared to the other directions. Those gates are much busier, and therefore better appointed."

Still, Sal thought, it was hardly unimpressive. On the far side of the wall was a brick tunnel two metres higher and wider than the gates. The floor was made of time-polished slate. Numerous glass-capped holes in the roof above let in long beams of sunlight. At first he had trouble seeing, but his eyes soon adjusted.

The tunnel led for quite a long distance without branching or deviating from its course. Just as Sal was beginning to feel as though it might never end, a door slid open ahead of them and they filed through into a very different space.

The first thing he noticed was the noise: there were other people here, their voices distant and echoing. The air had the same quality that a very large building did, but the area was much larger still. When they emerged fully into the enormous chamber, he saw that it was constructed like a hall: the arched ceiling lay high above, pierced by skylights and supported by numerous columns, some slender, others thicker than five people across. The walls were concealed behind these columns, so the true extent of the chamber could not be seen. The only thing Sal could be sure of, intuitively, was that it completely enclosed them. Nowhere that he could see was there an entrance larger than the one through which they had just passed. The air *smelt* contained.

Yet it wasn't stifling. Giant, sail-like fans turned to keep air circulating. There were roads and small buildings dotted across the floor of the chamber, and plants growing in the relative gloom. The voices he heard came from a group of twenty or so people in the distance, standing in a pool of light and conversing cheerfully about something which he couldn't make out. They were robed in many colours — contrasting with the uniform blues and greys of the chamber — and didn't look up to notice the arrival of the caravan.

"This isn't Ulum," said Brokate, anticipating their questions. "This is just one of the upper levels; an antechamber, if you like. The city itself is spread out through numerous cavities below us, some of them much larger than this. As well as roads, it has tunnels to take you from place to place. Apart from that slight difference it is very much like any surface town. It's certainly easier than living under the sun all the time. Stay here long enough and you soon forget to miss the clouds. Or so they say."

She sounded sceptical, and Sal sympathised. There was a certain magnificence to building a city underground, but he was sure he would miss the open space. Even if they piped sunlight through the hollow columns, along with air, what about the stars? What about trees? What about birdsong?

He soon discovered that birds did live in the mighty chambers comprising the city. There were trees, too, tended in wide copses near fields where animals were herded in flocks numbering in the hundreds. Starlight was hidden behind many metres of rock, but there were species of fluorescent algae that grew on the ceilings and walls; when the sun went down on the world above, and the great lamps were extinguished at midnight, patches of brightness were faintly visible, glowing like ghostly writing in the otherwise utter darkness.

But that lay ahead of him. For now, as the caravan crawled like a string of ants under the mighty upper roof of Ulum, his mind was caught by another marvel.

Shilly pointed it out first. "The buildings we saw above us," she said, her neck craning to look out of the wagon and up at the roof. "They're hollow, aren't they?"

"Indeed they are," said Brokate. "The towers are the tops of air vents; the domes match the contours of the ceiling above us. The roads between them are pure artifice, for no one lives up there to use them." Her smile carried more than a hint of admiration for the city builders. "Ulum was founded in a series of natural caves, it is said, but soon outgrew them. Excavations conducted over the centuries to create more space resulted in vast amounts of excess rock. Some went into the shield wall we passed through on the way in here; the rest was used to make the floor of this chamber and the roof above us. The ancient architects designed the latter so that from a distance it might appear to be an ordinary city, with buildings and streets waiting to be ransacked and burned." The look in her eye sharpened. "An invading army would find nothing but a steep fall if they broke into one of those buildings and the streets all lead in circles."

"Has anyone tried to invade?" Shilly asked.

"Several times. They say Sky Wardens tried once. None of them succeeded."

Brokate's attention was taken by the approach of a man in bright yellow robes on the back of a small horse. His black hair hung free and his lower face was hidden behind a beard of the same colour, a shocking contrast to his fish-white skin. His age was impossible to determine.

"Hey, Beli!" he called. "Welcome back."

She raised a hand in reply. "Hey, Wyath. You haven't been waiting here all this time, have you?"

"Me? No. But I've had lookouts posted. They saw you on the road and sent me word. It's good to see you again." The man's horse settled into a gentle lope alongside the lead wagon. His eyes smiled warmly, although his actual expression was impossible to read behind the beard.

Brokate's expression was similarly inscrutable. "Yes, well. As you say."

"You didn't send word about under-age passengers." Wyath leaned closer to peer at Sal and Shilly. "Are you picking up waifs on the road, now?"

"Not waifs. They paid their way."

"A long way, by the looks of them," he said. "Do they have names?"

"Sal and Shilly. They'll need somewhere to stay. Can you help with that?"

"How long for?"

"Tonight. They'll make other arrangements tomorrow."

"Naturally." Wyath adjusted the neck of his yellow robes. "They could use my spare room."

"That's what I was thinking."

"Were you, indeed? How interesting."

"I thought you might find it so."

Wyath uttered an uninterpretable chuckle, and winked at Sal. "Well, you know me better than anyone, Beli. I'll let you get on with things. Come by when your cargo is unloaded. I'll have a meal ready."

"Thank you, Wyath."

The man nodded at Brokate, Shilly and Sal in turn, then spurred his horse. With a clatter of hooves, he sped ahead and disappeared behind the base of a large column. When he didn't reappear out the other side, Sal realised that it hid a means of getting to the levels below.

"Who was he?" asked Shilly.

"Wyath Gyory. A friend," Brokate replied simply. Someone wolf whistled from behind them, and Brokate almost flushed. Leaning back in her seat, she turned to face the rest of her team and yelled, "Another word from you lot and you'll muck out the pens tonight!"

She turned back to Sal and Shilly. "Wyath has family connections with the city council. He'll be able to help you two if you decide to stay here, so it'll pay not to be shy."

Shilly nodded seriously, and Sal, although mystified by the exchange, did likewise a second later. They needed all the assistance they could get, wherever they were going.

They headed down a narrow ramp set in the floor of the massive antechamber. The echoes of camel hooves, wagon wheels and engines drowned out any attempt at conversation. Shadow enfolded them, and for a brief moment all was pitch black.

Had his mother come this way, once? Sal imagined her riding in a caravan much like Brokate's, descending into the bowels of the earth. Had she, too, wondered if the darkness would ever end?

Then the corridor opened up into a space as wide and crowded as the biggest market Sal had ever seen — and noisier, for the sounds of animals and people were magnified by the walls of stone around them and flung back as a cacophony that threatened to overwhelm the senses.

"Welcome to Ulum!" shouted Brokate in his ear.

He couldn't think of anything to say in reply. They had arrived. That was enough to deal with for the time being.

CHAPTER 7

WITHIN AND BELOW

Shilly spent most of that day in the wagon watching Brokate conduct business with buyers, traders and other customers. At first it was interesting. The goods were varied and Brokate dealt briskly with everyone, especially those who tried to short-change her. But as time wore on and the routine became familiar, Shilly's attention wandered. Unlike Sal, whose eyes were practically falling out of their sockets, she was unable to find something to interest her.

When a bell rang to announce midday, he went for a stroll and returned with a local delicacy: spicy meat and vegetables rolled up in a white pastry sheet. But she didn't find it particularly appetising, and ate only a small portion.

"There are so many people," he said, stating the obvious around mouthfuls of her leftovers. "The market goes forever — and most days there's more than one going at the same time!"

Who'd want more than one, Shilly asked herself, *when they're such ugly places?* Compared to the Fundelry markets, where the traders at least had time to talk to each other, this was a rabble. What she had considered heated barter was nothing compared to the brawling going on around her and much of what they were arguing over was incomprehensible.

Where she came from, salt was cheap; here it was expensive, and chocolate was common instead. The prices of tea leaf and coffee beans were similarly reversed. Nothing was as she expected it to be.

To top it all off, the markets stank even worse than dried camel shit.

The only good thing she could think of to say about it was that the flies had been left outside. But she knew she was reacting to more than just the noise and the smells and the sense of barely-controlled chaos. She saw endlessly varied tattoos, and rings and studs poked through bits of flesh she would have thought impossible to pierce. Where she was used to seeing wood or ceramics, the people around her used metal: fashioned into clasps, hairpins, spectacle frames, and bracelets. Only a few people had dark-coloured skins like her, and all those who noticed her sitting in the back of the wagon stared at her a split-second longer than was necessary.

Without a doubt, she thought, this was how Sal had felt in Fundelry. She had once assumed that he was immune to such reactions, having travelled all his life, but the borderlands contained a mix of all sorts of people, as her brief glimpse at the Lookout and Yor had attested. He wouldn't have been used to the blatant racism of Alder Sproule and his son, Kemp. Being so deeply in the minority would have been a new experience for him.

Now, in Ulum, he was part of the majority and *she* stood out. She wondered if that was why he seemed to be feeling so much at home, and why she was beginning to hate it.

As the sun, far above, started to set, the light issuing from the mirrored pipes dotting the roof above began to dim. The fuss died down. Brokate secured the caravan in a fenced compound and left some of her riders to mind it for the night. Then she packed her two charges into a buggy and drove them to Wyath's apartment.

The half-hour journey afforded Shilly another, quite different, view of the city. Outside the market, the roads were narrow and crowded, as were the houses. The air rang with the sound and smells of thousands of ordinary people all living under one vast roof. The city filled more than this single chamber, as Brokate had said, and the same air circulated through them all. Giant brass turbines turned the fans that in turn stirred the air. Shilly smelled smoke from wood fires, cooking aromas, incense, and a faint tang of effluence underlying everything. She marvelled that everyone she met didn't smell vile, until she learned that the perfume trade did brisk business in Ulum. After the stink of the markets, she wasn't surprised.

But for the first time she saw some order to the city. Such a crowded place simply had to be well maintained to exist for long, and the large numbers of maintenance and civic workers she saw on the streets confirmed the effort that took. Numerous people filed into and out of large buildings that, she supposed, contained factories, offices, or other sorts of workplaces. In the Strand, administration and industry was distributed evenly across the entire nation, in villages and small towns for the most part. Within the Interior, it was concentrated in only a few places and its produce distributed elsewhere. In a relative handful of semi-independent city states, such as Ulum, bureaucrats made decisions that could affect incredibly large areas; according to Mrs Milka, artisans produced goods that could be shipped to the far side of the Interior. Everything was on a much larger scale than Shilly was used to dealing with. Painfully so.

How the Stone Mages kept everything under control she didn't know for sure. According to Brokate, Wyath's father was on some sort of city council, which Shilly presumed answered ultimately to the Stone Mages, who in turn reported to their Advisory Synod when they met at the Nine Stars, wherever that was. She guessed that there were numerous other administrative layers she knew nothing about, filling in the gaps. Someone had to conduct the censuses Brokate had mentioned. This joined a growing list of things she didn't know about the Interior: where the metal she saw was mined and smelted; where the fuel came to keep all the fan motors running; how the diverse parts of the cities coordinated their activities — and indeed how the cities themselves communicated with each other.

Instead of filling in these blanks, Brokate pointed out landmarks as she drove. In the growing gloom they were hard to see and even harder to understand. What happened in the Year of the Quake for it to be honoured by a marble triangular monument? Who were the Maxteds and why did they deserve such a magnificent garden on top of a stepped terrace? Shilly just nodded, overwhelmed by the unfamiliar. This was only the beginning, she suspected.

Wyath Gyory's apartment was situated near — and partly in — the summit of an underground hill built in the shape of a cone beneath a vaulted ceiling that seemed almost impossibly high. The lane they followed wound around the hill three times, getting higher with every turn until the city's main cavern lay spread out below them. At night, yellow lamps fuelled by natural gas hung everywhere, above and below, so it was like floating in the middle of a cloud of stars. Shilly admired the view and decided it was one of the most beautiful things she had ever seen. For the first time, as the smell and the chaos fell behind them, Shilly could see why someone might want to live there.

Could *she*? She didn't know, yet.

"Come in, come in," called Wyath when they arrived at the entrance to his apartment. While Brokate secured the wagon, he waved them inside. "Welcome to my home. You must be starving."

Shilly crutched her way into the apartment's main room, marvelling at what she saw. The floor consisted of boards of wood stained so dark it was almost impossible to see the grain. There were shelves covered with fragile ornaments and wall hangings of every conceivable colour. Everything in the room was delicate and fine, quite a contrast to Wyath's shaggy appearance. The soap in his bathroom, when she washed before eating, left a faint honey scent on her hands and face.

"This is Ori," Wyath said, indicating a slender man with hair as pale as his skin. "He's on my father's staff. I've asked him to make us something with seafood for dinner. We thought it might make you feel more at home."

"Thank you," Shilly said, trying to be nice, as Brokate had instructed them. It wasn't hard. "That's very kind of you."

"No problem at all." Their host smiled widely, and for the first time she saw his mouth through the beard. His teeth were white and evenly spaced. "It does Ori good to be kept busy."

The cook stuck out his tongue. The table where they would eat dinner sat low to the ground, surrounded by cushions. A special place had been set for her, with room to stretch out her leg. Slightly embarrassed by their hospitality, she let Sal take the crutches and eased herself onto the cushions. They were soft and covered with embroidered silk.

When Brokate returned, dinner was served. While they made small talk, Ori spooned the meal into pottery bowls, produced vegetables and rice he had also prepared, then joined them at the table. They ate with metal utensils, the finest Shilly had ever seen. The fish, a rarity in the Interior, had been marinated in spices and tasted quite unrecognisable. She watched what her hosts did before doing anything, studying their customs and interactions, while at the same time waiting for the time when she could politely bring up Skender Van Haasteren. That was the purpose underlying everything, after all.

"Wyath's servant?" said Ori good-naturedly in response to Sal's curious question. "Far from it, although here some stewards do eat with their employers." Ori was, in fact, a lawyer on the rise through Wyath's father's department. "Wyath and I attended university together and have found many ways to assist each other. That's what friends are for, after all. One of Wyath's failings is his inability to prepare decent food for guests."

"For anyone," said Brokate, rolling her eyes.

"And I'm happy to trade the service for the pottery dishes he produces in his spare time. The barter system makes us both richer."

"I made these, you know," said Wyath, lifting the bowl he was eating from and showing Sal and Shilly the glaze with evident pride. "We're generally not as good at ceramics as you are in the Strand, so this is a skill I'm particularly proud of. I've been taught to be as good with my hands as I am with my mind."

"I'll toast to that," said Brokate.

Ori laughed heartily, and Wyath raised his glass.

"Yes, a toast," he said, then looked at the water in front of Shilly and Sal's plates. "Do you kids drink wine? My parents were liberal souls, thank the Goddess, but I know they're in the minority. What would yours say to a sip?"

"I never knew my parents," said Shilly with more emotion than she'd intended.

"And mine are dead," said Sal.

"Well." Some of the impetus went out of Wyath's bluster, but only for a second. "Let's toast *them*, then, wherever they are." Ori poured two half-measures of golden liquid into delicate glasses and passed them across the table. "To our ancestors," Wyath said, raising his glass again. "May we escape their sins and reap the benefits of their wisdom."

Shilly sipped when the adults did, and was surprised that the wine wasn't sweet at all, but had a dry, fruity taste that left her tongue tingling. The wine was so cold it brought beads of condensation to the glass, yet it made her stomach feel warm. She wasn't certain she liked it, but at the same time didn't find it unpleasant.

Sal, on the other hand, failed to hide a slight grimace when the liquid hit his palate. He swallowed quickly and put the glass back down in front of him.

"Delicious," said Wyath, smacking his lips. "Your lack of parents explains, I guess, why neither of you are giving family names."

"Sal has both his family names," said Brokate, "if he's willing to share them."

"There's no reason why he should," said Wyath. "I'm only making conversation."

Sal had looked uncomfortable since the subject of families had come up. Shilly could guess what lay at the heart of it:

although he had said that his parents were dead, his real father was very much alive and still living in the Haunted City. The name Sparre wasn't one that he was willing to adopt, however.

"My father is of the Cloud Line Hrvati," he said, taking the family name of the man he had thought was his true father instead. "From the east."

"Leonora?" asked Ori, looking up from his bowl.

"East *and* south," Wyath corrected his friend. "Beli said the kids are from the Strand. Everywhere in the Strand is south of here. But you must have some Interior blood in you as well, Sal, to have such colouring. I assumed you were one of us when I first saw you."

"My mother belonged to the Earth Clan Mierlo."

Ori's eyebrows went up. "Really?"

"You know them?"

"Not that I'd admit to anyone." Then he winced as though someone had kicked him under the table.

"Ori doesn't mean to be disrespectful, Sal," said Brokate.

"No, that's okay." Sal looked in puzzlement from one to the other. "What's wrong? Why don't you like them?"

It was Wyath who answered. "They have a reputation. Let's put it like that. They are as ruthless in business as they are unlucky. And tenacious. If they weren't so cunning no one would give them a second thought. Every time you think they've been knocked down for the last time, they rise back up again like a wounded snake, twice as angry and three times more deadly." He shrugged and raised his glass. "Sins and wisdom, Sal. You can't help who you came from, and there's no point in denying them, but it's your choice what you take from them. Remember that."

"And be careful who you tell," said Ori, earning himself another kick from Brokate. "Ah, hell, it's true! They're not popular and the boy would do best to know. Do you want him to tell the wrong person at the wrong time and suffer for it?"

"Where are they?" asked Sal.

"Mount Birrinah, the last I heard," Wyath replied. "Their usual bolt-hole. That's where you're heading next, I presume."

Shilly opened her mouth to point out that that wasn't where she was heading at all, but Brokate beat her to it.

"That's not why they're here, Wy," she said. "They're looking for a Stone Mage who might help them."

"Which one?"

Brokate shrugged and passed the question over to Sal.

"He's a teacher," Sal said. "Is there a school in Ulum where we might find him?"

"There's the Keep." Wyath glanced at Brokate, then back at Sal. "You could try there."

"I thought of that," said Brokate, "but how will they get in?"

"There's only one way to find out, and that's to try. Maybe tomorrow."

"I don't understand," said Sal. "Why wouldn't we get in?"

"You'll see," said Wyath with a sharp nod. "There's no point losing sleep over it. Van Haasteren lives by his own rules up there. Nothing you can do will change that."

Shilly stiffened. *Van Haasteren*. Tomorrow! Her ears rang with the thought that they might be so close to the end of their journey.

"Hey, that's good," said Ori, leaning across the table to point at the plate in front of Shilly. While her mind had been concentrating on the conversation during dinner, her hand had been using a fishbone to absently sketch a likeness of Wyath into the oily residue left behind by her meal. She had emphasised his beard and hair, and sent his eyes far back into his profile, so he looked both comical and sinister at the same time. "Wy, take a look at this. She's nailed you perfectly!"

Their host peered over the water jug to see. His face broke out into a smile. "I don't know whether to be offended or flattered."

Shilly put down the sliver of bone, mortified. If she blew her chance of finding Van Haasteren because of a stupid doodle ... "I'm sorry. I didn't mean to —"

"Don't be sorry. Ori is right. That is very good. I'd frame it if my housekeeper would let me."

"Uh, thank you," she managed.

"Were you taught to draw like that, or is it just a knack?"

She thought of Lodo's visualisation exercises and the emphasis he had placed on likenesses being the key to controlling the Change. He had taught her to use what talents she had to make up for those she lacked. "Some training," she said, "but mostly it's a knack. It's nothing special."

"Don't dismiss yourself so readily, Shilly." Wyath nodded appreciatively. "Talent doesn't grow on bushes, you know. There's good money in portraits, from the right buyers. If things don't work out at the Keep tomorrow, let me know. We might be able to find you work."

Shilly nodded, amazed at the thought. She had never considered her ability to draw anything more than a game she played for her own amusement. Being able to think in terms of pictures and symbols made it easier for her to reinforce the images Lodo gave her to meditate on — but to use them to make money simply hadn't occurred to her. She had so focused her entire life on being a Change-worker, somehow, that the chance of finding any other vocation had slipped her by.

That, and the fact that the market for drawings was non-existent in the villages she had grown up in. In Ulum there were so many more people in one spot, presumably there were so many buyers, too. Perhaps, she thought, it might not be such a bad place, after all.

Conversation dwindled from that point; four of the five around the table were tired and distracted by other things. Only as they saw Ori off and made arrangements for sleeping did Shilly really begin to understand why Wyath was being so good-natured.

His spare room consisted of a narrow chamber deep in the underground hillside from which the apartment had been carved. It had one bed dressed in white linen, above which hung two long, iridescent feathers, crossed like swords.

"You can have the bed," Brokate said to her, putting Shilly's pack beside it and Sal's on the floor near a rolled mattress. "It's very comfortable."

"You've slept in it?"

"Normally this is where I sleep when I come to Ulum."

"What about tonight? If we're putting you out —"

"Not at all." There was an amused sparkle in her eyes. "You're not putting me out at all. Giving me a nudge in the right direction, perhaps."

"But —" Shilly fell silent as Sal walked into the room, followed by Wyath. The older man had the same amused expression as Brokate, behind his facial hair. "Well, then," he said. "Help yourself to anything you need. I'll make arrangements for you to go to the Keep tomorrow morning. Until then, you kids just concentrate on getting a good night's rest."

"And don't wake us up in the morning," said Brokate with a wink, putting an arm around Wyath and guiding him from the room.

Shilly's face burned as she realised, finally, what was going on.

"Is your leg okay?" asked Sal, apparently oblivious to the exchange.

"Fine," she said shortly, even though the bone was aching. Turning her back on him, she hobbled on the crutches over to the bed and turned down the lamp. He unrolled the mattress next to Shilly's bed and draped a sheet and blanket across it. The room was cool and would be pitch black when the lamp was out. There were no windows, and the door was shut.

"Goodnight, Shilly."

"Goodnight."

She waited until he was under the covers before turning out the light, undressing herself and hopping awkwardly onto the soft mattress of Wyath's spare bed. With the light out, everything was still and peaceful, much to her relief. The only things she could hear were Sal's breathing and the occasional hiss as his limbs moved against the stiff sheets. Those sounds seemed unreasonably loud, startling her every time they broke the stillness. Adding to her restlessness, her stomach was unsettled by all the spices in their meal. Anything, however, was better than the twisting cramps of her first period, now thankfully behind her.

Don't think, she told herself. *Just sleep. We'll find Van Haasteren tomorrow, and everything will change for the better.*

But sleep, when it came, held dreams of being chased and unable to get away. Her legs folded beneath her, and the man pursuing her caught her with ease, looming out of the darkness and looking down at her as though she was a broken toy someone had left in his path. At first she thought he was Wyath, his face obscured behind the thick curls of his beard. Only later, when she woke properly, did she realise that it was Sal — an older Sal, tattooed and bedecked with rings and other forms of

Interior decoration. Sayed Mierlo of the Earth Clan rather then Sayed Sparre of the Cloud Line. He was much taller and stronger than the Sal she knew, and his clothes consisted of dark robes, gathered into his waist by a black leather belt studded with silver. She was afraid of him, and the touch of his hand on her leg in the dream, as he bent down to pick her up, made her jerk awake with an involuntary scream.

She didn't know where she was for a moment. It was the silence that reminded her. She couldn't remember the last time she had slept under a solid roof, away from nature. Fundelry was an age ago. Since then, her life had been conducted in a rushed succession of roadsides, tumbledown dwellings or wagons. She prayed that it wouldn't be like that forever. She couldn't stand it.

The darkness seduced her back to sleep within minutes, and she didn't wake until she felt the real Sal's hands on her injured leg, massaging her through the bedclothes. Shimmering waves of the Change spread through the still-tender limb, and she let her mind dance with them, half-dreaming. It was like floating on a sea of light, made all the better by the knowledge that it was doing her good.

When his hands fell away, she groaned and opened her eyes. She was surprised to find that, even though something inside her told her that the sun had risen, the room was still utterly black. It occurred to her that they were sleeping in a windowless box in an underground city where varying degrees of darkness were the norm. She would have to learn to rely on her instincts if she was ever to know the time of day.

Sal fumbled at the head of the bed and, with a hiss, the lamp flared on. He lay back down next to her, dressed in the same stained and torn cotton shift that he had worn since she had known him.

"Sorry to disturb you," he said. "I woke early and couldn't get back to sleep. Decided I might as well make myself useful."

"You could've made us both breakfast."

"Ah, well, no. We're not the only ones awake. I made the mistake of going out there before. I don't think they saw me, but..." He shrugged. "I figured they'd rather be alone for a while."

She couldn't meet his eyes and felt her face burning again. She was surprised at how little embarrassment he was showing; maybe it was the slight difference in their ages making itself known again. But he wasn't completely ignorant. He seemed to be enjoying her discomfort, for one.

Two could play at that game, she thought.

"Did your father ever have a girlfriend?"

"What?" The look of surprise and alarm on his face suggested that the question had never occurred to him before. "How could he?"

"Well, you know. He travelled around a lot. Women would've noticed him. He could've had a lover in every town for all I know. Did he?"

"No." The answer came so quickly she was sure he had no idea. "We were running. The whole point was not to be noticed by anyone."

"Fair enough. And it would've been difficult with you in tow."

"I suppose so." His gaze danced away. "What about you, Shilly? Did you ever have a boyfriend back in Fundelry?"

She'd expected that. "That's none of your business."

"No, it's not. But I remember you saying once that you thought Tait was cute."

"Yes, but —" She stopped. *Yes*, she had been about to say, *but he had been a candidate for Selection and I was three years younger than him. Why would he ever notice me, an apprentice to some scruffy hobo?*

She couldn't say that: it would only confirm that his shot had hit home.

"No," she said, with complete honesty, "I never had a boyfriend."

He didn't say anything in response to that. Feigning an interest in something in his pack, he turned away while she rebound her leg and settled back to wait for rescue.

After breakfast — eggs and bread, delivered to their room by a sheet-wrapped and apologetic Brokate — Wyath delayed going to work long enough to explain that he would arrange for someone to take them to the Keep, where they could ask about the Stone Mage they sought. A cab driver would meet them at the market clearing-house where Brokate would be for most of the day. They would wait with her until the cab came. This could take a while, apparently, since few cabs would drive that far. If their visit to the Keep was unsuccessful, then they could stay one more night in Wyath's apartment before finding more suitable accommodation.

"What *is* the Keep?" Shilly asked before he left, while Sal was bathing.

"Something like a college or university," Wyath said. "It's where they train novices from this area before sending them to the Nine Stars for induction. I've never passed through the entrance so I can't tell you much more than that. It's ... Well, you'll understand when you see it."

Then Ori knocked on the door, and Wyath had to go. There was no affectionate display between him and Brokate when he left, but Shilly sensed a new relaxation between them, as though a tightly wound spring had been eased overnight. Neither acted tired, despite the bags under their eyes.

"That's our cue to leave," Brokate said, helping Shilly onto her crutches and taking her pack out to the buggy waiting for them. "I'll be busy today, so I'm sorry if it looks like I'm ignoring you. I'd let it go if I could, and show you about the place, but the thieves here will steal half my percentage before I've even calculated it. Maybe we'll get a chance another day when things settle down for both of us."

Shilly's thoughts were focused on the journey ahead, not Ulum. Her imagination was full of mysterious and powerful figures in red robes shaping fire and stone as easily as she would mould clay. Skender Van Haasteren was the tallest and most powerful of them all, his face hidden in shadow. Would he judge her worthy, or would he send her away into a future devoid of hope? Her chest felt as fragile as birds' wings, as though a slight squeeze would crush her ribcage and collapse her.

"When do you go back to the Divide?" Sal asked Brokate.

"In two weeks. There are a couple of repairs I need to look at before then, and some of the team deserve a bit of a break, myself included. Your buggy guaranteed a profit, so I can take my time going back for more." Her smile was quick, but very much alive. "This is me talking *now*, of course. After a couple of days in this place, I'll probably change my mind."

Shilly appreciated why, all too well, as they descended back into the filth and stench that had appalled her the previous day. A night off had not made the markets any more presentable. She assumed it rained occasionally even in the arid lands around the city, but here the cobbles never received a refreshing flood to scour away the grime. Dirt was layering dirt until what lay beneath had been completely buried.

The morning dragged, broken only by half-hearted attempts to join in with Sal as he tried to guess what was in the containers Brokate had carried from the Divide. He was better at it than she was; whenever they interrupted Brokate to ask, the small flasks of golden oil invariably turned out to be from olives, not whale carcasses, and the flat, silver tins contained dried fish rather than herbs for curing fevers. For lunch Sal bought her slivers of grilled meat and vegetables dusted with red spices that made her tongue burn. She ground her teeth, and forced herself to remember that patience would probably pay off. Wyath had said that he would make sure they got there at some point, and if Brokate trusted him then she could too. The frustration of being so close and not moving, however, was almost unbearable.

The time finally came when a swarthy man appeared and interrupted a dispute about the cost of two barrels of southern wine. The caravan leader pointed to the two of them sitting in the wagon. He came over and looked them up and down.

"Going to the Keep?" he asked with a voice like Von's, the hostel-keeper in Fundelry. Perhaps, Shilly thought, his vocal chords had been burned too.

"Yes," said Sal, hopping down and helping Shilly to follow. "Will you take us?"

"That's the idea. You got money?"

"How much is it going to cost?"

"Fifty."

They had just twice that in their purse, but Shilly would have paid it happily if it meant getting where they needed to be.

Sal, however, stared at the man in disbelief. "Twenty is the most we can afford."

"Then you'll be walking, boy. Forty won't even cover my costs."

"Twenty-five. We're from out of town, not stupid."

"And I'm not a charity. Thirty-five."

"Thirty is as high as I can go."

"It'll have to do, then. In advance." When paid, the man shouldered the two packs and pushed through the crowd to a horse-drawn cab waiting nearby.

Brokate concluded the argument over the wine and joined them as Shilly was boarding the cab.

"Good luck," she said. "If I don't see you tonight, I'll know it went well."

"Thank you," said Sal. There were tears in his eyes. "For everything."

Brokate brushed it off. "It's nothing. I made a profit, remember." To Shilly she simply said: "Look after yourself, young woman. If you need help, you know where to find me. Or Wyath. I'll make sure he looks after you."

"Thanks." Shilly was surprised to find a lump in her throat. "Goodbye."

Then the driver of the cab cracked his whip, and they were on their way. The fuss and bustle of the market covered the silence for the first few minutes of their journey. They stared out at the city on either side of the cab. Shilly wondered if they would ever see the caravan leader again. The safety she had felt under the woman's care was rapidly falling behind. Her stomach felt as unsettled as it had after her dinner the previous night.

"How long to the Keep?" asked Sal, leaning forward to talk to the driver.

"One hour." The driver yelled at someone who cut them off, and spat noisily into the street.

Sal fell back into his seat. "Are you going to be okay for that long?" he asked, indicating her leg, squashed awkwardly into the small amount of space allowed them.

"I'll survive." She hesitated, not knowing how to voice her doubts. What if it all went horribly wrong? The fact that she didn't know how it might go wrong didn't mean that it wouldn't. "When we get there —"

"Are you two from the Strand?" the driver rasped, half-turned to look at them.

Shilly forced her uncertainty back down. It would be hard enough to admit it to Sal alone, impossible with the driver listening.

"Yes," Sal replied awkwardly. "We're from the Strand."

"I thought so. You must be on holiday, then."

"Sort of."

"Well, there's lots to see here. Funny place to start, the Keep."

"A friend suggested we go there," Sal said.

"Good luck to you, that's all I can say. I've been driving these streets for twenty years, and I've never taken anyone before who got in there. Or came out, for that matter. Maybe your friend knows the right people." The driver laughed humourlessly, deep in his throat and spat again.

Neither Sal nor Shilly said anything to this, but that didn't seem to bother him. As though their silence gave him permission, he launched into a guttural diatribe on the benefits and costs — mostly the latter — of living in Ulum. He had an opinion on everything: taxes, the city council, the state of the roads, the height of the ceilings, water quality, manners, his neighbours, the lack of respect for honest working citizens such as himself ... and more. Shilly had heard similar complaints many times from the tradespeople in Fundelry, and she wondered if citizens everywhere were unhappy with their governments.

Whether the complaints were serious or not, they didn't need to reply beyond grunts to acknowledge points driven home with particular force. Neither did they get much chance to add comments of their own. Shilly soon learned to switch off the sound of the driver's voice, letting it blend in with the regular rhythms of hooves on cobbles and wheels creaking over ruts.

Meanwhile, they progressed slowly through the city. The main chamber, containing the markets and the hill in which Wyath's apartment had been carved, was several kilometres across. The driver led them to its furthest edge and through a high, brick-lined tunnel to another chamber filled with factories and sweatshops. The tunnel was lit by gas lanterns every few metres, but it seemed oppressively dark to Shilly, who felt that she was already beginning to forget what normal daylight looked like; after the searing blast of the desert sun, the underground city made a ridiculous contrast. The second chamber was much the same as the first, quashing her hopes of splendid vistas awaiting them elsewhere, and they trundled their way through it exactly as before, with the driver passing judgment on everything as they passed.

Soon enough, though, they reached the far wall of the second chamber, and followed it a short distance to another tunnel, much smaller than the first. This led for several hundred metres through nearly airless gloom to a circular intersection carved out of naked rock upon which many tunnels converged. The driver chose one of the tunnel mouths without hesitation, following signs written in languages Shilly couldn't understand, to another junction, then another. If she hadn't been completely disoriented since they'd left the first chamber, she would have become so by now. The network of tunnels was a maze she simply couldn't follow.

At the fourth junction, the driver stopped to light lamps on his cab and to water the horses at a shallow bowl that cupped water dripping from a metal pipe. The path he chose was the smallest of the ones before them and clearly the least travelled. It led down at a steady rate and was lit only every five metres or so. Shilly assumed that the light came from gas lamps, as in the other tunnels, until the cab slowed so the driver could point out that the light in fact came from smooth nuggets of golden stone fixed in brackets to the carved walls.

"That's the Change, that is," announced the driver with a mixture of pride and awe.

"Like in the Ruin," Sal hissed to her.

She nodded, thinking not only of the stone she had taught him to summon light from back in Fundelry but of all the strange artefacts filling Lodo's workshop. The Stone Mages worked light and stone: the Keep *had* to be nearby.

As the buggy picked up speed again, her eyes strained through the darkness to see the road ahead. There was a faint sense of the Change in the air — glimmering, trembling just below the level of her conscious senses — and she thought the echoes of the horse's hooves might be returning differently than before. But it was hard to tell below the constant droning of the driver, currently expounding his theory of why living on the surface was infinitely inferior to life below ground.

"It stains you, see? The sun and air, and all that rain falling on you whenever it wants. You might say it's just light and wind and water — but what *else* is there in it? There's bird shit and sky dust and pollen and only the Goddess knows what else. It gets into your skin. It pollutes. Look at you, for example." His eyes glanced back again at Shilly, at her dark skin. "You live under the sun all day and you go black. I stay under shelter and I'm white. That's the way it's supposed to be, I reckon. You'd be better off living like us, if you don't mind me saying so, because then you'd look right. You wouldn't be, well, *stained*, as I said."

"Have you met many people from the Strand before?" asked Sal. If the driver noted the edge to his voice, he didn't rise to it.

"A few. They all look the same. They're nice people, mind — I don't mean to give offence — but they've all got the same problem. Too much sun and air and rain is bad for you. No wonder those Sky Wardens are so crazy. Open spaces are hell on the temperament, as well as the skin. And you know what?" Shilly was about to say that she didn't *want* to know what, but she wasn't quick enough. "It's not just the Strand. That's how I know I'm right. There are people who live in forests north and east of here, past the northern desert, right outside the Interior. Explorers come back with stories. These people live in the tops of giant trees filled with birds of every colour, and lizards so green you'd think a plant had come to life! They call it the Canopy, and they drink nectar from flowers and eat animals that look like tiny people. And the men and women who live in the trees, among all this greenery, they have yellow skins, see? As yellow as old paper. The world rubs off on them, and they look different. Now, if they built a big hut out of all those trees and lived in it, maybe then —"

"Excuse me," said Shilly, forcing the words out through clenched teeth. "How much further is the Keep, now?"

The driver chuckled. "Don't worry, miss. We're almost there. Old Lebesh isn't taking you off to a dark corner of the city to murder and rob you. Not like some drivers would, these days. I could tell you some stories that'd turn your hair white. Standards are slipping, I tell you. Standards are slipping fast."

And he was off again. Shilly sank back into the seat, grateful at least that the subject had changed. *Skender Van Haasteren,* she thought, *you had better let me in at the end of this because I don't think I could stand a return trip.*

Down they went along the tunnel, deeper and deeper into the Earth. Shilly wondered how far they had descended. It felt like kilometres. There was something wrong with the air — it left her feeling slightly breathless, as though it didn't quite fill her lungs — and all around her was the pressure of rock. She felt that the muscles of the Earth might flex at any moment and crush her beneath a million tonnes of stone. The only sign that people had ever come this way before were the rocks lighting the way, stretching ahead of them in two converging lines, meeting in the impossible distance.

At that intersection, finally, a stronger light appeared. Whatever lay at the end of this tunnel was a long way off still, but it was well lit and yellow in colour. She craned her neck to see better, as did Sal. There was nothing else to be made out, at first — just light growing brighter and brighter with every minute.

As they neared the light, the cab driver finally fell silent. For the first time, she sensed that he was nervous about where they were going. Perhaps, she thought, that was why he had chattered so incessantly: to keep his mind off their destination. It wasn't a reassuring thought.

Then the mouth of the tunnel was upon them. The naked rock from which the tunnel had been hacked was lined with wide, grey slabs that slotted together without mortar. For the last dozen metres it ballooned outward, tripling in width and height. The rough and rutted road beneath the cab's wheels was paved at the very end, and their passage became very quiet a heartbeat before they shot out the tunnel and into the light.

The light! It was impossibly bright, like a thousand lanterns all shining at once, blinding her. The horses whinnied and the cab jerked to the left. The driver cracked his whip, straightening its course with a determined curse. The wheels jolted over something, bumping Shilly's leg. She hissed with pain, but not loud enough to cover Sal's muttered exclamation:

"I don't believe it!"

She forced her eyes open and confronted the glare. The first thing she realised was that, despite having travelled down at a steady rate for more than a half an hour, down through solid rock into the heart of the Earth, the light that blinded her didn't come from lanterns or any form of Stone Mage Change-working. It came from a point above and ahead of her — and when she glanced at it, she had to look immediately away with her eyes watering.

It was the sun!

But that was impossible, she told herself. They had to be underground. A strong gust of wind told her otherwise, bringing with it scents of dust and dirt. She could no longer smell people, or smoke, or perfumes. The air was fresh and baked by the desert into a dry wind that stung her eyes as much as the light.

With the wind came a sensation of movement overhead. A voice boomed down at them:

"*Stop*!"

The horses whinnied again and shied back. Through the crack between her eyelids, she glimpsed something enormous leaning over them like the column of a fallen arch. There was another on the far side of the road, just as large.

The driver reined the horses in, his indrawn breath audible over their stamping.

"I — I can take you no further," he stammered to his passengers.

"Are we at the Keep?" Sal asked.

"Whether we are or not, you get out here."

The jittery horses tugged the cab under the shadow of one of the looming things, and Shilly took the opportunity to open her eyes properly.

The towering shapes on either side of the road turned out to be worn statues of men, pockmarked and eroded by the weather. Six metres tall or more, they leaned like trees over the cab, faces downcast and brooding. Faded writing on their bases might have announced their identities, or — most likely, Shilly thought — advised the traveller that a toll was due ahead, but the script was unfamiliar to her so she couldn't tell for sure. The only way ahead was to go between them.

She looked around, unable to see what had made the horses so skittish or who had ordered them to halt. Both the driver and Sal were looking up, and she naturally followed their gaze.

"I — I'm sorry to disturb you," said the driver, and Shilly still couldn't work out who he was addressing.

"Who are you talking to?" she asked. "Why can't you take us the rest of the way?"

"*They* wouldn't let me go any further, even if I wanted to."

He indicated the statues with a fearful nod of his head, and she was about to point out the blatant absurdity of this — for the road passed unimpeded between them, as safe as any other — when the statue on her right turned its head with one impossible, rapid movement and fixed its stony stare on her.

She almost wet herself when it spoke with the same voice she had heard before:

"*Set them down and leave this place!*"

"Yes, yes, of course." The driver hurried to obey. He jumped out of his seat and unloaded their packs, then helped Shilly onto her crutches with indelicate haste. Barely had her good foot touched the ground when he was back in his seat.

"Wait!" she yelled. "What if they won't let *us* pass, either?"

"That's your problem!" The driver didn't meet her eyes as he tried to untangle the reins, only knotting them further in the process. "I'm not going to do anything but exactly what they tell me."

"We'll be stranded!"

He didn't seem to care about that. With one frantic tug, the reins were free, and he urged the horses forward. They didn't need much encouragement.

"You can't do this!" she yelled at the driver.

The cab turned and rattled off into the tunnel, leaving nothing but a cloud of brown dust in its wake. Shilly watched it go with a feeling of dread in her heart. They were trapped under the bright, impossible sun. And they weren't alone.

"*Speak*," said the voice.

They turned as one to face the statues.

CHAPTER 8

FOUND WANTING

"We're looking for Skender Van Haasteren," said Shilly. She found her voice before Sal did, and that impressed him. All he could do was gawp dizzily up at the statues towering over them, his mind stuck as much on their size and weight as on the fact that they had moved and talked.

"*He is here*," the nearest replied. Now that Sal was watching he could see that its lips didn't actually move. The words issued from it like smoke from burning wood, or steam from boiling water. When it did move, it flickered in and out of reality, as though it started off frozen in one position, jumped instantaneously to a new position — which might be only slightly different to the old one — froze again, then repeated the process an instant later.

How they did that when they were undoubtedly made of solid stone — shaped in the fashion of armoured guards, with eroded helmets hanging low over their frowning brows, swords longer than Sal was tall in scabbards at their sides, and ornate armour bearing unfamiliar coats of arms on their trunks and limbs — eluded Sal completely. They made no sound at all when they moved, even though they must have weighed many tonnes. There was no evidence of the Change that he could sense. There was only dust drifting down from the fine cracks in their surfaces, and the sun, blasting down on the stone with a power that could not be denied.

"Where do we go to meet him?" asked Shilly, a mixture of fear and excitement in her voice.

The statue simply repeated: "*He is here.*"

"In the Keep? Is this the way to go?" She pointed between the statues. The road led out of sight behind a yellow cliff face. There was nothing visible except a perfectly barren landscape: cliffs behind them, cliffs to either side, and a tall mountain ahead of them. They had emerged from the tunnel into a canyon cul-de-sac with nowhere else to go but up the road ahead or back through the tunnel to Ulum.

"*That is the way to the Keep,*" said one the statues; Sal couldn't tell which.

"Good. We'll be on our way, then."

Shilly took a determined step forward on her crutches, intending to walk between the two statues and up the road.

"Wait!" The voice came from above them and to their right. The head of a young boy wearing a wide-brimmed sunhat appeared from behind a spur of rock. He waved his arms to make sure he had their attention, then disappeared. They heard a series of loud scrabbling noises, as if a miniature landslide had begun behind the outcrop. Pebbles and dust rolled in a cloud to the bottom of the canyon and came to a halt not far from where Sal stood.

He backed cautiously away. Shilly cast him a look that said: *What now?*

"Don't move!" said the voice. Seconds later, the dusty figure of the boy emerged from behind the base of the spur and rushed forward. "Wait! I'm Skender Van Haasteren. What do you want?"

"You're not Skender Van Haasteren," Shilly said.

"I am so."

"You can't be."

"Why not?" the boy asked indignantly.

"Because Skender Van Haasteren is a Stone Mage, that's why."

"Ahhh." Comprehension dawned on the boy's face. "You'll be looking for my father, then. He's Skender Van Haasteren too. But don't call him Skender. He hates it. *I'm* Skender. Call *him* Mage Van Haasteren, if you have to call him anything, and watch out for his temper. He's not good in the mornings. Have you come to take the Test?"

Both Sal and Shilly stared at the boy. Skender junior was shorter than both of them and looked at least two years younger. His colouring was similar to Sal's, with pale skin and black hair, but there was no resemblance beyond that. His face was round and boyish and the hair peeking out from under his sun hat did so in wild disarray. He moved with restless energy, always shifting his feet, or brushing his robes, or looking around. He would have been easy to dismiss as an ordinary kid but for one thing: all around him was the faint buzz that Sal had learned to associate with the Change. The statues didn't have it, but Skender did. That was enough to convince Sal that he was telling the truth about his name.

"Where is this place?" Sal asked, ignoring the boy's own question. The size of the mountain ahead was bothering him.

He didn't recall anything like it on his father's maps. "We're nowhere near Ulum any more, are we?"

"You tell me," said the boy, a sly smile on his face. "Can you read the stars?"

"I might be able to, when the sun sets."

"That's a long wait. Why not read them now? There's Kienan and Sadaqah." The boy pointed up at the sky with a stiff, insistent finger. "And Ghafur and Girvin and Dzik." He looked back at Sal and Shilly, relishing the puzzled looks on their faces. "What? Don't tell me you can't see them."

"Of course we can't," Shilly snapped. "The sun's still out. They're invisible."

"That's why they're called the Invisible Stars. There are seventeen of them, but only nine are in the sky at any time. You have to know how to look."

"Never heard of them."

"Well, they're there."

"So what? You've demonstrated that we don't know about them. Does that mean we've failed that test of yours?"

"That wasn't *the* Test," he said, facing her squarely. "You'll know all about that when you get to it. They make you do all sorts of things to work out what you can do. Only the best make it through, and even then it's never easy for them."

"Tests like the Scourge of Aneshti, you mean?" asked Sal, remembering the awful test Lodo had put him through.

The boy looked startled. "What do you know about that?"

Shilly shook her head in annoyance. "Look, we can't stand around here talking all day. It's hot and we have somewhere to go. Will you show us the way to your father or not?"

"Sure. He's up there." Skender nodded along the road, between the two statues.

"In the Keep?"

"Yes."

"Thank you." She turned and began to hobble up the road.

Skender watched her retreating back for a moment, as though warring with himself, then said to Sal: "You'd better go with her, if you're coming in together."

Together, thought Sal. *Yes*. That was the point. "What about you?"

"I'll wait for a second."

"Why?"

"To see what happens. Be on your toes."

The boy's tone was ominous. Sal sensed that they were being tested again. Even if it was just Skender's childish game of one-upmanship, he couldn't let Shilly walk alone between the statues and into possible danger.

He caught up with her and slowed to match her pace. They walked side by side under the shadow of the nearest statue, the dusty surface of the road crunching beneath their feet. Two more steps took them into the space between the two statues, and a silence fell about them. Sal waited for the ground to open up beneath their feet or for a mighty stone sword to come crashing down before them, barring their way.

Nothing happened. They walked between the statues and emerged on the other side.

They kept walking. The sound of scampering footsteps came from behind them.

"That's it?" Skender shouted. "That's *it*?"

Sal turned. Skender was addressing the statues from a point on the road between them. One of them was bent almost double at its waist, so that it looked like an ungainly puppet, albeit one over five times as large as the boy it addressed:

"*We have better things to do with our time.*"

"Like what, huh?" Skender kicked dust in frustration. "The first newcomers in months. *And* they asked for my dad by name. You could at least have given me a little fun!"

The statue didn't reply to that. With silent, impossible grace, it straightened and turned its attention back to the tunnel entrance.

Skender waved his hands above his head, blew a raspberry, then gave up trying to regain its attention. He glanced at his small audience, shrugged, and ambled amiably over to them.

"Dumb as posts," he said.

"What are they?" asked Sal.

"They guard the way. They make sure only suitable people get through, and like Dad they can get quite cranky. I've seen them actually throw people back into the tunnel for being too insistent. Not to hurt them, mind, but to make sure they get the idea."

Before Sal could ask what made him and Shilly "suitable" — and which particular outcome Skender had been hoping for — Shilly broke in.

"So they're guards. I guessed that much. But you haven't told us what they *are*. How do they talk and move like that?"

"They're man'kin, of course. That's what they do." He looked from Sal to Shilly in confusion. "You don't have them where you're from?"

"Not that I've seen."

"Oh. They must have given you a bit of a fright, then. Sorry." He smiled innocently — but with relief, it seemed to Sal, as though their encounter with the guards hadn't been totally unsatisfying. He had still managed to come out of it demonstrating his superiority. "Come on, and I'll take you to meet dad."

Skender headed up the road. Shilly hesitated, a pained expression on her face, then followed. Sal delayed longest of all.

Man'kin? He had heard the name before. Lodo had mentioned it, back in Fundelry. Their exact nature escaped him: were they made objects or natural phenomena that happened to look like statues? They were ignoring him now — the pressure of their stony gaze had passed the moment he and Shilly stepped out from under them — and perhaps they would ignore him forever. But they stood between him and Ulum. Would they let him through if he decided to leave the Keep?

The tunnel mouth gaped invitingly behind the guardians. Sal presumed that it was similar, in principle, to the entrance to Lodo's workshop, which had opened onto the dunes near Fundelry and, although it led only a few metres underground, somehow managed to transport people the hundred or so kilometres inland to where the workshop actually resided. He wondered if the Change required to make it work took effect at the entrance and exit, or somewhere along the tunnel, or across the whole structure one bit at a time.

The man'kin and the tunnel were just two of many perplexing things he had encountered in only a few weeks. The Change was opening a whole new world before him, and he had no idea where to begin exploring now that he was here. The stone guardians had let him pass. That had to be a good thing. He was about to meet someone fully trained in the Change who might tell him what to do next. He needed the advice, that was for certain. He needed *something*, even if it was only a new direction in which to travel.

Turning his back on the long road behind him, he hurried after Skender and Shilly.

The road ahead wasn't easy.

"I suggest you save your breath for walking, not talking," Skender said, interrupting a snappy inquiry from Shilly. "We're about two thousand kilometres northeast of Ulum and about three times higher up. Don't be fooled by the heat during the day. The air is thin up here."

Shilly looked as though she thought Skender was making excuses to avoid answering questions they might ask, but Sal remembered his lightness of breath in the tunnel, and the sensation of dizziness upon facing the statues. He *was* breathing more heavily, although he hadn't consciously noted it. And although the sun was hot, the thin air didn't retain the heat. Every breeze brought with it a hint of ice.

The road to the Keep led around a bend and up the side of the cliff in a series of stepped doglegs. Shilly's progress was slow but determined. The only concession she made to her injury was to let Sal carry her pack. He was happy to do that; there was no way she could have done it on her own, and it held him back to her pace. Still, after half an hour under the burning sun, with the thin air eating into his stamina and no sign of an end to the road in sight, he was beginning to regret making the offer.

"Is the Keep much further?" Shilly gasped.

"Why?" Skender shot back. "Is this too much for you?"

"No." Sal could see the pain in the lines around her eyes, but he knew she would never admit to it in front of their guide.

"Well, it's too much for me," Sal said, dropping both packs and sitting heavily on one of them. Shilly considered her options for a moment, then sat on the other. Sal couldn't tell whose breathing was more laboured, his or hers.

"You go on ahead," he said to Skender. "Wait for us at the top. We'll catch up eventually."

"I'll give you five minutes," the boy said, with a tone of extreme reluctance. But he was sweating too, and dropped to the road surface with an air of relief he probably didn't realise was so transparent.

"Is this the only way in?" Sal asked, ignoring the opportunity to score a point and thinking of students climbing and descending the path every day instead.

"No. There are several others. They don't all lead to Ulum, of course. The way you came is the only one the public knows about."

"Why the secrecy?"

"If everyone knew about the Ways, everyone would want one. And we certainly don't need people dropping in to snoop around."

"What about students? How do they come in?"

"New students come in the same way as you. That's why the guards are there: to sort out the diamonds from the quartz. Roughly speaking."

"I assumed they'd be brought here by Selectors. It seems a bit pointless Testing people *twice*."

"We don't do things the Strand way. That's where you're from, isn't it? I can tell by your accent. We don't have Selectors here, we have *Guides*. Their job is to encourage kids who think they might have potential to come here, or to one of the other schools, where they can be properly examined. The Test is in the stages of the journey itself; it either makes them or breaks them. Stopping for a rest halfway up the hill isn't usually a good sign, but under the circumstances it could be forgiven."

"Who made *you* our examiner?" asked Shilly.

Skender's eyes twinkled. "No one," he said. "Your sense of timing was impeccable. I had a feeling someone was coming up the Way, and I came down to see who it was. I was just about to give up when you appeared. The look on your cabby's face was worth the wait. Normal people never know what to expect at the end of the Way. To them it's just a road few people take, and even fewer return along."

Shilly's face had frozen at the phrase *normal people*. "What would've happened if the guards hadn't let us through? We'd have been stranded!"

"They wouldn't have let your cabby go. They pretty much make their decision before you get between them, you see, although you can never tell for sure. I wasn't sure what they'd do in your case, since only one of you has the knack."

Shilly opened her mouth.

"Perhaps we should get moving again," said Sal quickly. "If we've got as far again still to go —"

"We haven't," the boy said. "It's just around the corner."

"Oh, great," said Shilly. "Why didn't you tell us that before?"

"You'd made up your mind to stop, regardless of what I said." Skender smiled. "Would you have believed me if I *had* told you?"

"I'm not sure I believe you now," she said. He laughed and held out a hand to help her to her feet. She pulled so hard on it he winced.

Sal shouldered the packs and groaned at the weight on his aching muscles. The sun was well on the way toward the horizon behind them, burning with less force than before. He was hungry, and the constant sniping between Shilly and Skender was getting on his nerves. He forced himself to put one foot in front of the other, telling himself to be grateful he had the full use of both legs.

Skender led the way as before, with a return to his normal energy level. He skipped ahead then waited for them to catch up, swinging his arms and kicking stones over the edge of the path. When they caught up to him, he was off again. Sal couldn't imagine where his vigour came from.

Sal had never known many kids Skender's age; the last he had met was Tom, Tait's brother, and the two boys couldn't have been more different. Withdrawn and tightly focused, Tom had been obsessively determined to be Selected as soon as possible in order to join his brother in the Haunted City. He had been crushed when his brother was stationed in Fundelry just as his dream came true. Successful applicants never turned down Selection, according to the Alcaide, so Tom's wish to change his mind and remain home with his brother had been ignored. Tait had followed that disappointment by mocking Tom for wanting to stay in Fundelry, then by betraying his trust. Without Tom's help, Sal and Shilly would never have found the buggy and would have been caught. They owed him as much as they owed Lodo, in a way. Sal couldn't imagine Skender doing anything quite so noble, unless it was to show off.

There was another difference between Tom and Skender that wasn't obvious: beyond occasional prophetic dreams, Tom didn't have the Change yet, whereas Skender most definitely did. Generally, the talent blossomed at puberty. Either Skender's natural ability was so pronounced as to make it stand out even in someone so young, or else Sal's own talent had matured to the point where he could sense its potential, not just its presence. The latter was certainly possible, he thought. He had done things that barely weeks ago he couldn't have dreamed of: heard Behenna's thought from hundreds of kilometres away, healed Shilly's torn arteries, and spoken to a golem. Being able to instantly recognise someone else with the Change didn't seem unreasonable.

Pondering where his innate ability might lead him kept his mind occupied while he walked. And so it was that he didn't immediately notice when they arrived. He missed Skender's proud announcement and almost walked into the boy, who had planted himself in their path with arms wide to symbolically embrace what lay ahead.

"Home!"

Home consisted of a Ruin the size of a small city carved out of the side of the cliff face. While "the Keep" had encouraged Sal to imagine a fort or castle, like something out of a story, the actual place was far from that.

Terraces and steep stairways connected more than two hundred dwellings which clung to the cliff like barnacles or beehives, all carved or built from the same, yellow-white stone that comprised the cliffs themselves. Its age was obvious. Birds nested in its crumbling brick facades. Bushes reached at odd angles from cornices and collapsed balconies. Canopies swept like sails across absent ceilings and walls, stretched taut and anchored by hooks planted firmly in solid rock. Wind chimes sung softly from a thousand locations, sending up a delicate but atonal symphony that neither paused nor took shape. All in all, it looked as though someone had haphazardly stuck some rough houses onto the sheer cliff face and called it a town.

Sal could feel the Change buzzing through it like wind across a wire.

Shilly's response was ambiguous in tone. "This is the Keep?"

"Of course. Home, I said."

"You live here, not in town?"

"I'm a student," Skender said, puffing himself up proudly. "So yes, I do live here, with the others. Dad would rather I didn't, but he can't kick me out now. I got in fair and square, past the guards and everything." He deflated slightly and added: "I'd probably be there anyway, to be honest. I don't have anywhere else to go. Mother's always out in the desert, looking for stuff to dig up."

Skender's explanation was at odds with the appearance of the place. The cliff dwellings looked neither safe nor comfortable.

"Down here." Skender led them along the path toward the town. As they came closer, around the side of the mountain slope they had climbed, Sal could see ladders and stairways going up the side of the cliff, between and among the barnacle dwellings. Looking away from the town, out into a yawning space, he saw a discordant jumble of jagged mountains stretching into the distance — real mountains, this time, not the hills he was used to. Their sides were bare and their summits white with snow, which Shilly stared at, agog. Sal had never seen such beautiful, rugged emptiness.

The mountain whose flanks they were skirting was one of the highest in the range. Perhaps that was why people lived in such an isolated location, he thought. It would be worth it for the view.

Sal half-expected people to appear as they approached, but no one did. Every one of the scores of windows that he could see was empty; every doorway remained closed. As they drew closer, he realised that he couldn't hear anything, either: no voices, no banging of tools, no animal calls. The only sign the place was inhabited came on the air: a faint tang of smoke hung across the path like a mist, invisible but evocative.

"Sorry about the lack of reception," said Skender, answering Sal's unspoken question. "They'll be in classes for a while yet. I snuck out after lunch and didn't come back. Bethe — she's the student overseer — doesn't mind so much. It's Dad I have to watch out for. Seeing I'm bringing in some new recruits, I should be able to get away with it."

The path terminated in a short wooden bridge over a deep chasm. On the far side hung a blackened silver bell in a niche cut out of the rock. Skender picked it up and shook it firmly, sending up a clatter that echoed off all the stone faces around them. Sal put his fingers in his ears and Shilly winced as the racket went on and on. Finally, red in the face from his exertions, Skender returned the bell to its niche and settled back to wait for a response.

When his ears had recovered, Sal noted the sound of footsteps growing louder through the still, thin air. It was impossible to tell where exactly from, though. He looked from door to door, half-expecting a crowd of people to emerge all around them at once and engulf them.

When they did appear, it was almost an anti-climax. There was a wide tunnel entrance ten metres to their right and one level up. A dozen young men and women emerged from the tunnel and looked around. They were all dressed in burnt-red robes that hung loose around their arms and legs, revealing ordinary clothes beneath. One of them, a tall, thin boy with hair exactly the same colour as his robe, caught sight of Skender and his two companions standing by the bridge.

"Hola!" he called, leading the way down a narrow flight of stairs. "It's the little magpie with some bright young things from the West Gate. Have you been snooping again, Skender?"

"Easy, Raf," said a strong-looking, brown-haired woman at the back of the group. She had a double-triangle pattern tattooed on each of her cheeks and a brass ring in her left ear. She moved purposefully forward through the group to examine the newcomers.

"They're from the gate, Bethe." Skender's flush had returned at the comment from the redhead, and it didn't fade as the woman moved closer. At nineteen or twenty years, she was obviously the student overseer Skender had mentioned earlier.

Bethe looked at the boy before her, then at Sal and Shilly. "Welcome," she said with a slight smile. "I hope Skender has been polite."

"They arrived in a cab," the boy said before either of them could reply. "They asked for dad by name, and the guards let them through without even saying anything!"

"Really?" she asked, turning her attention back to him.

"Really. Bethe, it was amazing. The guards were unsure, at first, but then they didn't care at all. 'We have better things to do with our time,' they said. Honest."

"Are you sure they weren't talking about you?"

"Pretty sure. It makes a good story, anyway." He turned to Sal and winked. Sal found himself warming to the boy's precociousness, although he could see how it rubbed Shilly the wrong way.

"Where have you come from?" asked one of the younger students, pushing forward.

"What are your names?" asked another.

"I want to know what's going on here," said a deep voice from behind them which startled everyone into silence. Sal turned to see a very tall man with black hair and heavily lined skin standing in the entrance to another tunnel. His nose was a proud triangle in profile and the bones of his face stood out like a mask. He wore rich red robes lined with gold thread.

"Applicants, father," said Skender, nervously.

Sal looked at the man with amazement. This was Skender Van Haasteren, the man they had travelled all the way across the Strand to meet. Shilly went instantly rigid beside him, as though she couldn't believe that they'd actually found him.

"Where from?" asked the man, paying them no attention at all. His voice conveyed both authority and a faint air of irritation.

"The West Gate," answered his son.

"You brought them?"

"Yes, father."

"What were you doing there?"

Sal could see the way the conversation was going. Before Skender could get himself into more trouble, Sal stepped forward.

"We came to talk to you, Mage Van Haasteren."

The man's attention instantly shifted. Sal had just enough time to notice Skender exhale gratefully before Skender Van Haasteren's dark eyes were on him.

"Did you, now?"

"Yes, sir. I hope that wasn't presumptuous of us. If it is, we apologise. We've come a long way, you see, and we don't know the customs here."

"Yes," he said. "That much is obvious. You're from the borderlands, judging by your accent. And you —" He turned to Shilly. "You might be from further south."

"Fundelry," she said, her voice as stiff as her posture, "in Gooron."

The name of the region provoked a reaction: a slight flicker of puzzlement behind the man's deep frown.

"I *am* the Mage Van Haasteren," he said, looking back at Sal, "as you guessed, and these are my students." He indicated the small group behind him. "What do you want with me?"

Put so baldly, the question seemed impossible to answer. There was no single, simple answer. *Shilly wants you to finish her training. She wants to you to teach her all the things Lodo left out.* Sal was busy trying to decide what *he* wanted when Shilly opened her mouth.

"I thought you'd be older," she blurted out.

The dark eyes turned to her again. "What?" he snapped. "Why would you think that?"

"Because you were Lodo's teacher when he was younger, and he looked older than you. A lot older." She looked up at him with an awed expression and didn't seem to notice that she was beginning to babble. "I know the sea air ages you, and he wasn't one for appearances, but it still doesn't seem right. Your son is younger than Sal, which means you could be younger than Sal's dad. You're not *that* young — but I'm older than Sal and Lodo was old enough to be my grandfather. How could you be his teacher when you're obviously younger than him? Unless you've found a way to stay young as you get older, it just doesn't work out." She stopped suddenly, as though her brain had caught up with what her mouth was saying. "That's all," she added, looking like she might be sick any moment.

Again that strange flicker of puzzlement. "Lodo, you say? I never knew a Lodo."

"His old use-name was Payat Misseri," put in Sal.

"Him I do remember." A darker emotion fell down behind Mage Van Haasteren's eyes like shutters over a window. "Yes. I see now. We will talk in private. Bethe." He waved the student overseer forward. "Is the audience chamber clean?"

"I aired it yesterday," she said. "Would you like me to bring some water?"

"That would be good of you. These two look like they could use it. Thank you."

The Mage Van Haasteren nodded with unexpected gentility, and Bethe hurried off to see to his instructions. Then the mage raised his arms to usher Sal and Shilly forward, into the stone tunnel from which he had emerged.

"Please, come with me."

Shilly glanced once at Sal — her eyes were wide and frightened, as though she thought she had ruined her chances by talking like a fool — then she was ahead of him, crutching down a long corridor cut into the heart of the stone.

"Not you, Skender," the mage said to his son, who moved automatically to follow them. "You have this afternoon's lessons to make up. I'll see you tonight to review your progress."

"But — but —" Sal could hear Skender protesting fruitlessly as the mage moved ahead to lead them deeper into the cliff wall. The redhead called Raf laughed at his obvious distress, then their voices fell behind them.

"This way," said the mage, urging them on.

The tunnel led only a short distance before doglegging, then doglegging again. It was barely high enough for the mage, and the ceiling was rough, but he was obviously well used to its irregularities, stooping to avoid the odd bump and skirting occasional cracks in the floor with familiar ease.

The walls weren't like the tunnels of Ulum; they looked as though they had been hacked out by hand, centuries ago, and worn smooth by the touch of fingers and robes as they passed. The only light came from stones in the walls, glowing as the mage approached then fading when he had passed.

Sal noted a handful of exits from the tunnel that all led off to the left. Although Sal's grasp on his bearings was uncertain, he received the impression that they weren't travelling deeper into the cliff face, but parallel to it. In that case, he reasoned, the passages they passed would lead even deeper into the mountain. The Keep was as much inside the cliff as attached to it.

They reached a closed doorway. The mage opened it and waved them inside. Pale yellow lights came up in a circular chamber ten metres across with a relatively high ceiling carved in the semblance of flames. A low stone table stood in the centre of the room, with twelve chairs arranged around it. Each was made of a greyish metal, simply yet elegantly fashioned. On the walls were hangings woven from a rough thread dyed in ochre, yellow and black.

The mage offered them seats. Shilly accepted hers with a sigh.

"My armpits have blisters," she said.

"You've travelled a long way," the mage commented in return, taking the seat opposite theirs. It wasn't a question.

"We came here to find you," Shilly said, and Sal didn't qualify her answer. "You taught Lodo. Or Payat Misseri, if that's what you called him. I didn't realise he had another name until Sal's father used it."

"Payat was a *very* old use-name. I'm not surprised he abandoned it." The mage's eyes were penetrating. "How well did you know him?"

"I was his apprentice from the age of five years."

"And I was his apprentice too," said Sal. "Briefly."

"Did he tell you his heart-name?"

"No," said Shilly, and Sal shook his head.

Mage Van Haasteren pinched the fingers of his right hand together and rested his forehead on them. Close up, Sal could see the resemblance between him and his son: when Skender grew up and lost his baby fat, he would have the same bony, angular face. Even if he didn't develop the same towering stature or brooding presence, he would still be striking.

There was one odd note about the mage that Sal only belatedly noticed: he possessed a bare minimum of tattoos and piercings. He had one pink-gold stud in each ear, and a sun-shaped tattoo on the back of his left hand. Apart from that, he was practically naked, compared to many of the people Sal had seen in the Interior. Given his status, and the fact that his father had once described such tattoos as rank-markings, Sal would have expected him to have more.

The mage sighed heavily, as though intensely weary, then looked up at them.

"'Oh, outcast of all outcasts most abandoned,'" he recited. "'To the earth art thou not forever dead? To its honours, to its flowers, to its golden aspirations? And a cloud, dense, dismal, and limitless, does it not hang eternally between thy hopes and heaven?'"

His eyes were sad, focused on distant times and places, not the two people in front of them. For the first time, Sal thought, he did look almost old — much older, certainly, than Sal's father.

"You're talking about Lodo," said Shilly. "Aren't you?"

"Yes." The stern mage came back with a frown. "I apologise for assuming that Payat's story has a bearing on why you are here. Perhaps I am wrong in that, if you don't know why I'm not happy to hear his name spoken here, in this of all places." He looked down at his hands, then up again. "You should start at the beginning and tell me everything that has brought you here. I will try not to jump to any conclusions. When you've finished, we will discuss what would be best to do next."

"I want you to teach me," said Shilly, her voice firm and determined.

"That decision lies at the end of the story," said the mage, raising a hand. "Begin, one of you."

Sal exchanged glances with Shilly. Her determination was a veneer, almost invisibly thin; one scratch and it would evaporate. He nodded to indicate that he would go first, and he supposed that that made sense: the story began with his parents, after all, and was continuing through him — although the thought of recounting it again made his stomach sink.

Only the realisation that he and Shilly would never have made it so far without simply starting in the first place encouraged him to open his mouth and begin the tale.

CHAPTER 9

A PARTING OF WAYS

Two things came out of Sal's story that Shilly had not known before. Both profoundly shook her.

The first emerged in a discussion of the events leading up to their last day in Fundelry, when Sal's father had been imprisoned and Lodo had taken Sal to the cells on his nightly awakening of the town lights. She could tell that the story was making him unsettled because he was shifting in his seat and barely looking at her, but she didn't realise the half of it. At the time, she was more concerned with observing the effect it had on the Mage Van Haasteren. The purpose of telling it was, after all, to convince him that he should finish their training in the Keep.

Later she would understand that Sal had warred with himself about revealing the secret, approaching the subject tangentially, then suddenly venting it as though relieved it was finally out.

"Lodo fixed a broken globe outside the cells where my father was kept," he said. "It was cracked. On the way back to the workshop..." He paused to take a sip of water from the jug Bethe had brought, then said, "On the way back, Lodo gave me a globe to keep. He told me it would come in handy one day."

"A globe?" asked Shilly and Mage Van Haasteren at exactly the same time, with a similar tone of disbelief.

"Only a small one. He made me promise to slip it in my pack when I got back to the workshop."

"You never told me," Shilly said, feeling blood rush to her face. Lodo had never let her touch the globes with more than a fingertip, let alone given her one to keep.

Sal's eyes didn't meet hers. "He didn't think you'd understand. I told him it was worth too much, but he wouldn't take no for an answer. He made me accept it, so I had to do as he wanted." His gaze fixed almost desperately on the mage. "He talked about his teacher, then. He told me your name, and said that you would be very old, possibly even dead. That's why it's so surprising to see you looking so young."

The mage shook his head, dismissing the point.

"The globe," he said. "Do you have it with you now?"

"Yes."

"Let me see it."

Sal reached deep into his pack and produced a leather-wrapped bundle. Inside was a slightly flattened polished glass ball as large as a man's fist. The globe's weight was obvious when Sal handed it to the mage, who had to exert more effort than expected to stop it dropping to the table. Inert, it possessed a smoky grey colour as dense as a thunderstorm.

The mage hefted it in his hand, and examined it from all angles.

"Did he show you how to work it?"

"No."

The mage turned to Shilly: "Have *you* ever seen this before? Did you see him make it?"

"No," she said, fighting to keep her emotions out of her voice. Lodo gave Sal a globe! Why not *her*? Hadn't *she* deserved one too? "I've never seen anything like it before in my life."

"Neither have I. Not from the Strand, anyway. This was in Fundelry, you said?" he asked both of them. "By the sea?"

"Yes," said Sal.

"*Wasted*," said the mage, in a voice so bitter it almost startled Shilly out of her resentment. He put the globe down on the table in front of them and thought for a moment. Sal's attention was on the globe, as though he was afraid the mage might take it away from him.

Van Haasteren nodded and said, "Continue."

Sal picked up the story, haltingly detailing his father's near escape from the Sky Wardens: how Lodo had argued that Sal wasn't the child they were looking for and that they should let their prisoner go. Then Tait had betrayed them to the Alcaide and the Syndic, and Sal's father had died. Not even Sal's innate talent had enabled them to escape. Only an earthquake summoned by Lodo had set them free.

And as a result, Shilly thought to herself, Lodo might be a golem like the creature they had met among the towers: hollow of all thought; filled with something *else*, something malignant, while his mind hung trapped in the Void Beneath.

There hadn't been time to go back to the workshop before fleeing Fundelry forever. All she had to remember Lodo by was the globe that Sal had.

She missed a chunk of the story, so wrapped in her thoughts was she. The mage asked her questions about the work Lodo had done in the village: small things mostly, such as repairing pots, heating water and keeping the town lit at night. But the mage was impressed by her description and, in some ways, more interested in Lodo than the two of them.

"The Scourge of Aneshti," he said at one point. "It's much like a whip, with —"

"We know it," said Shilly.

"Do you have it? Did Payat give you that, too?"

"No. It'd still be in the workshop — unless the Alcaide or the Syndic managed to get in."

"If that's where it is, it will be safe." The mage nodded, although he didn't seem especially happy with the answer. "Such places seal themselves upon their owner's death. The Ways that connect them through the Earth to the outside are very difficult to reopen — and doubly so for a Sky Warden."

"So it's all still there?" Shilly asked. "All of his stuff, just as it was?"

"Yes."

The thought appealed to a very deep part of her. She had spent a lot of her life in those small, underground chambers, and she had learned things that she would never forget. There, Lodo had taught her the ways of the Change; there, they had lived for more than half the years she had been alive. The workshop would always be a part of *her*, in her mind. She would find a way back in, somehow, one day.

"What exactly did he teach you?" the mage asked her, and she did her best to explain. The Change was a powerful gift and a terrible responsibility. It came on its own terms, or it didn't come at all, as in her case. But she had learned how to use other people's talent; if she was touching someone like Lodo or Sal she could reach into them, find the place in them that responded when they called it up, and bend it to her own will. But she couldn't use it if they didn't want her to, and she could only use as much as they had.

Within those limitations, she had been taught everything else she could learn. Not just visualisations, but an understanding of the balance implicit in the Change: if she altered the world in any way, there would always be a physical cost. The Change wasn't a bottomless well of wishes she could use to get whatever she wanted. Even someone born with it could only ever work within the limitations of their bodies, just as with everything else. She had seen both Lodo and Sal drained from over-exertion of their gifts, so she knew well what that meant, even if she didn't feel it herself.

The mage was fascinated by what she had been taught, but the sea also piqued his interest. She tried to explain, and failed completely. It was easy to grasp the concept of an ocean as a vast body of water under which the land lay hidden, but it was impossible to capture the complexity of it to someone who had never seen so much as a wide river: the waves, the tides, the sand, the shells, the sheer *vitality* of it all: it confounded the mage, who had only the concept to cling to in his dry, dusty land.

Soon enough, though, the story left Fundelry and rushed inland, and she found herself back in unfamiliar territory. She relived the awful, disorienting days early in their flight, when she had hardly spoken for fear of the emotions boiling inside her. She remembered Cleve's Well and Stonehouse, buying food outside Kittle and calling herself Elina to hide who she was. Nothing had been real; she remembered it as though it was a dream, and mostly let Sal recount it to the mage, who listened carefully to every detail.

Then came the Old Line, and the ravine, and the treacherous bridge . . . and her leg was broken all over again.

"Show me where it was injured," the mage requested.

Shilly balanced awkwardly on her good leg while he unbound the other and examined her injury. She had been using fewer and looser bindings every day, but the breaks in her thighbone still felt painful and fragile. The purple remnants of her bruises were still tender to the touch. She only placed any weight on the leg by accident, and knew well how much pain that caused.

"Hmm." She flushed as the mage traced a line down the scars on her thigh, even though she knew his interest to be purely clinical. "You did this?" he asked Sal. "You healed the break when it occurred?"

Sal nodded awkwardly. "I did what I could to save Shilly's life. She saved mine, and I couldn't let her bleed to death. It was hard, though, and I didn't really know what I was doing —"

"Who helped you?"

Sal hesitated, then answered as though he had misunderstood the question. "Shilly does, when she's awake. She's better at guiding what I need to do, when she uses my ability to —"

"No, Sal. Who helped you *at the time the break occurred*? This was a serious injury. Shilly would not have been conscious, and I doubt you could have done it on your own. Who was it, Sal?"

He looked down at his feet. "Shom Behenna helped me."

"The man who was chasing you?"

"Yes. He felt me trying from a long way away. He knew I wasn't getting anywhere. I called for help — from the Change, from anyone — and he answered. He reminded me of what I needed to do to make the Change work. And it *did* work."

"It worked well enough," the mage admitted thoughtfully.

Shilly — thrown into emotional turmoil by the revelation that it wasn't Sal alone who had saved her life — was allowed to sit back down. The mage wrapped her leg up, his hands moving expertly and quickly. The conversation flowed around her as though she wasn't even there. Inside her head, she might as well not have been. Her mind was stuck on the thought that, but for the help of the man chasing them, she would probably have died two weeks before, on one end of a bridge in the middle of nowhere. A man that she had thought of only as an enemy, or at best the enemy of a friend.

"Why do you think he helped you, Sal? Is he under orders to capture both of you alive?"

"I don't know."

"Perhaps he was trying to confuse you — make you think he was on your side, by doing you a good deed. Fine clothes do not always hide a black heart, after all."

"Maybe."

"I think it was good that you were wary of him, Sal. Behenna's motives are unclear to me in this matter. Helping you to help Shilly confirmed the fact that he was not just listening for you, but close on your tail. If he had done nothing to help you, he might have caught you easily. I'm at a loss to know why he would risk so much to save Shilly. After all, she knew nothing of you or your parents until you arrived, and she has no talent of her own. Her role in this situation, one presumes, is small."

The mage trailed off in thought, apparently oblivious to how his words stung her. *He's saying*, she thought, *that Behenna should have let me die because I was no use to the Sky Wardens*. Because she had no talent. Because her life was worth less to him than catching Sal.

Is that, she wondered, what the Mage Van Haasteren would have done?

Sal glanced at her, as though to check that she was okay. She kept her face carefully neutral. He hadn't told her about Behenna's involvement in the saving of her life, leading her to assume that it was all his work. She didn't know if she could forgive him for that deception; she wanted to know who she owed her life to, irrespective of the motive.

Shom Behenna had helped Sal save her life at the expense of his mission. Skender Van Haasteren thought the Sky Warden should have let her die. Lodo had given Sal one of his precious globes to keep. Her first meeting with the Stone Mage she'd hoped would be her teacher wasn't going at all as she had planned.

Sal concluded by outlining their escape across the Divide and their travels through the Interior. Shilly didn't have much to say from that point; she was beginning to realise that her role in the story had mostly ended after they had left Fundelry.

So much for *together*, she thought, feeling the old, protective silence creep over her.

"Very interesting," said Mage Van Haasteren when Sal had finished. "The bridge across the Divide will not allow acts of hostility against those who cross it. That's why it rose up against Shom Behenna when he tried to use the Change to stop you from escaping. It's a very old artefact — so old that its makers are unknown to us. I've not heard of it awakening for quite some time. There are those who mistrust a thing about which we know so little, but the truth is that it serves both sides of the Divide very well. Without it, crossing at that point would be difficult."

"I've always wondered why there are just two bridges," said Sal. "Why doesn't someone build another?"

"To do that would require crossing the valley floor. Things live there that make golems look pleasant."

"What sort of things?"

Van Haasteren waved the question away. "I think you were wise to run here from Warden Behenna. Even if his motives were pure, he was wrong to attempt to take you by force, on the bridge or anywhere. If he is hotheaded enough to make the attempt, it is better that you remain with us for the time being — at least until he cools down. Has there been no communication since?"

"No," Sal said, shaking his head. "I haven't sensed him once. Wouldn't he have given up trying to catch us, that night on the bridge?"

"I would imagine so. Sky Wardens rarely venture any distance into the Interior, for any reason. It is alien to them. That's not to say, of course, that your great-aunt, the Syndic, could not have sent ordinary spies or bounty hunters to find you, if she was keen enough. Do you think it likely?"

"I doubt I'll ever feel safe again," Sal said with disconcerting honesty. "I don't trust any of the Wardens, and I wouldn't put anything past them."

"What about your real father, though? Aren't you interested in meeting him, one day?"

"No. I don't think I'd like him very much."

How could you possibly know that? Shilly wanted to ask him. Sal knew very little about his real father. Only that he had been an ambitious Sky Warden who had married Sal's mother in the hope that it might better his career; that he had hunted for her and her journeyman lover all across the Strand; that he was still alive in the Haunted City. That wasn't much on which to base an impression.

Her patience with the story had run its course. She was weary of everything: the endless journey, the discomfort and pain, not knowing what waited for her at the end of it, being lied to . . .

"What now, then?" she asked. "I'm tired. You must have heard enough of our story to make some sort of decision. Did we waste our time coming to you? Are you going to help us or not?"

"Many things are indeed clear," said the Mage, placing his hands before him on the table. "Shilly, you are an Irregular, a latent talent. You come from a remote part of the Strand, far away from the Haunted City where any potential you might once have had would have been better understood. Lodo took you in, Shilly, to see if your talent would develop into anything. It didn't, ultimately, and that is to be regretted, but Lodo did manage to teach you the fundamentals that all people must know if they are to practice our art, at first or second hand. All you lack, apart from the Change itself, are the details."

Van Haasteren turned to Sal. "You, Sal, are another thing entirely. We know your heritage; where your ability comes from. Yet you are untrained even in the basics. You know a few tricks — that is all — and if your talent wasn't so substantial, you wouldn't be able to master even those. You impose your will upon the world like a poor blacksmith wields a hammer: with unnecessary force, and at great risk to those around you. Luckily, people like you are rare; they only occur when there is a crossing of great Lines or Clans — which is a rare occurrence, as you can imagine — and their development is monitored from birth. Those who spring up by chance, without any known heritage, are usually found young and brought into the fold where their abilities can be focused. Of the remainder, most destroy themselves before they know what they are doing. The awakening of their talent opens a floodgate they cannot control, and they are torn apart, erased. Only very infrequently does one such as yourself arise: caught just in time to avoid self-immolation, yet still powerful and raw, and wilful because of it. These we call wild talents, and they have the potential to teach us as much as we can teach them."

"What can *I* teach *you*?" asked Sal, frowning.

"Wild talents punch a hole through the fabric of routine and expose the inspiration that lies beneath. They can be a broom, sweeping out the cobwebs and exposing new corners to explore that we didn't know were there. They illuminate the depths of our knowledge and show us what we have forgotten. They open our eyes, and force us to see again." The mage steepled his fingers before them, and studied Sal closely. "They can also destroy. Their light can be so bright that it burns, blinds all who look at it. It is not always good to see into the dark places; some things are forgotten for good reason. I'm not saying that they do this deliberately, out of evil intent. Motivation is never simple to decipher out at the edge of things, beyond what is considered normal. Some say, for instance, that a wild talent created the Divide. Who are we, now, to say whether that was to the benefit of good or evil? Power in any form is ambiguous, and those who desire it ignore that truth at their peril."

Van Haasteren reached across the table, past the smoke-grey globe, and patted Sal's hand. "This sounds incredible to you, I imagine. Not so long ago, you didn't even suspect that you had the Change. And now this. Well, that is the way of it, I'm afraid. I'm not guaranteeing that you will be a wild talent in the senses I have described. You are powerful, yes, and you are new to the knowledge, but you may go no further than that. You might not be a broom of any kind. But you do need training to ensure that you do not use your talent incorrectly. You must be polished to see what sort of gem you are. The conjunction of your two minds must be explored."

"Both of us?" asked Shilly, unable to keep the urgency out of her voice.

"You are a wild talent and a latent talent, working in concert. Do you have any idea, Shilly, how unlikely this is? Did Lodo never tell you? An Irregular such as yourself might be born, somewhere, once every year or so, and most of them make no use of their ability. Wild talents are rarer — perhaps one a century — and few of those survive at all. To see both in one place is almost inconceivable. I myself have never heard of it, in all the literature."

"So?"

"So, Shilly, I will give you what you want. I will help you find your feet. I will give you shelter from those who pursue you. I will Test you to see how best your talents might be utilised."

"And you'll teach us," she asked, "like you taught Lodo?"

"Alas," said the mage, his face stiffening, "I cannot do that."

Her stomach fell. "But —"

"Wait. Let me finish. I cannot teach you in the same fashion Lodo was taught, because I did not teach Lodo. That was my father, the eighth in a long line of Skender Van Haasterens like my son and me. He was a teacher, too, and I have inherited some of his ways — but I can only teach you the way *I* would teach you. Not him. Will you accept that?"

Shilly felt like she was riding a wild river of emotions. This latest revelation barely had the capacity to surprise her. "So *that's* why you're so young. I thought something was wrong. Did you know Lodo? Did you learn with him when he was young?"

"Yes, I knew him well." Again, a dark emotion clouded the mind behind the mage's eyes. "But that is of no concern, now. His story is irrelevant to yours, and you have told me once already that you are tired. It would be ungracious of me to delay your rest any longer."

He stood and held his hand out to Shilly. She took it awkwardly, leaning on the table to keep the weight off her leg. "We'll find you a room and give you a meal. Tomorrow we'll look at your situation more closely, and see to that leg, too. You two have a done a good job under the circumstances, but we can do it better. There is a wealth of medical experience recorded here. We'll have you up and about in no time." He handed her the crutches and she gingerly put her armpits over them.

"Wait," said Sal. He too stood, facing the mage across the table. "There's just one other thing I have to ask you."

"Of course. What is it?"

Sal's expression betrayed his uncertainty. "It's about my mother's family."

"The Mierlos?"

"Yes. I know what people think of them here, but they're the only link I have left to my mother. I owe it to her to find them, I think."

"I thought you might want that." The mage nodded slowly. "I can make enquiries for you. A meeting might be arranged, if they're interested."

Sal nodded slowly. "Thank you. Please." Then he moved away from the table to help Shilly with her pack. She clutched it in her left hand and managed to use her crutches while carrying it. It was awkward, but worth the effort. Rebuffed, he put the globe back into his own pack, and Van Haasteren led them away.

They were given a room high in the cliff town, accessible by tunnels through the rock rather than by ladder or external stairway. It was dusty and hadn't been slept in for a while, but it had a stone balcony granting a perfect view of the mountains to the south. The sun had set by the time they arrived and the air coming in the window was already cold. Bethe appeared in the doorway, hot on their heels, with some cold meat, salad and cheeses, and turned back the rugs on the beds.

"It's not much," she said. "If you need them, there are extra rugs in here. Everyone complains about the weather when they first arrive." She showed them a small cupboard by the door.

"It's much better than we're used to." Sal smiled at her and helped himself to the food. Shilly ignored both of them and stood silently in the middle of the room.

"I'll leave you now," said Van Haasteren when Bethe had gone. "There's a bell at the end of the hall. Ring it once — just once — if you need assistance. Otherwise we'll come for you shortly after dawn. The Keep wakes early, you'll find."

"Thank you," said Sal. Shilly found his gratitude grating, although it seemed genuine. He was more at ease than he had been since she had known him, and that only made her more annoyed than ever.

The mage hesitated a moment before leaving, filling the room with his sombre presence, then he wished them a good night and left.

The moment the door was closed behind him, Shilly took the crutch out from under her left arm and threw it at Sal. It struck him hard on the shoulder — not as hard as she would have liked — and fell to the floor with a clatter.

"Hey!" He backed away from her, rubbing his arm. "What was *that* for?"

"You don't know?" His words echoed through her mind: *Lodo gave me a globe to keep ... Shom Behenna helped me ...*

"No! How could I?"

"It was for lying to me."

"I didn't lie to you."

"For keeping secrets, then. It's the same thing!"

"It's *not* the same thing." He shook his head in hurt puzzlement. "I'm sorry I didn't tell you about the globe before,

207

Shilly, only I didn't know how to. I was confused, and Lodo made me promise."

"What about Behenna?"

"You were hurt, and then we were in the Broken Lands and there just wasn't time. By the time there *was* time, it just didn't seem important any more." His eyes pleaded with her to understand. "It wasn't that I didn't want you to know. I just didn't know how to tell you."

She turned away from him, blinking back tears. It didn't really matter what he had to say in his defence. If she was honest with herself, she knew that the betrayal of her trust was only part of the problem. She just wanted to hurt him the same way she was hurting.

Lodo took you in, Shilly, to see if your talent would develop into anything. It didn't, ultimately . . .

The thing she wanted most in all the world was the one thing she could never truly have.

"Shilly? Sal? Hello?"

The voice came from the window, and both of them turned in surprise. A pale face peered back at them over the balcony.

"*Skender?*"

"Give me a hand up, Sal. I'd rather not make a mistake at this point."

Sal hurried to the balcony and grabbed the boy's hand. With a couple of good heaves, he was standing before them, dusting himself off.

"Thanks," Skender said, his eyes bright. "Climbing around here is easy once you get the hang of it — and safer than the hallways if you don't want to be seen — but it can be messy at night. Especially if you fall."

"What are you *doing* here?"

"I came to find out what happened." He studied them

expectantly, oblivious to the tension in the air. "What did Dad say? Are you staying? Tell me you're staying, please."

"It looks like we're staying," Shilly said, and winced at the ragged edge to her voice. This was what she'd wanted, wasn't it?

"Well, good!" Skender rubbed his hands together. "It'll be great to have you guys around. You're my age, or nearly, and that'll be something."

Why? Shilly wanted to ask. *Why will it be something just because we're around your age?*

"I doubt we'll be in the same classes," said Sal, sitting nervously on the edge of the bed, his eyes avoiding Shilly.

"Don't be so sure. We tend to learn together, helping each other along — but you'll see that when we start. Are you going to be Tested tomorrow?"

"He didn't say anything about that."

"No? Oh, well. You'll find out in the morning." Skender practically bounced up and down with excitement. "This is going to be so much fun."

Shilly couldn't deal with his energy. Throwing her remaining crutch to the floor, she collapsed backwards onto the bed, not caring about jarring her leg. The pain cut through her distress and gave her something concrete to focus on. She put a hand over her eyes and was surprised to find moisture there.

"Listen, Skender, I'm sorry," Sal stammered. "It's late, and we need to sleep. Do you want a hand out the window?"

"I'll leave by the door, thanks. The lights go out soon." As though on cue, the glowing stones on two of the walls decreased in brightness. "There you go. I'll be off. See you tomorrow, fellow students."

With that, he slipped through the door and away, leaving the two of them together in the gathering darkness. Shilly rolled over deliberately to turn her back on him. She felt him staring at her for a long moment. Neither of them said a word as he eventually turned away to prepare for bed.

Darkness fell. Shilly shivered and rolled herself into the musty rugs. The air coming through the window was cold and thin and would no doubt get colder as the night progressed. Sal's breathing slowed and deepened almost immediately, but she couldn't sleep so easily. The trials of the day — a very long day, when she considered how much they had done — weighed heavily upon her mind.

Sal. Everything always came back to him. Lodo had given him one of the precious globes that she'd never been allowed to touch, demonstrating that he was favoured over her. Shom Behenna had helped him save her life, most likely to bend him to the Sky Wardens' cause. Belilanca Brokate had brought them to Ulum because she had liked exchanging stories with him. And now the Mage Van Haasteren had accepted them into the Keep because of *his* potential, not hers.

It had been her idea to come here, she thought angrily to herself. Yet would she even have got through the guards without Sal? Would she have been accepted on her own merits? Wasn't she worth *anything*?

Nothing had gone as she'd hoped it would. There was no grand welcome, no sense of *togetherness*: there only bitterness, old hurts and lies. Still, she drifted off to sleep with the phrase *fellow students* ringing in her ears — the only thought that comforted her. No matter how she had got here, and no matter how overshadowed she was, she was still *here*. She had achieved her goal. She had met the Mage Van Haasteren and had probably been accepted into the Keep. The ends justified using the means.

Maybe it needed time for everything to settle down, she told herself. The last two weeks had certainly been the most painful of her life. Maybe in another week or two everything would be better ...

When she dreamed, she dreamed of Lodo. He held a bright light in his hands. She reached out for it, but he withdrew it from her. Shaking his head, he pitched one arm back and threw the light into a mighty crack in the earth, where it vanished and went out. She looked back and he was gone, swallowed by the darkness.

CHAPTER 10

THE LIGHT-KEEPER

Sal woke shivering, and opened his eyes to find a lizard clinging to the wall in front of his face. The vision had an unreal edge to it, at first, as though he might still be dreaming. The lizard's skin was a vivid yellow colour, almost glowing in the near darkness, and its eyes seemed to be looking right back at him. Time froze for a moment as they contemplated each other — then it blinked once, lightning fast, and Sal jumped back in fright.

He almost fell out of bed. That was when he truly accepted that he was awake. The lizard watched his sleepy over-reaction without surprise, then crawled slowly across the wall to the corner, and up to the ceiling. From that new vantage point it watched Sal as he shook his head, ran his fingers through his hair, and got up.

The air was icy. He took a rug with him and walked to the balcony, where he watched the grey dregs of night evaporate into the new day. The sunlight rolled in sluggish waves across the jagged, barren mountaintops before him. It wouldn't strike the Keep directly for some time yet, since the small town was partially sheltered behind a jagged tongue of stone sticking out of the cliff like a ship's keel. He wondered what the Keep would be like during the winter months, when the nights were longer. Very cold, he imagined, tightening the rug around him. He didn't envy Skender and the other students those mornings.

Perhaps, he thought, he might find out what it felt like in person. Training would prevent him from hurting people by accident, if what the Mage Van Haasteren had said about wild talents were true. He would need to learn how to control himself. He didn't want to go rushing off to meet his mother's family, only to hurt them somehow. He could wait to meet them, if he had to.

And there was Shilly, too. She had fallen asleep fully dressed, with covers wrapped awkwardly around her. The look of unhappiness on her face made his own concerns seem much smaller. The injury still dominated her day-to-day life, with the loss of Lodo and her home a constant counterpoint. He wouldn't shirk his responsibility to her. Even with the argument still fresh in his mind — the sense of guilt it woke in him — he could never have contemplated leaving her to look after herself just yet.

Besides, Sal didn't know exactly where she stood in the Keep, without him. Even though the mage had said that he would teach both of them, Brokate's doubt about the Stone Mages' motives was still in his mind, niggling away at his relief in arriving safely. He didn't know for sure that the mage wasn't simply letting her in so the Stone Mages could get their hands on *him*. But there was nothing he could do about that without seeming ungrateful. He could only assume that everything would work out perfectly well. The Keep could turn out to be the home he had never had, and he could become its greatest student. He would use his wild talent to divine new ways of understanding and using the Change; he would justify all the risks Lodo took on his behalf; he would make the memory of his father proud ...

A knock at the door interrupted his fantasies. It opened a second later, revealing Bethe, dressed in the dark-red robes that were the uniform of the Keep. Today's looked cleaner, however, as though she was putting on her best for the visitors. His clothes, in a pile by the end of the bed, seemed dusty and worn in comparison.

"Hello, Sal," she said, smiling brightly. "You're up. I thought I'd have to wake you." She put a small pile of towels on the empty bed and stooped to gently shake Shilly's shoulder. "Good morning!"

Shilly groaned. "What? Who ...?"

"Time to start your first day." Bethe straightened and winked at Sal. "I'll show you where to bathe. Breakfast is in the dining hall between first and second bells. I'll come back shortly to take you there." She indicated that Sal should follow her. He grabbed a towel and let her lead him down the hall and around the corner. There, a communal bathroom awaited him, empty. He had the choice of seven shower stalls and twice as many toilet cubicles, none as luxurious as Wyath Gyory's, but much better than he had become used to on their long trek. Bethe left him and he showered quickly, scrubbing at his dirty skin and washing his hair with soap. The water was as hot as the air was cold. The icy stone beneath his feet made him wince as he hurried back to the room.

Shilly was up and waiting for him, her towel around her neck along with a change of bandages.

"Where do I go?" she asked. Obviously his assistance wasn't required, beyond giving directions. Her anger hadn't abated overnight, then.

He told her the way, then finished getting dressed. When he was done, he sat on the balcony and waited. Shilly's mood would pass, he hoped. Once they got down to lessons, she would have plenty to distract her.

She returned at the same time as Bethe. "Ready?" the student overseer asked.

"Couldn't be readier," Shilly said, her jaw set as though responding to a challenge.

"I'm starving, to be honest," added Sal, hoping to counter the frost in Shilly's tone. "I feel like I could eat an emu."

"Well, we don't serve meat for breakfast," Bethe said, "but you'll find plenty else to fill your plate. It's Raf and Mereki's turn to cook this morning, and they never skimp on quantity."

"You cook for yourselves?"

"Oh, yes. This isn't a school for the soft. That's why it's regarded as one of the best. There are no servants here. We all have housekeeping duties to perform. It was my turn to clean the unused rooms last week, so I'm a bit embarrassed that yours was so dusty. I'm not often caught redhanded like that." She laughed, and the sound of it echoed off the stone walls of the corridor around them. Shilly didn't respond, but Sal liked the sound of it. It made him feel welcome, part of the joke.

He had imagined the dining hall to be enormous, filled with trestle tables for hundreds of students, but the reality was much more modest: a high-ceilinged chamber open to the morning air with a dozen tables arranged in a haphazard fashion. Food was dished out through a hole in the wall that led to the kitchens. The redhead who had poked fun at Skender the previous day

215

served them large portions of porridge, stewed fruit and toasted bread piled high with mushrooms and beans. Sal wondered where the food came from, and Bethe explained that produce came from Ulum once every week, brought along the Way by a dedicated trader. Very little would grow among the barren mountains, as long years of trying had demonstrated. Students with an interest in horticulture had tried to cultivate small crops in unoccupied chambers, using rainwater and soil carried up from the valley below, but with only minor successes, certainly not enough to feed the entire Keep. In the end, Sal gathered, trade with Ulum was maintained in order to maintain links between the school and the greater community at the other end of the Way.

Skender was sitting by himself in the centre of the room, waving furiously to attract their attention. They joined him, Sal and Shilly mindful of the stares of the other people in the room.

"Everyone," the boy announced, "this is Sal and Shilly, our new recruits."

There were muttered good mornings and a few well-meaning grunts. Not everyone, obviously, enjoyed the early starts as much as Bethe or Skender.

"We'll introduce you properly as the day goes on," the student overseer said through a mouthful of beans. "For now, eat. You've got a lot ahead of you."

"First up," said Skender, "is to tell us how you got here. Where are you from? How far have you come? Did you have any adventures on the way?"

Bethe shot him a warning look, but he just pulled a face back. Sal resigned himself to the fact that he would have to tell their story yet again, and composed an abbreviated version for discussion over breakfast. They were orphans exiled from the Strand looking for training and hoping to find it among the

Stone Mages. This only whetted Skender's appetite, however, and he demanded detail upon detail until Sal despaired of finishing his breakfast before the second bell, and Bethe had to rescue him.

"Enough, Skender!" she snapped, mock-stern. "If your father won't tell you, then it's none of your business."

Skender pouted and threatened to catapult a spoonful of porridge in her direction. She raised a warning finger, and he rolled his eyes in amused indignation. Sal got the feeling that this was a familiar rivalry, one they both enjoyed.

Throughout it all, Shilly sat in silence, taking everything in but not responding. Only once, when addressed directly in a way she couldn't avoid, did she volunteer anything.

"We haven't known each other long," she said. "My teacher took in Sal to protect him from the Sky Wardens, and because he had more potential than me. I can't blame Lodo for that, I guess."

"He thought the two of us were *destined*," Sal added with a smile.

Shilly cast Sal a look he couldn't interpret, then turned her attention back to her plate. "Destined for *what* is anyone's guess."

Sal avoided Bethe's searching gaze, and was relieved when the bell rang not long after, announcing the end of breakfast. It was true: he and Shilly hadn't known each other very long. Their knowledge might not run very deep, but in all his years of travelling, he had known her longer than anyone apart from his father, and he remembered clearly the day she had offered to be his friend. She was possibly the only real friend he had ever had.

He wondered if the same could be said for her. She hadn't been popular in Fundelry, that was for sure. Had she known *anyone* well, apart from Lodo?

The Mage Van Haasteren — the only adult they had seen in the Keep thus far — appeared in the doorway.

"Good morning," he said, striding forward to loom over the table. "I have a new schedule for today, Bethe. You'll find it in my office. I'm going to be busy with Sal and Shilly until lunchtime. The Mage Erentaite arrived an hour ago and is ready to examine them now."

"Can I —?"

"No, Skender, you cannot. Go with Bethe and attend to your work."

"But I'm already a year ahead, father —"

"Then now is not the time to fall behind. Go!"

The boy scowled as deeply as his father and moved off, muttering.

"Good luck," Bethe said to the both of them. The mage led them out of the room, mindful of Shilly's crutches through the chaos of students in the room.

"This way." The Mage Van Haasteren took them along a wide, low corridor with a rustle of robes. He had to stoop slightly to enter a doorway on their right, beyond which they found a large room lit by yellow glow stones. The room contained a table carved from grey marble, behind which, in the room's only chair, sat an extremely old woman dressed in black robes. Her head was slumped forward over hands folded carefully in front of her. Her hair was as grey as steel and cropped short, exposing thinning patches and a spotted scalp.

"Jarmila," said Mage Van Haasteren in a hushed tone.

The elderly mage, whom Sal had assumed was sleeping, looked up. Her eyes were gold in the light of the stones and seemed startlingly alert.

"I see you." Her voice was thin but very clear. "These are the two?"

"Yes, Jarmila."

"I sensed them coming up the hall. They have already been Tested, you know."

"I did wonder."

"The boy most recently. Come forward, both of you." The Mage Van Haasteren nudged them closer. "Ah, yes. The Scourge of Aneshti has cracked over them, if I'm not mistaken. What was its diagnosis, Sal?"

The Mage Van Haasteren stiffened beside him, but Sal ignored him, trying to remember. The Scourge had taken him on an imaginary series of deaths by drowning, freezing, burning and suffocation. Somehow, Lodo had determined from this what his inclination was regarding the Change.

"My heart chose air," he said, hoping he wouldn't have to go through the experience again, "and my head chose fire; I have a natural predilection for stone over water. Shilly was the opposite."

"Ah." The elderly mage nodded. "An unusual pairing, but an effective one."

"Why do we have to be a pairing?" Shilly asked. "We came here together, but that doesn't mean we do *everything* together."

"But you *are* paired," the Mage Erentaite said, "more than you realise. Your hands, please." She reached for them across the table.

They obeyed, letting the woman clasp their hands in hers. Her skin was dry and soft, and she smelt of old age. Her eyes closed, and she breathed in deeply. Sal felt a strange tingling move up his arm and into his neck, like goosebumps. Only when her eyes opened did he realise that the reflection of the glowing stones hid a disturbing truth: the woman's irises were white with cataracts. She was completely blind.

"Yes," she breathed. "They must be trained — to defend themselves, if nothing else."

"Against what?" asked Van Haasteren.

The elderly mage didn't answer the question. "Do you think you're up to it, Skender?"

The use of the mage's first name took Sal by surprise. "Of course, Jarmila. Why wouldn't I be?"

"Don't let pride lead you, my boy. These are no ordinary strays. Payat knew that, and do you see what it cost him?"

"Payat was a fool."

"He was not, and you would do well to remember that. Your father trusted him."

"My father was betrayed by him."

The elderly mage sighed. "Skender, you need to be careful. The Weavers will be interested in this one, if they aren't already." She indicated Sal with a nod of her head, but spoke as if neither he nor Shilly were there. "Where their eye is drawn few can predict, and none can stand in their way. Don't be caught in the middle, that's my advice. Do only what you can, then surrender the limelight."

"Who are the Weavers?" Sal asked, remembering what Brokate had said about them on the way to Ulum: that they were legendary figures who stole children.

"They are the ones your parents angered, unintentionally." The Mage Erentaite looked at him with her blind, white eyes, and he felt that she was seeing the depths of his being. "They are everywhere, yet nowhere. Their work is of vital importance to both our lands, yet is conducted in absolute secrecy. They destroy as often as they create, and they are not to be crossed."

"They are a myth," snorted Mage Van Haasteren, coming up behind them and putting a hand on each of their shoulders. "Jarmila, the children will learn more from lessons than they will from such common tales. I don't want you making things more difficult than they already are."

The elderly mage looked up at Van Haasteren with a crooked smile. "It is not I making things difficult, Skender."

"Nor is it ghosts. Tell me what you advise for their training. That's why I asked you here. Should they be separated?"

"No. They must be taught together. They are less opposites than complements. That I see very clearly." The elderly mage let go of their hands and stood. She barely came up to Sal's shoulder, and he wasn't remotely tall. "Will you do as I say in this respect, Skender, if no other?"

"Of course, Jarmila." Mage Van Haasteren bowed his head so low behind them that his black hair brushed Sal's cheek. "I respect your judgment in these matters."

"Indeed." She smiled more widely still at that, then uttered a single, barking laugh. "Ha!" With a brisk wave, she commanded that Shilly come around the table and sit in the chair she had vacated. "Let's take a look at that leg of yours, my girl."

Van Haasteren guided Sal away as the elderly mage unbound Shilly's dressing and examined the scars. Although they were some distance across the room, Sal could feel the buzzing of the Change as she did so, and saw a startled expression cross Shilly's face. The old woman's knobbled fingers traced strange patterns across the leg, lingering in some places for almost a minute, then darting elsewhere without warning, like a bird looking for seeds in the grass.

"Does this hurt?" she asked Shilly.

"No."

"This?"

"Ouch, yes!"

"Good. Tell me if you feel anything here."

The probing intensified around the knee, then continued down her shin.

"What's she doing?" Sal whispered to Van Haasteren.

"Laying the groundwork for true healing," said the mage in a soft voice. "You don't repair a major wound by sticking the pieces together and forcing them to bind. That's like building a house by stacking chunks of wood one on top of the other. You have to shape the pieces, guide them as they bond, make them one. You paint a map for the tissue to follow, then leave it to grow into the shape you desire. If Jarmila is successful, this will be the last time Shilly or you will use the Change upon her leg. It must be allowed to mend at its own pace, or else it will not mend true."

Sal thought about this for a second, then asked, "Does this mean she might not be lame?"

"If Jarmila is successful, she might not be, yes."

A measure of relief trickled through him. Not having the leg between them would make things easier. Shilly might have absolved him of blame, but he wouldn't be surprised if her present resentment of him was grounded in part in that injury. He was the cause of it all, ultimately.

The Mage Erentaite finished her examination by gripping Shilly's foot with both her hands and breathing deeply over it. She didn't seem to be doing anything at all, as far as Sal could tell, but he knew better than to discount the old woman's skill. The hairs on the back of his neck were still tingling, and he knew too little about the Change to make any judgment.

The elderly mage stirred, but still she wasn't finished. She reached out with one hand, cupped it around Shilly's head, and drew her close. They whispered softly to each other for a moment, then drew apart. Shilly was released with one last pat. She gathered up her crutches and stood, looking puzzled.

"Teach them, Skender." The Mage Erentaite folded herself gently into the chair and closed her eyes. "I will return in one week to see how things are going. If you approve, I will take them to Ulum to give them their robes."

"Yes, Jarmila." Van Haasteren bowed once, and led them out of the room. As they passed through the door, Sal caught a flicker of movement high up in one shadowy corner. He pulled back just long enough to see what caused it.

It was another lizard. Not the same sort as the one in his bedroom, but around the same size. Its eyes reflected the light as he let himself be guided from the room, and he wondered if the Keep was full of such creatures. Maybe they kept insects down, and were encouraged to stay. There might be hundreds of them sharing the spaces with the humans who lived there. He hoped not. Their unblinking intensity unnerved him.

The Mage Van Haasteren, silent, as though the elderly mage had given him much to think about, led them along a series of corridors until they reached the main tutoring room. There he introduced them to the rest of the students and outlined what they could expect to do in the coming days. Their acceptance into the Keep wasn't final until it was ceremonially formalised by the Mage Erentaite in Ulum granting them the rust-red robes of the school, but Sal saw the light in Shilly's eyes and could tell what she was thinking.

She was on her way. The second stage of her education had begun. It was up to her, now, to prove that she was worthy. Her fate rested in no one else's hands but her own.

As did *his* fate, Sal supposed. He found himself unexpectedly envying Shilly's certainty. She'd known exactly what she wanted and where she wanted to be, and now she had it. If only, he thought, his own journey could end so neatly.

When they had been welcomed near the bridge the previous day, Sal had been surprised at the small number of people to appear. He had assumed that there were more elsewhere. But at breakfast that morning, the number had still been small, and when Raf confirmed during their introductory lesson that there were only eighteen full-time students at the Keep and just the one full-time teacher — the Mage Van Haasteren — and that it had always been that way, Sal had been less disappointed than he would have expected. He had imagined the Keep as a teeming community of scholars and students at the heart of the Interior. Instead, it was an outpost on the fringes of society — a retreat rather than the sort of university he had read about. Deep down, he was relieved not to be thrust into the centre of an enormous educational machine, as he imagined the Haunted City to be.

Their introductory session gave them an overview of how the lessons generally worked. The Mage Van Haasteren tutored the senior students who, in turn, tutored the juniors. That way, lessons were repeatedly reinforced and no one was permitted to coast along. Easily the least experienced of anyone at the Keep, Sal tried to make up for it with sheer determination. After the first visualisation session he knew the patterns they had been asked to memorise at least as well as he knew the Cellaton Mandala.

Bethe took them for theory that afternoon, reintroducing them to some of the concepts that Lodo had already touched on — briefly with Sal, in more detail with Shilly. He got the feeling that the student overseer was sounding the depths of their knowledge to see just how much they would need to be taught. Sal did his best to imply that he knew more than he did, but he didn't think she was fooled. After the session, Bethe took Skender aside and arranged for Sal to receive special tuition from him in the evenings. The boy was initially reluctant to receive more work but, upon realising that it would give him more time with his new friends, soon cheered up.

"We'll have you up to speed in no time, old boy," he said, clapping Sal on the shoulder and grinning like a wild cat. "I'll show you how to get around this place without being seen, too, if you like," he added in an undertone.

Sal wasn't keen on the idea of crawling up and down the crumbling cliff face, but he was warmed by the boy's ready acceptance and trust. A new chore roster was drawn up to include the new students. Shilly wasn't exempt, even with her leg, although she would be confined to cooking duties for the time being: preparing vegetables, washing dishes, and other work she could do while seated. Sal had cleaning, with Bethe, and was glad for that. She was friendly to him outside of classes, and he could tell that Raf was slightly jealous of the attention he was getting, even though the redhead was a lot older and a lot better at the Change. He kept finding ways to keep Sal, Shilly and Skender busy.

"Concentrate," said Raf fiercely, during their third lesson with him. The redhead held Sal's left hand in his right one. Raf's right hand was in Shilly's left. The three of them and four other students, Skender among them, all with hands linked, formed a ring in one corner of the main tutoring room. In the heart of the ring was a cloudy white glow. The cloud was a simple, confined version of the background potential, and the game they were playing was called Blind. Blind was normally played between two or three people in a kind of free-for-all. Sal had first played it in Lodo's workshop against both Lodo and Shilly. The version they were playing pitted two teams of three against each other, with Raf as a kind of adjudicator.

"Concentrate, Skender. I'm watching you." Raf's eyes were tightly closed; he didn't need sight to see the match before him. Each team had a hoop, a spike and a bulging cavity, shapes woven from the cloud itself — as though teased from cotton wool and able to move around the surface of the cloud, directed by the minds of the players. The objective of the game was to immobilise the opposition in any conceivable way: the spike could pin both hoop and cavity, while the hoop could be swallowed just as easily as it could capture. Blind was characterised by periods of intense scrutiny, as each team member sized up all the others, followed by flashes of rapid motion, almost too fast to follow.

Sal and Shilly had been snapped up by Skender to play with him. Cautious at first, and undisciplined, they had lost twice in a row. On the third game, Sal was determined to do better. The problem was, he didn't know how to go about it. Playing Blind as part of a team was very different to playing for himself.

"Careful," said Skender, their team's loop, warning Sal's cavity away from a feint by the other team. They spoke using a simple technique Shilly and Skender already knew, but which Sal had had to belatedly learn, using the background potential as a channel between them. It wasn't as simple as talking aloud, and he was awkward at it at first, but it saved them from exposing their tactics to their opponents. "Come around a bit to your left. Nudge Chema off course."

"Which one's she?" Sal asked.

"The spike. And the brown-haired girl opposite you, with the dangerous gleam in her eye."

"The one who almost pinned you before?"

"Exactly. Watch out for her. She's fast."

Sal edged closer to the spike, wary of any sudden moves. "So how come I get to be her shadow?"

"Concentrate, you two," snapped Shilly, her brooding silence broken by the need to compete. "They're about to try something."

"How —?" asked Skender, but didn't finish the sentence. As Shilly had predicted, their opponents suddenly burst into motion, their hook and cavity darting around behind Shilly and their spike stabbing at Skender, hoping to force him into a mistake. Swoop and clumsy counter-swoop followed. Sal was, for the most part, ignored. He blundered forward in an attempt to save his friends, and the other team abruptly called off the attack.

"Thanks, Sal," said Skender, swooping across the cloud to avoid one of the other players. "It was getting tight there for a moment."

"I didn't have a choice," he said. "I wouldn't last a second without you guys. I'm too slow."

"Being fast is no asset," said Shilly, "if you don't know where you're going."

"What's that supposed to mean?" asked Skender.

"It *means* we're tackling this the wrong way. What are they doing that we're not?"

"Winning, mainly."

The other team pounced again, scattering the three of them to the far corners of the cloud. The second wave of their attack concentrated on Sal this time, and he was hard-pressed to fend them off. Only by holding his ground with his cotton-wool maw opened as wide as he could make it, did he manage to deter them long enough for Shilly and Skender to find an opening. They managed to repel the advance, just. After a minute's chaotic posturing, it was back to the waiting game.

Raf, observing the activities in the cloud with his mind, chuckled softly. Sal took the chance to catch his breath, while Skender skated through the cloud like a mosquito, never staying still for longer than a split second.

"This is ridiculous," said Shilly.

"Except as an exercise," Skender responded.

"An exercise in futility."

"Now, now. You're honing your skills, aren't you?"

"Only our skills at losing. What are *you* getting out of it?"

"A much needed thrashing, as my father might say. So maybe you're right." Sal didn't need to check Skender's face to confirm that he was joking. "We might as well forfeit and save ourselves the embarrassment."

"No! There has to be a way." Shilly's determination rose in proportion to her frustration. "They're not winning because they're better than us. They're winning because they're working as a team. We're just running in circles around each other. If we could somehow put your speed and Sal's brute force together ..."

"One thing's for sure. We'd surprise the pants off them." Skender dodged a brief attempt to trap him in one corner of the cloud. "Any ideas?"

"Well, I can see what they're doing, even if I don't know what the tactics are called. They're not moving randomly, like us. They only *pretend* to until it's time to attack. You can tell when they're about to attack because they freeze for a second to check that everyone's ready — then they move."

"You can see that?" Skender sounded as surprised as Sal felt. "I just fly by the seat of my pants and assume everyone else does too."

"No, there's definitely some sort of pattern behind this." Shilly watched closely as their opposing team wafted around them, feinting then pulling back. "See? The loop's trying to edge you out of the way, Skender, so she can take that upper point. Once she's there, we won't be able to shift her. While Sal's in the middle, their own cavity is forced to one side as well, and they won't want that. They'll try to push Sal out soon, then bring their spike down here —" an image came with her words, indicating a spot near her that was currently empty "— and then they'll make their move."

"You think so?" Skender sounded dubious.

"Yes. There's more to winning this game than just flying fast."

"Apparently so. Okay, then. What do we do in response?"

"We let them think we're falling for it. Sal, move out of the centre like they want, but not too far. Skender, stay roughly where you are until I say. I'll come around here, like this..." Her spike dodged past the other team's loop, then flew in a tight figure eight in front of her.

As predicted, their opponent's cavity took the centre position, once Sal had moved.

Sal participated in the strange ballet with distant fascination. He could see what Shilly meant about the other team's tactics, but only after she described it to him. He couldn't predict it. There were too many variables to take into account, too many dimensions. A simple game of Advance, on a flat board with only two players, was complicated enough for him.

"Okay, Skender, move to your left and down, but don't make it look like you're going anywhere in particular. I want you on the opposite side to Sal."

Skender moved, and the other loop instantly took his place. The opposing three players held that position for a bare instant — just as Shilly had said they would — then they attacked.

The loop swooped down on Shilly, who was forced to duck out of the way, toward the hostile cavity. Skender rushed forward to help her, but their spike was in the way. When Sal clumsily propelled himself forward, their opponents backed away for a brief moment, but then regrouped in a new position with Shilly pinned between their cavity and Sal able to retreat in one less direction.

Their loop jumped forward to enclose her. She saw the threat before Skender could point it out to her.

"Watch out, Shilly!"

"I see it! Sal, back up. Skender, come round and down right. Further. Now jump forward. That's it! Sal — to your right, into that opening — quickly! Good."

Sal felt himself caught up in the rush of her directions. Even if they didn't make sense at first, they always proved to be sensible. She managed to extricate herself from her sticky position and almost immediately turned the attack back on their opponents. Sal found himself as surprised as the other team's spike when he bore down on her from above and almost swallowed her whole. Then their opponents' cavity was under a combined attack from Skender and Shilly, and it looked as though the tables might finally have been turned.

So intent was Sal on trying to swallow the other team's spike that he didn't see the loop come up behind and past him. It darted for Shilly, swinging like a lasso. When Sal saw it, he put all his effort into one powerful leap forward — so powerful it set the cloud between the six contestants sloshing like water in a barrel. He misjudged his leap and missed the loop, but the strange currents circulating as a result of his effort put everyone off balance. Sal himself reeled from both the visual disorientation combined with an odd dragging sensation, as though the universe was drifting out from under him.

The opponent's spike was the first to recover. She speared Sal and Skender before Shilly even noticed, and by then it was too late. The game was lost.

Shilly broke the circle with a curse, and the cloud vanished.

"Much better," said Raf, opening his eyes and stretching. The other team accepted his praise with pride, particularly Chema, the girl who had appeared as their spike in the game. She nodded at Sal without any trace of gloating.

"Promising indeed," Raf went on. "Sorry, Sal and Shilly, that you had Skender to hold you back. We'll try again tomorrow and see if we can't rearrange the teams a little." Skender thumbed his nose at the redhead, who ignored him completely. The rest of the students climbed to their feet and picked up their books. It was time for meditation, then lunch. In the afternoon they had visualisations and mnemonics, in groups according to their ability, and after that they had a theory refresher. Chores would keep them busy until the evening meal was ready, then the rest of the night was theirs to study or relax.

To Sal it was daunting and stimulating at the same time. He had so much to learn, even with Skender's help, and he didn't want to distract Shilly from her own studies. Although her anger had cooled to the point where she tolerated his presence outside lessons, she was barely talking to him unless she had to. There had been no repeat of the crutch-throwing incident, but the tension was still there, bubbling in the background. Ever since the decision to accept them into the Keep, she had been grimly determined to work hard and she would let little distract her. Whatever the Mage Erentaite had whispered to her that day, it appeared to have left her focused completely on the job at hand, rather than her feelings.

Sometimes the cracks showed. They rarely saw the mage, except at meal times, and they were never alone when they did. Whenever the mage *was* there, Shilly tried to bring up Lodo and his relationship with the Keep. Every time she did, however, her questions were met with blank silence. None of the younger ones had ever heard of Shilly's first teacher, and before she could explain, the Mage Van Haasteren would firmly change the subject.

Sal himself never found a reason to talk to the mage after their first day at the Keep. Instead, he relied on Bethe to tell him what to do, and listened to information filtered down through the other students, mainly Skender. As a result, he learned some details about the Keep that he presumed didn't fall into the official history.

On one occasion, Skender was supposed to be introducing Sal to something called the Interconnectivity Dictum, but was instead showing him five rooms that no one else knew existed in the Keep. Only a tiny percentage of the cliff town's many rooms were inhabited: the rest were empty. Along the way, Sal learned that the responsibility for the school and its students had been in Van Haasteren hands for more than ten generations. A long line of Stone Mages had sprung from their Clan, the talent passed through parent and child to the most recent generation, the adult Skender. The heirs weren't always male; only since Skender's grandfather had they been so. Before that, the senior members of the Clan had been female for four generations, an alternating series of mothers and daughters overseeing the education of the region's most prominent would-be Stone Mages.

"We almost lost it, though," said Skender, as he guided Sal past a rockfall that appeared to have blocked a tunnel, but had in fact left a small crack that they could squeeze through. "My grandfather did something before I was born. I don't know what. My dad won't talk about it. It got us into trouble."

"How do you know about it?"

"I hear rumours. Other mages come here to visit and to teach. You met Jarmila Erentaite, right? She's on the Synod, and it's her job to make sure the various schools are running properly. She talks to me sometimes; she tells me things. Maybe she thinks I'll take over the Keep one day, when Dad retires, and she wants me to be informed."

"Will you do that?" asked Sal.

"Take over the Keep? I don't know." The boy shrugged with the gravity of an old man. "I'd want to see the world first. Dad's been here all his life, you know. Sometimes I think he forgets there's a world out there. I don't want to end up like him. I'd rather be like my mother, wherever she is right now."

Skender's mother, Abi, was a Surveyor who travelled the fringes of the Interior looking for Ruins. Sal could understand her unwillingness to stay cooped up here for too long, as Skender was. Anywhere would begin to chafe for someone used to travelling — even somewhere as interesting as the Keep. And the Keep *was* interesting, full of nooks and crannies and all sorts of oddities that few people visited. The views from the empty rooms were all the more spectacular for knowing that he and Skender might be the only ones who had seen them for decades. There were massive storage chambers deep in the hillside, large enough to hold entire ships. Natural caves led deeper still, containing delicate crystals and carrying echoes from underground rivers kilometres distant. Skender said that the cliff town was ancient, and had once been a winter retreat for an ancient queen. Sal could believe it. Even being responsible for cleaning the many empty rooms and sweeping the endless corridors didn't take the shine off the Keep's novelty.

He thought about this while writing a short, belated note to send to Belilanca Brokate, letting her know that they had arrived and settled in. For the first time in a very long while, he began to feel something approaching safety. The work was hard, but that was all he had to worry about. There was no threat from the

Sky Wardens. There was no Shom Behenna on his tail. There was nothing to threaten him at all, if he ignored the Mage Erentaite's vague warning about the Weavers, whoever they were, and the fear of failing. If he worried, regardless of all this, he told himself he was just being stupid. Running was a hard habit to break, and he had been running his entire life. The time had come to stand his ground. If anything or anyone *did* get in his way, he would meet the challenge head-on, on his own terms, rather than let himself be pushed around again.

It was at this time, when he was feeling the beginnings of independence and self-confidence, that his voice broke.

"Squeak, squeak."

"Shut up!"

"What's that, little mouse? I can't hear you."

"I said, shut up!" He'd thought his voice breaking would be a cause for relief, since it meant that his talent for the Change wasn't going to evaporate after all, but in fact it had proved to be nothing of the sort. "I can't help it."

His vocal chords betrayed him again on the last word, prompting another wave of laughter from Skender.

"Be quiet, *both* of you!" called Shilly from the balcony. "I'm trying to study."

Sal threw Skender a dirty look and followed it up with a pillow. The boy ducked, and the pillow hit the wall, startling the yellow lizard that had taken up permanent residence in the corner. It scuttled for cover under the bed while Skender scrabbled for something more solid to throw back. His hand fell on Sal's pack.

"Don't touch that." Sal was across the room before Skender's fingers could close. He pulled the pack reassuringly close to his chest, feeling the heavy weight of the globe in his arms.

"Why? What's in it?" Skender teased, dancing around him like a restless puppy. "Love letters from a little mouse's girlfriend? Or a lock of Bethe's hair?"

Sal gritted his teeth. He should never have told Skender that he enjoyed doing his chores with the student overseer. The teasing had been merciless ever since.

"Nothing," he said. "It's none of your business."

Skender flopped back on the bed and rested his head on one hand. "Which one is it? You can't have it both ways."

Sal sighed. Skender had a way of getting what he wanted, either by resourcefulness or sheer persistence. The chances were it would be easier to just tell him, now that his interest was piqued. It didn't come easy, though. He had kept the globe secret even from Shilly. How could he justify revealing it to a complete stranger?

He glanced at where she sat in the balcony of the room they still shared, reading by the light of the evening sun. How she ignored the yawning gulf on her right he didn't know, but she seemed unperturbed by it. Their chores were over, and they all were supposed to be studying.

He was, however, certain she was paying close attention to what went on between him and Skender. Even if she never joined in on the teasing about Bethe — a fact for which he was distinctly grateful, since Skender was more than enough to deal with at one time — she wouldn't want to miss out on anything. She certainly wouldn't want to miss out on what he was increasingly sure he was about to do. He had to do it, he thought, to repay some of the trust Skender had shown him. And maybe to get a reaction from her, too . . .

He took a deep breath and reached into his pack.

"This is a secret, Skender, so you have to promise not to tell anyone about it."

"I promise," said the boy, sitting up with eyes wide.

"Our first teacher gave this to me before we left Fundelry." He heard a faint creak as Shilly shifted in her chair. "He didn't tell me how to use it, but he said it might come in handy, one day. I've been carrying it around ever since." He put the leather-wrapped bundle in his lap and began to unfold it.

Skender's eyes opened even wider when he saw what it contained. "It's a light-sink!" he exclaimed.

"Is that what it's called?"

"Or a light-keeper." The boy inched closer so he could get a better look. "Different types have specific names — the Orb of Ardanoi, for instance — but they all do pretty much the same thing. Where did you say you got it from?"

Sal described Lodo and Fundelry in more detail. Skender listened with interest. The fact that it had come from — and presumably been made in — a small town as deep as you could get in the Strand fascinated him as it had fascinated his father.

"Amazing," Skender said, clearly wanting to touch the globe for himself, but, strangely enough, not bold enough to ask outright. "Only trained Stone Mages can make light-sinks, you know, and even then only under exactly the right circumstances. I can't imagine how this Lodo of yours managed it so far on the wrong side of the Divide."

"What makes them so hard to make?" asked Sal. "I mean, there are hundreds of glowing stones all over this place. Isn't this just something like that?"

"'Something *like*,' yes, but the difference is crucial. What makes light-sinks really tricky is not that they store light or emit it, because doing either of those is easy; it's doing *both* of them that's hard. You've got to tell them to stop storing and start emitting, and that's not easy. Fixed matter like glass and stone doesn't want to change. You have to force it — and force it gently, or it'll break. You have to *seduce* it."

"You know how to do that, then?" asked Shilly sceptically, moving from the chair on the balcony and coming into the room.

"Only in theory. I've read about it and I've heard Dad talk to the more advanced students about it."

"I'll bet he was the one who said 'seduce'," she said.

"It was. So what? If he used it, it must be the right word."

"You've never tried to use one?" asked Sal.

"No, but only because I've never had access to a globe like this. Making them is a whole other matter entirely." Sal held the globe gently up to the window so it caught the last rays of the sun and Skender's gaze followed it. "It's *beautiful*, Sal. You're very lucky."

Shilly's lips tightened.

"Wha—" Sal started, but stopped as the word came out as a squawk. Skender chortled.

"What do you think?" he asked, handing it to Shilly. "Skender seems to think he knows how to make it work. Is it worth a go?"

She took the globe as though he had offered her a very fragile, enormously precious jewel.

"You're asking me?"

"Yes. I am."

"Then no. It's not that I don't believe you, Skender —"

"Not just Skender," Sal said. "All of us. Together."

The word caught her attention. She thought about it. "No," she said again. "We still might break it."

"I'd be curious to try anyway," said Sal. Still fresh in his mind was his dream of a bright light shining when everything else around was dark. "Lodo said I might need it one day. It's not going to be much use to me if I don't know how to make it work."

"But it's too valuable," she said, shaking her head.

"Exactly!" Skender exclaimed. "Who knows how old it is? Who knows how much light is stored inside it? Look how grey it is. I think that correlates to how charged it is, in which case —"

"It might even be dangerous," she finished for him. "To *us*, I mean."

"Nonsense. What could happen?"

"It could blow up, that's what."

"I've never heard of globes exploding under any circumstances."

"We saw a bunch go off in Fundelry," said Sal, remembering all too well the sudden violence and the showers of glass dust that had rained down after each one. "Shilly's got a point. We could really be hurt."

"Aw, you're nothing but a pair of spoilsports." Skender flopped back onto the bed with a sulky expression. "I thought you were here to learn."

"We are," said Shilly, "but —"

"So learn! Look, extending yourself beyond the syllabus is the only way to excel, right? And don't tell me you've never taken a chance before, Shilly. You struck me as a troublemaker the moment I first saw you, for all that you're on your best behaviour now. Why the act? Who are you trying to impress? Me? I'm not my father, you know."

She pulled back from him, and Sal could tell that Skender's words had stung.

"All right, then," she said, measuring every word. "Let's try — but carefully. We stop if it looks like we don't know what we're doing."

"Okay." Skender nodded happily. "If we screw this up, anything could happen."

"Not just anything. You can be certain that I'll kill you, for starters."

Shilly made herself more comfortable on the floor, stretching her leg out to one side. The pain of her injury didn't seem to bother her as much, since their visit to see the Mage Erentaite. Sal and Skender sat down in front of her with the globe in the space between them. The last rays of the sun were draining from the sky behind her; her dark skin was dissolving into the gloom.

"Do we need light for this?" Sal asked.

"If this works, we'll have as much light as we could possibly want." Skender reached out and took his right hand. They formed a triangle on the floor of the room with the globe between them. A sense of *flow* that was difficult to pin down swept through them. Sal felt his skin tingle all over, and could see his two friends quite clearly, despite the darkness.

"So, how do we do it?" Shilly asked.

"Well..." Skender paused. "Hmm. I hadn't thought that far ahead. I know in theory —"

"So you said. You made it sound easy a minute ago."

"Well, it's not, okay? The patterns are very complicated."

"Tell us how to visualise them," said Sal. "And we'll all try at the same time."

"No, there's a better way," Shilly said. "We're linked, right? You show us through the link, just like we did playing Blind, and we'll look at it together. It can't be *that* difficult."

"Something that most mages struggle to master? Sure. Not difficult at all." Despite Skender's scepticism, Sal felt his hand tighten in readiness. "I'll show you what I know."

Through the link, a complicated image surfaced. It appeared in Sal's mind like a thought of his own, although it came with a flavour that he knew belonged to Skender. The image was difficult to fathom, consisting of an uncountable array of spheres dancing around and, sometimes, through each other. The spheres were transparent and solid, but weren't glassy. Their centres were connected by thin, black lines that whipped around like the antennae of an army of agitated ants.

Sal tried, but he couldn't follow it.

"Are you getting this, Shilly?" asked Skender. "You picture the balls, and you imagine them moving —"

"Shh," she said. Sal could feel her concentrating so much that she was reluctant to interrupt herself. "I'm thinking."

As she thought, something happened to the image. The balls began to form a pattern. It wasn't a fixed pattern, or one that repeated with any regularity, but Sal could sense that there was reason to the dance, unlike before.

Shilly sat back slightly, as though seeking a different perspective. "Does that look any better to you?"

It looked to Sal as though all the myriad winds on a gusty day had suddenly got together to form a willy-willy, sweeping across a plain. The transition felt natural, not forced. Watching it, Sal could see how she manipulated the image, applying pressure to the illusion to make the balls slow down or speed up. A nudge in one spot changed their behaviour completely; a simple push sent a new order cascading through the pattern.

"Indeed it does," said Skender. "I've never made it look so good." He sounded impressed. "That's a really high-level adjustment."

Barely had he said it when the pattern dissolved into chaos again. Shilly harumphed in annoyance.

"Where did you say you learned to do this?" she asked Skender.

"I saw the pattern in a book."

"And you just happened to remember it?"

Skender didn't answer. Shilly concentrated furiously, and the pattern reformed. Skender let it wobble for a moment before suggesting a slight adjustment based on another text he had read. Shilly applied it and the pattern stabilised immediately. They watched it dance in their mind's eye for several minutes until Shilly was certain she had it more or less under control.

"So what now?" Sal's voice squeaked again, but this time no one commented.

"I suppose we try it," said Skender.

"That *was* the whole point," Shilly commented.

"But what if someone senses us?" It was Sal's turn to be nervous. "Lodo could always tell when we'd been mucking around with the Change."

"Not here," said Skender. "This place is a Ruin. It's full of background potential. You'd have to really let something go before — well, you know what I mean. We'll be okay."

"If this thing does blow up," said Shilly, "getting caught will be the last thing on our minds."

"True." Sal nodded and tried to ease the nervousness nibbling at his gut. "Let's go, then. Slowly at first. We don't want to take it too far all at once ..."

He stiffened as the will of the others slid through him, like something slippery yet sharp crawling up the inside of each of his arms and down his backbone. A deep hum arose out of nowhere, throbbing silently in the air as though the earth itself was vibrating. Unlike the first time his talent had brought light from a stone — in a cave under another Ruin, at Shilly's instigation — he didn't feel a sudden blossoming of energy from all around him. He could feel the Change gathering within him and concentrating itself into a single point just above floor level in front of him, where the globe rested.

"That's it," breathed Shilly. "Hold the pattern and let it move, like it's alive."

The image in his mind swirled around the point between them, fiercely energetic yet focused at the same time. For every element that spun away, as though about to tear itself free, another fell back to the centre with even more momentum than before. It was almost like watching an explosion in reverse. He put every iota of his energy into encouraging the implosion to collapse, figuring that that was what it needed.

Just when he thought something was about to give, the pattern deflated and the feeling of gathering energies ebbed. He looked around, startled.

"What happened?"

"Not enough grunt," said Skender, his hand slippery with sweat. "You'll have to push harder, Sal."

"It's more than that," said Shilly. "We're not going to crack this by hammering at it. I have to help Sal push in the right spot while you help me keep my focus. We have to support each other in order to make it work."

Sal's doubts grew stronger. "Maybe it's too much."

"No," Shilly said sternly. "We can do it. We *will*. All we have to do is concentrate."

Encouraged by her determination, Sal again put every effort into their second attempt. He felt Skender's pattern swirling through their minds, and Shilly's insight into its nature guided him along. When the pattern was in place, Sal dipped deep into himself — into the reserves of the Change which he pictured as the muscles of invisible limbs, stretching back into the darkness of his imagination — and willed the pattern to change along the lines the other two provided. He felt them willing with him, guiding him in the right direction.

It happened so quickly he almost missed it. The swirling condensed into a tight, spinning lattice, then collapsed into a point at the heart of Lodo's globe. It hung there for a split second, like a spark trembling on the verge of creating flame. Sal had just enough time to wonder if anything more was going to happen when the surface of the globe began to emit a warm, golden light. It wasn't bright, at first; the light was similar to that cast by a campfire, but without the flickering. The glow revealed Shilly and Skender's faces in the darkened room, gazing in wonderment at the globe, and Sal had no doubt his face showed the same expression.

The light grew brighter and whiter. Sal distinctly saw Shilly's pupils contract. There was no heat or sound, but he began to feel an energy rushing through the air, as though something new was building up momentum. Staring at the globe left a purple afterimage on his retina. Soon he could barely look at it, and it was getting brighter. There was still no sound, but he felt as though they were sitting at the centre of a gathering storm.

Then something else happened. The light changed texture, became more fluid and more penetrating at the same time. He felt as though the light was cutting through him, stripping away his flesh to reveal the bones beneath. With a shock he realised that he actually *could* see the bones of his friends sitting beside him, as though their flesh had turned to glass. Their faces seemed to melt away and he saw their eye sockets, cheekbones and jaws standing out. He was reminded of the skulls he had seen in the Ruin the very first time he had consciously used his talent — and of the story of the baker, of the world's bones and death.

"Do you see it?" he asked.

"It's beautiful!" said Shilly. Her hand gripped his tightly.

"How do we turn it off?"

"Turn it off?" Skender's skeletal face turned to confront him. His bony fingers clutched Sal's. "Why would you want to do that?"

Shilly's hair had melted back to a bleached skull white. She was gazing around her rapturously. Clearly neither of them could see what he saw.

"Why waste it?" he said anxiously. Their bones themselves were beginning to look faint. He didn't want to know what happened when they vanished completely. "We don't want to drain it, do we?"

"Good point," Skender conceded. "Okay. We turn it off by reversing the pattern."

"Like this?" An image from Shilly cut through the increasing disorientation of the glare.

"No. It won't just turn off on its own if we stop pushing it. You have to turn it around and put it into reverse."

Shilly struggled with the new pattern while Sal tried to maintain his composure. It was hard for Shilly to visualise while the light of a small sun was blasting between them. Twice she came close, and Sal felt a drain on him as Skender tested the pattern to see if it would work, but both times it fell apart and reverted to the original form. As his friends melted away, Sal tried to concentrate. Even when he closed his eyes, the ghostly images cast by the light were still visible. He could feel the light blossoming around him, as though he was a skull lying in the desert, experiencing a thousand years of bleaching sunlight in less than a minute. He was being burned away to dust, blasted into a stream of particles too small to see . . .

"That's it!" Skender's voice brought him back to reality. The boy's expression was invisible, just bones, but Sal heard the grimace of effort in his voice. "Got it, Sal? Push now, while Shilly has it."

Sal clutched at every shred of his willpower and focused on the pattern, guided by his two friends. The invisible muscles of the Change flexed, then flexed again. The bright point at the heart of the globe resisted. He gritted his teeth and tried again.

It was like willing the sun to set. He pushed a third time, but still nothing happened. He felt as though something was sucking him dry, taking all the strength he had before he could use it. But what would do that? It couldn't be the globe itself; Lodo wouldn't have given him something dangerous. It had to be something outside — or some*one*.

Then the resistance unwound and instantly the pressure eased. At the same time, the globe responded to the pattern that Skender and Shilly had given him to impose upon it. A shadow passed over him as the spinning image assumed a new pattern. The glare flickered and began to die. Immense relief rushed through him. He must've just managed to get it right, when he really needed to.

He dared to open his eyes and he saw the light fading, retreating back into the globe like water down a drain, returning to normal as it did so. The faces of his friends returned.

Blinding afterimages danced across his vision for a disconcertingly long time. When they were gone, the globe was back to its initial, warm-yellow state, and all three of them were staring at it. Shilly's expression was one of shock.

Sal flexed one more time, and the globe went out. He felt drained, weak. There was a moment's silence during which their hands stayed linked. As his eyes adjusted to the darkness,

Sal could see stars shining through the window. A cold, refreshing wind played across his sweat-drenched skin. He felt like the baker in Belilanca Brokate's story, freshly back from the land of the dead. Exactly what had just happened, he wasn't sure. Maybe he had imagined the light boiling through flesh. Maybe he had imagined, too, the sense of being drained, or hollowed out from the inside.

Worried that he had over-exerted himself, he said nothing. He didn't want them thinking that he was weak. As no harm had been done, there seemed no point alarming them.

Shilly was the first to move. Her hand slid damply from Sal's. He heard her get up and reach for her crutches.

"Well," said Skender, likewise letting go. "That was interesting."

Light of a gentler kind entered the room. Shilly had brought a glow stone from the corridor and put it on the end of her bed. By its light, her eyes were glowing.

Sal's gaze strayed to the open window.

"Do you think —" He swallowed back a squeak. "Do you think anyone saw it?"

Skender followed his gaze, then shook his head. "Maybe," he said, without his usual flippancy. "I can't hear anything, so even if they did it hasn't caused any alarm. We aren't the only ones likely to experiment around here. You get used to odd things going bang in the middle of the night."

A sense of accomplishment rose in Sal and drowned out the fear that they might get into trouble, or that he had pushed himself too hard. They had done what they set out to do. They had brought the light-sink to life. That was something to be proud of, he told himself, even if it hadn't given him exactly what he had expected.

"We did it," he said.

"We did, indeed," said Skender, staring at him.

"I wonder what else we can do? With your knowledge, Shilly's understanding, my —"

"We can sleep," said Shilly. She seemed very tall as she stood over them, her shadow cast onto the ceiling by the gentle light of the glow stone below her. Her expression was unreadable. "It's late and I'm tired. It's all very well for you, Skender. You've got years on us. And you, Sal: you come with talent to spare. But me, the only advantage I've got is the ability to work hard, and I'll bet we won't be allowed to work as a team when it comes to exams. So if you don't mind . . ."

She turned away to tug back the covers of her bed, and Skender pulled a mock-terrified face.

"Okay, Shilly," he said. "I understand." He climbed to his feet. "Goodnight, squeaker. See you in the morning."

"'Ni — oh, hell. Goodnight."

"Goodnight to you too, Shilly."

"Take this with you." She handed him the glow stone, and he took it out into the hallway with surprising obedience.

They got ready for bed by starlight. Shilly said nothing, and seemed to fall asleep straight away. Sal lay awake, looking out at the stars. The feeling of the globe coming to life stayed with him, tingling in his bones. He felt as though he had exercised vigorously: completely exhausted yet strangely invigorated at the same time. He wondered how Shilly could sleep if she felt anything remotely the same. She was wrong about herself, he knew that much. She could do more than just work hard. She understood Blind better than either of them. She instantly grasped things that even Skender failed to understand. He suspected that her comprehension of the deeper workings of the Change was greater than his would ever be. The Mage Erentaite had said that he and Shilly complemented each other almost perfectly, and that simply wouldn't be true if she had nothing to offer.

His invisible muscles twitched, like wings waiting to unfurl and propel him upward, into a waiting sky.

When he finally fell asleep, it was to the sound of soft crying from the bed next to his, but he was too deep in his own imagination to hear.

CHAPTER 11

DEAD WOOD

Life in the terraced cliff-city had changed little for generations, judging by the paths worn in stone steps. The cycle of cold nights and burning days seemed unchanging, too, and Shilly imagined that students had been going through the same motions as she for hundreds of years, constantly putting on and taking off layers of clothes, depending on the time of day. The extremes of temperature were taking their toll on the old stone walls, however. She could see where brickwork had been repaired or the cliff itself had collapsed. One whole wing of the city had been swept clean away in an avalanche two hundred years earlier, Raf told her, and she believed him. But for the students whose duty it was to maintain the ancient structure, it might have fallen completely away long ago.

She was beginning to feel that way herself, after just one week. Stretched in one direction, pressured in another — her first few days in the Keep had almost been enough to make her snap, after everything that had brought her there. The security she had hoped for was painfully absent, leaving her feeling over-extended, dangerously off-balance.

She refused to let it get to her. Instead of snapping, she devoted herself to her studies with a determination so great that she almost managed to convince herself that she was enjoying them. And in truth the lessons on theory *were* fascinating. They took everything she had learned from Lodo and raised it to new levels. Almost immediately she began to understand just how much more there was to learn. She was a child who had been locked in a cupboard all her life, able to see the outside only through a keyhole. A key had been inserted into that lock, blocking her sight for a moment; then the key had turned, the door had opened, and now she had the entire world before her, vast and mysterious.

The trouble was, she couldn't explore it on her own. Because she had no innate talent, she was forced to rely on others just as she relied on the crutches to walk. Nothing brought that fact home harder than the practical lessons, where they learned the basics of lifting, forming, binding, shaping. While the others did what came naturally, she could only watch and imagine what it was like. If she did have the opportunity to try for herself, using the talent of one of the other students, she was conscious of the fact that she was holding someone else back by doing so. What she took, they missed. And she had already taken enough from Sal. After the night experimenting with the light-sink, guilt nagged at her every time he offered.

The suspicion that, given talent or an unlimited source, she could be better than any of them, made her fate harder to accept. Her skill at drawing, which Lodo had fostered and Wyath had encouraged, served her in very good stead, assisting her when it came to visualising and experimenting with known patterns. Raf noticed her ability almost immediately, and even Mage Van Haasteren commented on it. If just half his students had half her intelligence, he said privately after one lesson, the Keep would have the highest graduation rate of any school in the Interior. She became more angry about it the more she thought about it. The talented ones like Sal had it so *easy*. They didn't appreciate how lucky they were.

Worst of all was the fact that they had an expression for people like her. She overheard it a couple of times, when they thought she wasn't listening. They called people without the Change *dead wood*. They spoke about *dead wood* in derogatory tones and laughed at the things *dead wood* couldn't do. Shilly was *dead wood*. She knew it, and they certainly knew it, and it didn't seem to matter that she was in the Keep, anyway, determined to prove them all wrong. The reminders of what she was were constant.

She *was* in the Keep, yes. There were mountains visible from her window and there was snow on them. She was being taught the Change; she had made it to the end of her journey. But it wasn't anything like she had expected. She was being taught the things she longed to learn, but everything else was wrong. The Mage Van Haasteren was hardly to be seen around the Keep. Senior students took all their lessons, and they thought she was *dead wood*. They knew as little about Lodo's past as she did.

Only the Mage Erentaite's words, whispered to her at the end of her healing session with the old woman, kept her going.

"Endure." The old woman's depthless sight had filled the world. "Be the stone wall that stands against the storm. Be strong and resilient. You will find your place."

She tried to be the wall the elderly mage wanted her to be, to remember that she was supposedly part of a one-of-a-kind pairing. It was hard when the storm came from inside her —

when the feelings that threatened to snap her in two wouldn't let her rest, even at night. Resenting Sal for having the Change solved nothing, she told herself, and wanting to hurt him solved even less. It shouldn't matter that he was fitting so effortlessly into the place she so desperately wanted to be hers, or that he had lied to her about Behenna and kept the light-sink to himself. That was old news. She shouldn't let it get to her.

But it did. It left her feeling isolated from him, and ignored by him, her supposed partner in whatever it was that made everyone think that she and Sal were special. And she was frightened by the ease with which she *could* hurt him, if she wanted to. It was clear he hadn't noticed what she had done during the light-sink experiment — or *almost* done, she told herself. It hadn't even felt like her doing it, more as if she had been outside her body watching someone else. Sal probably thought it was nothing more than the effort of making the globe shine, and it would be better if he continued to think that, she decided. She hadn't *quite* snapped, after all. It would never happen again. No one needed to know.

The night before the Mage Erentaite was due to return, she was sitting in her usual spot on the balcony with a blanket draped over her shoulders, reading as the sun set. There were books on hundreds of subjects in the Keep's library. As well as learning about the Change, she was attempting to fill in some of the blanks she had uncovered on arriving in Ulum. She read about vast paper mills, tanneries and iron refineries; a complicated bureaucracy consisting of clerks trained to expedite the many tasks required to keep the giant cities working; an equally complicated system of checks and balances designed to ensure the cities traded as equals, with communication between them encouraged by messengers and Stone Mages. The decisions of the Synod filtered down through Interior society in much the same way those of the Sky Wardens' Conclave spread from the Haunted City. When the Synod gathered at the Nine Stars every month, it did so both to provide broad guidelines and to judge specific cases in which an injustice might have occurred.

The Nine Stars hadn't appeared on the maps Sal's father had kept in the buggy. When she finally found out where it was, she hadn't believed it at first. The northern edge of most of the maps of the Interior ended at the Long Sleep Plains from where, Brokate had explained, much of the country's grain and stock came. Beyond that, she learned, lay an unnamed desert. In the very heart of that desert was the Nine Stars. What sort of place it was, the map didn't reveal, but the fact that the nearest town was easily five hundred kilometres away was remarkable enough. Only one road led from Ulum to the place where every major decision affecting the country was made.

It was a strange arrangement, Shilly thought, but no less strange than the many other things she had to assimilate before she would ever feel comfortable here. She was still having trouble with the food. They put spices in everything.

Sal was out cleaning with Bethe when Skender turned up early for his evening tutoring session. A *psst* from the empty void behind her made her jump.

She turned. "Don't *do* that!" The boy had scaled the cliff face to reach them, and become stuck again.

"Give me a hand," he said, reaching up for her. "I'm not sure I'm ever going to crack this. Maybe that's why Dad put you here."

She begrudgingly helped him over the edge and waited while he dusted himself off. "You're looking for Sal, I presume."

He looked once around the room, saw that Sal was absent, then flopped down on a bed.

"Mind if I wait?" he asked.

"What if I do? You're here now." She sat down in her chair and put the blanket back over her shoulder. Her knee ached in the cold evening air, but the rest of her enjoyed the rising chill.

Skender rolled restlessly onto his side. She thought for a moment about asking Skender why his father hadn't liked Lodo. Old family gossip would probably fascinate him as much as the everyday type, she was sure. But he beat her to it.

"Can I ask you something?" he said.

"If you have to."

"Why don't you like me?"

The similarity to her own question stopped her in her tracks, for a moment, and she had to think carefully about what to say. *It's not you*, perhaps; *it's what you have. It's what you stand for, which I can never be part of. It's for being everything that I want to be, and not realising how damned* lucky *you are* ...

"I'm tired," she eventually said. "Let's not get into this."

"No, Shilly. I want to know." His eyes glinted. "I know I'm just a kid, and I'm enough like you to be annoying, but there's more to it than just getting on your nerves. What have I done or said to put you off?"

As much as she hated the implication that they were in any way similar, she admired his directness. She doubted she could have been so forthright.

"I'm just jealous," she said. "That's all."

"Really?"

"Honest."

He nodded. "I get that, you know. People think: Oh, he's the son of the great Mage Van Haasteren; he must have it easy. Look at how much further ahead he is than us. Look at all the exciting things he gets to do that we haven't learned yet. It must be easy when the person doing the grading is your father." He shook his head. "Is that what you're thinking?"

"No," she said, and meant it. "If anything, I imagine it's harder having your father here, with all that history behind you. All those expectations."

"Exactly." He looked somewhat relieved. "I can't help being good at learning things, and neither could Dad. It's a family trait, you see. We have the Change, yes, but not buckets of it. If we did, we'd be out in the real world, doing real things with the other Stone Mages. All we're good for is to ask how things should be done." He hesitated for a second, then went on. "Do you see what I'm saying? Knowing things is different to *doing* things. That's the main reason why I've never mucked around with light-sinks before. Even if I could get my head around the pattern like you did, I don't have the knack to make it work. I could only do it with Sal or someone like him behind me."

"Are you trying to make me feel *sorry* for you?"

She didn't intend the question to come out with so much emotion behind it, but he winced. "No."

"What, then?"

"Maybe I was just trying to make conversation." He sat up straighter, abandoning all pretence of being comfortable. "Look, do you want to know my deep, dark secret — the reason why I find it so easy to learn things?"

"Not really."

"I'm going to tell you anyway. It's all to do with memory. I don't forget anything. That's what I inherited from my father, and he from his. That's what makes my family such good teachers. Show us a textbook once and we have it for life, in our heads. Demonstrate a pattern, and we can reproduce it in an instant, any time. Even if we don't understand it, we can trot it out on demand. And we never forget our students' names. Perfect, eh?"

It was her turn to feel besieged by the outpouring of emotion. "What's all this got to do with me?"

"Jealousy, of course," he said. "I'm going to be a teacher one day, like my father, since I'm no good for anything else. I'm trapped here forever, condemned to reciting things I don't really comprehend. But *you* — you've been to places I've never heard of. You've seen the sea; you've seen the Divide; you've seen the Broken Lands; you've seen the city in the salt lake, one of the three great cities mentioned in the Book of Towers! You've seen more in a month than I ever dreamed of seeing in a lifetime. If I could trade places with you, I'd do it right now. I just wanted you to know that."

For a moment they stared at each other. All trace of his usual levity was gone. He didn't look like a kid any more. He just looked lonely — as lonely as she had been in Fundelry, perhaps. Behind all the cheerful banter, Skender was as insecure as anyone.

She remembered his comment that it would be good to have them around, and her scepticism at hearing it. It wasn't really their age he had been talking about, she realised, but the fact that they were outsiders, too. She had gravitated to Sal for the same reason in Fundelry.

And look where that got me, she thought. The insight into Skender's motivations didn't ease her own uncertainties at all. The fact that her resentment had been so obvious appalled her. She had to keep a tighter lid on her emotions; that was becoming *very* clear. What else had he seen?

"Is that why you came here early?" she asked. "To tell me all this?"

A smile crept slowly over his features. "Partly. I knew it'd feel good to get it off my chest."

"Well, thanks, I think."

"My pleasure. I'd appreciate it if you didn't tell anyone else about it. Not even Sal. I think I've got him fooled, for the time being."

She nodded, hoping that was the end of it.

It wasn't. He leaned forward conspiratorially.

"I felt what you did the other night, when we mucked around with the light-sink."

The night air was warm compared to the chill that spread through her. "You felt —?"

"You were Taking," he said. "That's what we call it when you use someone else's talent without their knowledge. You were Taking from Sal, and you were Taking hard. Did you see how he looked afterwards? He was as pale as a sheet. You can hurt someone doing that, you know." He leaned back. "It's okay," he said. "My lips are sealed. I just wanted you to know that I knew."

"No, it's *not* okay," she said, feeling tears well up in her eyes, completely beyond her control. Her secret was out! "I wanted to do more than just watch him make the light-sink work. I wanted to do it myself. He lets me use him and I guess I took that for granted. Then I didn't want to give it back. I wanted to take all of what he had and make it mine!"

The feelings were painfully clear in her mind, even though she had felt strangely removed from them at the time and had been avoiding them ever since. She had wanted nothing more than to prove her mastery over the globe — to prove that she was as worthy of it as Sal. The only trouble was, she had almost had to drain him dry to do it.

"I nearly ruined everything," she sobbed, "because I was jealous and wanted what he has."

"It was a mistake —"

"It was a *terrible* mistake!"

"But don't be too hard on yourself. Really." He didn't make any move to comfort her beyond a softening of his voice. "I told you we have a lot in common."

She swallowed back the tears with an effort and wiped her eyes on her sleeve. This wasn't like her, she told herself furiously; this wasn't what the Mage Erentaite wanted her to be. "You're jealous of him?"

"Of course." Skender's gaze met hers. "Who wouldn't be? He makes it all look easy — even though I'm sure that, for him, it isn't really."

The sound of footsteps came echoing up the corridor outside, growing rapidly nearer, and Skender leaned close again. "We all make mistakes," he whispered. "That's the other thing learning is all about. No one will know about yours, I swear. Unless," he added, "it happens again."

"It won't," she swore, as much to herself as to him. *I'll never use Sal's talent again, even if he asks me to. It's too dangerous for both of us.*

Then Sal was in the doorway, breathing heavily. "Sorry I'm late," he said. "Bethe needed a hand carrying some boxes down to one of the cellars."

Skender was instantly back to his old self, bouncing up on the bed. "Oh, Bethe needed a hand, did she? Far be it from me to come between you and your lady love."

Sal flushed. "Hey —"

"Don't pay him any attention," said Shilly. "He's just trying to get on your nerves."

"And succeeding, I hope." Skender dragged a pile of looseleaf paper out from under the bed. "Let's get revising. You've got a big day tomorrow."

Shilly forced herself to concentrate on the book on her lap, although her thoughts were in a tangle. *Yes*, she thought, *we do have a big day tomorrow*. The biggest in her life, perhaps, if she didn't blow it. Maybe she already had. She found herself believing Skender when he said that he wouldn't tell anyone about what she'd done to Sal. *Almost* done. They knew each other's secrets now, and she could trust him with hers so long as she kept her feelings in check in future. Which she would. She had come close to ruining her chances forever, but she had backed away from the precipice and now, she told herself, everything would be simple.

It had to be. That was the thought turning through her mind constantly throughout the night. It had to be, because there was nothing else for her, anywhere.

The roster that morning called for illusions with Raf. The redhead's interest lay in extravagant uses of the Change, including doppelgangers and *grande mirages* as well as illusions, the principles of which Shilly already knew. Breakfast came and went with no sign of the mage. Shilly nonetheless hoped to hear that, instead of illusions, the time had arrived for them to meet the Mage Erentaite for the second time.

But Raf walked into the room when the bell rang and proceeded to take the lesson, joining Skender in his usual game of provocation and response. Shilly had found such games irritating at first, wishing Skender's father would give him more attention so those around him could be spared his attempts to get it from them. She felt a little more sympathy for him now, though, and did her best to see through it to the lesson taking place around them.

But illusions weren't sufficient to keep her mind off the Mage Erentaite and the robes of the school. Although Raf had a lot of finesse when it came to his craft — summoning lifelike images of animals and plants, even making the walls of the tutoring room dissolve so it seemed as though they were standing on the summit of the mountain behind them — illusion-making was something she was good at and she soon found herself bored.

She wished he could show her how to make the images real, or how to create images of people. Instead, time dragged painfully.

The moment she had been dreading all night came during group demonstrations. Their task was to summon a simple, lifelike flower from the empty air, something Shilly would have found incredibly easy had she had a drop of talent. Sal offered her a hand to lend her some of his, and she pulled away, remembering her promise of the previous night, never to Take from him again.

"No, really," he said. "Go on. I don't mind."

She wouldn't. She *couldn't*. But she couldn't tell him why, either. All was awkward between them until Skender offered her some of his instead, along with a look of understanding and approval as she gratefully took his arm.

"The girl has taste," he joked, but Sal's quick laugh didn't hide a brief flash of hurt.

The bells for lunchtime sounded, and still there was no word. Disastrous scenarios formed in her mind: their progress had been so poor that the Mage Van Haasteren had contacted the Mage Erentaite to inform her that she shouldn't bother to make the journey; the elderly mage had died, which Shilly presumed happened to all Stone Mages at some point, no matter how powerful; a war had broken out, requiring a gathering of the Synod to which the mage belonged, placing all other concerns on hold; Skender had revealed her secret even though he said he wouldn't. If any of the above were true, Shilly dreaded to think what would happen to *dead wood* like her. Sal had fitted in so well, and he had talent to spare. But not her; she would just get in the way. They would kick her out of the school, and she would be lost far from home with no one to turn to. Then she would have to follow Wyath's suggestion and turn to painting to keep her alive. She had no other skills.

Her mood was at its darkest during afternoon visualisations. All attempts to concentrate failed her. Patterns she had mastered years ago fragmented in her mind like glass. What had gone wrong? What was she going to do?

The appearance of the Mage Van Haasteren in the doorway prompted a bolt of simultaneous hope and dread through her body.

"Sal and Shilly," he said, ignoring the other heads that turned to look at him. "I need to talk to you in private."

He looked very serious. Her muscles felt like water as they stood and left the room. Shilly didn't ask any questions for fear of hearing bad news. She wondered how he would tell them if they *had* been rejected. A startling rush of annoyance went through her. Why couldn't the mage be more like Lodo, she wondered, who had always, despite his moods and long silences, made it clear that he cared?

The mage led them to the same room in which they had met the Mage Erentaite before. This time, though, the room was empty, and there were just three chairs at the table.

"Sit." They did so, side by side but not touching. The mage took the seat facing them and rested his red-robed elbows on the table. "As you know," he began, "I was hoping to formally induct you into the Keep, today, with the blessing of the Mage Erentaite. That can't happen, I'm afraid. There has been a change of plans."

Shilly waited breathlessly to hear that all her dreams had been for nothing.

"I have been instructed to take you to Ulum instead," said the mage. "You will meet Jarmila there, instead of here, and assume your robes then."

She almost melted down the chair and onto the floor.

"You're not sending us back?" said Sal with a squawk.

"No. It's my decision, based on the potential you show and the work you've put in this week, that you should both stay here at the Keep until your training is complete. Unless you choose to leave —?"

"No way," said Shilly quickly.

"I didn't think so." He smiled fleetingly. "The robing ceremony is just a formality, really, albeit an important one. I know Jarmila approves of you too, so only the full Synod could override our decision now. It's up to us, and we have made our decision. Welcome to the Keep."

Her relief was profound. After all the uncertainty of the previous week, at least she could be sure of one thing: she had made it. They had been accepted! A smile came to her face and she didn't think it would ever come off. Not even the trip to Ulum could tarnish it. She was keen to get the ceremony over with and return to her studies. Everything was going to work out just fine.

But the mage's smile had been brief and barely hid an underlying concern. Shilly's joy faded. She sensed that not everything else was going to go according to plan either.

"There is one other thing, another reason why we must go to Ulum," the mage said. "Your grandmother, Sal, wishes to meet you immediately."

Sal's face went a greyish colour. "She is? I mean, she does? How ...?"

"You asked me to contact your family on your behalf. I tried to do so, but my message to Mount Birrinah went unheard. They were elsewhere, or so I was told by a very unhelpful secretary. I was just beginning to search more thoroughly for them when word reached me that they were in Ulum. Business must have called them there about the time you arrived, and my message therefore passed them in transit. I approached them through different channels, this time with success. Once I explained who you are, they were very keen. Your mother, Seirian, was a favourite of your grandmother, I'm told. They had their differences, but she has been sorely missed. Your grandmother will be very glad to see you, if you are prepared to meet her in Ulum."

There was a strange cast to Van Haasteren's expression that Shilly couldn't interpret. It was similar to the one on Ori's face when the topic of the Mierlos had come up over dinner at Wyath's. Distaste, perhaps, or dislike; or even distrust.

"Why don't they come here?" she asked. Sal's family were irrelevant to her; she had forgotten they even existed. The possibility that he might leave the Keep — leave *her* — to join them returned with surprising force.

"They wouldn't be allowed," the mage explained. "The guardians are very specific about who they let into the Keep. As Sal's grandmother is neither student nor teacher..." He trailed off into a shrug.

When Sal spoke, his voice was deeper than Shilly had ever heard it, and almost frighteningly adult.

"What is my grandmother's name?"

"Radi. Radi Mierlo."

"And she said she wants to meet me?"

"Yes."

"Who else is with her?"

"I'm not sure exactly. If the Mierlo family travels as a strict family unit, like a lot of families do, that unit could consist of anything. One or more of your uncles and aunts, perhaps; there might be cousins. Customs have undergone many changes down the years, and I am removed from such things here." The mage looked around the room, seeming as baffled by the details as Shilly was. "I understand that your grandmother will be putting us up tonight, though. The business that brought them to Ulum must have seen them well, since they are offering to treat all of us, not just Sal."

Shilly leaned forward. "We're *all* staying with them?"

"Yes."

"So I'll meet them, too?"

"Yes, Shilly. My letter included a brief description of you both, and you have been included in their return invitation. I will be there, of course. You may not have your robes just yet, but you are still my responsibility. Jarmila would never forgive me if something were to happen to you."

"When are we leaving?" asked Sal. Shilly couldn't tell if he was looking forward to it or afraid.

"In two hours. We'll stay the night and meet Jarmila in the morning."

"Is two hours long enough to get past the guardians and through the Way?"

"That's not the route we're taking, this time." The mage's smile returned, albeit briefly. "I should also explain that I am taking a basic staff with me, along with Skender. He will be too much for Bethe to handle on her own, I fear, and he does need to be set free of the cage every once in a while. He takes after his mother in that respect." His smile slipped a notch, but he continued without taking a breath. "I have also arranged a change of attire for you, to see you through until you receive your robes. I could hardly have you meeting your family in your travel clothes, could I?"

Not *my* family, Shilly wanted to say. But she kept quiet for Sal's sake. He was having enough trouble absorbing the news without her making it any more difficult.

"Do you have any questions?" asked the mage.

"Only one," she said. "When are we coming back?"

"Tomorrow. Unless Radi Mierlo makes Sal a better offer, we'll all be home in time for the evening meal."

The mage took them to their room and instructed them to pack. Their new clothes were laid out on their beds, ready for them to wear. Sal hurried off for a quick shower, and Shilly struggled into her clean leggings and overdress without anyone's help. When she thought of Ulum, only Wyath's elegant apartment, among the ceiling lights, inspired her to return. She would have been annoyed to go to the underground city for any reason, but having to meet Sal's family made it doubly worse. His great-aunt, the Syndic, had been nothing but unpleasant.

Unless Radi Mierlo makes Sal a better offer . . .

When Sal returned, the floodgates opened. "I wonder what they're doing in Ulum?" he asked her the moment he walked in the door, as though continuing a conversation she didn't remember beginning. "Maybe they're traders and they've come to sell their goods at the market. Or they're artists, or weather-workers, or . . ." His vocal chords emitted a strangled noise, but he didn't seem to notice. "I can't believe it. They want to meet me. They're waiting for me now. Shilly, do you think they're as bad as everyone says?"

"Maybe they're mercenaries," she said. "Swords for hire."

"Do you think so?"

"I have no idea, Sal. Why don't you wait until you meet them so you can ask for yourself?"

"It doesn't seem real. I'm meeting my mother's family!"

Shilly didn't need to respond to his outpouring of words and Sal didn't seem to notice that she was doing little more than nodding after a while. By the time he was dressed and waiting for someone to come take them away, he had run out of momentum and fallen silent, staring at the view through the open window. She didn't think he was actually seeing it, and his words confirmed that.

"This is as close as I'm ever going to get to meeting my mother."

"At least you're that close," she said.

He looked at her, then, and his focus returned from the unseeable. "I'm sorry, Shilly. I forget sometimes —"

"It's okay," she said. "Most of the time I don't think of them either." But that wasn't true. Whenever someone mentioned their parents or siblings, her own family came to mind, the people who had abandoned her as a child because of her shortlived flashes of talent. It was strange, she thought, that these people could have any impact on her at all, since in the realest possible sense Lodo had been all the family she'd ever needed. Perhaps part of her still remembered them and missed them, even if she wasn't conscious of it. She remembered their *absence*.

Or perhaps people just responded to the *idea* of family, even if they had never met them — or didn't need one. That would explain Sal's feverish excitement at meeting his own when, really, he had everything he could ever want right where he was.

She couldn't share in his excitement. She was curious, but that was all. The news that they were going to Ulum to meet the Mierlos had taken all the shine off her relief on being accepted into the Keep and the other reasons for the trip. Now she was feeling as anxious as she had been before, only it was about something completely different. She had made her decision and now had to simply deal with the consequences. Sal, on the other hand, had yet to make his. Since crossing the Divide he had been coasting along with her; it had been easy to assume that he would always do so. The time had come for him — and her — to face the fact that he had at least one other option.

Finally Raf appeared in the doorway. "We're off," he said. "Sorry to hold you up. Skender's so excited he completely forgot to pack. Are you ready?"

Shilly let him take her bag. It was much lighter than usual, containing only what she thought she might need for an overnight stay. She hadn't had much to start with, having left Fundelry with little more than what she was wearing at the time. Sal carried his, and she could tell from the way he lifted it that he had brought everything. She could understand that, even if it stung a little. There was always a chance that he might not come back.

Perhaps it wouldn't be a bad thing, then, she thought, if his grandmother turned out to be no different to the Syndic.

Raf took them to meet the Mage Van Haasteren, not down at the bridge where they had arrived, but at the highest point of the cliff face town. There, at the top of a long series of stairways — difficult to negotiate with her crutches — and on a shelf of rock wide enough to create the impression that there wasn't a yawning gulf below, were two statues facing each other, similar in appearance to the guardians below but smaller and less weathered. Between them was an iron door, shut, with a keyhole in its exact centre. Waiting with the mage were Skender, Chema and another student called Amahl. Thin with a yellowish complexion, he was only a couple of years older than Shilly, and looked more nervous than Sal. Skender was uncharacteristically restrained, as though saving his energy for the outside world.

"Good," said the mage, studying them all sternly. "We're all here. We'll leave in a moment. I'm sure I don't need to remind you that, even though we're no longer at the Keep, the normal rules still apply. You will be sure to represent me in a suitable fashion, no matter where we go. I have high expectations of you all only because I know that you are capable of meeting those expectations. That is why I have chosen you to come with me." He directed proportionately more of his warning at Skender, who nodded quite seriously.

"I think," Raf said, "that I speak for us all when I say that I won't let you down. I want to go next time, after all." He shot Skender a quick wink. "We'll be good, I promise."

Satisfied, the mage turned to the doors. Walking forward between the statues, both of which bowed slightly in acknowledgement, he produced a key. It fitted into the keyhole and turned smoothly. A mechanism clunked deep inside the door and the mage pushed it open, revealing a ramp sloping upward into the cliff. Then he reached up and touched a brass switch on the ceiling, awakening a series of glow stones to guide their way.

The statues didn't move as the students filed through behind him, one after the other, but Shilly could tell that she was being studied very closely. She assumed they would remember when she returned, with or without Sal. That she *would* return, she had no doubt, if the mage would have her.

Then she was through and standing with the others on the far side. Raf came last. The mage closed and locked the door behind him, then led the way up the slope. It was steep but flattened out after a hundred metres and widened into a large chamber with pillars supporting a high, vaulted ceiling. The stonework was elegant and very old, a faint tracery all that remained of what might once have been elegant frescoes on every surface. The walls were arched, and each archway led to another tunnel identical to the one through which they had entered.

Looking around, Shilly quickly became disoriented. The archway to the Keep was the third from the right on the wall behind her — or was it the wall to her left? She couldn't be sure. The glow stones in the tunnel had died, and the walls looked the same on every side.

The mage unhesitatingly led the students across the room, through the forest of pillars, and to an archway on the far side. There he reached up again and brought another line of glow stones to life. This tunnel led downward at as steep a pitch as they had gone up before and became wide, shallow stairs at about the same time as it began to turn in a lazy spiral. Shilly tried to count how many times the passageway completed an entire circle. It might have been four when the way — or *Way* — ended in another door.

The mage produced another key, opened the door, and waved them through.

The smell of humanity and its refuse hit her first. The stench was undiminished since she had last experienced it, thick and cloying after the thin, clear air of the mountains. Sound came next. People were all around her — walking, talking, shouting, running, hammering — and their animals were with them. She could distinguish chickens, camels and desert dogs easily, with hints of emu and alpaca. It sounded like they were in the middle of a vast animal pen.

The second-hand daylight was dim and gloomy. She didn't realise how quickly she had become used to the serene clarity of the Keep until dunked back into the mess of humanity that was Ulum. The realisation surprised her. She longed to be back on her balcony, reading by natural sunlight again. The sooner they left, the better.

The doorway had opened in a cul de sac lined with blank walls and sheltered from view by an overhang above. A narrow metal gate sealed the cul de sac from the street outside. When they were through that last doorway, they stood in a group together on the sidewalk and waited to be told where to go next.

It was hotter than she remembered. Her new clothes were stiff and heavy against her skin, and she longed for a refreshing breeze, or just a moment to sit down. But the mage was relentless. He led them along the street to the nearest corner, looked around to get his bearings, then nodded.

"Right on time," he said as two four-seater cabs pulled up in front of them. Raf, Chema and Amahl took one; the mage travelled with the three younger members of the party in the other. He exchanged a few words with the driver that Shilly didn't quite catch, then they were off through the busy streets, ducking and weaving among numerous other vehicles and bicycles mainly travelling in the opposite direction.

Skender barely took his eyes off the scenery as they passed. There were shops, multi-storey residences, animal pens, administrative buildings, food and water stores, entertainment halls ... He soaked it up with rapt interest. Black-uniformed police officers, looking very much like officers of the Syndic, coordinated the traffic flow with whistles and emphatic hand signals, intervening to restore order after occasional, inevitable altercations.

It was too much for Shilly. She stared upward at the roof of the cab and wondered what time it was in the outside world. She had completely lost track during the brief journey. It was inconceivable that they had travelled so far during their walk along the Way, but instead of letting it get to her, she resolved to learn how it was done — if only in the hope that it would help her find a way back into Lodo's workshop. All she had to do was get through *this* day, and the next morning, and her position at the Keep would be permanent. The rest was up to her.

Endure, the Mage Erentaite had said. *You will find your place ...*

She clung to the elderly woman's words as tightly as she clung to the edge of her seat while the cab negotiated its way through the city.

After what felt like a small eternity, they pulled up outside a large, stone building in a relatively sedate suburb. There were miniature trees on the corner of each block and gas lamps at the entrance to each yard. The Mage Van Haasteren got out first and brushed down his robes. He looked around with a mildly suspicious air, then waved the others out. Shilly brushed away Sal and Skender's helping hands, and bit her lip when she stumbled on her injured leg. The crutches fitted into their familiar places under her armpits, where her blisters had turned to calluses, and she took a few paces to stretch her good leg.

"Is this where we're staying?" asked Raf, bringing the others up to join them.

"Apparently," said the mage.

"Very fancy. You'll have to mind your manners, Skender."

The boy rolled his eyes. The building was a giant cube, with narrow windows on three storeys. There was little ornamentation to be seen anywhere upon it, but that spareness was part of its elegance. Shilly thought it looked like the sort of house an architect would build for their own home — simple, efficient, and well made — or one owned by a very wealthy person, with no need to be ostentatious.

The mage led them along a narrow path through a gravel garden to the door. Sal's hand brushed hers, and she was reminded of the time she had taken him to the beach at Fundelry so he could see the sea for the first time in his life. He had held her hand then, and she had been glad for the comfort it had given him. Now, even if he wanted such comfort again, she couldn't have given it to him. She needed both hands just to walk — and she wasn't sure she had enough strength to spare any more.

A stone sign above the door announced that it belonged to Gourlay House. The mage knocked three times then stepped back. They heard footsteps from within, coming closer, then the lock clicked and the door swung back to reveal a woman dressed in formal attire. Her gaze swept across the small group standing at the step, and Shilly felt Sal stiffen expectantly beside her.

"Hello," said the woman in an imperious tone. "You must be Mage Van Haasteren."

"I am."

"Come in, please. All of you. I am Melantha, the steward of this house."

Some of the tension left Sal when he realised — along with Shilly — that the woman was a servant, not his grandmother. The woman held the door open until the seven of them were standing in the entrance hall. It was as spacious and austere as the outside. The walls were plastered white and the wood was dark-stained. The air smelled of roses.

The steward took a second to look them all over. "Which one of you is Sal?"

"I —" His voice broke, and Shilly felt embarrassed on his behalf. "I mean, I am."

"You're here in good time." She nodded approvingly, then turned to the others. "I have prepared a small meal for the rest of you in here." She opened a door to their right and showed them a large sitting room in which a table had been laden with food. "If you require anything, please ring the bell and I will attend you. Sal will rejoin you after dinner."

She gestured that Sal was to accompany her and he stepped forward as though pulled by strings.

"I will go with him," said the Mage Van Haasteren firmly, putting his hand on Sal's shoulder.

"And I'm coming too," said Shilly, crutching up on the other side, surprising herself in the process. "I don't want to miss this."

Sal looked gratefully at both of them. "Is that okay?" he asked the steward.

She smiled. "Of course. If you wish them there, they may come. Your grandmother anticipated as much. She is waiting for you through here."

She took them along the hallway and to a door set deeper in the house. The smell of roses grew more pronounced as they walked. Shilly was acutely conscious of the sound her crutches made every time she stepped forward, clunking ungracefully on the polished floorboards, but there was nothing she could do to silence them. With a deep breath to calm herself, she plunged after Sal through the door.

The room was as sparsely elegant as the rest of the house, lined with bookcases filled with ornaments and trophies. What little wall space remained was crammed with maps and sketches of plants. Three high-backed chairs stood in a half-circle on a thick, red rug, and in one of those chairs sat Sal's grandmother.

Radi Mierlo was a woman in her late fifties with long white hair held back by a silver clasp. She wore a graceful blue robe that matched the jewel in a ring on the third finger of her right hand. Her posture was straight and her skin pale. Like the Mage Van Haasteren, she appeared to have no tattoos that Shilly could see.

The first thing that struck her about Radi Mierlo, though, was how much she reminded her of Sal. It wasn't in her bone structure or hair, nor was it in the way she spoke. It took Shilly a while to realise that it was her eyes: they were the same blue flecked with white, like a summer sky, and possessed the same depthless quality.

A tall, thin man with long brown hair and a drooping nose stood in one corner with hands folded in front of him. He barely glanced at them as they entered the room.

Radi Mierlo stood with a rustle of silk.

"At last," she said, her voice soft and low-pitched. Her eyes scanned them, one by one, then fixed on Sal. "It is a great pleasure to meet you."

Sal opened his mouth, but nothing came out. There was an awkward silence until the Mage Van Haasteren came to his rescue

"Good evening, Mrs Mierlo," he said. "It's a pleasure to meet you in person."

"And you, Mage Van Haasteren. You are very welcome."

"Your generosity in putting us up tonight is exceptional. The Keep maintains accommodations for our visits to Ulum, but this is infinitely more comfortable."

She clucked her tongue. "I wouldn't dream of seeing you stay anywhere else. It would be impolite of me after the lengths you have gone to to see my family reunited."

"I did only what Sal requested."

Radi Mierlo took a step closer and studied Sal with an appraising eye. "Yes," she said, "you *are* my daughter's son. You could only have our blood flowing through your veins. Even if I had any doubts, this would convince me." She reached out to touch the ward in his ear. "It used to belong to your mother, you know. Sahen, her father, made it for her when she was half your age. She inherited his natural talent, although it bloomed late. He loved her very much."

Sal nodded but still hadn't found his voice. His grandmother smiled, and turned her charm on Shilly.

"You must be Shilly, Sal's friend." The force of Radi Mierlo's stare was more powerful than Shilly had expected — even more disconcerting than the elaborate pleasantries. She was also the source of the rose scent; it poured off her in waves. "I'm pleased to meet you, too. You will always be welcome in my house."

"Th-thanks," Shilly stammered, not knowing what else to say in response.

"It's the least I can do, dear." Sal's grandmother turned in a graceful manoeuvre to cross the room. "When I heard you were here, I could barely contain my excitement. I would have come to the Keep immediately, if I'd been allowed to. I'm so happy to meet you, and so proud of everything you've done. You are remarkable young people. It's a pleasure to make your acquaintance."

Sal remembered how to talk at that moment.

"Thank you, um, grandmother," he said, hesitating over the title but continuing when she nodded encouragement. He sounded very young again. "I've been wanting to meet you too, since I learned about you."

"When did you learn? Did Seirian tell you about me?"

"I never knew my mother. She was taken from me when I was very young, and she died before my father and I could find her again."

"You're in touch with your father?" she asked, her tone sharpening. "Highson has never mentioned this to me."

"Not him," Sal corrected her. "I don't consider him my father."

A look of confusion passed across her face, then suddenly cleared. "Of course. No, you wouldn't. You have no reason to, as yet. You mean Dafis Hrvati, the man your mother eloped with."

"My father," he repeated.

"Yes." Her gaze didn't waver. "What happened to him?"

"He is dead." The family resemblance was stronger than ever, Shilly thought, when Sal was keeping a lid on his emotions. She wondered if Radi Mierlo was hiding something too, and if so what it was.

Sal's grandmother was the first to look away. She turned gracefully and indicated the man standing in the corner, who had yet to utter a sound.

"Forgive my rudeness," she said. "I haven't completed my introductions. This is Manton Gourlay, our host for the evening. He is the sole surviving heir of the great explorer, Jack Gourlay. This lovely abode belongs to him. He allows me to use it when business brings me to town. Come forward and say hello, Manton."

The slender giant stepped out of the corner and offered a very large hand to the mage. Then he bowed briefly to Sal and Shilly. "Welcome to my house," he said in a voice soft and tremulous. Shilly had never heard of any "great explorer" called Jack Gourlay, but understood now the significance of the trinkets and the maps on the walls.

"Manton lives here alone," Sal's grandmother said, reaching up to adjust their host's lapel as one would for a child. "He enjoys the company. Don't you, my dear? He would be offended if we stayed elsewhere, and accepting the gift honours the giver, as they say."

Manton Gourlay nodded patiently, apparently deaf to the patronising tone that put Shilly's teeth on edge. Shilly wondered if he had missed out on some of the traits that had made his ancestor great. Or maybe he just liked being told what to do when he was off duty. She had seen couples like that in Fundelry — fishermen who could haul a shark onto a boat with their bare hands but barely spoke up at home.

"Nobody is so generous as those with nothing to give," said the Mage Van Haasteren.

Radi Mierlo chuckled. "Indeed. But I am a great believer in generosity. Generosity and family. There is no bond greater than blood, and no gift greater than forgiveness. Do you understand what I'm trying to say, Sal?" Her full attention was back on him, and her voice had a subtly commanding edge that Shilly suspected could turn to steel if required. "No matter what your mother did — no matter how much she damaged her family's ascendance and hurt me — I would forgive her now, if she were here before me. As she is not, and I will never have the opportunity to welcome her back into our family, I can only welcome you, instead, and say that you will always be forgiven, no matter what you do. The Mierlos are your blood, and we are yours. No person can change that. It is written in the stone that is the symbol of our Clan. The Earth itself is witness to the bond between us — a bond that I have no desire to break, now that it has been acknowledged. Now that I have seen you with my own eyes." A smile softened her features, and her eyes gleamed as though filled with tears. "My daughter's son. My grandson."

"Do you —" Sal's voice broke again. He shook his head in annoyance. "Do you have other grandchildren?"

"Why, yes, of course. Your mother had a sister and a brother, both older than her. They have two and three children respectively. You will meet your cousins in due course. No doubt you wish to learn more about the rest of your family. I have pictures of your mother at home in Mount Birrinah, when she was young. Your resemblance to her is very strong. Would you like to see them?"

"Yes, very much." He glanced up at mage beside him. "Would I be allowed to?"

"We are open to familial visits," said the mage, "although not usually so soon in training. The children are to be given their robes tomorrow," he explained to Radi Mierlo. "They have their studies waiting for them back at the Keep."

"Of course, Mage Van Haasteren," she said. "I understand your concern and I am sure something can be arranged. I feel that a child learns best in the company of those who love and nurture him, and will do all in my power to ensure that nothing comes between them and him."

The mage smiled in response, but it was thin, with a tension Shilly could only guess at. Didn't the mage *want* Sal to go? The thought suddenly struck her that they might expect her to go with him to Mount Birrinah, and she almost groaned aloud.

"But I am remiss," said Sal's grandmother, as though sensing Shilly's restlessness. "You must be hungry. Melantha, is everything ready for dinner?"

"All is as you requested." The steward bowed and left the room.

"Excellent. We will retire in a moment to eat. I have requested that we six sit apart from the others so we can talk in private. I hope that will be in order, Mage Van Haasteren?"

"Whatever suits Sal, Mrs Mierlo. As his temporary guardian and teacher I give him permission to choose in this instance."

"Indeed. Well, Sal. Would you like to eat with me?"

"Yes," he said.

"Very good." She smiled broadly and put her hands on his shoulders. Sal stared up at her as though hypnotised. Shilly had never seen him like this.

"You said six," she blurted out.

"What's that?" Radi Mierlo's pale blue eyes turned on her.

"You said there could be six of us for dinner. I count only five."

"Ah, yes." She addressed Sal again, her voice solemn. "We have another guest for dinner this evening, my grandson. He's been looking forward to meeting you very much, I know. He has come a long way to talk to you about your future."

"What *about* his future?" asked the Mage Van Haasteren.

"About whether Sal should return home," said a voice from the doorway behind them, "to the place where he was born."

Hardly believing her ears, Shilly turned at the same time as Sal to see a man they'd assumed they'd left far behind them.

"Where he belongs," said the Sky Warden, Shom Behenna.

PART THREE

JUDGING

CHAPTER 12

LUST FOR POWER

For a moment, Sal was unable to move. All he could do was stare at the Sky Warden — at the man who had somehow managed to follow them all the way from the Strand into the heart of the Interior — with a feeling like a cold knife point running down his spine. The only outward sign that Behenna was enjoying his surprise was a faint smile playing across his lips.

"No," Sal said. "It's not possible. You can't be here."

"Oh, it is, and I am. It's nice to see you again." Sal sensed gloating behind the pleasant facade. "And you too, Shilly. How's your leg feeling now? Tait has been hoping we'd catch up with you."

She just gaped at him. Sal couldn't blame her.

The Sky Warden folded his hands in front of his blue robe as he waited for them to say something. His skin was darker than anyone else's in the room, even Shilly's. Tiny whorls and details in the delicately fashioned crystal torc fastened around his neck caught the light and reflected rainbow flashes. His deep blue robes seemed undamaged by the journey. Maybe he had a spare set, Sal thought feverishly, trying to accept the revelation.

He hadn't felt the Warden *tap-tapping* once! How had he *known* ...?

"How —?" he began, but stopped when his voice dropped down into its new, deeper register. "No," he said again. "I don't care how you got here. I'm not going to eat with you, and I'm not going back to the Strand. I'm here now, and I'm going to stay here."

"At least hear the alternative, Sal."

"There's no point. I'm not going back."

"You're just going to throw away everything you've ever known? All those places and people? Your home?"

"The only home I ever had was with my father on the road, and you took that away from me."

"Not I, Sal. I have never harmed you. In fact, I've helped you. Doesn't that count for something?"

Sal felt an anger rise in him from a place so deep he had never suspected its existence. "Don't play with me," he said, barely able to keep his voice level. "I'm not stupid. The Syndic and her schemes killed my father, and you're on her side. I'm not going to talk to you, let alone go back to *her*."

A sensation like wind rushed through the room. Sal felt it all over his skin, as though he had been wrapped in a miniature hurricane. Small inhalations from Shilly and the mage at his side told him that they had also felt it. Behenna took a step back. But it wasn't a wind that anyone else could hear. It was the Change, gathering like clouds before a storm. Sal wasn't aware of where it came from until the Mage Van Haasteren stepped between him and the Sky Warden and raised a hand in command.

"Enough!" he said in a commanding tone Sal had not heard before. "Stop it, Sal. Do not do this. You don't have to listen to him. You've done enough. Leave it there."

Sal was confused for a moment. The wind strengthened. Shilly edged away from him, looking frightened. Behenna's eyes widened in alarm — and only then did the mage's words sink in. The wind was coming from *Sal*. The Change was swirling around him in readiness to attack almost without his conscious control. He could feel its eagerness and its strength coursing through his body. It was all he could do to hold it back.

"I will not go home, and you can't make me." He forced himself to speak calmly, despite the rage still coursing inside him. He urged the Change to recede, and it did ebb slightly, reluctantly. "Tell the Syndic to leave me alone."

"Your grandmother — along with your great-aunt — would gladly release you into the world, Sal, if the decision was yours." Behenna's posture lost some of its tension as the threat of attack eased. His face assumed an expression of wary nonchalance. "But you're a minor. You're not old enough to do whatever you want. You can't possibly expect your families to be so uncaring."

"They don't know me, so how can they care about me?"

"But we do, Sal," said Radi Mierlo from behind him. "Give me a chance to prove that, and we can deal with the Syndic as one. We will be stronger working together than you would be on your own."

Sal turned to face her, but felt uncomfortable with Behenna behind him. He walked backward until he could see both of them, even though it meant going deeper into the room, away from Shilly and the mage. "You said we should listen to him."

"I did, yes." She came across the room until she was standing right in front of him again, near enough to touch. This time she didn't touch him, but her eyes never left his. "You should at least do that much. His case is convincing. I would be keen to hear why you are so opposed to it. After all, you do have family there."

"I have family here, too," he said.

"Yes. But we have lived in the Strand before. I would accompany you back to make certain of your safety. There would be nothing to fear, Sal. I would let nothing happen to you, I promise."

Van Haasteren laughed humourlessly. "Now I know your game, Radi Mierlo."

Sal's grandmother's gaze whipped across the room. "Do you, mage?"

"A child could see through it. You are as transparent as you are ambitious, and care no more about Sal than those who killed his father."

"And what about you?" she snapped back. "You who put yourself so easily in Payat Misseri's shoes. Do you, too, want to tutor a wild talent? Is that how you hope to earn your place? To succeed where he failed?"

The mage went a shade whiter. "I have earned the right to teach anyone who comes to the Keep. Payat has no bearing on what is best for Sal —"

"And neither do you," said Behenna, stepping forward. "Sal *is* a minor, and he's also a citizen of the Strand. Our law applies. He must be returned to his family there."

"But he's not in the Strand any more. How can your law apply here?"

"That's a very good point," the warden admitted, although his expression lost none of its triumph. "That is why we have petitioned the Synod to hear our case. The decision will be taken out of all our hands and placed in theirs. *They* will decide what happens to Sal — not you or me, or Radi. When the law of *your* land determines what is best, you will have to accede to it, will you not?"

The Mage Van Haasteren looked from Behenna to Radi Mierlo, then back to Sal. He was trapped. Sal glanced at Shilly, but her eyes, wide with surprise, were fixed on the Sky Warden. His grandmother waited to see what the mage would say, while Manton Gourlay, the descendant of the great explorer, stood as patiently as a statue in his corner.

Sal was frozen in the moment and wished he hadn't reined in the Change. It would have felt good to vindicate the alarm in the warden's eyes. Everything would have unravelled if he had set the Change free. All of the Syndic's schemes to get him back would have come to nothing without Behenna in the Interior. And the warden, so far away from the sea, would have been unable to resist.

But Sal knew it would have been wrong. It would make him no better than the Syndic herself. When he had struck out at her and the Alcaide before, the feeling of it had been uncontrolled and dangerous, just as it had felt when Behenna had confronted him. Van Haasteren had said that people with the wild talent could tear themselves apart using it, and he could see why. It was an enticing thought, but it could ultimately lead to disaster.

And besides, the Alcaide's retaliation to his attack in Fundelry had killed his father. He didn't want another backlash to hurt someone else he cared about. It might have been Shilly, this time. She had suffered enough because of him.

Blind force would solve nothing. He needed to be clever.

The mage's jaw worked, then he said, "I will accede to the decision of the Synod, as is my duty."

"Good," said Behenna. "They meet at the next full moon, in six days. That gives us just enough time to travel to the Nine

Stars to present our cases. You may travel with us, if you like, for safety of numbers."

"I can make my own arrangements."

"I'm sure you can." The warden waved the matter away as though unimportant. "We can discuss the details over dinner. I don't know about you, but I'm starving."

"Yes," said Radi Mierlo, adopting the role of perfect hostess as smoothly as though it was a mask. "Our meal is waiting. Melantha." The steward appeared instantly in the doorway. "Be so kind as to show our guests to the dining room."

Sal stood his ground as his grandmother tried to sweep him with her to the door.

"I told you," Sal said, looking at Behenna and wishing he could erase the smug expression from his face. The Sky Warden thought he had already won. "I'm not going to eat with him."

"Don't be ridiculous, my dear," she said. "You must let bygones be bygones, if only long enough to fill your stomach."

"You can't force me to," he said, "and if you try, I'll know you don't have my best interests at heart."

An identical flash of anger, brief but potent, passed over the faces of the warden and his grandmother. "Oh, very well," she said. "If you insist. Manton, you lead the way while Melantha takes Sal to the boys' quarters. If he doesn't want dinner, we won't force him to eat."

The owner of the house stirred and walked through the door, waving for people to follow. They did so awkwardly, in embarrassed silence. The mage cast him a warning look, but followed the others. Sal wanted to shout to Shilly for help, to ask her if she thought he was wrong, but Behenna swept her off with him and he remembered the way she had pulled away from him during their last lesson in the Keep. Was that how it was to go? She didn't need him any more, so she threw him to the dogs?

No, he thought. *She wouldn't do that.* But he was still alone in the room with his grandmother and the steward, when he most needed help.

Radi Mierlo leaned close. "I'm giving you this time to think, Sayed Graaff," she said, using the surname his real father, Highson Sparre, and his mother had chosen after their marriage. His hackles rose on hearing it. "What you do now will decide the course of not just your life but the lives of all those around you. The selfish path may be the easiest for you, but that doesn't make it right. Remember that, and think hard."

The selfish path? he wanted to say. *Travelling for thousands of kilometres with nothing certain waiting at the end of it — that's supposed to be easy? Giving up at any point in the journey would have been far simpler. It would also have been wrong.*

It was still wrong. He could feel it, deep inside him, just as the surname "Graaff" felt wrong. His parents had chosen that name to commemorate their union, and that union had turned out to be hollow. He was Sayed Hrvati, the son of the man he had always believed to be his father. That's how he thought of himself, and that's what the golem had called him among the towers.

And then there was the Syndic. No matter what anyone said, his great-aunt didn't mean him well. She had imprisoned his mother so that she died of a broken heart. Why would Radi Mierlo even *consider* dealing with the woman who had done that to her daughter?

But he said nothing. His grandmother studied him closely for a long minute before releasing him from her gaze. The silk of her robes sighed as she left the room, then the steward's hand was on his shoulder and he let himself be guided away.

The dormitory to which he and the other young men in the party had been assigned was on the top floor at the front of the building. It was a long room with a sloping ceiling containing three double bunks and lit by a single gas lamp on the interior wall. There was one small window; through it came the sounds of traffic and a slight breeze. He examined it, looking for a way to get out, but it was barred. Below, there was only a steep drop to the ground.

The room was empty and unwelcoming. Although the steward didn't lock the door behind him, he was under no illusions that he was not a prisoner. He would never get down the stairs and out the front door without being seen. All he could do was wait to see what happened to him next. Choosing the bed furthest from the door, he sat down and did just that.

Time passed slowly. His stomach rumbled, as much from nerves as from lack of food. He tried not to think about the scene in the sitting room but he was unable to let it go. So much had happened in the last hour that defied explanation. How had Behenna beaten him to his grandmother? Why was she listening to the warden? Why would she want to go back to the Strand? Was everything she had said to him about family and forgiveness the truth?

He dug into his pack until he found the clasp that had once belonged to his mother. Silver, with threads woven into a hemispherical design that Lodo had said represented the Earth, it was tarnished black in places, but structurally whole, clearly very fine work to have survived ten years at the bottom of his father's pack. He held it tightly in both hands and wondered what his parents would have done in his shoes. Would they have stood up to Radi Mierlo? They must have done, he supposed, when they declared their love for each other, in defiance of her marriage to Highson Sparre. Their union had been forbidden, Lodo had said, because it would have hindered the Mierlos' rise through the Strand's social ranks. Was that, then, what this was all about? Social standing?

His head hurt and his eyes ached with the effort of not crying. He was determined to deal with this in an adult way, in a way his parents would have been proud of. But his thoughts were confused. He kept coming back to seeing Behenna in the doorway and feeling the world fall out from underneath him.

And there was something else nagging at him: a memory of a dream … he had seen his grandmother's face before. In the cell at Fundelry, he had dreamed of three women. One was Shilly; the Syndic had been another. The third was his grandmother, Radi Mierlo. He had not known what she looked like then, but her identity was obvious now that he did know. The thought that all three of them might turn out to mean him ill rose up inside him, but he thrust it down as hard as he could. Surely not Shilly, after all they had been through together.

On leaving Fundelry, his grandmother had appeared in another dream, the one in which he had seen Shom Behenna and Tait. She had been talking to a statue — a man'kin, he assumed — although that particular dream image had yet to be realised.

So much of that dream had already come true: the Sky Warden following him; the globe Lodo had given him burning brightly in the darkness (although he sensed that this image was in a different darkness, a different time to the Keep); the city half-buried in the sand, inhabited by ghosts; Lodo, crippled and hollow, maybe a golem; his grandmother, crouching jealously, waiting to pounce. There were other images: Kemp and a golden tower; a tunnel leading down into the ground with corpses swinging on either side; the man'kin. He didn't know when or if they would ever come to pass. Among them, nothing suggested a happy ending to his situation.

The door clicked open, and he sat bolt upright. So lost in his thoughts had he been that he hadn't worked out what to say if his grandmother tried to convince him to talk to Behenna again.

It was the mage. Van Haasteren shut the door carefully behind him and came to where Sal sat on the bed.

"I'm sorry, Sal," the mage said, his usually looming presence seeming diminished, his face even longer than usual. He sat down next to Sal and reached into his robes. His hand emerged containing food wrapped in a serviette. Giving it to Sal, he said again, "I'm sorry. I swear I had no knowledge of this. Neither does Jarmila, I'm sure, although she will hear about it soon if the Synod is involved."

Sal knew that he was telling the truth. Officious and distant the Mage Van Haasteren might be, but he didn't seem the deceitful type. Sal accepted the offer of food gratefully, and picked at it while they talked.

"You're probably wondering why I don't just take you away from here," the mage said. "The truth is, I'm not strong enough to show any sign of weakness. Running will make us look guilty, and the last thing we should do is give Behenna any advantages. Especially if he's bluffing."

"Do you think he might be?"

"Not really. But if he is, we'll be able to find out more quickly from here than at the Keep."

Sal nodded, although his mind ached from trying to follow the web of double-crosses around him.

"If he's not bluffing," he asked, "will we really have to go to the Synod? Is it really up to them to send me back?"

"We do, I'm afraid, and it is. We'll still be seeing Jarmila tomorrow, as planned, but I suspect it will be to confirm what lies ahead. When the Synod convenes at the Nine Stars, we will have to be there or our side won't be heard."

"Can we get there in time?" Sal had seen maps of the Interior. The place where the Synod convened was in the middle of a desert a great distance away. Six days didn't seem a very long time in which to make such a journey.

"We can," said the mage, "with the right sort of transport. By tradition, there are no Ways connecting any of the Interior cities to the Nine Stars, so we must travel by road — and as much as I hate to admit it, Behenna does make sense when he suggests we travel together. Two small caravans are no match for one large one on this sort of journey. We might have to combine our resources to make the most of them."

"But —"

"I know what you're about to say. There's no reason to worry. You'll be safe. He may be as cunning as a snake, but he's toothless. Don't forget that. He's thousands of kilometres away from the sea, and that's where his power comes from. He won't be able to hurt you."

That hasn't stopped him from trying so far, Sal wanted to say, but he knew that would sound petulant. "Will that really stop him?" he asked instead, wanting reassurance on this score. "I mean, *I* can use the Change both here and in the Strand, so why can't he?"

"Your abilities are part of what it means to be a wild talent, Sal. You tap into what you find around you, regardless of its source, but the results of your efforts are blunt, unfocused. Everyone who learns to use the Change properly learns to refine not just the end results but also the places they originally come from. It's like making a diamond, or manufacturing a blade: if you don't start out with the very best source materials, the product will be flawed. And they are not interchangeable. If you made a blade out of diamond, it would shatter, and steel has none of the properties that make diamonds precious.

"Sky Wardens are born exposed to the natural ambience of the Strand, which contains a mixture of background potential that is biased in the direction of wind and water. So they develop naturally to use that ambience. Training emphasises it. Ultimately, that is all they know. And it is the same with Stone Mages: we grow surrounded by, and are trained in, the ways of fire and earth. It becomes more than just our relative strengths. It becomes what we are."

"Doesn't the Change all come from the same place?" Sal asked.

"Ultimately, perhaps, but that is like saying that all life on the Earth comes from the Sun. It may be true, but it doesn't mean that we can eat sunlight. We eat plants that convert the sun's rays into fruit, or we eat animals that eat the plants. We are not equipped to tap directly into the Change. It is not natural."

"But what's to stop someone from trying? The background potential is all around us, no matter where we're from. If they really needed to —"

"No Stone Mage or Sky Warden would do it, Sal, because it would destroy them." The Stone Mage's voice was firm. "As I said, our different uses of the Change are more than just matters of convenience; they *define* us. Stone Mages and Sky Wardens use different tools to manipulate the Change, and these tools change us in the process. The calluses on a mechanic's hand are different to those of a musician, for instance, because the two crafts are fundamentally different. Likewise, were we to break the patterns of a lifetime, it would destroy the foundations of our training. The reflexes we spent our lives developing would be undermined and we wouldn't have new ones to take their place. We could take nothing for granted any more: the source of our power and the ways we manipulate it are so delicately balanced that the slightest shift can render our efforts worthless. Even the way we fit into society would be ruined, for such a thing is impossible to hide. It would be like changing our skin colour or sex as opposed to simply taking a new nationality or name. For both Stone Mages and Sky Wardens, there is no other way than the ones we have learned."

Sal absorbed this. If it was true, then he was as safe from Behenna as he was from any other person. But there was one obvious exception — apart from him — to the rule Van Haasteren was trying to hammer home.

"What about Lodo?" Sal said.

The mage's face instantly clouded. "What about him?"

"He was born in the Strand but he trained as a Stone Mage."

"That's true. Some people are like that. That's why we Test all applicants, to see if they are developing askew and need to be relocated."

"But then he left to come back to the Strand, to the beach. He said..." Sal thought back to remember the old man's precise words. *The Change doesn't sit well with most people*, he had said, *because they think it's for big things. It's a powerful gift and a terrible responsibility, and big things don't mix well with little people.* "'I prefer the small magic,'" Sal repeated aloud, "'the magic of the everyday, and I came to Fundelry because the beach has its own magic, a magic that is neither water nor earth, neither fire nor air, but a mixture of them all. Here, on the edge of one world, I have found a bridge between two.'"

"He said that?" the mage asked, his expression darker than the shadows around them.

"Yes. Maybe he found another way."

"Well, he was wrong, Sal. There *is* no other way."

Sal was nervous about speaking for a long moment. The mage's mood was almost frightening. He didn't want to exacerbate it by saying the wrong thing.

It didn't last, though. The mage took in a deep breath and slowly let it go.

"You know," he said, "my father would have chosen him over me — to run the Keep, I mean. That's why he gave Lodo the Scourge. Did he ever tell you that?"

Sal shook his head, surprised. "No, he didn't. He told me your father had had high hopes for him, but that he had let him down, turned his back on him and everything he stood for. I wondered what he meant by that." Sal understood, now, what his grandmother had meant when she had accused the mage of putting himself in Lodo's shoes: she thought he was trying to prove himself by succeeding where the old man, his father's favourite, had failed. And he understood why the absence of the Scourge bothered the mage so much. As a means of Testing students, it would have been a fundamental symbol of the school. Losing it would have both undermined the Keep's reputation and created the opportunity for someone else to start a new one in competition.

"We were friends once," the mage said. "He told me his heart-name."

The sadness in the man's eyes made Sal feel uncomfortable. "He said your father knew that he could never go back."

"Exactly. And that's what I'm saying about Behenna. Once you cross the line, there's no returning. You're trapped in between, belonging to neither one nor the other. There is no in between, no matter what he said. If there's one thing worse than being born a wild talent, it's making one of yourself."

"Lodo tried to fit into the Haunted City but he said that he had threatened the establishment there. I got the impression that they kicked him out on the basis of some made-up charge. I suppose that was why."

"He was accused of necromancy," said the mage. "Do you know what that is?"

"Trying to revive the dead?"

"Not only the dead, but the un-living as well. You know that you can only create illusions of animals and things, not people. People have a spark that the Change cannot reproduce. They said that Lodo tried to create such human illusions, regardless of this fact. I don't know if it's true, or, if it is, whether he succeeded. If he *had* succeeded, the illusions would have been as bad as golems, empty vessels looking for occupants, and where better to search for such occupants than the Void Beneath? They would have been abominable things to bring into the world."

Sal tried to reconcile such a practice with the old man, and found that he could not. It had to be untrue. "They lied about him, then," he said. "They lied to get rid of him."

"I suspect so," said the mage. "Here was this man who dared teach that their way was not omnipotent, that it could be undermined. The fact that it worked for him didn't matter; he was a threat to them. Similarly, the fact that it worked *only* for him didn't matter to Payat; he refused to acknowledge the danger that he was putting himself into. So they got rid of him, as you say. He was expelled from the city and forced to live in the wilds as little better than an outlaw. He should have known that there was no other way it could end. All that talent was wasted." The bitterness in the mage's voice surprised Sal. The mage's jealousy of his old friend was mixed up with feelings of betrayal and regret as well. "That's how it would be for Shom

Behenna if he attempted to use his powers here, Sal. Even if it worked, which it wouldn't, it would change him irrevocably, and his superiors would know when he returned. He would be marked as an outsider and outcast just like Lodo. Unlike Lodo, though, I don't think this man has enough native wisdom to survive on his own, let alone find a new meaning to his life, as you say Lodo did. He is too ambitious, too hungry for the power he knows already exists. He has too much to lose. And he has obviously found other ways to get what he wants."

Sal nodded. "My grandmother."

"It seems so. She was expelled from the Strand after the scandal your parents caused, and you are her best means of getting back. But I don't know exactly what's going through her mind. I could be misrepresenting her. She hasn't survived the last ten years by being simple-minded, after all. I fear there are so many layers to her scheming that sometimes not even she knows the full truth of what's going on."

"If only I hadn't asked you to contact her," Sal said. "If she hadn't known I was here —"

"She did know. Behenna went straight to her. He didn't know exactly where *you* were going, but he knew about your mother's family, and they are easy to track down. All he had to do was tell your grandmother the story, and between them they guessed the rest. They knew where you had crossed the Divide and where your caravan was headed. Anyone in Ulum would tell you to try the Keep, if you were looking for training, so they came to Ulum to see if they could get close. There was no business bringing them here: it was all for you. When I contacted them to see if they would like to meet you, everything fell into place for them." The mage hung his head. "Again, Sal, I'm sorry. I don't think my actions have changed events terribly much, but it has certainly made finding you easier for them.

The only good thing is that it will soon be out of all of our hands. The Synod are the ones we'll have to worry about."

The mage would have said more, but the door opened. Skender, Amahl and Raf entered the room, chatting animatedly among themselves. They stopped in the middle of the room when they saw their teacher sitting with Sal.

"I was just leaving," the mage said, squeezing Sal firmly on the shoulder and standing. "If you've finished eating, I suggest you all get some rest. I don't know what tomorrow will bring."

"Yes, Dad." Skender was more cautious than usual of his father. "Is everything all right?"

"No. Everything most certainly is not."

The mage swept out of the room and closed the door behind him. They listened to his footsteps recede down the hallway. When they were gone, Skender was instantly onto Sal.

"What's going on? What happened? What did we miss? Tell us!"

Sal considered refusing but knew he would have to endure the boy's nagging all night if he didn't. He gave them an abbreviated version of what had happened during his meeting with Radi Mierlo and Behenna. He didn't mention Shilly or what Skender's father had told him. Skender sat raptly through it, eyes wide, and seemed to pick up more than Sal had intended to say. When the story was over, Raf and Amahl expressed their indignation by promising to do anything Sal needed to help him get back at his grandmother for betraying him like that. But Skender didn't join in. He just sat on the bed with Sal for a long while.

"Maybe it's a misunderstanding," he finally said. "Behenna got to her first, so she sees his side of the story. When you talk to her again, I'm sure you'll be able to convince her that she's made a mistake, and that going back to the Strand would only make things worse."

Sal nodded, knowing that this was exactly what he wanted to hear. His grandmother wasn't selfish and manipulative; he wouldn't be forced to go somewhere he didn't want to; he could stay at the Keep with Shilly and forget all about his mother's family; Behenna would be sent home empty-handed, and that would be the end of it.

But he wasn't stupid. It would never be that easy. This wasn't a situation he could wriggle out of with a few well chosen words. In order to escape the Sky Wardens once and for all, he would have to think of another way to thwart them — something cleverer than just running away. Something he could do on his own, without anyone's help.

Without Shilly. She had turned away from him at the Keep and again when Behenna appeared. If she thought their deal was over, so be it. He had gone most of his life without friends to rely on, and he could do it again if he had to.

"Thanks, Skender," he said. "I hope you're right. But right now, all I really want to do is get some sleep."

"Of course. Tomorrow will be better. You'll see." Skender and the others turned down the lamp to let him rest. In silence, they undressed and got into their own bunks. The only sounds came from the creaking of the house around them and the faint sounds of traffic from the street outside.

The scraps of the Mage Van Haasteren's dinner in his belly did nothing to quell an ache that came from a different part of him entirely.

Alone, Sal slid under the covers and thought for his life.

CHAPTER 13

IRON AND GLASS

Shilly woke the next morning to hear her two bunkmates discussing Tait. Behenna's journeyman had joined them in the dining room after Sal had been taken away, not to eat but to ensure that the Sky Warden he served was being looked after.

"His hair, his eyes —"

"Are you kidding? I can't get past his skin. It's so black!"

"But that's the best bit. It's so soft looking. He looks like he's made of chocolate."

"Now I *know* you're kidding." The young women laughed softly. "You don't really think he's cute, do you?"

"The competition pales in comparison, Chema. Literally." That meant it was Vita talking, the local girl who had waited at the table the previous night and who had shared the room with the two visitors afterward. "He just looks so ... *different*."

"Well, there's no accounting for taste. I'll settle for picking his brains, thanks. The places he's been, the things he's seen ..."

Shilly stirred. "Don't let him fool you," she muttered, opening her eyes a crack. "He's no genius."

Vita laughed again. "I can live with that, for long enough."

"Of course," said Chema, moving onto Shilly's bed. "You come from the same place as him — that village, whatever it's called. It must be weird seeing him here."

Shilly didn't answer at first. It *was* strange, yes, to bump into someone she'd known most of her life so far away from their home, just when she'd given up all thoughts of seeing anything like home again.

But that wasn't what she was feeling. She had grown up with him around. She knew his face as well as anyone's from Fundelry. His narrow, handsome features and his dense mat of black hair; even though he had been at the Haunted City, training with the Sky Wardens for over three years, his voice was exactly the same as she remembered.

"Good weird," she said, wishing she could just go back to sleep. Whatever she felt, she wasn't interested in sharing it with perfect strangers.

"Told you," said Vita, punching her new friend lightly on the arm. "He *is* cute. If only Mr Gourlay was going with you to the Nine Stars —"

"Well, you two can fight over him until then," Chema said. "I'm not interested. There are plenty of ordinary boys like Raf around to keep me busy."

The conversation shifted to whether or not Chema's redheaded fellow student was more interested in her or Bethe, the student overseer, and Shilly let her attention wander. Judging by the pale light creeping through the dormitory's sole narrow window, the day was only just dawning on the world far above the underground city. She'd never been an early riser, and missed the days with Lodo, when she could sleep in. As long as she'd finished her chores before bed each night, the old man had let her organise her own daily schedule.

The memory of him brought tears to her eyes. She fought them down, not wanting to face the interrogation of the other girls. The memory of what the golem had told her was still too painful to talk about. That he could be adrift in some terrible Void, unable to call for help while his body lay helpless, made her angry and upset. She wished there was something she could do to find him, but she didn't even know where his body was, let alone the rest of him.

There was a knock at the door and Melantha, the steward, stuck her head through. "Vita. Help me with breakfast, please." To Chema and Shilly she added: "The mage is up and asking for you two. I think he intends leaving early."

The steward backed out and shut the door. Chema offered to help her dress, but Shilly said no. She forced herself out of bed and into her clothes. Her leg complained at being moved and the rest of her joined in. She could have stayed in that warm, soft bed all day, given the chance. Negotiating two flights of stairs with her crutches didn't make her mood any better. Only when she reached the dining room and saw the generous spread waiting for them did she begin to feel like being awake. There were bowls of eggs, porridge, crispy-fried bacon, mushrooms and fruit. Not a spice stronger than pepper to be seen. Her mouth watered at the sight and smell of it.

Chema loaded up a plate and followed the sound of voices into the next room. Shilly juggled a bowl and a serving spoon and her crutches, all at the same time, not having much success with any of them.

"Can I help you with that, Shilly?" asked a voice from behind her.

She looked up with a mixture of embarrassment and relief. It was Tait, dressed in a less elegant version of his warden's blue robes. He had no torc around his neck, just a simple necklace of glass beads. "Thanks."

He took the plate from her. "What are you after?"

"Some toast and eggs."

Tait served her what she asked for. "What about a drink while I'm here? They have freshly squeezed orange juice, or coffee."

"Just water. Thanks again."

He poured her a glass. "We didn't get a chance to talk last night," he said. "I wanted to say how good it is to see a familiar face here."

She shrugged awkwardly, afraid to admit to the same feeling. It was better to seem worldly-wise. After all, they were both well travelled now. "You were probably the last person I expected to see."

"Yes, well. Who'd have thought either of us would get this far?" His smile was warm and open. "I'm just glad you're doing okay."

"Apart from this." She swung her leg like the dead weight it was.

"You're on the mend, anyway. Come on. You look like you could eat a camel."

He indicated the door, and she crutched through it. Everyone except Sal was seated around a very long table, and her hosts welcomed her to breakfast when she appeared. Even the mage nodded politely as she took a seat on the opposite side of the table. Tait put her plate and glass in front of her, then took his own seat not far away. Vita nudged her as she went past with a load of dirty dishes, and Chema rolled her eyes.

"I was just saying," said Radi Mierlo at one end of the table, opposite Manton Gourlay, their nominal host, "that I'm looking forward to seeing the Nine Stars. It's somewhere you hear about all the time, but never visit. I don't know why the Advisory Synod conducts their meetings so far away from everywhere. They make it very hard for the ordinary person to be part of the decision-making process."

"We have elections," said Skender, through a mouthful of bacon. His hair was standing on end at the back, and his father tried in vain to pat it down.

"Yes, but to be part of the discussion, to see the faces of the Judges as they consider their decisions, to have the opportunity to speak..." Her face was alive with the thought of it, reflecting an internal vision that probably, Shilly thought, had no bearing on what the reality would be like. "That would be a supreme moment."

"It's a long and difficult journey," said the mage.

"It can't be that bad. Some of the members of the Synod are very old, and they make it there every month."

"They are there, yes, but there are ways to make the journey easier." The mage considered his words carefully. "Ways we will not have access to. We can only take the road."

"And it is a long and difficult one — yes, you said." Radi Mierlo was clearly enjoying the verbal sparring. "We'll have plenty of time to get to know each other then."

"Great," said Skender, rolling his eyes. "That should be fun."

"Who says *you're* going?" asked Raf, always ready to provoke the boy. "I've a crate for you back at the Keep, strong enough to keep you in until your dad gets back."

"I have to come!" Skender exclaimed. "Dad. You can't really be thinking of —"

"I'm not, son," said the mage. "You can come along, if you behave."

Skender whooped with joy, and Raf looked surprised and more than a little disappointed.

"Really?" he asked.

"Really," said the mage, with a resigned look. "It's time Skender saw where his future lies. And I know most of my colleagues are eager to see how the latest Van Haasteren has turned out."

Shilly concentrated on her food while talk rolled around her. She hated morning people, and Sal's grandmother was most definitely one of them, directing conversation with a firm, occasionally unsubtle, hand. Shilly wondered how Manton Gourlay put up with her, and supposed that this was one reason why people in the Interior didn't like her or her family. Luckily for Sal, he had inherited none of her arrogance. Shilly doubted she could have stood more than a day on the road with him otherwise.

"Where is Sal?" she asked, the thought of him making her wonder, and the fleeting, irritated look on his grandmother's face made speaking up worthwhile.

"Upstairs," said Shom Behenna. "He'll come down when he's ready, I'm sure."

"We're going to see the Mage Erentaite after breakfast," said Van Haasteren, "to discuss the Synod's intentions. Sal has assured me that he will attend."

"Not much point going without him," said Skender, still flushed at the thought of the journey.

"Indeed," said Shom Behenna. "Or Shilly."

"Of course. What about you, dear?" Radi Mierlo asked the question lightly while she stirred a glass of a potent-smelling hot beverage. "No one's asked you what you think about going to the Nine Stars."

Exactly, she thought. *I'm just dead wood*. But she didn't say that. "I didn't know I'd be going."

"I'm sure they'll need you to testify."

"Well, I don't really know what to expect, so I don't know how I think about it."

"What about going home, then?" There was a glint in Sal's grandmother's eye. "How would you feel about that, if you had the chance?"

Shilly felt like she'd been led into a trap. Everyone's eyes were suddenly on her as though her answer was critically important. She couldn't understand why it should be. Wasn't it obvious that she missed her home? At the same time, though, she had worked very hard to find herself a teacher of the Change, and she wouldn't throw that away in a hurry.

Besides, she thought, who said she would go with Sal, if he was sent away? It was him they wanted not her.

"I've been there, you know," said a soft voice from the far end of the table. Manton Gourlay had uttered his first words of the morning. Everyone who had previously been watching her leaned closer to hear what he had to say.

"*Where* have you been?" Radi Mierlo prompted.

"The Strand," he said. "Went there on a delegation with Mage Seto. Remember him? Complete fool, but knew how to drum up patrons when he had to."

"And what did you think?" asked Shom Behenna. "Of the Strand, I mean."

"It's a wonderful place. Well worth the effort. Wouldn't want to live there, though. Too soft. Too much water. Life's too easy. Give me sand and the sun over a sea breeze any day. And fish?" He pulled a face. "But the Haunted City is interesting. Never understood how the place managed to look so beautiful yet so ugly at the same time ..."

The memory overwhelmed him and he trailed off into silence. For a moment no one spoke. The thin, wasted man stared vacantly into space, saying nothing at all — yet still commanding more genuine interest than the woman at the opposite end of the table.

"Well," said Radi Mierlo. "Thank you, Manton, for sharing that with us. It has certainly brought back memories of my own. I must tell you about a wonderful restaurant on the Laudato Promenade, where we used to meet the Grey Wardens of the Novitiate for dinner. Do you know them, Warden Behenna? They were very influential in my time."

And she was off again, tugging the reins and cracking the whip over the conversation until she had broken its spirit. Shilly watched Manton Gourlay retreat back into his shell and felt sorry for him. She didn't doubt that Radi Mierlo was bleeding him as dry as she wanted to bleed Sal.

Her thoughts must have shown on her face, for Tait caught her eye and shrugged meaningfully. She smiled back, and he toasted her with his glass of juice.

Shilly returned her attention to her meal, hating the warm flush rising up her neck and into her cheeks. She didn't hear what Sal's grandmother had to say after that, and she didn't much care, either.

The meeting with the Mage Erentaite took place in a large, temple-like structure on the far side of the city. A motorised vehicle was waiting for them when they stepped out of the house. The driver handed the wheel to Manton Gourlay, who explained that he had bought the bus in a distant, lawless town called Mayr and occasionally enjoyed taking it for a drive. It was easily large enough for the entire party, comprising the Sky Warden and his assistant, the Stone Mage and his entourage, Shilly, and Sal, and Radi Mierlo.

Sal emerged as promised at the last minute, looking tired and small but determined, like an animal wrapped defensively around itself. He said nothing, just walked out of the door as soon as it opened and headed out to the bus. He appeared to have slept in his clothes. Although Shilly sat near him in the vehicle, he said as little to her as he did to anyone, giving nothing freely. His attention was drawn tightly inward — but at the same time he was aware of everything around him. Shilly could practically hear his mind ticking over, analysing everything, thinking every action through.

He was up to something, she thought. Once she might have tried to get him to tell her, but things had changed. There were too many people around, for one, and she had learned at the Keep just how good he was at keeping secrets from her. She was still angry that he had taken some of the credit away from Sky Warden Behenna for saving her.

"Did you sleep well, my dear?" his grandmother asked him when they were settled in their seats and Gourlay pulled smoothly away from the curb.

"I slept enough, thank you," he said, with equal measures of distance and politeness.

"I'm sorry you missed breakfast." Radi Mierlo radiated nothing but concern. "If you're hungry, we can —"

"I'm not hungry," he interrupted her, his eyes flicking for a split second to the Mage Van Haasteren, "but thank you. Again."

She pulled back with a slightly pained expression, and Shilly wondered how deep the socialite facade went and where the real woman began. Was she really hurt that Sal had rejected her, or just bothered that Sal wouldn't cooperate in her grand scheme? Shilly couldn't decide which.

She tried to catch his eye but he wouldn't look at her. Feeling hurt, she retreated into her seat and folded her arms. Had

Skender told him about the Taking? She doubted it, but could think of no other reason for him to be so cold to her. She hadn't done anything to him. It was the other way around, if anything: it was he, after all, who had considered leaving her behind while he went gallivanting after his family. It served him right, she thought, whatever happened.

The bus bounced and rattled through the streets, adding more smoke to the miasma that already filled the city. Shilly was glad when they arrived. Skender's father had described the place where the elderly mage awaited them as a communal hall for philosophers and physicians. The Grand Minster, as he called it, looked like nothing so much as a giant, up-turned flowerpot with ornamental spires added as an afterthought. Four wide archways led into the interior, a maze of halls and corridors, many of them open to the "sky" above. The air was thick with incense; brands burned at every corner, barely making up for the smoke they issued by giving a little extra light.

The Mage Erentaite rose to her feet as a hooded guide showed them into the minster's heart. She wore the same black robes as before, only this time they were trimmed in red, and her eyes were the same unbroken white. Over her patchy scalp she wore a skullcap with the same colouring that somehow managed to make her look even smaller and more frail than before. Her expression was tight-lipped and her blind eyes seemed to see everyone with perfect clarity.

She spoke without welcome or preamble.

"On behalf of the Synod, I witness the request from Sky Warden Shom Behenna to speak before the Judges of the Interior. It is his wish that two children be returned to the Strand, their place of birth, whether it is their wish to be so returned or not. Do I speak correctly?"

"What?" blurted Shilly. "*Two* —?"

An urgent hiss stopped her in mid-sentence. Radi Mierlo was glaring at her, and she fell into a shocked silence.

"Do I speak correctly?" the elderly mage repeated.

Behenna stepped forward, bowed formally, then answered in a clear voice. "Yes, Stone Mage Jarmila Erentaite. You speak correctly. I appreciate that the matter is a sensitive one. That is why I have taken it through the correct and proper channels. I pursue this request in the hope that it will be heard with all due compassion and impartiality."

The warden stepped back, and the Mage Erentaite regarded him coldly with her blind stare. "This is more than just a dispute over custody or citizenship. You realise that, don't you?"

"My only concern is for the wellbeing of the children. I trust that is your concern, too."

"I have no doubt about my concerns," she said, and for a moment her cool reserve gave way. Shilly saw impatience pass across the elderly mage's features, followed almost immediately by weariness. Then the formal mask returned. "Very well. The case will be heard. Present yourself to the appropriate place at the next full moon for the Synod to hear your petitions and for the Judges to determine which has the most merit. Any decision made at that time will be final. Do you agree to this?"

"Yes," said the warden, but the question was directed to everyone, not just him, and the Mage Erentaite required them all to answer.

"I will abide by the wisdom of the Judges," said Radi Mierlo with smug certainty.

"This is a waste of time and resources," said the Mage Van Haasteren irritably. "The children have already been accepted into the Keep —"

"But they haven't taken their robes yet," said Behenna, "so no oaths have been sworn in, or to, the Interior."

"Your opinion is noted, Mage Van Haasteren," said the Mage Erentaite, her expression clouding again. "Do you agree to abide by the Judges' decision?"

"I suppose I have no option." He didn't look happy about it, though.

"Thank you. What about you, young Skender?"

"Sure." The boy nodded vigorously. "I'll agree to anything if it means I get to go to the Nine Stars."

"And you, Shilly of Gooron?"

Shilly was brought out of her shock by the mention of her name. "Me? I didn't know I had a choice."

"We would never deprive you of the freedom to choose to speak to us," said the elderly mage.

"So they're not just going to tell us what to do without asking us first?"

"No. They will listen to anyone who agrees to abide by their judgment. *Do* you agree?"

She wanted to tell the Judges that she didn't want to go home, that the Keep might not be perfect but it was all she had.

"I have to, I guess."

The elderly mage nodded. "Sal Hrvati," she said, last of all. "Is this the name you choose — not Mierlo, Sparre or Graaff?"

Sal stood a little straighter when attention shifted to him, last of all. "Yes."

"And how do you decide?"

"First, I want to know something. Will the Judges kick us out even if we don't want to go?"

"If that is their decision, yes."

"So you want me to agree to be sent back to the Strand against my wishes."

"If it comes to that, Sal, yes, in exchange for being allowed to testify on your behalf."

Sal took a deep breath. "I will never return to the Strand except by my own free will," he said, "so I can't accept what you're asking me to do."

"Is that your answer? Think very carefully about it. Understand that by refusing to accept the Judges' decision you also rescind the right to speak in front of them."

"I understand." Sal held the steady gaze of the elderly mage without blinking once. "I do not agree to your terms."

A wave of surprise spread through the guides and attendants in the room. Shilly couldn't believe what she was hearing. Her face flushed with a mixture of anger and shame. Why was he being so stupid? Where did he find the courage to stick so stubbornly to his principles? If he was hoping to embarrass the Judges into rejecting Behenna's case, or banking on his silence to speak more loudly than words, then he was taking an awful chance. If it didn't work, he would lose his last opportunity to speak out against Behenna, to tell the Judges what had happened to him and his father, and to Lodo. The Mage Van Haasteren might know, and so might she, but it wouldn't have the same impact as it would coming from his lips.

"So be it," said the Mage Erentaite. Shilly couldn't tell what she was thinking, whether she was annoyed by Sal's reticence or hiding admiration behind her stern mask. "Your refusal is noted. You will, however, be required to attend the hearing anyway. Your presence has been requested by the Synod."

Sal nodded. Instead of looking annoyed at having to make the trip, he seemed intensely relieved that the moment of decision was over. He was committed, now, to whatever it was he had in mind to do.

"That concludes the proceedings for today," said the Mage Erentaite, sitting down. "This matter will conclude only when the Judges' decision is made. Until then, the law of the Interior will regard it as being open. No other negotiations will be honoured. I'll see you all again in five days."

She lowered her blind gaze to the table before her, and the hooded guides motioned that they should follow them out of the room. Behenna bowed and did as he was told. The elderly mage didn't acknowledge the gesture. Sal followed, propelled by his grandmother.

Shilly didn't move. *Is that it?* She wanted to shout. *We came all the way across this stinking town just for this?*

The Mage Van Haasteren came up behind Shilly and put his hand firmly on her shoulder, as though to reassure her that everything would be all right.

She was surprised by the gesture, but not half as surprised as she was when the voice of Mage Erentaite spoke directly into her head.

"*You are angry*," said the elderly mage, her mental voice soft but insistent. "*I don't blame you.*"

Shilly stifled a gasp, realising that Van Haasteren was allowing the frail-looking woman's words to flow through him to her. The corners of her eyes twinkled with the Change; it felt like tears.

"*I'm sick of all this travelling*," she said, assuming she could reply the same way. "*We only just got here. Why do we have to go all this way so soon? Why can't the Judges decide here? Why do we have to go anywhere at all?*"

"*That's not the way it's done. Not in the Interior, or in the Strand. Behenna has forced our hand. If it was up to me, I would let you rest.*" The mage's head tilted forward, as though she was about to fall asleep. "*Since what happens to you is not* up to me, all I can do is say that I'm sorry. One day, perhaps, you will be glad that this matter was resolved this way, rather than another."

"*Big deal.*" Shilly didn't know if Van Haasteren could hear or not. She hoped he could. Her sense of betrayal was very great — greater than it had been when she had found out about Sal's lies. "*I don't care about one day. I care about now. I came to you for help, and some help you've been. All you care about is Sal.*"

"*That's not true. I would do more if I could. Believe me.*" The elderly woman's voice radiated warmth and sincerity, and quite against her will, Shilly felt it melt some of her anger and frustration. "*Endure, Shilly. Don't forget that I'll be there at the Nine Stars, watching over you both.*"

That thought reassured her, even though she couldn't have said why. "*Are you coming with us?*"

"*No. I have my own means of getting there.*" Van Haasteren's grip tightened on her shoulder, and Shilly let herself be propelled toward the door. The old woman didn't move. "*Travel well. And don't be afraid to follow your heart. It's a journey we all must take, if only once in our lives.*"

On that note, the link between them was severed, and Shilly pulled herself out of Mage Van Haasteren's grasp. She didn't know what the elderly mage had meant by her closing comments, but she could feel the weariness in them, the debilitating fatigue of great age. Her anger ebbed even further.

"She's so old," she said to the mage beside her, "and it's such a long trip. Will she make it?"

The Mage Van Haasteren seemed much taller in the smoky air of the Grand Minster, and his face was even more remote than usual. "She will do whatever she can," he said, "but I share your concern. To lose her would be a terrible blow to us all."

Shilly looked up at him, annoyed that he had taken her concern a completely different way than she had intended it. She didn't care about him and the Stone Mages. All she was worried about was that a frail, well-meaning old woman wouldn't die over something so stupid as Behenna's petition to send her back to the Strand.

By the time they reached the bus, her old melancholy returned. The Mage Van Haasteren didn't care what she needed, and neither did Sal. They were just looking after themselves, like Radi Mierlo. None of them really cared what happened to her. She was just *dead wood*.

So when Tait waited until everyone else had boarded to take her crutches and help her up the steps, one hand under her arm and another at her back, she couldn't help the warm feeling in her stomach that carried her through the rest of the journey back to Gourlay house, where they immediately began to prepare for the much larger journey ahead. Familiar, good-looking Tait was nothing but friendly to her when everyone else made her feel like a burden. He didn't make demands of her, or threaten her with talent. He was pleasantly *ordinary* — the opposite of Sal in almost every way.

Perhaps, she surprised herself by deciding, she should look forward at least in part to going to the Nine Stars — and be glad that Vita, the girl in Gourlay House who had thought Tait handsome, wouldn't be coming with them.

CHAPTER 14

THE DESERT CRAFT

*T*he Mierlos are your blood, the sign read, *and we are yours.* Sal stared at the words. They were carved in letters taller than a person out of the rock wall in front of him. The line to his left said: *No person can change that.* The letters continued all around him.

Sal hunted for a way over the wall, but it was too high. There was no break anywhere along its length. He felt despair, then. They had everything covered. There was no way out.

It is written in the stone that is the symbol of our Clan.

Then he remembered the Change. Yes: he could blast his way through the wall! That was the simplest way to escape. When the wall came down, he would be free again.

So he concentrated, gathering all his potential into a ball of light that he raised in one hand and held behind his head, poised and ready to fly.

The Earth itself is witness to the bond between us.

He struck at the word *bond*. The wall exploded into dozens of large fragments. The force of the blast knocked him flat. With a noise like an avalanche, rubble poured down, burying him.

It had worked too well, he thought as everything went dark. Or else it hadn't worked at all . . .

He woke to the gentle chugging of an engine and the insistent rock-and-bounce of travel across rough terrain. For a moment he was confused, and thought he was lying in the back of the buggy with his father at the wheel, driving through the borderlands to the next town on the map. The air was warm; his nostrils were full of burnt, desert air.

But he could hear camels, too, and there were spices as well as sand on the wind. He was wearing robes rather than his usual cotton pants and top. His head rested against wood instead of metal, and there was an ache in his chest. He had lost something important. He had been dreaming about it. Or had he? That really *was* a buggy he could hear grumbling in the near distance . . .

I won't think about that, he told himself. *I* won't. *There's no point.*

He sat up with a groan and rubbed his head. His bed was on the back of a wagon comprising part of the Black Jade Caravan, led by a bald, wiry man with triangular tattoos on his lips, like teeth, who Radi Mierlo had contracted to get them all to the Nine Stars. His name was Zevan — just Zevan — and he usually spoke in a mixture of normal speech and trader tongues in bursts too fast to follow. He and his riders kept to themselves, concentrating on covering the vast distance to the Nine Stars with as little disturbance to their passengers as possible. For the most part, Sal and the rest might as well have not been there. They were just cargo.

That was fine with Sal. It gave him time to think. He reached for a water bottle and took a deep drink. Beside him, snoring gently, Skender lay in a tightly wound knot. Through the fabric wagon top, the sun was riding up the sky toward noon on the third day of their journey. The landscape around them was completely flat, all the way to the horizon on every side, and consisted of little more than rocks and red-brown dirt. The road the caravan was following cut across the stony desert in a perfectly straight line, heading northeast. They were travelling at a brisk, running pace, leaving a cloud of dust in their wake that took hours to settle.

It was hard to believe that just three days ago they had farewelled the other students of the Keep and started their long journey. It was even harder to believe that in just over another three he might be heading back to the Strand.

Not if I can help it, he thought.

He crawled forward through the wagon, to the front. There he found the Mage Van Haasteren meditating behind an open leather-bound book full of repeating geometric designs — aids for visualisation, he guessed, or new charms the mage was catching up on. The big man would have filled the small space even without the boxes of supplies and luggage stacked around him, and Sal felt nervous about disturbing him. Pushing through the forward flap, he found himself next to the driver, exposed to the sun. It was no cooler there, but at least the air was fresh.

Grabbing a hat from under the seat, he made himself as unobtrusively comfortable as possible. The sun was bright and hot, and had burned the drivers' normally pale skins to brown. The drivers of Zevan's caravan used a secret mixture of charms and tattoos to protect themselves from the ravages of the desert. Unprotected skin blistered within hours, and Sal wasn't about to test the efficacy of his mother's ward on sunburn.

Like the caravan leader, the driver of their wagon had made no moves to befriend his passengers, so Sal felt no need to try in return. He was content to sit in silence as the desert plain rolled slowly by. The sky was a powerful white-blue, unbroken anywhere by cloud.

The road didn't deviate even slightly, ahead or behind. As far as he knew, it pointed as straight as an arrow at the Nine Stars. Putting all thoughts of his destination out of his mind, he concentrated on the Cellaton Mandala, as Lodo had taught him to do, and imagined himself to be invisible. *An advanced student learns how to visualise them as spheres*, Lodo had said, *completely enclosing themselves*. Sal tried to do just that.

Time passed in an unmarked blur. The wagon rocked beneath him; the buggy chugged softly behind them. Every now and again, a camel would call out to its fellows, but apart from that the day was still and silent, as though the sun had evaporated all the life from the world. There were no engines, no caravan, no sense of Shilly aching in his chest, no . . .

"Kalish," said the driver suddenly, pointing.

Sal blinked out of his trance. "*Favi* Kalish?" he asked, thinking of the caravan leader Lutz had colluded with at the Divide. "Here?"

"No." The driver, a dirty, cotton-swaddled man with two missing teeth at the front of his mouth pointed again. "*Kalish*."

Sal followed the man's finger to where a bird wheeled in the porcelain sky, so far away it was barely a dot. In whatever dialect the driver was speaking, "kalish" obviously meant "bird." It was the only one he recalled seeing since entering the stony plains.

"I wonder what it's eating," Sal said. His voice had settled down during the days since Ulum. He liked the sound of it but was still surprised at the stranger's voice coming out of his own mouth.

"*Ouce.*" The driver, grinning, made a scampering gesture with one hand: rodents or possibly lizards. Sal repeated the word, although it was an odd time to give him a language lesson.

The driver's face sobered. "Sun," he said, pointing this time directly above them. "Takes." Then he pointed at Sal.

"The sun takes me?" Sal guessed. "Takes me where?"

The driver made a fist out of his hand, then pulled it in close to his chest.

"Oh, *takes.* It takes *from* me." That earned him a pat and a wink. "Or *of* me."

The driver returned his attention to the road, satisfied that he had delivered his message. Sal wondered how it had been intended. As a warning, perhaps — but if so, what was he supposed to do about it? Avoid the sun for fear of it stealing his talent away? He couldn't stay under cover all day. Maybe it was just at noon he had to be careful, or of meditating too long. It seemed crazy to him, either way.

But he *had* lost track of himself for a while, there. He was surprised to see just how much of the day had passed. It was now late afternoon, and his stomach rumbled to tell him that he'd missed lunchtime. Once the caravan was underway in the morning, it didn't stop until evening, but there were supplies to get them through the day in the back. He would get them later.

Chastened, he watched the bird spiralling gracefully through the air as they slowly drew abreast of it, then past it. He was wondering how it would find a place to nest — let alone a mate — when Skender stuck his head through the wagon flap.

"Here you are," said the boy, squinting blearily at the day. "Are we there yet?"

Sal didn't take the question seriously. They were making good time, as far as he could tell, having left the relatively fertile soils of the Long Sleep Plains behind them on the second day. They had almost reached the halfway point. There, at a small town called Three Wells, they would stop briefly to water the camels and re-supply, then head on into the wilderness.

And there, he reminded himself, he would have to put his plan into effect. Unless he changed his mind or thought of another solution ...

"Dreamt I was a fish and a shark ate me," the boy went on, either not noticing or not caring that Sal was more interested in thinking than talking. "Except, now that I think about it, I'm not sure what a shark actually looks like. Do they have arms?"

"I don't think so." Sal knew only a little more than Skender about the sea and the creatures that lived in it.

"Maybe it wasn't a shark, then. Anyway, whatever it was, it ate me, gulped me down whole, and I found a golem living in its stomach. It was annoyed to see me. 'I don't eat meat,' it said. It pulled a lever and the shark vomited me up. Then I was standing on a ledge in a city made entirely of brass, and I was polishing a wall with a cloth. Dad stuck his head out of a window and said —"

"To keep it down, I imagine," said the real mage Van Haasteren from inside the tent. "People are trying to concentrate."

"Only crazy people," said Skender. "We're on holidays!"

Some holiday, Sal thought. "The driver isn't," he said.

"Oh, sorry." Abashed, Skender reversed back into the wagon and disappeared. Sal followed.

Inside, it was cramped and hotter than ever. After Sal had eaten, he and Skender played Double Blind while the mage flipped through pages in the book, glancing cursorily at some, pausing for long minutes to stare at others. The time passed more slowly than it had outside, even though Sal had the game to distract him. The rocking of the wagon, the creak of the wheels and the ever-present rumble of the buggy's engine were the only reference points they had for the outside world.

Eventually a piercing whistle announced that Zevan was calling a halt. Skender broke the circle and rushed forward again to see what was going on. Sal followed at a more sedate pace and emerged to see the caravan looping around a collection of small, stone buildings, huddling for shelter in what looked like a crack in the earth. A long time ago, something had caused the otherwise perfectly flat landscape to buckle, resulting in a split that was tiny in the context of the hundreds of kilometres of emptiness around it but easily large enough to accommodate a small settlement. The disturbance must also have altered the flow of deep groundwater, for Sal could smell moisture in the air as clearly as if it had been smoke. Pockets of green plants — a welcome change after the ever-present browns and reds of the stony plain — took advantage of both the shade and the water and flourished in whatever fashion was available to them.

Clouds of dust wrapped around the caravan as it parked near the settlement. Camels snorted and, one by one, the wagons rattled to a halt. With one last grumble, the buggy also fell quiet. The ambience of the desert collapsed instantly upon them, soaking up the cries of drivers and passengers alike without echoes, brushing away the slight human intrusion with a gust of wind that might be travelling unhindered from one side of the plain to the other.

Sal hopped down to stretch his legs, and noticed the other passengers doing the same. His grandmother climbed awkwardly from a wagon not far away, helped to the ground by one of her grandchildren, a well-built, white-haired young man called Aron who, thus far, had shown little interest in the family's new addition from the south. He behaved more like an attendant than a grandson, and she showed no interest in making it otherwise.

Two Stone Mages Sal didn't know emerged from another wagon. They and a combined staff of five were travelling to the Nine Stars for the Synod and had booked Zevan's caravan through his grandmother. Sal gathered that the caravan leader made a reasonable living going backward and forward across the desert each month, being one of the few people who could endure the repetition without going slightly crazy.

Or maybe he was already crazy, Sal thought, watching the wiry man ducking and weaving between wagons, barking orders in his guttural mishmash of languages. Quite apart from the alarming, jagged tattoos on his lips, there was a whiteness to his eyes that most people didn't have.

Sal walked between the wagons, wanting a closer look at Three Wells. Skender came too, kicking up a small cloud of dust under his fast-moving feet.

"Doesn't it *ever* rain out here?"

"Rarely," said his father, moving after them both in a more dignified fashion. His reddish robes blended almost perfectly into the background. "When it does, though, it's quite spectacular. There is a pent-up energy to this land that, when released, can cause deluges. Afterward, the desert comes alive with flowers that sprout and bloom almost overnight. Everywhere you look, as far as the eye can see, is colour. They last as long as the water, then die, leaving seeds behind for the next storm to bring to life. I know it's hard to imagine on a day like this, but it does happen."

Sal kept quiet, wondering if the Stone Mage had seen it himself, or if he'd only read about it. Sal had experienced such monsoonal flourishes in the lesser deserts of the Strand — such as the storm that had swept away the road in the Broken Lands and killed the caravan leader called Diamond Fargher — but he knew nothing about the flowers. Fortunately, Skender was intrigued by the thought of so much rain in so much emptiness. It was a thought Sal wanted to pursue, later that evening.

People from the small town moved among the wagons, filling waterbags and topping up rations. Sal found his way to a better vantage point and watched unobtrusively as Zevan negotiated with someone in charge. His arms gestured violently, but the woman he was speaking to didn't flinch. One hand held a piece of paper; her index finger stabbed at something written on it for emphasis. Zevan grinned his alarming grin — with no trace of humour — then stalked away.

Sal didn't have to move to learn what was going on. Just out of sight, the caravan leader held a brief but intense conversation with Radi Mierlo. Sal would recognise her ingratiating yet rock-hard tones anywhere.

"Prices," said Zevan without preamble. "They go up."

"You said —"

"I said, they said. Things change. You want to go on?"

"Yes, of course, but —"

"Prices go up. You pay four hundred extra. No questions."

"I'll pay you when we get back."

"No good. Pay now."

"I *can't* pay you now. I don't have the money on me. Do you think I'm stupid? There are bandits on roads like this. There are people like *you*. I hired you to protect me, not rob me, remember?"

"Business, not robbery," said the caravan leader, and Sal could imagine his lips tight, his tattooed teeth grinding together. "You pay six hundred, then."

"*Six* hundred? You said four before!"

"Six hundred when we get back. Or four hundred now. Your choice"

"Thief!"

"*Pizta*! You want to walk home?"

There was a tense silence, then: "All right. Six hundred it will have to be. I simply don't have the money to pay you now. Satisfied?"

"When I see money." The caravan leader loped off to talk to the woman with the piece of paper. Sal's grandmother, meanwhile, went away to renegotiate her deals with the Stone Mages sharing the caravan with her, muttering under her breath.

Sal didn't listen for long. He had already guessed that the Mierlo family was broke and that any extra fee would be difficult for them to pay. The way his grandmother had leaned so heavily on Manton Gourlay's generosity, the subtle hints he had picked up from Wyath Gyory and his friend Ori, the determination with which his grandmother clung to her chance to return to the Strand — a place she clearly associated with golden opportunity, so briefly in her clutches and so tragically lost — all spoke volumes to Sal. He didn't need to hear her beg to know that she was desperate, even if it was buried under bargaining or outright lies.

He retreated back to the wagon he shared with Skender and Skender's father and sat on the running board, looking up at the cloudless sky, trying as always not to dwell on the things that hurt him most, but in the main, not succeeding. When the time came to move on, he was no surer about what he would do about them, but he was more certain than ever that he had to try.

Over the camels and wagons stirring reluctantly back into motion, he heard the buggy's engine turning over. Through the wheels of the wagon, before he could turn away, he caught a glimpse of the Sky Warden driving it into position at the rear of the caravan. Tait sat beside the warden in the passenger seat, facing backward to talk to Shilly, where she sat propped up on the tray as she had been on their journey together through the Broken Lands.

The problem wasn't going away, bringing tears of anger as well as sadness to his eyes. He couldn't stop thinking about it, although he tried; he was constantly confronted by reality, no matter how hard it was to believe, or to what lengths he went to avoid it.

He blinked away the tears. If he couldn't change the situation, at least he could deal with it more maturely. It made sense that Shilly ride in the buggy. There was more space and she could be more comfortable there. She didn't need him to change her dressings any more, or to help her to the toilet, or to drive her around. Once they had reached the Keep, they hadn't really needed to stick together any more, even though everyone else seemed to want them to. It was perfectly natural that she might go her own way, without him.

But — with *them*?

He wished he didn't care. But wishing didn't solve anything, he told himself. He had only himself to rely on, now, and that would have to be enough.

The mystery of how Behenna had overtaken them in the Interior — not just beating them to Ulum, but going beyond the underground city to Mount Birrinah, where the Mierlo family lived — had been solved on the first day of their trip to the Nine Stars.

Behenna had the buggy. Not just any buggy, but the very same Comet copy his father had once owned, and which he and Shilly had driven from Fundelry to the Divide. When Belilanca Brokate had sold it on the far side of the Divide, neither she nor

Sal had suspected that Behenna might see it for sale upon crossing himself, two days later, and recognise it for what it was. He had immediately bought it with Sky Warden funds — the irony not lost on him — and used it to set off after Sal, travelling more quickly than any caravan could manage.

Luckily for Sal, the warden had assumed he would be heading for his mother's family in Mount Birrinah, and had overshot Ulum completely. But he had soon turned the disadvantage around. It was Behenna who had brought Sal's grandmother to the underground city in order to press for the Keep to let them in. And now he added it to the caravan as his own personal means of transport.

No doubt he had enjoyed the look on Sal's face when the buggy had appeared. It had seemed a miracle at first, until the truth had been revealed. Behenna had the keys. The symbol of Sal's freedom now belonged to the Sky Wardens.

It didn't change anything, though — or so Sal tried to tell himself. He had sold it to Brokate, who had sold it in turn. If a complete stranger had owned it, it would have bothered him less. The best thing to do was to pretend it was a different buggy entirely. If that felt like pretending to be a completely different person, then maybe he should do that too. He had to get used to disappointment, especially if his plan failed and he ended up being returned to the Strand.

The caravan rode for another hour, then stopped just before sunset at a stone cairn where, judging by the wide space worn into the desert plain around it, caravans had stopped for generations. Zevan didn't waste any time setting up provisions for the evening meal; barely had the fattening moon risen over the eastern horizon than dinner was over, the dishes were being cleaned, and all there was left to do was settle in for the night. Like most deserts, it was going to be cold.

Although the landscape hadn't changed at any point in the previous two days, it was easy enough to encourage Skender to set off on an expedition of discovery. You never knew what might lie hidden among the boulders and the dust, Sal told him: coins dropped by other caravans, fragments of pottery, old charms ...

When they were out of earshot of the camp, but still within easy sight of the campfire, Sal felt safe to begin probing.

"Do you think people might have lived here, once?"

"Not likely. There's nothing to eat but dirt."

"Maybe it hasn't always been like this. What if the weather changed one year and the rain stopped coming? Things like that happened elsewhere, you know. Crops failed; rivers dried up; settlements were abandoned. If it was long enough ago, there might not even be ruins left."

"We could be standing on one of them," said Skender, his eyes wide in the moonlight.

"There might have been forests from horizon to horizon right here, and we'd never know."

"There would be stories about that, if a forest suddenly vanished."

"Maybe there *were* stories, but it happened so long ago that people don't tell them any more. It's all forgotten. Dried up like the land."

"Why didn't they use weather-workers?" Skender asked. "Rain doesn't just stop overnight."

"Could they summon enough to live on?"

"I don't know. It depends on how much rain there is floating around up there." Skender pointed vaguely up at the sky, then added: "Whatever. You can't get blood from a stone."

Or flowers from a desert, Sal thought to himself. But he remembered what Skender's father had said about the stony plain being a deluge waiting to happen. All the weather needed was a nudge in the right direction.

"Do you know how to summon rain?" he asked as innocently as he could.

"Probably. I've seen the pages in Dad's books. The patterns are reasonably simple. You just need a bit of grunt behind you to make it work, as always."

"My dad bought a jar of pearl shell and blood mix from a vendor in the Strand." The vendor had been Lodo, but Sal didn't feel it was necessary to explain that. "That's supposed to be good for getting rain, isn't it?"

"Pastes and ointments are generally applied to the place you want a charm to take effect, then activated by the Change. I don't know how that would work with weather." The boy looked at Sal through narrowed eyes. "If you're about to suggest we extend the syllabus again, I'm definitely interested."

"I don't know." Sal feigned uncertainty. "I'm just curious. If the people who lived here couldn't do it, I doubt we could."

"That's if there *were* ever any people here. Maybe no one's tried before. Do you want to or not?"

"I suppose we can muck around. See what happens." He thought of what Skender's father had said. "It'd be nice to see the flowers, if it worked."

"We should get Shilly in on it too," Skender said. "She's great with patterns. Remember how well the trick with the light-sink worked?"

"I remember."

"I'll go get her, if you want."

"No," said Sal, a little too sharply, and Skender noticed.

"What's going on with you two?" he asked. "You're barely talking to each other these days."

"It's nothing. She'll be tired after the trip, and I don't want to bother her."

"You sure? She hasn't done anything to you?" the boy asked sharply.

Sal feigned innocence. He didn't want to risk Behenna or Tait finding out what he was up to. Everything would be ruined if that happened, and he simply wasn't sure he could trust Shilly not to mention what they had been doing — even if he didn't tell her *why* he wanted to do it.

"No. We're just — not getting on, I guess."

The half-truth seemed to satisfy the boy. He shrugged and looked around. "Well, here's as good a place as any." He squatted and held out his hands. Sal took them and formed the circle they used to share images and words without speech. "Okay. Here's one pattern. See it? The idea is to make the lines turn — not like tops, but like a stick rolling between your hands. Pretty simple, huh? Or there's this one: you visualise little clouds forming out of nothing then collapsing into points, like flowers in reverse. You combine that with this one — the spinning boxes — and that's supposed to do something. I don't know what, exactly, but that's what the book says."

They ran through several such patterns, from the simple to the fiendishly complex, and Sal committed as many of them as he could to memory. He made a few token efforts to see if the patterns would work, but he always stopped short of trying too hard. They didn't want to attract the attention of the mages in the caravan — let alone the sole Sky Warden — any one of whom might put a stop to things. Behenna might have been toothless, but he wasn't blind as well.

They gave up when the moon was halfway up the sky. In two more nights, it would be full, and at that time the Synod would sit.

"Do you know how long it would take for rain to come," he asked Skender as they walked back to the camp, "if we could get it to work?"

"No idea," said the boy. "That would depend on the place you tried it. Here, we didn't even get a nibble, so it might take days. Maybe it would never come. In the Strand it might just blow in off the sea in minutes. If the people who lived here had had *that*, maybe they'd still be here now."

"If there *was* a sea here," said Sal, "the place would be crawling with Sky Wardens."

"True." The boy yawned. "One's quite enough for me, thanks."

Sal waited until he was certain Skender was asleep, then waited another half-hour to make sure that no one else in the camp was awake. When even the crackle of the fire had died down, he crept out of the wagon and dropped to the ground in his bare feet, the jar of pearl and blood paste in his hand. The desert night was still and cold. Dispassionate stars crowded in the sky above. A camel coughed as Sal wound his way through the darkness, but nothing else stirred. Zevan didn't mount sentries, since potential bandits rarely came so deep in the desert. The dangerous portion of their journey had been on the plains, long past.

Sal came to a halt when he was within a few metres of the buggy. Behenna was asleep on a bedroll by the passenger side. For a moment, he couldn't find Tait, but the journeyman turned out to be propped up by the fire, dead to the world. Shilly was asleep on the tray, and she stirred as Sal approached. He held his breath, but she just turned over and muttered something under her breath.

Sal moved closer, one careful step at a time. The keys weren't in the ignition, and he was grateful to be spared that temptation. He doubted his father would have approved. He had to be cleverer than that.

He hoped he *was* being clever. Crouching in the dark by the buggy's right fender, terrified that he was about to be caught, he was pretty sure his father would have discouraged what he was about to do as well. But no other plan had come to mind, and he had given it plenty of thought. He had thought until he'd realised that thinking had become a means of avoiding action. He had only one chance, and he had to take it.

Opening the jar, he scooped out a portion of the paste on the tip of one finger. Reaching under the fender, he painted a thick, curving line, then repeated the motion in reverse to complete a circle. Inching his way back along the buggy, he repeated the procedure at the rear. With half the jar left, he reached under the chassis and painted another circle by the exhaust pipe, then moved back to the front and put the last behind the bumper. No one would see any of the marks, he was sure. If all went well, he'd soon know if the paste was just a sop for wishful buyers, or if Lodo had known his stuff.

Really known his stuff, Sal thought. When it came down to it, his plan rested on Lodo being right and the Mage Van Haasteren being wrong. Given that the mage's own father had chosen Lodo over his own son to run the Keep, breaking generations of tradition, Sal felt as though he should be confident of his decision, but if there was one thing he *was* certain of it was that there were few certainties where the Change was concerned. How could anyone hope to pin down something as nebulous as change itself?

When the job was done, he wiped his finger on one leg and backed away from the buggy.

"Sal? Sal, is that you?"

Shilly's whisper froze him to the spot. Barely an arm's reach away from him, she stirred on the tray and blinked around her in the darkness. Sal couldn't guess what had disturbed her: maybe the same sixth sense that told him when she was nearby. He had become so accustomed to it that he worried that the loss of it would hurt more than her silence when they were together — but he hadn't known that she felt it too.

He waited. She didn't seem entirely awake, and he couldn't be sure that she had actually seen him.

"Sal?"

Tempted though he was to answer, he knew that doing so would be foolish. She had made her choice. No one was making her ride with the Sky Warden and his journeyman. She didn't need him or his problems any more.

He took five slow steps backward until the corner of a wagon stood between him and the buggy. Shilly didn't call again. He was free to finish the job he had to do.

An hour later, he returned from the desert with Skender's patterns still turning in his mind. He had felt something this time, when he had really tried: a potential right at the edge of his senses like storm clouds lurking just below the horizon. And the paste had responded, burning like tiny brands in the darkness. If rain would come or not, he couldn't tell. But he had found *something*, and it had heard him in return.

Crawling into the wagon, he fell exhausted into bed. The mage rolled over as the wagon shifted slightly beneath them, but Sal had worn out any fear of being caught. He was too tired to worry.

The first proper charm he had ever performed on his own was done. He had set the Change loose, and all he could do now was wait to see what effect it had on the world.

CHAPTER 15

A KIND OF CHARM

"You're kidding," said Shilly, not believing her ears.

"No, it's true." The sound of Tait's voice was a musical contrast to the abrasive chugging of the buggy. "I'm telling you, there used to be creatures everywhere in the desert. They weren't alive like animals, but they weren't properly machines, either. They looked like a cross between a box kite and a..." He struggled for the right word, literally clutching with one hand as though to pluck it out of the dry, desert air. "... and a ..."

"A ladder," supplied the Sky Warden in the driver's seat beside him, glancing away from the road for a second to join in on the story. "Several ladders that have been in an accident and ended up wrapped around each other."

"That's exactly it!" Tait gesticulated enthusiastically. "And they've got sails, see, that catch the wind. The wind tips the sails forward, which rotates a wheel, which in turn moves some of the tangled ladders ahead a step, then the sails tip back, and it all goes round again. They can't control where they're going. The wind just drives them along like tumbleweeds — only they're a lot bigger than that. Bigger than this buggy. Wider than all the wagons in this caravan tied together end to end. But not very deep. They're like hedges that have come to life and gone marching across the land."

"Or a wave," said Behenna. "A wave of ingenious clockwork driven by the wind."

"There were thousands of them! All over the desert!"

Shilly could barely picture the image Tait was painting for her. "Here? *This* desert?"

"Maybe. They certainly had them in the Strand, once, up north by the Divide."

"Do any of them still exist?"

"I don't know about that." Tait looked at Behenna for the answer.

"The stories about them date back a long way," the warden supplied, "and they were considered ancient even then. But there might be working survivors somewhere. Perhaps here. I can't see why not."

Shilly looked around her, at the horizon, half-expecting one of the strange machines to appear at any moment, still marching endlessly nowhere. It was a peculiar thought: unnerving and exciting at the same time.

"Who made them?"

"No one remembers," Behenna said, "but the things themselves were called strandbeasts. That much we do know."

"If we had one now," said Tait, "we could sail the desert like we do the sea. No more camels; no more smelly drivers; no more lugging fuel around for machines like this old thing. All you'd have to do was point it in the right direction, then sit back and relax. The wind would do the work for us."

He reclined in his chair as though imagining himself on such a voyage. Behenna slowed the buggy to avoid running up the back of the wagon in front. The warden was a reasonable driver, but heavy on the accelerator. He was constantly in a hurry, as though full of impatience he could barely contain. It was obvious to Shilly that, had he been able to convince Sal to ride with them, he would have left the caravan behind to travel at speed for the Nine Stars, and waited there for everyone else to catch up.

But Sal had refused, even when Behenna had offered to let him drive. Shilly could tell that the sight of the buggy in the warden's possession had upset him, but she didn't understand why he was being so stubborn about it. Had she been in his position she might have taken the chance to enjoy it one last time, even if she refused to have anything else to do with the Sky Warden who now owned it. He had sold the buggy in good faith and Behenna had bought it on the same terms; Sal couldn't fairly expect it back, just like that. And despite Tait's best efforts at keeping her entertained, she wasn't entirely comfortable driving with the Sky Warden and his journeyman without Sal as well.

The thought of Sal cast a pall over the conversation. There were a lot of things she didn't understand about him, and she had told herself that she was no longer going to try to work him out. It wasn't easy, though. His decision not to speak before the Judges had made her realise just how stubborn he was. She had assumed he was coasting along behind her burning desire to get to Skender Van Haasteren, but it might not have been that way at all. She remembered little things, like the way he had got past Behenna at the Divide without consulting her. They had been working together, hadn't they? Not all the time, apparently. She wondered how far she would have lasted with him had she not wanted to go north in the first place. She might have found herself abandoned in the middle of nowhere while he followed his own counsel, alone.

Then there were his secrets: about the globe and the way Behenna had helped save her life by the ravine. She knew that she had told him "no blame" about the accident itself, but she wasn't sure how *completely* blameless he really was, now. Everything had gone wrong since he had come into her life. She had told him once that she didn't want to be dragged into his family curse, and with every day she was leaning more toward the opinion that that had been the right attitude to take all along.

"Did you learn about these things in the Haunted City?" she asked, trying to recapture the spirit of the conversation.

"In a book called *Historical Artefacts and Ruins*," Tait said. "There are lots of amazing things lying around out there, Shilly. You should see them. Talking statues like the ones they have up here; ice that never melts; crystals that reveal views of far-off places; and weapons that can kill people without even touching them. You have to be very, very careful in the wilds of the Strand."

"You've been Surveying?" she asked, hoping her envy wasn't as obvious as it felt.

"Not personally, no." He looked uncomfortable for a moment. "But there are museums bigger than Fundelry, full of stuff the Surveyors brought back. You'd love it!"

She was certain she would. It sounded much more exciting than theory and meditation at the Keep.

Tait reached down for his water bottle and swigged from it. Scowling up at the sun as though it had personally offended him, he poured a measure of the precious liquid over his face and revelled in its coolness. Shilly could sympathise. She was sweating like a fish. The day had been a long one, for the caravan had fallen slightly behind schedule. The camels were jittery, and Zevan was wary enough of their nerves to lengthen rest stops throughout the day. If they were going to reach the Nine Stars before the following evening, they were going to have to push on through part of the night. The thought dismayed her.

Shilly wasn't looking forward to spending any more time on the back of the buggy than she had to, no matter who kept her company. She had considered moving into one of the wagons for the extra space to stretch her leg, but Tait and Behenna had talked her out of it.

"I'm sick of this place," the journeyman had said the previous day, near Three Wells, after she had admitted to him that, no, there was no one in the caravan who knew anything much about where she and Tait had come from. Not even Sal, for he had come from the borderlands. "I can't wait to get home and have some decent food. I'd kill for a nice fish fillet. Not to mention decent clothes." He looked disdainfully down at the robes he was wearing. "Whoever thought something like this would make sense in a desert must have been crazy."

"It stops your sweat evaporating too quickly," said the warden, "and saves you from dehydration."

"I don't care about that. It's hot, and I'm *still* thirsty. If the sea was right here, I'd throw it all off and go for a swim." He looked longingly at the mirages dancing on the horizon. "If only . . ."

Indeed, Shilly had thought, wondering how Vita the serving girl would have reacted to that sight. Probably swoon, she decided.

"The rest of them might take it badly if you did that," she had said.

"So?" Tait had kneeled on the passenger seat to face her. "You're with us, now. What does it matter what they think?"

His vehemence had surprised her.

"I may not fully subscribe to my young friend's summary of the situation," Behenna had said, "but in essence he's right about how frustrating it is. Although we are travelling of our own accord, we are in effect captives of their system. We have no alternative but to go to the Nine Stars. Should we decide not to, for whatever reason, we will be held in contempt. Their ridiculous legal process has forced us into something we shouldn't have to do, in order to do the right thing. Which is, of course, to get you home again, where you belong."

She wanted to ask him how he could be so certain where she belonged, when she herself was having doubts. It wasn't Fundelry itself she missed — not really. The town had been claustrophobically small and its people petty-minded. Apart from a few of Lodo's friends, there was little there she actually wanted back in her life. What she missed was the *idea* of home, of a place where she could feel safe and loved, an environment she found familiar. She had hoped that the Mage Van Haasteren might provide her with such a place, but she now realised that hope to have been naive. Nowhere in the Interior so far had even come close to meeting that expectation. It was too hot, and the food tasted weird to her still. And the mage had never been more than a distant figure at best.

But was it really a home she was after? She remembered thinking before leaving Ulum that Lodo had been all the family she had ever needed. A father figure, friend and teacher, the old man had been there for her for most of her life, and it was him she missed more than Fundelry, the sea or the Strand as a whole. More than anything else, she wanted to reel back time and go back to the days before Sal and his father arrived, and her world had been turned inside out.

She doubted the Sky Warden could offer her that. But would a new *family* fill the same need?

Tait poked her in the side and she snapped back to the present. He had been talking about museums and her mind had wandered.

"I said it would be great to take you there, one day," he repeated, and she nodded. Yes, she thought, it would be great — but what about the Keep and her studies?

"You don't look convinced," he said, poking her again. "You're not having second thoughts, are you?"

"I..." She didn't finish the sentence, being unsure if she had completed her *first* thought, let alone her second, or was, in fact, so confused that she'd reached her third or fourth without even noticing. It was great that Tait had come back into her life and befriended her; she hadn't realised how lonely she had become, and how much of her life revolved around Sal's concerns rather than her own. But she didn't entirely agree with some of what the warden and his journeyman said, and that made her wonder again what her concerns actually were. Simply finding the Mage Van Haasteren obviously hadn't eased them.

"Go easy on her, Tait," said Behenna. "She's nervous, and you can't blame her for that. If I'd been through what she's been through — stolen from my home, injured, taken to a strange place where I didn't know anyone — I'd be a little unsure of things, too."

"It's just..." Again, she faltered, remembering the clear sense of threat that she and Sal had run from after his father had died. Lodo had sacrificed himself so they, or at least Sal, could get away. Should that be so easily forgotten?

It all came down to what she *actually* wanted. Was it the Change alone, or something more fundamental? Perhaps the answer was as simple as control over her own life, the ability to make her own decisions without having to worry about someone else.

She took a deep breath. "I came here to look for a teacher," she said, trying to sound strong, "and I found one."

"A Stone Mage," sneered Tait.

"I didn't have any other options. He was all I had."

"And you're reluctant to give that up so soon." Behenna nodded. "I understand. But remember the old saying: a bad beginning leads to a bad ending. You must take everything into account before you head along this path. If you don't learn correctly, you will learn badly. Trust me."

The Sky Warden's eyes were on the road, but Shilly felt herself being weighed by him nonetheless.

"I think it's time we found you a proper teacher," he said. "Back home, I mean. In the Haunted City."

For a moment she goggled at him. "But — but I don't have the Change."

"That's no impediment. You know that Sal's father was a journeyman, and he didn't have a drop of the Change in him. Nor does your friend Tom at the moment. He was Selected as much for his intelligence as his latent talent. Why shouldn't you be treated the same way?"

"No one's wanted to before," she said, remembering the Selectors and their assistants who had come through Fundelry and never paid her the slightest attention.

"That was clearly a mistake," the warden said, "one I am keen to rectify. Lodo kept you hidden from us for too long, and when you did come to our attention, Amele Centofanti proved too incompetent to realise what she'd found. That's why I replaced her — and why, also, I am here, doing this for you. As much as I disagree with their methods, I respect the opinions of people like Lodo and Mage Van Haasteren. They both saw something in you that had potential, something that slipped through our net. I don't want to lose you, Shilly — what you could be. You deserve us just as much as we deserve you."

This was all a bit too much for her to take in one chunk. "Lodo Tested me with the Scourge of Aneshti. He said I should be taught along the ways of air and water, but that I could learn his way because I had no talent of my own." She thought of the word Skender had used — *Taking* — and flushed. "I use what other people offer. It's what *they* have that counts, not what I would have had if I had any."

"That's true," Behenna admitted, "but it always works better if inclinations match. Have you never tried to do it with someone trained our way?"

She shook her head. Apart from the village seer, Aunty Merinda, she had only ever borrowed the talent belonging to Lodo, Sal and those in the Keep who would let her. Aunty Merinda had had little enough of her own that there hadn't been much for Shilly to use. Maybe there simply hadn't been enough for her to notice the difference.

"You should try it," the warden said. "Tait, let her use you."

The journeyman nodded and offered her his hand. Confronted with it, she didn't know what to do. The night of the light-sink was still fresh in her mind. It had been so easy to keep Taking Sal's wild talent, even though she had known it was the wrong thing to do. She hadn't tried it with anyone since the day after, when Skender had loaned her his talent to cover for the fact that she didn't want to use Sal's. Did she dare do it without him around?

But that was just stupid, she told herself. She couldn't rely on Skender for the rest of her life. She had to learn to trust herself at some point — and it was only Sal she had promised not to use again.

She took Tait's hand and held it gently in hers, wondering nervously what would happen next.

"Here." The warden slipped the torc from around his neck and gave it to her. She took it with her other hand and held it even more gingerly than she did Tait.

"Don't be afraid of it," said the warden. "It won't hurt you. The torcs contain a variety of charms woven into the glass, in the same way that Stone Mages capture charms in their tattoos. Every warden makes something like this to demonstrate their skill in particular areas." She nodded. "See the bubbles? Pick one and stare at it. Concentrate as hard as you can. Now think of a bath full of water and lie in it. Let the water accept you and roll over you. Sink into it and float for a moment. Then open your eyes."

Shilly did exactly as the warden said. She had never been in a bath containing enough water to float outstretched, so she imagined the sea instead. It was a still, cool day and the sun floated high and pale above her. The water was welcoming and familiar as it rose around her. She took a deep breath and went under. The sun receded and the air fell away above her. For a moment, she felt as though she was rising, not falling — floating face up into a dark, starless sky.

When she opened her eyes, she found herself in a place she had never visited before. She was high up — on a balcony, she presumed — and looking out over a city of glass towers that reminded her of the one she and Sal had found in the Broken Lands, only this one was inhabited. Walkways and staircases connected the towers like silver threads, glinting in the sun.

People moved along them, and behind the many glass windows, everywhere she looked. Men and women, even children, all going about their errands with a sense of purpose that made her feel, although she had no real reason to, that they would ignore her if she tried to talk to them. They were aloof, these people: remote, isolated, apart. She knew somehow that she could never be one of them.

With an effort, she tore her eyes away from the people in the buildings and had barely noticed two things — that the sun to her right was setting into a bright blue sea, and that she appeared to be standing on thin air — when the image was suddenly gone. It faded into blue like a cloud burned away by the sun.

She blinked and was back on the buggy, clutching Tait in one hand and the Sky Warden's torc in the other.

"Did you see it?" Behenna asked.

"I did. A city ..."

"The Haunted City through the eyes of a seagull. Impressive, isn't it?"

She nodded, even though elements of the vision bothered her. The people she had seen: were they the inhabitants of the city — the wardens, the members of the Conclave and the families they came from — or were they the ghosts the city was named after? Where was the golden tower, the one Kemp had to be careful of, according to a warning the Change had granted her? And why did Manton Gourlay describe the city as "so beautiful, yet so ugly at the same time" when it was so unambiguously the most incredible place she had ever seen?

She didn't know, and that ignorance bothered her. It was easy to create illusions of things that weren't real.

"You're saying I could go there?" she asked.

"Absolutely. You have the potential to learn even if you don't have the Change itself. You're clever and you're not afraid to aspire to what you want. Are you, Shilly? I see the look in your eyes when we talk about the Change. I know what you want more than anything else — and you can have it. We will give it to you freely. All you have to do is come home with us, and it's yours."

Shilly was so hypnotised by the warden's words that she didn't notice that she was still holding Tait's hand. Whether Behenna's illusion of the Haunted City was true or false didn't matter: the thought that she would see it with her own eyes was even more amazing. But it would mean leaving the Keep. It might mean leaving Sal, if the Synod decided in his favour.

The journeyman cleared his throat and she let him free with a jerk.

"Oh, I'm sorry."

"No worries, really." Tait smiled and took the torc from her.

"Did you feel how easy that was, Shilly?" asked the warden. "That was because you and Tait match. You resonate nicely together. I think you'll agree that it's easier this way."

It was true. She hadn't even noticed that she was using Tait's talent. It had all happened as naturally as though it was her own. Was this, she wondered, what Sal took for granted? What any of the naturally gifted lived with every day? If so, she envied them even more deeply. It was like dreaming she had wings and waking full of the joy of flight, only to be dashed to the ground when reality asserted itself again.

We will give it to you freely, Behenna had said. *All you have to do is come home . . .*

She was too afraid to ask, *Just me?*

Tait launched into another tale of his exploits in the Haunted City. She couldn't concentrate on it. Feigning tiredness from the exercise, she lay back on the buggy's tray and tried to think. So lost in her thoughts was she that she barely noticed the lengthening shadows as the sun set upon the stony plains. Neither did she see the looming darkness on the horizon ahead, like a giant wave about to crash over the land. Wisps of cloud fled before it, whipped along by a rising wind.

They stopped at sunset to study the phenomenon. The camels were very nervous by then, their restless hoof-falls and groans loud over the wind. Zevan strolled along the road ahead of them, one hand cupping his eyes as though to shield them from the sun. But the sun was behind them, and cast a blood-red pall over the cloudbank to the east.

Shilly could understand why the camels were wary of walking in that direction. The clouds looked like a solid wall blocking their path. Lightning crackled in the darkness beneath them. The wind carried occasional rumbles of thunder, as though the earth was complaining. The air smelled of moisture, thick and portentous. The Van Haasterens had come out of their wagon to look, and Sal stood between them, his expression apprehensive.

Behenna guided the buggy close to where the wagon containing Radi Mierlo had stopped. He jumped out, and Shilly took the chance to stretch her good leg. Hopping off the tray, she gathered her crutches and followed to where the warden and his journeyman had entered the wagon.

Inside, she saw a very peculiar sight. Sal's grandmother was seated on a low camp bed, dressed in a pale blue cotton robe with her grey hair tied back in a practical bun. Her grandson, the enormous, white-haired Aron, sat opposite her, steadying on his lap what looked like the bust of a stern-looking man with a high forehead and long nose. The head was slightly larger than a normal person's, and it was obviously heavy; Aron's muscles bunched as he held the bust upright before his grandmother.

Shilly couldn't see why he would possibly be doing that, until the bust spoke.

"*I know nothing of this storm you say is approaching.*" Its mouth didn't move and its voice was a buzz of insects from a great distance, yet its words were perfectly understandable. She eyed the man'kin with fascination. The Mage Van Haasteren had explained at the Keep only that the man'kin were relics from a bygone era, creatures of stone animated by the Change but not controllable by Change-workers. They existed more deeply in the background potential than humans, and that gave them subtle insights into the past, present and future. Some people kept them as advisors, and Shilly assumed that Radi Mierlo was one such person, even though "taming" the stone intelligences was apparently very difficult. Perhaps that explained the legendary tenacity of the Mierlo family.

"Nothing at all?" asked Sal's grandmother.

"*Water and air are not my field of expertise,*" it said. "*At a guess, I'd say you're going to get wet.*"

"Who sent it, then? Can you at least tell us that?"

"*I do sense a charm at work.*" The bust turned at the neck to look at Behenna. Like the giant statues guarding the way to the keep, it moved in tiny but discrete steps, lending the motion a slight jerkiness. "*As you know,*" it said, "*the spoor of weather-working is difficult to follow. It is probably aimed at us, or something nearby.*"

"Could it be someone trying to stop us getting to the Nine Stars?" Radi Mierlo asked.

"*Of course it could.*" The man'kin head didn't look at her. Its stony gaze slid past the warden to where Shilly peered through the flap. "*That face. I recognise it.*"

She stood rooted to the spot as Radi Mierlo glanced at her in surprise. "Shilly? How?"

"Yadeh-tash *knows her*."

The familiar name snapped Shilly out of her daze. "Lodo's necklace?"

"*It feels storms in the bones of the Earth. Were it here, it could help you determine the nature of the one approaching.*"

"But it's not, is it?" snapped Sal's grandmother. "You're worse than useless, Mawson. I don't know why I bothered to bring you."

"*Neither do I,*" shot back the man'kin with a flash of irritation.

"Put him away, Aron."

Her enormous grandson went to take the bust off his lap, but it wasn't quite done with Shilly. "*I will tell* yadeh-tash *that you are safe,*" Mawson told her. "*It wonders.*"

"What about Lodo?" she blurted. "Is *tash* with him?"

The man'kin hesitated. "*Yes and no. The essence of your friend is in the Void.*"

"But he's still alive? His *body* is alive?"

"*Yes. It still lives, and* yadeh-tash *is with it.*"

A giddy sense of relief mixed with dread rushed through her. Lodo wasn't dead! But she was sobered by the thought that he wasn't really alive, either. It was just as the golem had hinted in the ruined city: Lodo had pushed himself too hard in summoning the earthquake that had helped Sal and Shilly escape and, in doing so, had emptied himself. He was either still empty or something else had moved in.

She owed it to her old teacher to try to save him. This was much more important than just trying to open his workshop. "Where is he? His body, I mean."

"*In the place you call the Haunted City. The Wardens have it in their care.*"

"What?" Shilly turned, appalled, on Behenna. "Did you know about this?"

The warden looked cornered for a moment. He shot an angry glance at Radi Mierlo, then his attention was firmly on placating Shilly. "I did, yes, but didn't know how to tell you. It's not good news, on top of everything else."

"But I still deserved to be told!"

"Would you have believed me? Or would you have thought I was using the promise of Lodo as a lure to get you to agree to come home?"

She acknowledged the point to herself but refused to admit it aloud. "If it was the truth —"

"There's no way I could have proved it to you. In fact, I can only assume that what *I've* been told is true. What if I'd been wrong and given you false hope?" The Sky Warden's eyes held nothing but a desire to convince her. "Lodo's body was found after you and Sal escaped. He was still alive, but in a coma. The Syndic tried to reach him, but he was beyond even her, so they sent him to the Haunted City where he could be treated by experts. His condition is grave." He touched her arm. "All isn't lost, but it would be wrong of me to promise anything. I can only assure you that we're doing all we can."

She nodded, feeling tears on her cheeks and Tait's gaze, in turn, on the tears, as though he couldn't believe what he was seeing. But she didn't care what people thought of her. Lodo was alive and needed her help. That was more important than anything else — more important than any new family she might find, more important than Sal, more important even than learning the Change. Lodo *was* her family. She couldn't live with herself if she didn't try to help him.

"If I went home with you," she asked, "would he be there?"

"Should he survive that long, yes." The warden's face was grave in the greying light. "Feeding them is the problem, I understand."

"This is all very well," broke in Radi Mierlo. "But what do we tell Zevan? Keep moving or wait here for the storm to pass?"

Behenna looked up at the sky. Shilly hadn't noticed the sunset, and was surprised to see several stars already gleaming above. To the east, however, was nothing but blackness and lightning. The thunder was louder, clearly audible over the whipping wind.

"If we stay still, we'll only lose time," Behenna eventually said. "At the very least, we must avoid that. We can't afford to miss the full moon."

"We might not see it," said Tait, nodding eastward, "under all *that*."

"Irrelevant," said Sal's grandmother. She waved at Aron, who lifted the granite bust and put it aside with effort. The man'kin's attention stayed on Shilly as though fascinated by her. "Shom is right. We must keep moving. It's only a thunderstorm."

Behenna gestured with his left hand and Tait ran off to pass on the news. A gust of wind sent dust rising between them and the flaps at the rear of the wagon rattled. Shilly shivered, even though the air was still warm. There was a rising sense of electricity in the air.

She hugged herself, thinking of the Void Beneath. She had never experienced it, but she imagined awful things. What would it be like, she wondered, to be trapped alone in there as Lodo was?

"*Be careful, child,*" said the man'kin.

She turned to meet its stare. "Be careful of what?"

Everyone looked at her. "What did you say?" asked Radi Mierlo.

She stared back at them. Clearly they hadn't heard the man'kin speak.

"*Be careful of the Void.*"

Shilly glanced at Behenna, confused. The man'kin was trying to tell her something privately, and she knew she should listen. Because of it, she had learned something very important: that her old teacher's body was still alive and in the Haunted City. She didn't know when Behenna would have told her that, without its prompting. What else did it know that was being kept from her? And what did it mean by warning her to be careful of the Void?

She wanted to ask it what it was talking about, but she couldn't with everyone around.

"Can we take him with us, on the buggy?" she asked Radi Mierlo. Maybe she could whisper to it over the sound of the engine.

"Why?" Sal's grandmother shot back, suspiciously. "And it's an *it*, not a *he*."

Shilly couldn't very well say that she thought Behenna might be lying to her, so she lied herself. "I'm curious about it. I've never seen a man'kin this close before."

"Well, it's heavy and no good for conversation," she was told. Behenna added: "All they do is lie, anyway. You can wait until the next rest stop."

She let herself be led away from Radi Mierlo's caravan by the firm pressure of the Sky Warden's hand on her shoulder.

"*Choose well,*" the man'kin said as the canvas flaps were drawn closed over it. "*We will talk another time.*"

Shilly was still trying to work out what it had meant an hour later, when the storm hit.

*   *   *

Only a thunderstorm.

Radi Mierlo's words came back to Shilly as she huddled in the lee of a wagon, deafened by rain, wind and thunder. The night was utterly black apart from the frequent flashing of lightning. Earlier, one of the Stone Mages in the caravan had tried to activate a handful of glow stones he carried in his pack, shouting over the wind that they would at least keep them warm. But there was too much background potential in the air to do it successfully. The first didn't work at all. A bolt of electricity stabbed out of the sky and destroyed the second stone. He abandoned the attempt after that, and joined the others in finding what shelter they could.

The wagon creaked and swayed beside her like the sides of a leaky ship. Shilly had no idea what time it was or how long the storm had lasted. She was soaked right through, hungry and more than a little frightened. The ferocity of the storm belied Sal's grandmother's words with such violence that their inaccuracy was hard to forget. For a brief moment Shilly had been pleased to see the rain, since she had experienced none of any kind during her journeys in the Interior. It had been refreshing, although heavy, as the fringes had passed over them, washing away the dust and the dirt. It had become heavier as the cloud cover thickened over them, until no stars at all could be seen. And it had kept getting heavier; it seemed to Shilly as though they were receiving an entire year's rainfall in one night.

Now there was only the storm, crushing her beneath the combined weight of water, wind and thunder. Fundelry was renowned for the storms that blew off the southern ocean, and she had endured a few mighty ones — but there had been nothing like this. The wind had ripped the roof off one of the wagons and tipped another onto its side. One of Zevan's riders had broken her arm when a piece of debris carried by the wind had struck without warning from the darkness. The only other time Shilly had felt such weather had been when the Alcaide and the Syndic had arrived on their great ship of bone, *Os*, to take Sal away.

Something pressed into her from the darkness.

"Are you all right?" The words were shouted into her ear, but she could barely hear them.

Lightning flashed, revealing a very wet face. It was Tait.

"Yes!" she shouted back, brushing her saturated fringe from her forehead.

"What are you doing here?"

"I was going to get my crutches!" They were on the buggy's tray, tied down to stop them being swept away.

"On your own?"

She didn't try to explain. Tait and Behenna had moved her from the buggy once it had become clear that the storm wasn't going to abate. They had covered the buggy with a tarp then disappeared into the storm — to join Radi Mierlo, she had assumed. She had been left alone in one of the food wagons, wondering what everyone else was doing, wherever they were. Eventually she had let frustration get the better of her, and attempted to fix the problem herself. And then she had got stuck.

"I think it's easing!" Tait shouted.

She stared at him as lightning flashed again. Was he serious or just trying to cheer her up? Either way, it was so patently ridiculous that she didn't honour it with a reply.

"Any idea who sent it yet?"

"No. Maybe it was no one. After all, who could make something like this, eh? Only one of the great weather masters in the Haunted City, and they're a long way from here!"

She shook her head, not disagreeing with his conclusion, necessarily, but disagreeing with the reason he offered. Weather-workers didn't *make* weather; the Change didn't work that way. They simply guided the weather along, coaxing it into more suitable forms with the help of subtle charms. They were more like shepherds than smiths, urging rather than forcing.

"Couldn't Warden Behenna at least tone it down a bit?" she asked.

Tait shook his head. "He can't. That's what he's trying to explain to Mrs Mierlo. He doesn't have any power in the Interior."

Shilly acknowledged the point with a grunt, even though it seemed stupid to her that a Sky Warden, with supposed influence over water and air, could have no effect on a thunderstorm. She was still irritated with him for not telling her about Lodo, and wasn't inclined to be charitable.

A prolonged squall rendered speech impossible for a minute or more. Shilly felt the wagon rock violently on its wheels and was briefly afraid that it might also tip over. But it held. In the centre of the ring of wagons she could just make out the camels, tied together and knowing better than to move anywhere. Their stolid dispositions were quite unchanged. She tried to imitate them as best she could.

"Shilly, you're here." Suddenly Behenna was standing over them, looming out of a flash of lighting like a primitive deity, his face grim.

"Where else would I go?" she shouted back

He ignored her. "Tait! Do you remember where we left the buggy?"

The journeyman pointed across the ring of wagons into the darkness. "Over there!" he yelled back. "By Zevan's wagon!"

"That's what I thought." The warden's face became even grimmer. "It's gone!"

"What?" But Behenna had vanished into the rain. Tait was instantly on his feet and following him without a word.

"Hey!" Shilly forced herself upright on her good leg. "What do you mean it's gone?"

Her question vanished into the stormy night, and she was left alone with her fears. Could the buggy have been blown away? No, she told herself, that couldn't be. Unnaturally strong though the wind was, the wagons around her were still there and the buggy was much heavier than them. Someone must have taken it away, then. But who?

There was only one person she could think of who was likely to do that.

"Damn you, Sal! I need my crutches!"

She forced herself to move anyway, hopping more than walking from wagon to wagon, using whatever handholds she could find to take her weight and ignoring the stabbing pain deep in her thighbone if she put her right leg down even for an instant. The distance wasn't great — not even half that across the square in Fundelry, she told herself, and that took only a moment to walk across — but it was the longest she had travelled on her own since the ravine. The muscles in her good leg were soon quivering with the strain and it took all her concentration not to slip in the mud.

What the hell did Sal think he was doing? Escaping? There was nowhere to run to, which made the attempt seem stupider than ever. The fact that he had run off without her wasn't helping either. He would have done it once before, in Yor, had she not caught him in time. Perhaps that had been his plan all along. She had always borne in mind the fact that they would part at some point — but that it might be real, there and then, this way, was a very different thing. She was suddenly struck by the reality that she might never see him again.

He didn't even say goodbye . . .

She hopped to where she thought Zevan's wagon might have been, judging by the direction in which Tait had pointed. As she awkwardly manoeuvred herself around one of the wagon's sturdy wheels, she heard voices growing louder. A group of people, shouting heatedly, were coming toward her. Before she could get a proper grip on the wheel, their leader, invisible in the darkness, knocked right into her.

Screaming, she went down. The night lit up as though lightning had struck the wagon beside her — but it wasn't light. It was pain. She clutched at her injured leg, and suddenly there were people all around her, lifting her, cursing, easing her leg back out into a straightened position.

Tait was one of them. He cradled her head while they put her in the nearest wagon — Radi Mierlo's, judging by the great stone head of Mawson watching her from the corner.

"Shilly, are you okay?" the journeyman asked, wiping her wet hair out of her face. "We didn't see you, honestly. Van Haasteren almost knocked you right off your feet!"

Of course it would be him, Shilly thought through the pain and embarrassment. "W-what's happening?" she gasped, struggling to sit up against the hands holding her down. "Is it Sal? Has he gone?"

"Well, he's not here," said the Sky Warden with a snarl, climbing into the wagon with Skender right behind him. The mage's son looked like a drowned rat.

"He's done a runner!" the boy said, his eyes bright with excitement. "He must have summoned the storm to cover his tracks. I should have known he wasn't going to take this lying down."

"You know something about this?" Behenna asked him, his expression one of too-intense calm. Outside, the storm raged like a living thing. The wagon shuddered from the force of it. It was inconceivable that Sal could have brought such a force into the world. "Did he tell you where he might go?"

"No, but anywhere apart from here would suit him, I imagine." The boy cocked his ear at the ceiling. "Listen. I think the rain's easing. Sal told me he had some sort of fixative — a blood and pearl mix he brought with him from the Strand. My guess is he's somehow rigged the buggy as the focus of the storm. It's following him wherever he goes, and will keep on doing so until it blows out. Unless he sets it free, of course, in which case it'll just go wherever it wills. There's no way of knowing what he's doing. Isn't this brilliant, Shilly?"

"Be quiet," said the warden, his voice low and dangerous, "unless you have something useful to say."

Skender glared at the Sky Warden. "I'm a damned sight more useful than you are, here. You'd better start being nice to us, if you want us to help you find him."

"*He does not want to be found by you*," said the man'kin, its voice cutting through the rain and wind.

Shilly glanced at the stone bust, and caught Skender doing the same. Tait and Behenna, however, didn't react.

"I'm sorry," said the warden, annoyance giving away to weariness and frustration, or at least a good imitation thereof. "I don't mean to be rude. *Will* you look for me? I'm worried about him, you see. The storm —"

"No need to go on," said Skender, frowning. Shilly could almost hear his thoughts racing, even if she couldn't understand them. "You want us to look? That's fine. We want to find him too. He has to be at the Nine Stars tomorrow whether he wants to be there or not. Dad's looking for him right now."

"*He does not want to be found by you,*" the man'kin repeated firmly. "*That is not his intention.*"

Not his intention, Shilly echoed to herself, frowning. Of course he didn't intend to be found, she thought. No one who ran away wanted to be caught. Why did the man'kin think that worth saying?

Skender opened his mouth, then shut it. He looked at Shilly with intense curiosity. Something was going on that she didn't quite understand.

Skender tried again. "It'll be tricky, though," he said. "The storm is huge, and all the energy it's kicked up will hide him pretty effectively. I reckon we've got a fifty-fifty chance, with so few of us looking."

"He *can't* get away," Behenna said. "He *must* be located."

"We can only do as much as we can do," said the boy, unfazed by the determination in the warden's gaze. "You can't ask for more than that."

Skender glanced at the man'kin and gave a very slight nod. It didn't repeat its assertion, although Shilly half-expected it to. Skender had said nothing different, so why didn't the man'kin protest yet again?

Then it hit her. Mawson hadn't said that Sal didn't want to be found. It had said: He does not want to be found *by you*.

Shilly leaned back into her seat as Skender slipped out of the wagon, presumably to talk to his father. Behenna would think he was going to pass on the word, to look for Sal, but she knew better. He would actually be telling them not to try too hard.

Tait put a hand on her shoulder as though to comfort her. The truth was that she no longer felt the pain. All she could think of was Sal driving off in the centre of a storm with all the minds of the Stone Mages looking for him, hoping that someone would realise what he was hoping to do in time.

And she was left behind. Was this to be her family, then —
Behenna and Tait and Mawson and Radi Mierlo? If she spoke
up, it certainly would be, even if they brought Sal back. She was
far from certain that that was what she wanted. But was staying
silent the same thing as supporting Sal's actions? Did being
indecisive mean that she had to let someone else make her
decisions for her?

Mawson watched her closely as she warred within herself
over whether to say anything or not. How had the man'kin
known? Had it just guessed from what people said around him?
Everyday wisdom told her that what Sal was hoping for simply
wasn't possible, but Lodo's own history had shown her that it
was very possible indeed, and had given her some idea of what
the consequences might be. The man'kin must have been aware
of that too — and, like her, knew that it would probably work.
Human nature told her that much.

She felt a small stab of pity, deep inside her — but ultimately
she said nothing. She wasn't the only one who knew the risks.

The rain had indeed eased slightly, but it kept coming down
heavily as, across the wagon from her, the Sky Warden Shom
Behenna closed his eyes in concentration.

CHAPTER 16

DANGEROUS SEDUCTION

Like everyone on the great desert in the north of the Interior, Sal knew of only two directions to run: west and slightly south would take him back to Ulum, while east and north led to the end of the road, where the Nine Stars and the Synod of Stone Mages awaited him. Beyond, there was only desert. As far as he knew, there was no other alternative, and the maps in the buggy's toolbox told the same story.

So it came as a surprise to him, an hour after leaving the camp, to encounter a crossroad.

He stopped the buggy and got out, braving the fury of the storm to take a closer look. The wind was deafening and threatened to knock him off balance. In his hour's travel, the ground beneath him had become sandier and less stony. It was hard to tell through all the rain, but the landscape was definitely beginning to undulate around him, as though the road was cutting through dunes rather than skimming across an endless plain. Both road surfaces were made from cracked, black bitumen across which the water ran like a multitude of snakes.

There were no markers to tell him where the new road led. He didn't know what might lie to the northwest of that point, since all the maps he had seen ended just north of the Nine Stars. Maybe it led to the jungles inhabited by the yellow-skinned people that Lebesh the cab driver had told him and Shilly about. He felt safe assuming that the road to the east ultimately ended up at the Divide, most probably at Tintenbar, the second of the two crossings that joined the Interior and the Strand. If he was trying to escape that way, a right turn would have been advisable.

He wasn't, but the thought of turning worried at him as he walked back to the buggy and kept driving northeast, toward the Nine Stars. Running to his fate rather than from it might confuse his pursuers for a while — it might even give him a slight margin of control that he had lacked thus far — but he was still running *to* it. The closer he came to his destination, the more ominously he felt the weight of his possible future pressing down on him.

Back to the Strand. Back to his great-aunt and the Alcaide. Back to the man who claimed him as a son: Highson Sparre, his mother's jilted husband. Back to face the consequences of his parents' defiant love.

He didn't want to go back. That much was certain. But he didn't want to run any more, either. Although going through life like a stone skimming over water had its appeal, he knew now that he needed to learn how to control the Change if he was ever going to live with it. The only way he could learn was to settle down somewhere, and he would never be able to do that with his relatives baying at his heels. He had to find an alternative. There simply *had* to be another way — and if hurrying to apparent doom was the means to make it happen, he thought, so be it.

Come on, Behenna. You can't know where I'm going yet. Don't let me get away that easily!

He gunned the buggy on through the rain. The storm was drifting south now that he had set it free. For a while he had travelled at its heart, marvelling at the raw power he had coaxed out of the desert atmosphere. It had been like driving in the centre of a hurricane, surrounded by lightning and a continuous wall of thunder. More than just water was carried by the wind: uprooted plants whipped out of the darkness then were snatched away again. He stung in a dozen places where more substantial objects had struck him. A couple of times the wind had been so severe that it threatened to make even driving impossible, snatching at the buggy's frame and rocking it violently, lifting one or more wheels from the ground. Had Sal himself not been firmly strapped in, just as the rear tray was firmly secured under the tarp, he could well have been snatched right out of the seat and tossed into the sky.

He hoped the caravan was enduring the downpour well enough. He didn't want to hurt Zevan or the riders — or Shilly.

But he couldn't make the storm selective; he could only summon it and look after himself. That alone was inconceivable enough. The thought *I did this?* ran through his mind like a mantra. It was inconceivable that he had been responsible for it. *I'm just a kid. What's the weather doing listening to* me?

But it wasn't the weather. It was the Change, ultimately, doing as he willed it. He had set it free for a moment, loosing the pent-up potential buried in the desert. The realisation of what lay at his fingertips sobered any brief fantasies he'd entertained in Fundelry of using the Change for fun. The wild talent was dangerous, Van Haasteren had said. Now he could really see why.

Although his destination lay northeast, he kept his thoughts firmly on southeast, as though he had in fact taken the right-hand turn. He'd felt the minds of the Stone Mages pass over him earlier, but they hadn't returned. They weren't the ones he wanted to succeed. If they found him first, it would all have been for nothing.

Come on, *Sky Warden. Show me what you're made of!*

The road was slippery, but thankfully almost perfectly straight. Had there been any other traffic, he doubted he would see it in time to stop. Slowly the rain eased. He began to feel surer of his command of the wheel. Within an hour the rain had almost completely abated. The nearly full moon peered through the northern fringes of the storm. Ragged clouds chased each other south, lagging behind the main body yet seeming eager to catch up. That was where all the action was. That was where, he presumed, most attention would be. Certainly, if he *had* been trying to escape, that would have been the place to do it, in the confusing mass of water and air, almost impenetrable to the Stone Mages, going anywhere but to the Nine Stars.

He was getting tired. The road was treacherous even without rain to make visibility poor. Huge sheets of water barely distinguishable from the asphalt occasionally lay across his path. His hands and arms grew tired from constantly working to hold his course. The Cellaton Mandala slipped more and more frequently from his mind as his concentration flagged. He began to wonder if he hadn't miscalculated, just as the tactics behind games like Blind and Advance sometimes eluded him.

I haven't got all night, you know!

When he finally felt it, he jerked upright in the seat as though starting awake from a light sleep. He looked around automatically, gathering his senses. The night was crisp and cool in the wake of the storm. There was only him and the stars and the road rushing by and —

tap

— at the back of his mind, like a guilty memory he couldn't shake loose.

Was it *him?* Sal concentrated on the faint sensation, wary of responding but not wanting to lose it. He didn't want to be *too* hard to find. His foot eased off on the accelerator and the buggy slowed to a halt in the middle of the road.

tap

It wasn't Van Haasteren or Skender. He could tell that much. It wasn't the other Stone Mages, either. Their minds had a different flavour. There was no one else it *could* be.

tap-tap

Yes. Shom Behenna had given in to temptation. He had dipped into the source of the Stone Mage's power and used it for his own. He had broken the golden rule. *Once you cross the line,* the Mage Van Haasteren had said, *there's no returning. You're trapped in between, belonging to neither one nor the other.* He had betrayed himself exactly as Sal had hoped he would.

Sal quashed a feeling of triumph. He had at best only won a small battle, not the war. He didn't know how far Behenna had gone to find him, and whether that amount was enough to mark him forever.

tap-tap

In order to give the warden a little encouragement, Sal eased back on the Cellaton Mandala so there could be no doubt at Behenna's end that Sal knew he had been found.

The words came immediately, travelling from mind to mind in the same way Behenna had spoken to Sal by the bridge over the ravine.

"*Not so clever this time, Sal.*" The warden was unable to hide the self-satisfaction in his thoughts. "*You didn't really think you could escape from me, did you?*"

Sal concentrated on replying. He had never before attempted such a communication without physically touching the other person. All he could do was imagine the trail of Behenna's words to their source, using the visualisation technique Shilly had taught him in Fundelry, and hope that his reply would follow.

"*No. I didn't think that.*"

It worked. The warden heard and replied instantly. "*Then what? You thought you could talk to them first, get them to change their minds? That's not going to work, either. They don't meet until the night after this one. Most of them won't even be there until tomorrow, and we'll have caught up by then. You're wasting your time.*"

"*So are you,*" Sal shot back.

Behenna chuckled. "*I admire your spirit; I really do. But you're coming back with me whether you want to or not — even if I have to drag you back by the hair, every step of the way. You really don't have any other options open to you.*"

The viciousness of the image surprised him. "*Why not?*" he asked, partly to give himself time to track the warden's exact location, but also to learn the answer. Why *did* someone follow a single boy for thousands of kilometres across little more than desert and wasteland? "*Why am I so important to you, Warden Behenna?*"

"*Not you, Sal, but what you represent, what you can help me obtain. Bringing you back will make me, Sal. At the very least, it'll guarantee that I'll never have to do anything like this again — and that's the point. Being a Selector is a minor honour, a desk job for bureaucrats and failures. I'm neither. I can do better. Fundelry was just one step up the ladder. What they give me when I come back with you will be more to my tastes."*

"You're risking everything just to get a promotion?"

"I won't fail, Sal. Don't consider that a possibility. I will bring you back with me, and I will be rewarded. And if you think I don't deserve it, ask yourself why there's only me talking to you now. Where are the others, the dozens of other Sky Wardens the Syndic sent out after you? There aren't any left: that's the answer. There aren't any because I'm the best, and I deserve recognition for it. If I'd been around when your parents eloped, they would never have got away with it. And neither will you.

"You've had your time in the sun, Sal. Are you going to stop the buggy and turn around now or do we have to go through this ridiculous charade all night?"

Sal didn't answer immediately. Behenna's arrogance woke an anger in him similar to that which he had felt for his grandmother. Radi Mierlo and the warden were perfectly matched, both more than happy to sacrifice someone else's chance at happiness in order to further their own ends. Sal's needs and feelings were irrelevant, except when they got in the way of their plans.

But it was good to know that, he told himself — to be certain of it. If they didn't care what happened to him, why should he care about them in return?

He had followed the thread of the man's voice back to its source. Behenna was moving north and west, presumably following the road toward the Nine Stars with the rest of the caravan. Sal knew the crossroad wouldn't fool him. He wouldn't let go, because he was right. Sal was trapped.

The warden's mind was hard to read clearly, unlike the storm, but it was clear enough. Sal had wondered once why Sky Wardens hadn't descended on him in Yor when he had accidentally given away his position. He knew now that Behenna had kept the slip to himself in order to maximise his gain. The Sky Warden's ambition, determination and pride shone like the sun through clouds of uncertainty and desperation. It was his desperation that Sal hoped to exploit. How far, he wondered, could he push it?

"*You think you're going to be a hero,*" he said.

"*For doing my job. That's all.*"

"*You're very confident of it. Are you sure they'll even want you back, after this?*"

"*Words are nothing, Sal, and neither is looking for someone. Minor charms requiring the bare minimum of potential. No one will ever know about them.*"

"*No?*" Sal closed his eyes and concentrated.

Using every iota of his raw, wild talent, he shouted down the thread connecting his mind and the warden's, putting all his anger and resentment into one wordless, primal roar.

The warden responded as he had hoped, by putting up barriers to resist the mental flood. But he did more than that: he fought back. Sal felt Behenna's resolve strengthen once the surprise ebbed. He was going to teach Sal a lesson. The defensive wall tightened, gathered itself around the warden's mind, formed a sharp point and lunged.

Sal felt the power of it, the rage that fuelled it, and didn't know how to resist it. It knocked his attack aside as easily as a knife through rain. He had just enough time to be afraid, to think that maybe he should have thought more carefully about attacking a fully-fledged Sky Warden, to steel himself however ineffectually for the impact —

— when it was gone. The attack vanished as abruptly as it had formed. The line between him and the warden had been cut from the other end. Behenna's mind was absent from his, leaving nothing but a faint aftertaste of annoyance in its wake.

Annoyed at whom? Sal wondered. Sal or himself? There was no way of telling, now that the line was broken.

He waited for a good ten minutes before starting the buggy and driving on. The long-distance conversation had exhausted him, left him feeling hollow and weak. One thing Lodo had taught him all too well was the inherent danger of sending even a part of himself to another, across any sort of distance. All that separated minds of every kind — talented or not — was the Void Beneath. Stretching across that emptiness took effort and attracted risk. He wondered, briefly, if part of him had been lost when Behenna had broken the link between them, but decided that if it had been, it wasn't much he would miss. The fading echoes of the shout, perhaps; maybe a gasp of surprise. Not even a fully formed word.

He waited. No *tap-tap*. Behenna knew where Sal was headed, and had decided to leave well enough alone. It was only a matter of time, now, before the caravan caught up. The trap had been sprung, Sal thought, but found himself wondering: *on whom?*

Dawn brought light to the still damp world, revealing just how much it had changed overnight. Instead of a vast, stony plain, Sal saw nothing but orange sand everywhere. The horizon appeared to be nearer, since the sand lay in dunes, some of them many metres high, but the lack of anything *other* than sand made the eye slip and skid in a way that was worse than flat infinity. A single rock would be enough, Sal thought, to give him something to look at.

The road was all that existed for him, stretching forward and behind in a perfectly straight line. Water still lay pooled in places. The sun would quickly evaporate what didn't soak into the sand, but until then the desert was a different place. Everything smelled fresh and sweet, with a strange pungency that Sal couldn't identify. Long-dormant seeds would already be stirring below the surface, revived by the water and warmed by the sun. Within days, if the Mage Van Haasteren was to be believed, the desert would be transformed again; life would return for a week or more, until the last drop burned away and this cycle ended. It might be months or even years before another storm visited the desert — but the times between rainfalls didn't matter. The life in the sand followed its own seasons, far removed from the ordinary procession. Winter and summer were irrelevant in a land like this.

He realised with surprise that he could feel the life all around him, itching at the back of his mind. It wasn't like the Change. It reminded him of the way he could feel Shilly when she was near, but more spread out, infusing the whole land. The storm had stirred the desert from its long slumber and he was there to witness its awakening. As a result he didn't feel alone as he drove. The sensation that he was, briefly, part of the desert's cycle of rebirth buoyed him along.

There was no fighting his exhaustion, though. The ancient paved road was treacherous. Apart from the water, the storm had deposited sand in small drifts, requiring him to concentrate in case the wheels slipped. Sal didn't know how long it would take the caravan to catch up, but camels were better suited to this sort of terrain and they wouldn't rest with Behenna urging them on. He didn't want to sleep for fear of waking in captivity again. He wanted to arrive at the Nine Stars free, even if he didn't leave that way.

The sun rose ahead of him, drying his clothes on him. When he stopped to stretch, his limbs felt as stiff as the fabric. He wondered what Shilly was doing, whether she knew what was going on or had missed the implications of what he had done. He imagined Behenna fuming at the loss of the buggy, being forced to travel with the other passengers. Sal wondered if he had done enough to undermine the warden's determination. Then it was back onto the road for another long stint driving endlessly onward. It was too late for doubts ...

Sal didn't see the turn until it was almost upon him. The road swung right without warning and his eyes, half-dazzled by the sun, had been lulled into complacency by the unchanging terrain. Spinning the wheel as hard as he could, he wrenched the buggy wildly into the turn, skidding on the sandy road surface and almost losing control. The back of the buggy slid for a split second and he spun the wheel the other way. It skidded again, then righted itself, heading due south along the new section of road.

He braked when he saw what lay ahead through the vast dunes, feeling a shock of recognition go through him — albeit one followed by a contrasting sense of strangeness. A mighty sandstone escarpment lay directly across his path, barely a kilometre away. There was a wide, mouth-like arch at its base that reminded him of the entrance to Ulum, but the scale was completely different. This archway was much bigger — and so was the city that loomed above it.

Where the escarpment was so substantial it looked like a mountain, the city was in a state of greatly advanced decay, almost a ghost of itself. Its towers were jagged and incomplete, many of them just girder frameworks held up by their neighbours, which were themselves crumbling away. No glass glinted in the sun; there was none of the cold beauty of the city in the salt lake. This city had been stripped by time back to its skeleton, and remained trembling on the edge of complete ruin like a vast and terrible monument to mortality.

Sal couldn't tell if the natural wall of rock hid the base of the city, or *was* its base. But if the escarpment formed the top of a buried giant's head, he thought, then the city was the giant's crown. A crown of iron thorns. The image grew increasingly powerful as he pressed his foot down on the accelerator and drove nearer.

It took a surprisingly long time. He didn't truly grasp the scale of the escarpment until he was in its maw, feeling like a bug braving a grain silo. The archway yawned over him like the mouth of a god.

As he drove into its shadow, the words of the golem returned to him: *Know this, Sayed Hrvati: there are three places to which creatures such as I are drawn. This one is in decay; the second is north of here, beyond my influence; the third lies far to the south.*

If this was the second place, Sal thought, maybe he had made a mistake coming there on his own. Even if it was beyond that particular golem's influence, others still might live there. He and Shilly hadn't escaped the first one so much as been allowed to leave. It wasn't safe to assume that he would be so lucky another time.

He kept driving. The tunnel mouth shrank behind him until it almost looked small. Just as he reached to switch on the buggy's headlights, a gate rumbled open ahead of him, dispelling the gloom. Light blinded him for a second, and he braked until he could see properly. The road led through the gate — a fraction of the size of the tunnel wall, but easily five metres across — and into the heart of the city.

Or so he had expected. He was surprised to find himself on the edge of a wide, stone bowl, easily a kilometre across. It looked like a giant crater, ringed by the jagged remains of the towers. The image of the city as the crown on a giant's head turned out to be perfectly apt, for it was completely hollow. The city was shaped in a ring, with the giant circular space in the middle.

He stopped the buggy before he went too far and looked around him. Sand had pooled where the walls met the floor of the bowl, but the rain of the previous night had disturbed the drifts, spreading them down and inward in large, feathery shapes. At the centre of the bowl was a cluster of structures that looked as though they had been added later. Sal couldn't quite make them out. Heat haze obscured the details. They looked like pillars of granite, or the trunks of branchless grey trees.

A ripple of light at the base of the pillars suggested that the bowl was partly full of water. The recent rains were obviously collected there, perhaps to be siphoned off into subterranean reservoirs rather than left to evaporate. Water would be precious, so deep in the desert.

Another thought struck him, then. The bowl and the city surrounding it appeared to be completely uninhabited — but someone must have opened the gate for him. The small of his back itched.

"Hello?" he shouted, cupping his hands around his mouth. "Is anyone there?"

A faint echo returned. A breeze swept through the bowl as though in reply. Apart from that, for a good thirty seconds, there was no other movement.

Then, from behind him, the gate mechanism clanked and began to shut. He turned in alarm — there was no way out of the bowl apart from that gate — and saw a skinny young woman standing in front of the wall.

"Hello, Sal." Her cheekbones were prominent and her brown hair looked unwashed. She seemed to have come out of nowhere. "I'm sorry to keep you waiting. We weren't expecting you so soon."

An inflection in her voice reminded him of someone. There was a weird feeling in the air, as though things were moving that he couldn't see.

"Do I know you?" he asked.

"Yes. I am the Mage Erentaite."

"What? That's —"

She raised a hand. "This will seem impossible to you, Sal, but I assure you that it is so. I am too old to undertake the journey here myself, in person, so I use this body as a temporary vessel instead. It is my thoughts alone that travel."

Understanding dawned. He had wondered how the Stone Mages could warrant such a long journey to and from the Nine Stars every month, and now he knew how they managed it. They sent their minds instead of their bodies.

But was it so simple? What happened, for instance, to the people who were in the bodies they took over? Did they swap places with the mages, or were they dislocated for a brief time, stuck nowhere at all in the Void Beneath.

A chill went through him. *Creatures such as I*, the golem had said. Sal had assumed it had meant other golems, but it might not have been talking about that at all.

"You look as though you've seen a ghost," the Mage Erentaite said through another woman's lips. "Apart from that, you look just as I imagined you."

Of course, he thought. *In her real body, she's blind.* He licked his lips and forced himself to speak. "I'm sorry. It's just I've never heard of anything like this before. It's…" He faltered, lacking the right word. *Horrible? Frightening?*

"Necessary," said the mage. "The mountain won't come to us, so we must go to the mountain. No harm is done to any of the vessels in the process. In fact, they are looked after rather better than they would be without us; they would have starved to death years ago without our care. The empty-minded are easy prey for those who hunt the weak, and it is our duty to ensure that they are protected. This way, we solve two problems with one action."

"So..." He struggled to get his head around it. "They're like this anyway? You didn't force your way in?"

"No, Sal. We would never do that. To force our way in when not wanted, or to stay any longer than was necessary, would be abominable."

He agreed wholeheartedly with that. There was nothing to stop a blind, old mage like Jarmila Erentaite from permanently taking over a young woman in order to live her remaining years fit and healthy instead of infirm and weak. It didn't matter that the woman's body would have been empty when the mage moved in; it wasn't *hers*. What if the young woman's mind ever tried to come back? She would have nowhere to go. She really would be lost, then.

He knew very little about what made a person who they were and where they went when their body was empty, but he couldn't believe that the body before him would function if its mind wasn't alive *somewhere*.

"What was her name?" he asked the mage, thinking: *If she can't answer, I'll know this is wrong.*

"Yeran," she said, without hesitation.

"And what happens to your body when your mind is — here?"

"It sleeps under the watchful eye of my assistant. If anything should go wrong at her end, I would be summoned immediately."

"Do all the Stone Mages do this?"

"Only the ones who are on the Synod, and then not everyone. All are required to travel in person at least once a year, and most usually choose the time of the solstices. Even I must do this. If I am unfit to take the journey, then I am unfit to be on the Synod. Does that seem reasonable to you?"

"I — I guess so." The answers to his questions didn't entirely satisfy him, proving that the matter wasn't so easy to resolve.

"Is there anything else you'd like to know?"

She smiled as he floundered for a moment. Who was he to question the ways of the Stone Mages? The decision the Synod would make should be most on his mind, not how they made it. But could he respect the decision of people who had anything at all in common with golems? He didn't know.

"When does it start?"

"At sunset tonight." The eyes of the mage's vessel were clear and blue, lighter than his grandmother's and his own. He couldn't quite bring himself to call her "Yeran", for that person was no longer there, but he still baulked at thinking of her as entirely Jarmila Erentaite. Sal wondered what it felt like to see again through such young eyes, even if it was only once a month.

She took his arm and directed his attention into the heart of the bowl. "We will gather here to decide the issues of the Interior until the sun rises and sets them into stone. There are many things to discuss. Your matter will not be the first, but it will not be the last, either. You'll need to rest in order to be ready. Even though you won't be talking, you will still find it exhausting. That I guarantee you."

He nodded, knowing it to be true. His entire body ached from the night's drive and the confrontation with Behenna. It was only his mind that resisted sleep.

"What about the Judges?" he asked, curious about those who would ultimately decide his fate. "Do they travel here like you?"

"Not all, Sal. Some of them live here permanently, in their own bodies." A slight hesitation caught his attention, but she didn't elaborate. "Come on," she said, her manner instantly more cheerful. "Let's go for a drive around the edge on the way. It'll be quicker — and I've always wanted to do this."

The surface of the bowl was smooth and never steep. Sal drove the buggy cautiously at first, but the Mage Erentaite urged him to go faster. Soon they were speeding rapidly around the inside of the bowl as though it were a racing track, with the decaying tower-skeletons as an audience and the sound of the engine growling off the walls. The mage in her younger body stood up on the seat and revelled in the wind sweeping through her hair.

"Yes!" She looked down at Sal, her smile wide and joyful. "There's always time for happiness, Sal, no matter the place or the circumstances. Remember that. Just a small amount of light can dispel the deepest darkness."

He smiled back and urged the buggy faster still, taking it in sweeping turns back and forth across the bowl, great figure eights that swayed them from side to side and made Shilly's crutches whip around on the tray. Only then did he realise that he had run off with them, and he instantly felt bad about it.

His attention was off driving long enough for gravity to override his steering. The buggy drifted naturally inward without him intending it to.

"No, don't go into the centre," said the mage, putting one of her vessel's hands firmly on his shoulder. "Leave that for tonight. Go back to the edge."

Her tone was no longer cheerful, almost warning, and he did exactly as she said, putting the relatively small collection of buildings and pillars, and the glistening pool of water half-drowning them, behind him. Closer to, the pillars hadn't seemed so small. Among them, he received the impression of giant upraised wings, although what they could belong to he had no idea.

"There." She pointed at a hole in the wall. It might have been the same tunnel through which he had entered. He had lost all orientation during the drive. "Drive right in. Slowly."

He did so, unable to see where he was going for a moment.

"Over there." She pointed. "Park under that overhang. The buggy will be safe there, I promise." He did so, feeling her gaze on him all the way. "You understand that you'll have to let Warden Behenna have it back when he arrives?"

He nodded, feeling a flush rise up his neck and into his cheeks. Erentaite hadn't mentioned the theft before then. He had hoped it wouldn't come up.

"Will it hurt my case?" he asked.

"That depends." The buggy's engine died and they were left in sudden, startling silence.

"Tell me why you ran here, Sal."

"To surprise Warden Behenna," he lied, hoping she didn't already know the truth. He didn't want the Synod to know that he had deliberately tried to ruin the career of another Change-worker. "To put him off guard. He thinks he's won, and I hate that. I want him to know that he could still fail."

She nodded. "And by running to *us*, you're telling your grandmother that you feel safer with us than her. That you can trust us to be objective. You're telling the Synod that, too."

He hadn't thought of that. "Do you think it'll help?"

"No more than talking to us would have. The theft can be used as much for you as against you. It's up to those speaking on your behalf to do it properly." Her gaze held him fixed a moment longer. "Whatever you do, Sal, let those words prevail or fail as the Judges decide. This is a council of reason, not passion. The Judges will not be swayed by shows of force, and such certainly cannot injure them. Strike out and you will only hurt yourself."

Sal nodded. The serious tone of her voice left him in no doubt as to what would happen if he let anger or frustration stir his wild talent.

"The Weavers —"

"Don't say their name here!" Her eyes darted past him, deeper into the shadows. "Don't even think of them."

Alarmed, he shrank back in the seat. "Sorry. I didn't know that I shouldn't."

"Don't be sorry, Sal. Just be careful. They have eyes everywhere." The Mage Erentaite startled him by slapping both hands on the thighs of her vessel body. "I'm the one who should be sorry, if anyone must. Neither Yeran nor you has been eating well lately. We both need food and rest." She climbed out of the buggy. "Come with me and we'll rustle up a meal, then it's off to bed. The ceremony will go for a long time tonight."

"What do I need to do?"

"Perhaps nothing. The fact that you have chosen not to speak will make it harder for you to defend what you think is right, but it will also make it harder for the Synod to ignore you. If that makes sense," she added with a smile.

"Do *you* think it's right?"

"It would be wrong of me to say in advance." She put a thin arm around his shoulder and pointed toward a door. "All I can do is ensure that you don't make things any worse for yourself."

With that, she launched into a long and detailed description of the history, rituals and protocols of the Synod. Whether it was her intention to bore him mindless with the litany of dos and don'ts she poured onto him, he didn't know for certain, but it worked anyway. He almost nodded off in the middle of the meal — simple bread and vegetable broth served in a kitchen deep under the ruined city, where other vessels served themselves or were handfed by the orderlies who tended them. He lost track of all the Judges and the decisions they'd made. The names, an endless litany of them, began to sound the same. By the time she showed him to an empty dormitory and he collapsed into bed, his thoughts were on nothing but sleep.

He didn't rest long, however. He was awoken from a dream in which he had asked the Mage Erentaite, in her original body, how the city of the Nine Stars had earned its name. She smiled and pointed upward. In the sky above shone nine bright lights that turned in a giant circle. They looked like stars but obviously weren't: apart from their unnatural motion, they were too bright and clear, too close. He soon became dizzy with his head tipped back, watching them spinning around, getting faster and faster with every turn until they were just a blur, a bright circle in the sky, and he lost his balance completely and fell upward, into the stars — into the Void, where all the little parts of his mind that he'd lost wrapped around him like a web, choking him.

He woke at the sound of a voice inside his head.

"*I'm sorry to disturb you, Sal.*"

"What?" He sat up, blinking, and found himself staring at a lizard frozen on the far side of the wall, splayed as though caught in mid-motion. Apart from that and the low cot he was lying on, the stone-walled room was empty. "Who —? *Where are you?*"

"*I'm not there with you,*" said the voice, "*although I soon will be.*"

Sal placed its source, finally. The voice belonged to the Mage Van Haasteren and came to him via the Change.

"*What time is it?*" The only light came from glow stones in the hall outside; it could have been either midnight or midday for all that he could tell.

"*Almost sunset. They'll come for you in a few minutes.*"

"*Where are you?*" he asked again.

"*We're within sight of the Nine Stars and will arrive in time for the beginning of the Synod. We'll certainly be there for your hearing.*"

Sal rubbed his eyes and thought of all the miles the caravan had travelled without a break. It had been hard enough in the buggy. "*I wasn't trying to hold you up.*"

"*I know, Sal. That's what I want to talk to you about. Your idea was a good one. Perhaps a little ruthless, but the victim did bring it on himself. You simply guided him — just as your grandmother guided you into his hands back in Ulum. Behind every powerful solution, as they say, there lies a powerful need.*"

"*But it worked, didn't it?*" Sal said, breaking into what sounded like the beginning of a lesson. "*He could use the Change, even though he wasn't trained the right way?*"

There was a slight pause, as though the mage was reluctant to admit that he had been wrong. But in the end he did so with only a slight edge of bitterness to his voice. "*Yes, that's true. Whether he knows what this means, though, I'm not sure. He is asleep at the moment. Hence this communication, while he won't notice.*"

"*Can Tait sense anything?*"

"*I doubt it. The journeyman isn't half as talented as he would like Shilly to believe. I gather the Haunted City sent him home before he finished training, and I can understand why.*"

That was pretty much what Lodo had said, back at Fundelry. And he had been right about the rest, too. But that was only half Sal's problem. "*What about Shilly? Is she okay?*"

"*She's angry, Sal, and confused. She suffered a minor injury during the storm, and she resents you for leaving without her. I haven't said anything to her about what you did, though, and neither has Behenna. He wouldn't, of course, even though he won't be able to hide what's happened to anyone sensitive.*"

"*Like the Synod?*"

"*Yes. Everyone there will know the moment they see him. His torc may not have exploded or turned green, but it might as well have. He's marked, now, like Lodo, as you wanted him to be.*"

Sal felt a moment of satisfaction. *Serves him right,* he thought to himself. Behenna had got exactly what he deserved.

A sudden and unexpected rush of shame followed that thought, though. Did he have any right to destroy the career of a Sky Warden to further his own ends? Even though that was what everyone around him, it seemed, was doing to him, he didn't want to adopt their strategies in return. That would make him as bad as them — one thing his father most definitely had not wanted for him.

He guessed that deep down he had thought it wouldn't work. That there would be no consequences. All he wanted was to stay in the Interior, his mother's birthplace. Hurting someone in the process of making that possible wasn't part of the plan.

He couldn't even say that he'd had no choice, because there were always choices. He knew that. His father could have chosen not to pursue his feelings for a married woman. His mother could have chosen not to encourage the advances of one of her husband's acquaintances. From those two choices had flowed so many ramifications — and they were still flowing.

Along with the questions. If anyone could use the Change, anywhere, why were the two schools of thought kept so separate, and where, ultimately, did the Change come from? There were so many secrets and mysteries surrounding something that had seemed relatively simple — if awe-inspiring — when he had first found out about it.

He almost asked about the Weavers, wondering if they were the ones the Mage Erentaite had hinted that he and Shilly had to learn to defend themselves against, but the elderly mage's warning not to even think the name stopped him from mentioning them, too.

"What do you think will happen?"

"Time will tell, Sal. If your plan doesn't work — and it hasn't yet, note — I don't know what will happen. Shom Behenna is not a man to be happily thwarted. You tried at the Divide and he persisted further than you or I ever expected him to. Perhaps he will simply accept it if the Judges' decision goes against him, but I doubt another loss at your hands will sit easily. If he doesn't decide that the cost already has been too great and lets you slip through his fingers, I'm sure he will make every effort to make sure you remain in his grasp."

"And he's not toothless now, is he?"

The mage hesitated a moment before answering. *"No, Sal. I won't lie to you. He's not. He has nothing left to lose."*

The thought hung between them for a good minute. A heavy dread settled into Sal's stomach and dragged his spirits down with it. The sense of accomplishment he had felt on the way to the Nine Stars was gone. All he had left now was the knowledge that he had done everything he could, whether he should have done it or not.

"We are almost there," said the mage. *"Tait will soon wake his master, and I don't want him to suspect that I've been*

talking to you. We'll see you at the Synod before long. Jarmila has met you, I gather?"

"Yes."

"Do as she says. She has only ever done the right thing, as long as I've known her, and only ever told the truth."

Just like a golem, Sal thought.

"I will," he promised.

"And one more thing," the mage added. *"In case I'm not able to talk to you afterward, in private, there's something you should know. Lodo's heart-name is Athim. Remember, and use it well."*

"How?"

"You will understand when the time is right."

Then the mage was gone. Sal was left alone with the lizard — and his puzzlement — for far too brief a space. But long enough. By the time the Mage Erentaite came to take him to the Synod, with Yeran's body washed and fully clothed in white formal robes, he could feel Shilly again. The caravan was therefore very close, and the moment of confrontation had almost come.

As he readied himself, he came to a sort of conclusion. No matter what happened next — whether he was dragged back to the Strand against his will or freed to return to the Keep — he would never regret his last, headlong flight in the buggy. As a farewell to the life he had loved with his father, it couldn't have been fitter. As a sign of what he could do when he put his mind to it, likewise. He had crossed a boundary in his life, and now it was time to move on.

Straightening his clothes, he went to face the Stone Mage Advisory Synod and the Judgment of the Interior.

CHAPTER 17

NINE STARS, ONE MIND

A frill-necked lizard hissed at Shom Behenna as he passed. Shilly, leaning on Tait not far away, saw the warden flinch as though struck.

"What's wrong now?" asked Radi Mierlo, at his side.

"Nothing," he said, although his dark skin had turned ashen. "There's nothing wrong."

The lizard watched him go, then scuttled into shadows cast by the torchlight guiding their way and disappeared.

"What was that all about?" asked Shilly. The warden's behaviour had been decidedly unusual since Sal had run off with the buggy: impatient and dismissive until Sal had been located again, then moody afterward, as though worried about something. Tait had been odd, too. Shilly couldn't understand what they had to worry about. Sal had been found and the Synod would go ahead as expected. The warden was getting exactly what he wanted.

"Lizards are the eyes and ears of the mages," Tait said, "just as seagulls are for Sky Wardens."

She nodded. That made sense; lizards were as common as gulls in the desert, and people tended not to notice them. But why had it hissed so venomously at the warden as he walked by and not the others? Because he had used the Change in the Interior? She didn't understand why that should make such a difference.

There was much more going on than appeared on the surface. All around her she could feel tension building, thrilling through the stone itself. Outside, the sun was setting in a wash of crimson fire, melting into the desert as though returning home. Soon the full moon would rise on the far horizon and the Synod would begin. The time would come for her fate to be decided. After all the effort she and Sal had put in to get to the Keep — to put their future in their own hands — she would never have guessed it would come to this.

Tait kept his arm tight around her waist as she hobbled along the great stone tunnel. There hadn't been time to find the buggy, even though one of the orderlies who had met them assured her it was nearby. Tait had offered to help her readily enough, but he was no substitute for her crutches. Her newly-bruised bone jarred with every step, making her wince. She tried to conceal the pain, but there was no hiding it from Tait. She was so close she could feel him breathe. Although she was grateful for his help, the intimacy made her uncomfortable in other ways.

Warden Behenna and Radi Mierlo hurried ahead, impatient for the Synod to begin. The Mage Van Haasteren and Skender came up behind Shilly and Tait and matched their pace.

"Are you nervous?" Skender asked. "I would be."

"I'm looking forward to it being over," she said.

"Me, too," said Tait. "Then we can go home."

"What's so good about that?" If Skender was trying to bait the journeyman, his voice held no hint of it. "This is your chance to see the world! Given the choice, I'd *never* go home."

"Not everyone's like you, Skender," said the Mage Van Haasteren.

"You can blame his mother for that," said a voice from the shadows.

Shilly turned to look past Tait as a woman in dusty red robes strode into the light. She was tall and carried herself proudly. Her head was bound tightly in cloth, like a turban, and in one hand she held a long, straight staff. Lines of unfamiliar letters ran across her temple and down both cheeks. Shilly had seen such decorations before in pictures of Surveyors. They were a breed apart from both Stone Mages and Sky Wardens.

When Skender saw her, his whole face lit up. "Mother!"

She took him into her arms and pressed her cheek against his forehead. "It's good to see you, kid."

"Hello, Abi." The Mage Van Haasteren took one stiff step forward.

She reached out to enfold his hand in both of hers. "It's good to see you, too. When I heard you were both coming, I rode from the dig as fast as I could. I thought I might not get here in time — and it turns out it was almost *you* who got here late."

"Well, that wasn't our fault." The mage's eyes glittered in the torchlight.

"Where have you *been*?" Skender wriggled in the woman's embrace, and looked up at her with something very much like awe. "Tell me everything!"

"Not now, Skender," said his father, glancing ahead to where Behenna waited impatiently at the end of the tunnel. "Wait until this is finished."

Skender's mother nodded. "I'll see you after, I promise. I'm not going back to the dig until the day after tomorrow."

Tait tugged Shilly along, and she dragged her eyes away from the family reunion. Another one for her to feel jealous of. Skender's mother looked nothing like her son, but she could see now where he got his wanderlust. How Skender's parents had ever found themselves in one place long enough to have a child was a mystery.

Behenna's face had lost some of its yellow pallor when they caught up with him. Between him and Sal's grandmother — who had set herself apart from the rest of her dusty entourage by donning a full-length azure robe just prior to arrival — stood a slender young man dressed in a simple cotton smock. He bowed slightly when Shilly and Tait joined them, sending a lock of golden-blond hair across his forehead.

He brushed it casually aside, revealing pale brown eyes. "Welcome." His voice was soft but firm. "My name is Othniel, and I have been assigned to ensure your wellbeing. We'll wait here for the others, then proceed to the commencement ceremony."

"Why can't we go on ahead and meet the rest there?" asked Behenna, glancing back to where Sal's beefy cousin, Aron, struggled under the weight of the man'kin Mawson, strapped to his back in a leather harness.

"Because that is not appropriate," Othniel said. "I appreciate that you are in a hurry, Warden Behenna, but I assure you that you will miss nothing important."

The warden wasn't going to acquiesce to the request with grace. "Is there anyone else I can speak to?"

"No. Please be patient."

"They send a boy to meet us and expect us not to take insult?" Radi Mierlo sniffed. "We've come a long way for this, you know."

"I know." Othniel smiled tightly and folded his arms. "And I am not as young as I seem."

The Mage Van Haasteren caught up at that moment. "Ah, Othniel," he said, reaching forward to shake the young man's hand. "It's good to see you again."

"You too, Skender — and you, young Skender. And Abi! It's been too long." Skender's mother embraced the young man. He barely came up to her shoulder.

"You must come by the Keep soon," said Van Haasteren. "The students could use a refresher course on optics."

"I'll see what I can do." Othniel nodded. "The spirit is willing, as you know, but the flesh . . ." He shrugged helplessly.

Shilly followed the exchange with growing confusion. "You're a Stone Mage?" she asked him.

Othniel bowed again. "At your beck and call, this evening."

"A very good one, too," Van Haasteren said with a smile. "Too good to play nursemaid to a bunch of tourists."

"Perhaps." Othniel took obvious pleasure at the look of consternation on Radi Mierlo's face. Behenna ignored him.

"But —" Shilly began.

"I'll explain later," whispered Skender, sidling up beside her. "Look ahead. That's where we're going!"

"It's a beautiful, clear night now the rain has gone," Othniel said. "Conditions couldn't be better. The Gathering isn't complete, but we have enough to begin. That's the main thing."

Shilly took the opportunity to let go of Tait and stood balanced on one leg, peering past the adults around her. Behind their guide, she could see a wide, flat surface sloping down into darkness. She received an impression of great space, open to the sky. There were lights, twinkling faintly in the twilight, and a patch of yellow in the distance. It looked like a bonfire, but if it was the flames weren't moving and there was no smoke.

The tangled framework of the ruined city — different both from the city in the Broken Lands and the Haunted City — stood out starkly against the greying sky. Within minutes it would be fully dark and the city would effectively vanish, but it would still be unmistakably present. Even with all the other novel sensations around her, Shilly could feel the Change emanating from it. Vast and impersonal, dwarfing her.

When the rest of the party had caught up, Othniel put a finger to his lips then indicated that they should follow him. Tait put his arm back around Shilly's waist and supported her while she walked. She endured the indignity purely because she had no choice, and she cursed Sal with every hobbled step for running off with her crutches. It was bad enough that she had been dragged into the centre of his mess; being unable to stand on her own only made it worse.

Othniel led them out into the night, down a gentle slope into the enormous stone bowl at the heart of the city. Shilly looked around as best she could. The deepening night was full of soft noises, as though a large group of people awaited them at the heart of the bowl, in the centre of the yellow glow. She sensed the enormous wall surrounding the bowl receding behind her, leaving her feeling stranded under the infinite sky. A dozen stars had emerged from the blue-black dome, hinting at constellations. More appeared as she watched. Some of them . . .

She stopped in her tracks and almost tripped up Tait. A longer look told her that her eyes weren't deceiving her. Some of the stars weren't in the sky at all, but hanging in the tangled mess that had once been a mighty city. She swung Tait with her as she turned on the spot, looking all around.

"Are you all right?" he asked, trying his best to avoid bumping her leg, but not entirely succeeding.

"They're not stars," she said. "They're something else."

"What?" His brow crinkled deeply. "What stars?"

"Those." She pointed with her free arm. "That one there, and that one there, and that one..." She stopped and did a quick count. Of course, she thought: there were nine of them.

"What are they?"

"*No one knows.*" The buzzing voice of the man'kin came from startlingly close on her right.

She turned to see that Aron had stopped to look as well. His eyes were wide and childlike with wonder. The granite bust twisted around to stare at her in a way she found unnerving.

"What do you mean, no one knows?"

"*Just that.*"

"Couldn't someone just climb up there in daylight and look?"

"*Certainly, but they would find nothing, just as nothing has been found on previous attempts.*" The man'kin looked smug. "*Besides, the lights are in a different place every full moon. And looking during a full moon is dangerous.*"

"Why?"

"*Try and you'll find out.*"

"Are there golems up there?"

"Is there a problem, Tait?" asked Warden Behenna, striding out of the darkness toward them, scowling deeply.

"Sorry," said Tait. "We just stopped to look."

"We're not here to sightsee."

"I know. Sorry." The warden stalked off ahead, and Tait urged Shilly along faster. Aron, Sal's cousin, maintained a slow, steady pace at their side, his face completely expressionless again. Every now and then he glanced at her as though making sure she was still there.

"Don't you ever talk?" she asked him.

"No," said the man'kin. "*He doesn't.*"

"I wasn't asking you."

"*Well enough, but this is the only way you'll get an answer.*" She felt the man'kin's stony gaze still on her, but she refused to acknowledge it by returning it. "*His silence is endearing. I've had many steeds, but few so compliant.*"

"Is that why you put up with her?"

"*With Radi? No. I owe a debt to her family that has yet to be discharged. Until then, I am bound, within certain limitations, to do her will.*"

"And in exchange you get Aron." She could appreciate that the young man was well suited to the task, but it still didn't seem fair. She could see muscles straining in his neck and shoulders with every step. "Why don't you have one of your own carry you?"

"*Never!*" The man'kin hissed like a snake. "*'Kin never carries 'kin. Don't you know anything, child?*"

The vehemence in its voice stung her. Her first instinct was to snap back an angry retort, but she didn't want to argue with it, if it could help her find Lodo. "If I don't, it's only because no one tells me anything."

That seemed to calm it down. "*Well, perhaps you're safer that way. You shouldn't believe everything you're told.*"

"I've been told to be careful of man'kin, as a matter of fact."

"*You will find that someone much closer to you than I is doing the lying.*"

"Someone close to me? Do you mean Sal?"

It said nothing.

She looked at Tait, who shrugged. "Do these things *ever* speak in a straight line?" she asked.

"I don't know," he said. "What did it say?"

Before she could answer, the rest of the party slowed them to a halt where Othniel waited.

Their guide raised a hand to indicate east. The sky in that direction was growing lighter as the moon rose behind the city wall.

"It is about to begin," Othniel said. "Please, sit."

Shilly's adjusting eyes took a moment to register a series of low, stone benches just ahead of them, facing the heart of the bowl. They stretched into the distance like the seating of an enormous stadium, and most of them were full. Tait guided her to one that had been kept free for them, and she collapsed gratefully into it, noticing as she did so that the ground beneath the benches appeared to have been recently wet. Aron chose a position nearby and unburdened himself of the man'kin, which he made sure was facing the right direction. Skender skidded up to Shilly and leaned in close.

"Are you ready?" he whispered.

"As ready as I'll ever be, given that I didn't ask to be here."

"Well, I'm on your side. Remember that. We made too good a team to break it up now." With a brief squeeze of her shoulder, he slipped away to join his parents, sitting together two rows down.

Shom Behenna stood behind Tait, a picture of barely restrained energy. Radi Mierlo sat on her own not far away. When they were all in place, Othniel nodded in satisfaction.

"I'll let them know you're here," he said, and vanished into the darkness.

Shilly waited impatiently for the moon to rise. They were much closer to the yellow heart of the bowl than they had been before, but still she could see surprisingly little apart from a number of slender pillars looming over the light. There was something about that yellow glow that bothered her: it didn't seem to cast any actual illumination, so everything around her looked like it was embedded in amber. It reminded her of the glow Lodo's light-sink had first made when she, Sal and Skender had brought it to life in the Keep. The pale silver haze to the east, heralding the full moon, was the only note of ice in an ambience that was otherwise just a little *too* warm.

"Theatrics," Behenna muttered, almost too softly for her to hear. She didn't know how the Sky Warden Conclave made its decisions, but doubted it aspired to anything less mysterious than the Stone Mage Synod.

When the first sliver of moon poked up over the city wall, a sigh went up around them as though the world itself had inhaled. Then a voice spoke.

"Welcome."

Shilly felt the word in her mind, not her ears, coming to her through the background potential surrounding her. Who was speaking, she didn't know; the voice had no accent and could have belonged to an old man or a young woman. It could even have belonged to a man'kin. Without seeing its source, she simply couldn't tell.

"Welcome, all, to this the Cold Moon Synod — the last of many for some, the first of many for others. As always, we have new members to welcome and old to mourn, and I'll move onto them in a moment. We have observers and petitioners from all parts. Their turn will come too. We have decisions to make and put into action. All things in their time, friends. For now, be welcomed and welcoming to those around you. We are here, we are the Synod, and we are united, burning with the desire to take the word of the world and write it into stone. We have many voices, yet we speak with one."

A murmur rose up around her and Shilly peered into the yellow-tinged haze. The more the moon rose above the wall, the more detail she could make out. She was surrounded by a great crowd of people, some of them in the full red robes of the Stone

Mages, others in more simple attire, like Othniel. All faced inward, except when asked to "be welcomed and welcoming", at which time they turned to their neighbours and renewed acquaintances in various ways.

Everyone seemed to know each other well. The Mage Van Haasteren and Skender's mother, Abi, exchanged warm greetings with several nearby people. Nobody spoke to anyone else in her party, however. Shilly felt invisible for all the attention they paid her, until a tap on her shoulder made her jump.

She swivelled in the seat, knowing who it was before looking. "Sal?"

"Here." He held both of her crutches in one hand. She took them silently. His face was drawn and his eyes held an imploring edge. She opened her mouth to thank him, but Tait beat her to it.

"Try thinking about someone else instead of yourself, next time," he said, taking the crutches from Shilly's hand and putting them between her and him on the bench.

Sal glanced at Tait, then at Shilly, and the hurt in his eyes grew strong.

Oh, hell, she thought. *Is he jealous?*

"Sal, listen —"

He turned to walk away from her and came face to face with Behenna. Both wore mixed expressions of determination and — strangely, she thought — confusion. They stared at each other for a timeless split second, then Sal was past, weaving through the crowd.

"We'll be seeing you afterward," shouted Tait after him, every inflection ringing with challenge.

"Shut up, Tait," muttered Behenna, turning his attention back into the heart of the bowl.

Tait winked at Shilly and did as he was told.

On the inside, she groaned at Sal and Tait's behaviour. *What have I done to deserve these two idiots?* That was all she needed, after everything else. She wanted to go after Sal, but he had disappeared among the pale faces.

The moon crept slowly into the sky as the voice launched into a summary of the night's agenda. If she had expected arcane pronouncements and cryptic ceremonies, she would have been disappointed. The truth was that she hadn't known what to expect. She had thought it would be more inspiring, though, as she sat through endless lists of names she didn't know.

Her own appeared in the middle of it:

"— the matter of Sal Hrvati and Shilly of Gooron as brought to us by Sky Warden Shom Behenna in Special Petition number forty-eight —"

Then it was back to the endless list of names. She wondered how they were going to fit it all in. Shifting restlessly in her seat, she cast her gaze around her and tried to find something interesting to look at. The crowd was universally focused inward, except for the odd pocket of restlessness. Other petitioners, she assumed. Among them had to be Sal, although she couldn't see him anywhere. Despite the growing clarity cast by the moon's silver orb, the interior of the bowl was still difficult to discern. The tall, looming objects reminded her of obelisks that had been stretched upward and twisted slightly in the process, so none of them stood quite true. There were a dozen or so of them in a very rough ring around the centre, in which stood several smaller, blockier constructions. She half saw people in the very centre and something tall and white moving among them. Maybe, she thought, she wasn't *supposed* to see very well. This was secret Interior business, after all, and there was a Sky Warden present. Her view could have been obscured along with his.

Finally, the list was done and the petitions themselves began. Instead of one voice speaking, there were several, and the discussions sometimes became quite animated. The hope that these might be entertaining soon faded. The topics were unfamiliar to her, and she rarely had time to work one out before it was over and the next had begun. Sometimes people moved forward from the crowd to address the Synod as a whole — one of them a man with dark skin, like hers — but, again, she didn't know anything about the issues so she couldn't follow the arguments. As far as she could tell, it was mostly about property settlements, mining rights, joint ventures and so on.

The Stone Mages didn't seem to find the process boring, though. They stood or sat through the whole thing with a patient intensity Shilly envied. The whole process felt increasingly unreal to her, until she almost believed that it was just a game, an act. It wasn't happening. They wouldn't really send her back because this was all make-believe. They were just going through the motions to unsettle her, or to lead Warden Behenna on. They would make their decision regardless of what happened here. Her presence was just a formality — or, worse, an irrelevance.

Still, the bench was real, and it became increasingly uncomfortable no matter how she squirmed. Eventually, she gave up and lay full-length upon it, rejecting Tait's offer to use his pack as a pillow. The voices in her head and the slow rising of the moon — which seemed to be taking much longer than usual, as though time itself had slowed — together conspired to lull her to sleep. She welcomed it, preferring rest after the day's journey to an impatient wait for her turn to come.

The last thing she saw was the sole Sky Warden in the crowd watching the proceedings with a silent, brooding intensity, as though daring the Synod to deny him what he desired.

*   *   *

When she awoke it was to a hand shaking her shoulder and a feeling that an enormous amount of time had passed. The night was cold and soundless. The moon was no longer before her, but above and slightly behind. A subtle breeze wound its way into her clothes, making her shiver.

She looked around her, still dazed but gradually regaining her senses. The hand stopped shaking her, satisfied that she was awake.

A face appeared before her, the Mage Van Haasteren. His long features looked even more serious than usual. For a moment she was reminded of Lodo, although she couldn't work out why.

"It's time," he said.

She sat up with his help. The Synod was unmoving and silent. She could feel its attention on her and those around her as though she was at the centre of a frozen whirlpool. The light was no longer warm and yellow, but icily blue, chilling. The air smelt like the Broken Lands, raw and primal, full of potential.

Tait gave her the crutches. Grateful that she could walk with some dignity, she followed the members of the party through the Synod and to the heart of the bowl. Othniel led the way forward, closely followed by Warden Behenna and Radi Mierlo. Tait and Shilly came next, with the Mage Van Haasteren and Skender bringing up the rear. Aron, Mawson, and Skender's mother, Abi, remained behind.

The subtle charm that had prevented her from seeing the centre of the bowl appeared to have lifted. As she approached, the ruins of the city rose around her like a multitude of skeletal limbs reaching for the sky. The nine stars hanging in their entangled fingers burned steadily, pinning her under their dispassionate stare. She felt the combined attention of all the Stone Mages upon her as Othniel guided them past one of the tall, twisted shapes — nothing more than granite, she noted; a giant stone splinter stuck into the ground — and beyond, to where the Judges waited.

There were nine of them, too, standing in a rough circle at the lowest point of the bowl. Three were male, five female. Four were old and dressed in black; four were young and clad only in pale shifts. The remaining judge was a man'kin: a tall, scowling, winged figure carved entirely out of marble, holding a downturned sword in both hands as though leaning on it. Its face was old and young, male and female, happy and sad all at the same time. Its expression, like the others, was stern. Two folded ice-white wings towered high above its head.

Sal was there, too, Shilly discovered when she tore her eyes off the statue. He was on the far side of the open space at the centre of the bowl, standing near a young woman with brown hair tied back in a plait. He looked very small and nervous.

Othniel led them to a point right at the heart of the bowl. Shilly felt the circle of Judges close in around her and the others, even though none came within three paces of them. Every word and every gesture was magnified, as though they were at the heart of the world. The attention of the Synod made the air feel thick and heavy.

She wanted to turn and run, but knew she couldn't back out. It was far too late for that.

"*Warden Behenna,*" said the voice that had opened the Synod, "*state your request as clearly and succinctly as possible.*"

The warden turned to face the man'kin — who, Shilly realised, was the one who had spoken — and took a deep breath.

"I request permission to return these two children —" He indicated Sal and Shilly. "— to their homes in the Strand."

"*That is all?*"

"You asked for 'clearly and succinctly' didn't you? Yes, that's all."

"*Does anyone wish to testify against this request?*"

The Mage Van Haasteren stepped forward. "I do."

"*For what reason?*"

"Returning Sal and Shilly to the Strand would not be in their best interests."

"*Very well.*" The winged man'kin shifted position, emitting a sound like stone grinding against stone. "*We will begin the examination.*"

"Thank you," said Warden Behenna with a slight bow. "I am confident that —"

"*Do not speak,*" interrupted the man'kin sternly, "*unless you are asked a direct question. You will be addressed in due course.*"

Behenna's skin grew a shade darker in the icy moonlight. In reluctant deference to the Judges' wishes, he shut his mouth and backed one step away.

"This is not an easy decision," said the young woman standing next to Sal to the gathering as a whole. "It is not one I would make, given the choice. Both children have recently lost their guardians; both came here of their own free will from the very depths of the Strand, and that is no small feat for anyone; both thought they had good reason to travel so far, fleeing what they perceived as a threat and hoping to find help here, from us. They have been through a lot and are yet to find their feet. Who are we to put Shilly and Sal through more?"

Shilly agreed wholeheartedly with the woman's final words, even though it was hard to remember how it had felt at the beginning of her flight with Sal from Fundelry. It felt like years ago.

"That is what we are here to discuss, Mage Erentaite," said a thin, white-bearded man on the far side of the ring of Judges. A shock of surprise went through Shilly. *Mage Erentaite?* The elderly woman had said that she would be there, watching over them, but how was this possible? "Tell us, child, why you came here."

The Judge was addressing Shilly, not Sal, and she fought to control her surprise in order to speak clearly. Othniel had been more than he had seemed. Why not the young woman before her, too?

"We, uh, well, we came here to find Mage Van Haasteren. Not *this* Mage Van Haasteren. His father. He was my first teacher's teacher, and I thought he might be able to help us."

"Help you how?" asked a woman in full robes like the bearded man. Her hair was pure black in the moonlight.

"By teaching us. Or just me. I don't know. Sal had family here, and I had no one. That was all I had to hope for: to learn."

"What happened to your first teacher?"

"He —" She stopped. "I thought he'd died helping us escape. We learned on the way here that he hasn't died at all, but become a golem. He's in the Haunted City now." *His body is*, she amended to herself. *I've no idea where* he *is*.

"Are we talking about Payat Misseri here?" asked a young, white-clad man to Shilly's left.

"Yes," said the woman near Sal — the one referred to as the Mage Erentaite.

"How ironic."

"We aren't here to discuss his case." The bearded man frowned at his colleague, then turned back to Shilly. "Forgive us if we ask you a lot of difficult questions, child. Although we already know some of your recent history, there is much we need to clarify in order to make our decision properly. You came here seeking teaching, you said."

"Yes."

"Even though you possess no talent of your own?"

"Of my own, no, but —"

"She is an Irregular," said the Mage Van Haasteren, "with residual predilection for the higher techniques."

"She's great with patterns," piped up Skender. "You should see her. She —"

"*Not you.*" The man'kin silenced the boy with a gesture. "*Your turn will come. Go on, Mage Van Haasteren.*"

"The truth is that, if she had the Change, she would be a powerful talent. That she does not is a tragedy, for she desires it greatly."

"Could you teach her?" asked the black-haired woman.

"Yes."

"Does her head and heart agree?"

"She . . ." The mage glanced at Shilly. "No, they do not," he admitted regretfully. "I can train her, but not fully."

"You took her in, anyway. Did you do so to gain access to the boy?"

"In part, yes. He I *am* able to train, and he needs it, badly. But I took them both in because they are suited. They complement each other almost perfectly. It seemed simpler to keep them together until I worked out what they needed as individuals." The mage took a deep breath. "I'm sorry. I'm not being as clear as I'd like to be. And in truth this insight doesn't belong wholly to me. Part of it has come to me second-hand from the girl's first teacher, who recognised that the two of them are linked."

"Payat again," snorted the white-clad man.

"Yes, him. He haunts us all, apparently."

Warden Behenna raised a hand. "May I speak now?"

"*No.*"

"But I have something to —"

"*You brought this matter before us,*" said the man'kin. "*You therefore speak last.*"

The warden subsided again, reluctantly. Shilly could feel the urgency radiating off him like heat.

"*The boy will not speak for himself. I find this strange and unhelpful. Why has he made this decision?*"

"As a protest against this proceeding," said the woman standing at Sal's side. "He will not willingly return to the Strand under any circumstances."

"Perhaps understandably," said another of the Judges, "given the effort he expended to get away from it. He has family here and he is best trained here. Why would we even consider making him leave?"

The question was directed to no one in particular, but it was Radi Mierlo who answered it.

"His father — his real father — is in the Strand," she said, her voice slow and dignified. "His great-aunt, Syndic Nu Zanshin, spent several years trying to find him while he was on the run with his de facto father. It was this man, Dafis Hrvati, who raised him to despise and fear the Sky Wardens, in ignorance of his heritage and potential."

"No training at all?"

"None."

"That explains his wild talent."

"Such ignorance was, perhaps, justified," said the Mage Van Haasteren. "Sal explained why when he arrived at the Keep. The reasons are complex and beyond the scope of this hearing.

I ask you to note that Sal has retained his adoptive father's name, Hrvati, despite everything he has learned in recent weeks. He has taken neither his mother's name nor his true father's, nor their married name."

"What else did Sal tell you?" asked the Judge with black hair. "Is there anything else we should know?"

"That I have little faith in those who say they would care for him." The mage prowled around the centre of the circle, pointing as he went. "His grandmother, for starters, seeks nothing but personal advancement from him."

"Nonsense," said Radi Mierlo. "I would freely abandon my holdings here to protect him if he has to return to the Strand."

"Exactly. And we all know how well the Mierlos have been received here since they returned from the Strand, ten years ago." The mage moved on to Tait. "This one betrayed his own brother's confidence to reveal that Sal had not left Fundelry — also in order to advance his own interests."

The journeyman shifted his feet awkwardly at Shilly's side. "I was doing my duty."

"Like any good warden." The mage came to Behenna. "Yes. A good Sky Warden knows where to draw the line. He doesn't abandon his constituents in order to go off on a half-baked quest to bring back one errant boy unless there's a very good reason. It's a big risk to take. Who knows what it might cost? But that's duty. Yes, indeed."

The Judges as one stared at Behenna as though he was something repugnant, and Shilly was reminded of the frill-necked lizard hissing at him. She didn't know what the Mage Van Haasteren was implying, but the Sky Warden glared right back at him, his lips a tight line. There was a hunted look in his eye that hadn't been there before, as though he was keeping his response carefully in check, for fear of what he might do.

"If these people truly have Sal and Shilly's best interests at heart," the Mage Van Haasteren concluded, "then I am not my father's son."

Shilly wondered what his case had to do with her, since most of it revolved around Sal. But she kept her mouth shut.

"*That is your argument, then?*" asked the man'kin, its wings shifting position with the sound of rock crunching underfoot. "*That the children will be improperly cared for if they return to the Strand?*"

"Primarily, yes." The mage nodded and backed down. "I see little need to jeopardise their wellbeing when we can give them all they need here, at least until they are old enough to choose for themselves."

"*Is there any extemporal information regarding these two that we might consult? Dreams? Prophecies?*"

"I, ah, suspect," said the thin, white-bearded man, "that these children might be of significance to certain concerns, both here and in the Strand."

The man'kin stared at him with its blank, marble eyes.

"I would prefer not to be more specific," he added.

The young woman next to Sal stirred. "Some desire Sal and Shilly in order to gain strength for their Line or Clan. This is likely to be true in Radi Mierlo's case. Others have a similar interest in their fate."

"*Would you care to name these people?*" asked the man'kin, turning heavily to face her.

"They know who they are."

The young woman looked around the circle of Judges. Shilly was reminded of the Weavers, and the warning the Mage Erentaite had given Van Haasteren at their first meeting. *They are everywhere, yet nowhere. Their work is of vital importance to both our lands, yet is conducted in absolute secrecy. They* destroy as often as they create, and they are not to be crossed. Were they, she wondered, the ones who were being hinted at here? Was one of them present, and did that explain why everyone was being so cautious?

What on Earth did the Stone Mage Synod have to be frightened of?

"*I fail to understand,*" the man'kin said. "*Do these mysterious third parties wish them here or in the Strand?*"

"That I don't know."

"*If neither their intentions nor their identities are clear, I do not see how we can be expected to take them into account.*"

No one said anything for a long minute. Shilly noted that some of the Judges were unsettled by the topic. Others kept their faces completely blank, as though nothing of any significance was being discussed. One, a square-faced woman of middle years, seemed bored, and it was she who broke the silence.

"Can we move on?" she asked. "Hints and rumours will get us nowhere. The interests of the children are all that should concern us."

"I agree," said the Mage Van Haasteren. "We can only base our decision on the facts, not speculation, and our time is not unlimited."

Shilly looked up at the moon. It hung frozen in the sky.

"*What else needs to be said in favour of keeping the children here?*" asked the man'kin, looking around the small group before it, one by one. "*Is that argument complete?*"

"You just *can't* send them back," said Skender. "That'd be crazy."

"*Why so?*"

"Because..." The boy looked surprised that he suddenly had the man'kin's permission to speak. "Well, it wouldn't be fair. They want to be here, so why shouldn't they be allowed to stay?"

"*It's not that simple. There are many things to take into account apart from their desires.*"

"Such as?" Skender took on the role of questioner with all the reckless confidence of a small dog barking at a very large man. "Who are you to decide what's best for them? How can you hope to know everything about them in just one sitting — especially when Sal won't even talk to you? What gives you the right to take over someone's life and change it in a way they don't want? They're not criminals. They're not refugees. They came here to learn from us, and you're actually thinking of turning them away. *That's* why I think it's crazy!"

He subsided, breathing heavily, as his father put a hand on his shoulder.

No one said anything. The night was still, poised on a cusp Shilly could half-sense but still wasn't quite sure she fully understood. Then:

"*Sky Warden Behenna.*"

The warden stepped forward at the mention of his name.

"*How do you respond to this? Why do you come to us to make this decision for the children?*"

"My response is simple." His gaze roamed the circle and settled on her. They were bright, eager for a fight. "Shilly? I want to ask you a single question. Do you want to stay here? Tell us now so we can all hear. Are you *convinced* that that would be the right thing to do?"

All attention turned to her. Her automatic response was to say *yes* because that was what Sal wanted, but the word wouldn't come out. It didn't feel right. The unexpected hesitation prompted a storm of emotions. What *did* she want? She hadn't found the security she had wanted in the Interior, and she had been seriously hurt. She might not walk properly again, despite the Mage Erentaite's ministrations. The Keep didn't offer the right sort of education — as Van Haasteren had admitted and Tait had demonstrated — whereas Warden Behenna had offered her a teacher in the Strand and access to talent more suited to her nature. Was it really such a bad thought, to go home, where Lodo's body lay waiting for her to rescue him? Was she *convinced*?

Sal was watching her — she could feel it. But she couldn't give him the answer he wanted to hear.

"I'm not sure," she said. "I thought I was, before, but now I don't know what I want. I'm sorry."

"But —" spluttered Skender. "But —"

"Don't be sorry," Behenna said, almost gently, ignoring the boy as though he wasn't there. "It's not a bad thing to be confused, especially at your age. Finding out who you are and what you should be is no easy process, and sometimes we take steps in the wrong direction along the way. Not usually as large as yours, I'll admit, but it's the same thing in principle. And it's never too late to turn back." He held her gaze for a moment then turned to address the Judges. "May I speak freely now?"

"*Yes.*"

"Then let me say this. Everything I have heard so far convinces me that I have done the right thing. Only one person has said anything sensible, and that is the one person I thought least likely. How dare *you* — who presumed to speak for these children without even knowing what one of them wanted — accuse *me* of not acting in their best interests? You can see the lengths I have gone to in order to ensure their safety. I have followed them a long way and at great personal cost. Are these the actions of a man who has only his self-interest at heart?

Aren't your misconceptions proof that I am more fit to make this decision than you?"

Across from Shilly, Sal's eyes narrowed, but he could say nothing.

"*Go on.*"

"Well, to begin with, I come from the same place as them, so I know what they're leaving behind. I also know the full story behind Sal's parents. I suspect that the version of events he has been told will turn out to be true only in fact, not in essence. He is too young to appreciate the subtleties. Exposure to his true father and the rest of his family, waiting for him right now in the Haunted City, will allow him the opportunity to make an informed decision about his future. Denying him that chance would be no better than caging him."

Behenna took several paces around the empty space between the Judges. "You question my motives, and I allow you that. But such questions can swing both ways. Mage Van Haasteren's grip on the Keep has been weak for a generation, since the Payat Misseri scandal. What better way for him to firm the school's reputation than taming a wild talent? I am not questioning his ability as a teacher but pointing out that his motivations are not necessarily so pure. He himself admits that he offered to teach Shilly because he wants to keep Sal. Is that the judgment of a man who has the best interests of the children at heart? If he was as ill-mannered as his own son when he was younger, it's no wonder his father wanted to divert the lineage elsewhere."

Veins stood out in the Mage Van Haasteren's neck, but he said nothing, and one strong hand on his son's shoulder kept him quiet too.

"He says that my journeyman betrayed his own brother." Behenna continued his stroll around the circle until he was abreast with Shilly. "Well, there's no denying that Tait did betray a confidence. But does he realise that Tait's brother, Tom, is the only candidate I have ever seen to turn down Selection directly to the Alcaide's face? What does that say about *his* judgment? Add to that the fact that Tom then helped Sal and Shilly escape in a vehicle that had been legally confiscated by the town's Alders in order to prevent just such an escape, and ask yourself again whose judgment is poor.

"My journeyman acted in good faith to protect Sal and Shilly from the lies they have been told. The friendship he has shown Shilly since demonstrates further that his heart is good. Don't be fooled by the surface. Do justice to what's at stake and dig deeper to find the truth."

He turned on Sal. "You, my boy, are the one I feel sorriest for. You despise me, steal from me and you seek to wound me, but I know that you only do so out of severe misunderstanding. It is not through any fault of your own. You deserve at least to know what your options are before you trap yourself here forever. You need to meet the rest of your family in order to know who you might become. At least let us take you that far. You should know by now that you can trust me to do only what is good for you."

Sal shook his head, slowly but definitely.

"Think of Shilly, then," the Sky Warden said. "I saved your friend's life. I've offered her a place in the Haunted City, where she will be taught as she deserves to be. All you can offer her is isolation and alienation. Allow me to show you the alternative before you drag her off on another pointless adventure. Would you deny her the chance to achieve her true potential in the place she calls home?"

Sal hesitated, his defiance undermined.

"*I see a clear dichotomy between the needs of each child,*" interrupted the man'kin. "*Is separation a possibility. The girl goes south with you while the boy stays here?*"

"No," said Behenna, turning to face the man'kin. "That is not a possibility."

"*Why not? Why must they be kept together?*"

"Their fates are linked," said Van Haasteren. "I feel this, and so did Payat Misseri. Although I disapproved of his methods —" The Stone Mage glanced in disdain at the Sky Warden. "— I'm not surprised that Behenna agrees."

"To break that bond," said the young woman standing beside Sal, "might have greater ramifications than we can see at present."

"But it is the simplest solution to the moral dilemma before us," said the Judge with dark hair, frowning. "Can we be expected to see beyond that, to follow hints and hunches in the face of hard facts?"

"We must consider all possibilities," said the woman who had looked bored earlier. Now she was paying close attention to proceedings. "How would the children themselves feel about studying apart?"

All eyes turned again to Shilly, since Sal was forbidden to speak. A surprising sense of dismay rolled through her at the thought of being separated from Sal. It was the same feeling she had felt during the storm, before Behenna had announced that Sal wasn't going to escape after all. They had known each other only a short time, but he had had such a powerful effect on her life. The sense of togetherness they had shared for a brief time had carried them such a huge distance that it was easy to see why everyone thought they might do even more, one day. Turning her back on that possibility would be as hard as it had been to leave Fundelry.

Judging by Sal's expression, he was feeling much the same way. His jaw worked as he waited for her to answer, and his blue eyes sparkled in the moonlight.

This time she was spared a difficult decision.

"This question is irrelevant," said Behenna. "I came for both of them, not one of them."

"*Are you saying you wouldn't take one if that was all we allowed you?*"

"No, that's not what I'm saying at all." Behenna looked uncertain, as though the possibility had thrown him completely. "I'm saying that I could hardly leave with half the job done."

"*You stated to the Mage Erentaite that you would abide by our ruling, no matter what it was.*"

"Yes, I did. But I —"

"*Would you take Shilly if our decision was to keep Sal here?*"

"That's a little unfair, don't you think? Asking me to choose between them?"

"*I'm not asking you to choose. I am asking you if you would be satisfied with such a decision.*"

"You're trying to trick me into something," the warden said. Shilly caught an urgent look flashing between Sal's grandmother and the warden. "You're trying to make it look as though I only want Sal by saying that I won't take Shilly without him. That's what you're trying to do."

"*Answer the question.*" The man'kin swung its massive body one step forward and raised the tip of its ceremonial sword to waist height. Its wings unfolded and seemed to absorb the moonlight, leaving the night dark.

Behenna swallowed, deflating. "No," he said, weakly at first. "No, I wouldn't take the girl alone. But not because —"

"*You do not need to say any more.*"

"Let me finish!" The warden faced the man'kin with wide, desperate eyes. "I wouldn't take just Shilly because I came for *both* of them! I wouldn't take just Sal, either, if you offered me that. One of them is no good; it has to be both."

"*That is for us to decide.*"

"No. I'm sick of this farce. As a ranking Sky Warden I demand that these children be allowed to return to where they belong immediately. It's time to stop playing games. These children are citizens of the Strand! Who gave you jurisdiction over them? More to the point, they're wards of the state. *My* state, the state I represent!" He was shouting with such intensity it was uncomfortable to watch. "How dare you tell me what I can and can't do with them?"

"You're not in your state any more," said the woman standing next to Sal.

"That doesn't change who I am. It doesn't change who I represent. I came here with the full authority of the Syndic. I speak with her voice. You —"

"*We have ourselves spoken with the Syndic,*" said the man'kin.

Behenna's mouth hung open for a second. "What? When?"

"*This evening. You are not acting with her authority. You do not speak for her.*"

"But — but —" The warden looked around him as though seeking help. "But she wants the children."

"*She does. That is true. She did not explicitly order you to go to such extremes, however, and she dismisses you from her service.*"

Behenna's dark skin went deathly grey. "What does that mean?"

"You broke your vows," said Van Haasteren. "You turned your back on your training. What do you *think* it means?"

"No." The warden looked as though he had been punched in the gut. "No."

"*Yes,*" said the man'kin. "*You did not have permission to extend the search beyond the boundaries of your prefecture.*"

You failed to inform her of your movements at all times. You appropriated warden funds without authorisation. The Syndic might have forgiven these breaches of trust, but for your flagrant disregard of your vows. You have been stripped of your rank, effective immediately. We are obliged to return you to the Strand for a disciplinary hearing. You therefore have no power over us as spokesperson for the Stand. You have no right to order us to do anything."

Behenna backed away, shaking his head. He stared around at the ring of white faces enclosing him as though considering making a break for it. Shilly imagined him running across the desert, the hunted rather than the hunter — and suddenly realised exactly what Sal had been hoping to do. By making the Sky Warden break his vows and lose his favour with the Syndic, Sal had effectively undermined his plea to the Synod. All Sal had had to do was give Behenna a reason to break them — and it had worked perfectly.

"So it's over?" asked a voice that had not spoken once through the entire proceedings. "We're free to go?"

The man'kin swung its sword in one swift, startling movement, sweeping it up and out so that it pointed directly at Sal.

"Silence! You are not allowed to speak here."

"But —"

"This matter is not resolved until we reach a decision!" The sword swung again, this time to point at the Judges one by one. *"Who raises a petition is not as important as the petition itself. This man's fate is irrelevant to the situation before us and the decision we must still make. Make it we must, now, unless anyone else wishes to speak."*

No one moved. Sal stood frozen as his clutch at freedom slipped through his fingers. It was truly out of his hands, now.

Shilly's heart went out to him, even though how she herself felt was still a mystery to her. She didn't know if she was hoping to stay or to go — with or without Sal. It seemed most likely to her that the Judges would choose separation, since Sal so clearly belonged in the Interior and she didn't, but that didn't ease her mind. She was afraid of what the future held — especially when, ultimately, she didn't know whose fate was really at stake. Where and how did she fit in? Why was everyone so determined to keep Sal and her together, regardless of what they wanted? For all she knew, she and Sal had no great destiny together at all, and she was little more than an impediment to him.

There was nothing Sal could do now except hope that they would choose to keep him in the Interior rather than send him to the Strand.

Her mind replayed images from the recent past while they all waited: of the buggy crushing her leg against the ravine wall; of Lodo urging them to run as the combined force of the Sky Wardens in Fundelry rose up against him; of the hurt in Sal's eyes when he thought she had rejected him; of the desperation on Behenna's face when success had been snatched from him.

The Sky Warden was a picture of anxiety. Shilly couldn't find it in herself to feel sorry for him. He was quite happy to sacrifice Sal's happiness by taking him back to the Strand, and he was equally unconcerned about her happiness, too. After all his talk of getting her a teacher in the Haunted City, he had in the end refused to take her alone. His promises were empty unless he got Sal as well. He had also kept Lodo's survival a secret from her when he had *known* what her first teacher had meant to her.

As far as Shilly was concerned, Behenna deserved everything he got.

The Judges said nothing for more than five minutes. She could tell that they were communicating furiously among themselves, although she couldn't hear what they were saying. The icy regard of the moon twinkled with the Change stirring in the air. So much was going on beneath the surface of things that the skin of her arm lifted into goosebumps. The tension rose until she thought she was going to scream —

"*We have decided,*" said the man'kin, lowering its sword to its usual position, point down in front of it. "*Both children will return to the Strand.*"

Shock rolled through her as though she had been dunked in icy water. Return to the Strand? *Both* of them?

She glanced around, wondering if she'd misheard. Sal was aghast; she could tell that just by looking at him. Behenna clearly didn't know what to think, still stunned as he was by the news that he had been stripped of his rank. Radi Mierlo displayed no such confusion: her smile was wide and triumphant. Identical looks of surprise were on the two Van Haasterens, old and young.

"But why?" asked Skender in disbelief.

"*It is in the children's best interest.*"

"Sal *and* Shilly?" said his father "I find that difficult to comprehend."

"*You do not need to comprehend. This is the Nine Stars, and we are of one mind. Our decision is final. You will abide by it.*"

The mage opened his mouth to protest. For a startling moment, the mage reminded her of Lodo, although physically they couldn't have been more different. Van Haasteren was tall and gloomy where Lodo had been short and grizzled, the only thing they had in common was the look in the mage's eyes. In them Shilly saw nothing but dismay for her and Sal. There was no thought for himself. For the first time she sensed that he really cared about them — *both* of them.

She remembered once wondering why the mage couldn't be more like Lodo. At that moment she realised that the mage's moods and silences made him *exactly* like Lodo. Only long experience with her former teacher had revealed what lay beneath — just as only the wrong decision, in the mage's eyes, had exposed the depth of his compassion.

In the instant it took to absorb that revelation, Van Haasteren gathered his resolve and stepped forward.

"Surrender the limelight, Skender," said the young-old woman standing by Sal, her voice cutting through the crystalline air like a bell.

The mage stared balefully at the woman, then backed down, and there was no one left to speak against the decision.

Othniel stepped forward. "It is over," he said. "The petition has been heard and the decision made. You must return to your seats."

Shilly turned, a sense of unreality creeping over her. The circle of Judges broke apart to give them a way out.

Tait put his arm around her and kissed her cheek.

"We did it!"

Although once she might have welcomed such a gesture, she awkwardly turned away. "You did it, not me."

"No, it was you too," he said. "You said exactly the right thing. We couldn't have done it without you, Shilly."

She stared at him

You said exactly the right thing.

He went to help her move through the rows of benches.

"Don't touch me," she said, pushing him back.

"What?"

"You heard me." She saw it now — too late, but better than never. Mawson had told her before the hearing that someone was lying to her: *someone much closer to you than I.* Tait had been letting her lean on him at the time, and he hadn't heard the man'kin's warning.

While Behenna and Tait might not have wanted her on her own, they had been quite happy to use her against Sal in the hope that where she went he might follow.

"If you think I don't know what's going on," she said, angry at herself for not realising sooner, "you're even more stupid than I thought you were."

Tait shook his head as though in confusion, but backed off to join his former master as the group moved back to their benches. Sal walked alone, listlessly, as though asleep. Shilly was afraid to approach him in case she only made him feel worse. If she had thought he might retaliate against the decision, she would have been wrong. He seemed dead to the world.

Behenna had the same look. He had won, but in the process lost everything.

By the time they had reached their bench and the people waiting there, the obscuring charm had closed back in and the centre of the bowl was no longer clearly visible. Mawson looked smug, but said nothing. She was glad for that, although she resolved to confront the man'kin later about what it knew. The Judges had proceeded to another case, and the moon had moved a short distance across the sky. The night wasn't done yet, but for them the difficult part was over. When the Synod closed, Shilly assumed, they would begin the long journey back to Ulum and there make arrangements for the journey south. Radi Mierlo would need to finalise things in Mount Birrinah, if she hadn't already. The Mage Van Haasteren would return to the Keep and his students. Skender would go back to his studies and soon forget the two visitors from the south who had so briefly enlivened his world. His mother would go back to her dig, wherever that was, and everything would soon be back to normal.

Under the cold sky of the Nine Stars, surrounded by mysterious ruins and people whose motives she was nervous of trusting any distance at all, Shilly wondered if she would ever have a normal life to look forward to.

SINS AND WISDOM

The caravan was ready to begin its long journey. Curled like a question mark, the long line of wagons — and one buggy — waited by the gates of Ulum for final farewells to be over. Moving east at first, through Lower Light and Carslake, then south to Leonora, it would enter the Strand at the crossing known as Tintenbar, the one normally taken by official travellers, then continue south through Millingen, Moombin and Gunida. The caravan would finally arrive at the Haunted City, where the Syndic would meet it personally, four weeks and two and a half thousand kilometres from where it had started.

In Sal's eyes, it wasn't travelling forward, but backward. After everything he had done to reach the Interior, he was being forced to return — and worse. Had he been going back to Fundelry, he wouldn't have minded so much. He knew what awaited him there, after all. Without Lodo it would be a very unfriendly place to live, full of racism and isolation. The Haunted City, on the other hand ...

With a shake of his head, he stopped himself from thinking that far ahead. Not yet. There would be plenty of time during the journey.

"Ready, Sal?"

He turned at the sound of the voice. Belilanca Brokate stood behind him, dressed in her riding gear, the thin lines on her face and the rings in her ears adding up to a very welcome sight. When she had heard that Sal was being sent home, she had pulled strings through Wyath's father to ensure that her caravan would be the one chosen to take him. She had been waiting for them when they had returned from the Synod, and Sal had been happier to see her than he could say. He suspected she knew.

"I'm not ready," he said. "But that never mattered."

She helped him up into the lead wagon, then climbed up herself, into the front.

"I hope you've heard some new stories," he said. "We've got a long time to kill."

"No happy ones." She lifted a shoulder in an economical shrug. "We'll manage."

The wagon moved forward with a lurch. Behind them, the caravan followed. It was much larger than the one that had carried him from Nesh to Ulum, and consisted of several quite distinct components. The Mierlo wagons were heavy with goods and people. His mother's family had no intention of coming back, if they could help it. Radi Mierlo rode as high as a queen by the driver of her wagon, eager to put her bad reputation behind her. Around her swarmed the uncles, aunts and cousins he had made no effort to meet, preferring to keep to himself rather than submit to their curiosity. He was their ticket to prosperity, and he, it had been made clear in no uncertain terms, wasn't going to cheat them out of it.

The other wagons contained a delegation from the Nine Stars, a party of five Stone Mages ostensibly sent to smooth the way for Sal's return but really, Sal suspected, intending to take a closer look at the heart of the neighbouring country. Relations were cool between the Nine Stars and the Haunted City and every opportunity to see behind the opposite side's lines was being taken with both hands.

Sal recognised one of them from the Synod: a fair-haired, middle aged female Judge who had looked bored during their hearing. She hadn't made any effort to talk to him, so Sal didn't know if his ability to get her into the Haunted City had played a part in the Synod's decision. Privately, he hoped not. There was enough complication in his life without adding politics to the mix.

The rest of the caravan consisted of small traders and exporters pooling resources to make the trip affordable. It wasn't often that a caravan was booked to make the journey from Ulum to the Haunted City in one unbroken stretch. Such an arrangement could also, Sal thought, make it easier to get past border guards. He didn't know what, exactly, the traders were bringing with them, but it was probably an eclectic mix.

They passed through the city gates and out into direct sunlight. Some of the drivers sang a short lament in another language that he remembered from his first trip with Brokate. It was a song of farewell, not just to a place but also to the people who lived there — to the *spirit* of a place. It perfectly matched his feelings. The plants, the sky, the earth, the smells — he would carry the memory of them all the way to the Haunted City, then follow them back, one day, to the land of his mother's birth. He was sure of it. The magic of the flowers that had bloomed in the desert, after the storm his charm had brought down, demanded that he return.

First, though, he had to sort out the unfinished business his parents had left him with.

Perhaps it was the gentle rocking of the wagon beneath him that brought the story of the baker of La Menz back to him. Or else it was the past that hung off him like a ball and chain, dragging him backward with grim fatalism. The baker and Sal had one unlikely thing in common: infidelity had cast their lives in unusual directions. In the story it had been the baker's infidelity that had saved him from a mysterious death. In real life it was Sal's parents who had propelled him on the journey of his life. Sal wondered now if the similarities really ended there.

The baker, in the beginning of the story, had done very little. He had endured the emotions of those around him, no matter how they battered him: his wife's hatred; Monca's love; the villagers' disdain. He subconsciously summoned death to him as a kind of solution to his problem, but found that even that wasn't what he wanted. If death was "the great Change-maker," as Brokate had said, then it wasn't a solution. It just made things different, and often not different enough to fix anything on its own. The baker had to take it upon himself to act in order to make things better.

The extra ending Sal had given the story now seemed trite to him, and had since they had left Ulum for the Nine Stars. When the baker had finally chosen to act, it was in a way that no one could have anticipated, and he had attained exactly what he wanted as a result: peace of mind. Perhaps Monca had come to understand that, in the end, she wasn't terribly relevant to the central conflict in her lover's life. The fact that she, too, had chosen death to achieve her own goals, in Sal's version of the story, only underscored the point that the rest of the story made. The baker had to act in order to take any control at all over his life, even if it was impossible to act without affecting someone.

Sal had acted, too. He felt as though he'd crossed a boundary when he had forced Warden Behenna to break his vows — or earlier, when he had defied the Synod by refusing to speak before them. The question was, would he get what he wanted as a result? Unlike the baker, he suspected that his story was far from over.

They stopped that night in a gully protected by a wall of dead tree trunks. Sal didn't leave the wagon except to bathe and relieve himself. He was too conscious of eyes watching him everywhere he went. Even under the cover of the wagon, he couldn't avoid that. He kept his head down and didn't meet anyone's gaze.

"Does it hurt?"

He looked up to see Shilly crutching toward his spot at the rear of the wagon, holding a plate of stew in her one free hand. They had barely spoken to each other since the Synod's decision. Her habit of hanging around the Mierlo camp during the day had made him wary, along with the incidents surrounding the Synod, and before. Back in Fundelry, he had wondered if she was only befriending him to get access to his power. He had convinced himself that it wasn't the case — but she had certainly jumped quickly enough at Behenna's offer to find her a teacher in the Strand, and he was sure Tait would be happy enough to let her use him. Maybe he had decided too quickly.

But here she was now, asking him a question. He glanced down to where he'd been fiddling with the charm around his wrist, then back up at her.

"No," he said.

"Good." She handed him the plate. "This could be the last red meat we'll see for a while. You should eat it."

"Thanks," he said. The stew did smell delicious. "What about you?"

"Is there room here for two?"

"I guess so."

"Good. The company out there is lousy."

She hobbled off and returned a moment later with another bowl. He wasn't sure yet how he felt about that, but he didn't let her new mobility fool him. Although she might be down to one crutch, the pain lines around her eyes were permanently etched. She winced when she propped herself next to him on the wagon's edge.

They ate in silence, which was fine by him. He hadn't told her the entire truth. The bracelet Behenna had wound around his left wrist hurt when he thought about it, and it was hard not to do that. Fashioned from knotted black leather and tied very tight, it was a constant reminder that he had lost his freedom. It was also proof that Lodo's theories were right: the Change came from one source, and all Stone Mages and Sky Wardens could use it, if they would only let themselves. Their teachings were simply two different methods of controlling it — and controlling the people who used it.

Behenna, now that he had broken his vows, had had no difficulty fashioning the charm even though he was as far from the sea as it was possible to get. Mentally, however, he suffered the worst indignities of an outcast. None of the Stone Mages on their journey back to Ulum had spoken a word to him, and Sal could tell that the thought of what awaited him at home weighed heavily upon him. The ex-Sky Warden watched the world moodily from the buggy's driving seat, answering Tait's questions in monosyllables.

"They've got you now, boy," Behenna had said to Sal via the Change, not long out of the Nine Stars. *"They've got you, and they're never going to let you go."*

Sal could still hear the thick edge in the man's mental voice. It wasn't gloating at all, but bitterness. Behenna had been talking about himself too, Sal suspected, although he didn't quite understand what that meant. Since then, Behenna had said nothing to Sal at all, mentally or out loud. Even while affixing the bracelet, he had worked in complete silence. It was his grandmother's acid-faced secretary who had explained what it would do: that it was designed to incapacitate him if he tried to sneak away or remove it. There would be no more tricks with the buggy this time, she had said. He wouldn't even get ten metres if he tried.

Sal hadn't tested it yet, but vowed to once he had worked up the courage. Whatever the bracelet would do to him, it was bound to be nasty. The way Behenna looked at him said so more clearly than words.

"Do you think Tom or Kemp will be there when we arrive?"

Shilly's question startled him out of his thoughts, and he was glad for it. Just thinking about removing the bracelet made it tighten, sending rhythmic pinpricks of pain up his arm.

"I don't know," he said. "It depends if the wardens forgave them for letting us get away."

"Do you remember when we left, though? Tom didn't come with us, but he did say —"

"*Later.* I do remember."

"If he dreamed it, like he dreamed the earthquake and Tait coming back, that probably means he at least will be there." The way she spoke left it unclear whether she thought it was a good thing or not.

Sal recalled something else Tom had told him. It had been outside School in Fundelry, just before Shilly had first suggested they be friends. "He told me that he thought I'd go to the Haunted City, one day."

"Did he?" She sniffed. "It's a shame he didn't tell us anything useful — like the details of how you'd get there. He could've saved us an awful amount of bother."

He looked at her, then looked away. Here he was again: thinking ahead. It was becoming a bad habit. He was caught between the past and the future like a bug between two fingers.

There was an awkward silence. Sal's stew was finished, and he put the bowl to one side. Shilly was still eating hers, and he watched her out of the corner of his eye. Her hair was getting long and straggly. The bleached sections were spreading too, thanks to the harsh Interior sun. The warm brown of her skin hid some of her gauntness, but not all of it. She looked exhausted thanks to large bags under her eyes. What, he wondered, had happened to the girl he had met in Fundelry, full of energy and always ready with a sharp comment? Where had she gone?

He had happened to her, he supposed. He had dragged her from one side of the country to the other, and now back again. No wonder she was looking tired. No wonder she had wanted to go home.

She looked up and he realised that he was staring at her.

"What?"

"Shilly, I'm —"

"No." She shook her head firmly. "Don't say it, Sal."

"Say what?"

"What you're about to say." She put down her food. "That you're sorry."

"How do you know that's what I was going to say?"

"It's obvious. How could you not be after all that's happened to us?"

"So why not say it and get it over with?"

"Because there's no point." Her expression was intense. "I want to say it, too. We've both done things we regret. I let Behenna use my hunger for the Change and my loneliness against you. But saying the words won't fix anything. What it really says is, *It's my fault*, and that's not the way it is with us. It's not our fault, really. It just happened. 'No blame.'"

"Whose fault is it, then?"

"Maybe it's no one's — or no one person's, anyway. Your mother is partly to blame, and so is your real father. And so is the man who you thought was your father, and your grandmother, and the Syndic —"

"I get it."

"And so is Lodo and the Mage Van Haasteren and the Alcaide and Warden Behenna. They're all mixed up in it with us. Hell, half of them probably blame us for most of it, so it doesn't seem fair that we should agree with them."

No, it didn't. He had no doubts that she was right on that point. And he remembered how he had felt in the Broken Lands when she had tried to thank him, and he wouldn't let her. This wasn't so different, perhaps. "What do we do, then?"

"We get on with making it better. That's all we *can* do."

"How?"

She shrugged in the fading light. "I've been talking to Mawson. He's been telling me things, in his own way. Did you know that he's been sworn to help your family in any way he can? It's like a curse for him, but he honours it anyway. His kind, he says, are bound by their words more tightly than we are, hence the way they talk. Curses and promises are prisons, he says, but riddles set you free."

Sal had glimpsed the bust and recognised it from his dream, but had never spoken to it himself. "What's that got to do with me?"

"Well, it was him who suggested I patch things up with you. You're part of the family he's supposed to protect, right? And he thinks I'm good for you. Maybe vice versa, too, but he's even more cagey than usual about that. He thinks we're going to have our work cut out for us, so we might as well start getting used to working together again, despite what we did to hurt each other the first time. If he's right, that does make a kind of sense."

"How do you feel about it?"

"I'm here, aren't I?" she said. Her expression was hard to read, though, and neither of them said anything for a long moment. He was glad she was there. Perhaps, he thought, Monca wasn't as irrelevant to the baker as he had initially assumed.

The stars came out one by one in the dome of the sky above them. They hadn't been at the Keep long enough to learn about the Invisible Stars Skender had taunted them with on their arrival — if they even existed. Sal preferred the ones he could see with his ordinary eyes. The world around him was more than enough for one person to deal with without adding whole unseen layers on top of it.

"I want to rescue Lodo," Shilly said with a ring of determination to her voice. "To do that, I have to go to the Haunted City. And as I'll probably need your help to do it, it would be wrong to lie about my motivations at the beginning. I've decided that Lodo told you not to tell me about the globe because that would only make me more determined to get it working. But no matter how determined I am, I still need you to help me do anything with the Change. I can't trust anyone else."

"How do you know you can trust me?" Sal asked.

"Maybe we should trade," she suggested, her eyes catching the light of the quarter moon in the darkness. "Really help each other, this time, instead of just pretend we're working together. Is there anything you want to do that I can help you with?"

Confront my problems, he thought, in a flash of insight. *If neither running from them nor into their embrace didn't work, then maybe confronting them head-on might.*

He wasn't ready to make that sort of a decision yet, or such a commitment, but it seemed as if someone might have guessed Shilly's desire well in advance.

Lodo's heart-name is Athim, the Mage Van Haasteren had said. *Remember it, and use it well.* It seemed certain to him that they would need that name to bring him back from the Void.

Even without it, Sal didn't doubt that Shilly would succeed. She, like her leg, had been put under pressure during their journey. Unlike her leg, which had snapped and might never heal, she was stronger than ever. *Not all bones heal the same way,* he thought, remembering the story of the baker yet again.

"It's a shame we don't have Skender here," he said. "He knows more than both of us put together, even if he doesn't understand it."

"Yes — and it's interesting you should mention him," said Shilly. "Mawson keeps talking about our 'third', the person we need in order to do what we have to do. I don't know who that is, though. Mawson sees the past, present and future all at once, so it's sometimes hard to tell what he's talking about. He must be referring to someone we haven't met yet, since Skender isn't coming with us."

"Has he told you what's going to happen to us?"

"Maybe." She looked uncertain. "If he has, I haven't understood it. He used to make me angry because I thought he was trying to confuse me, but it's not that. We just think differently, that's all. We confuse each other."

"That sounds familiar."

She laughed and reached across him to take his plate. Her smell, of cinnamon and sweat, filled his nostrils. "Don't think I'm going to do this for you every night," she said. "And I expect breakfast. You get up before me."

"I take it you're moving in?"

"If there's room." Hopping off the wagon and onto her one good leg, she peered at the shadowy recesses behind him. The wagon didn't contain much more than a large chest buried under rugs Brokate hoped would find a home in the Haunted City.

"I think there might be," he said.

"Good. Even if there weren't, it'd be better than bunking in a supply wagon."

"Is that where you've been sleeping?"

"Of course. Where did you think I'd been? With Tait and Behenna?"

He didn't answer.

Perhaps, in the darkness, he saw her smile.

Neither of them heard, in the dead of the desert night, a muffled sound from the chest at the front of the wagon. Sal rolled over, in the grip of an ominous dream, but he didn't wake. Even if he had, he would have assumed the noise came from Shilly, wound in a tight ball by his feet and breathing evenly, or from the outside where, somewhere on the ground she preferred as a bed, Brokate snored with patient regularity. He probably wouldn't have recognised the sound for what it was.

The glow stone seemed blindingly bright in the confines of the chest, but in fact it provided barely a glimmer, just enough to read by. The book passed the time, however little of it there was left. There was enough food and water in the chest to last another day.

The reader thought:

This is crazy! I wonder if dad's deciphered the note yet?

And:

But if I'd stayed I would've gone crazy, so it works out even.

And:

I wonder if they'll turn back when they find me?

Another page turned, rustling very faintly in the stillness.

In a nearby wagon, Mawson's marble eyes saw the past, present and future as one, and he never slept.

To be continued in
The Storm Weaver & the Sand.